Michelle Smart's love affair with books started when she was a baby and would cuddle them in her cot. A voracious reader of all genres, she found her love of romance established when she stumbled across her first Mills & Boon book at the age of twelve. She's been reading them—and writing them—ever since. Michelle lives in Northamptonshire, England, with her husband and two young Smarties.

After spending three years as a die-hard New Yorker, **Kate Hewitt** now lives in a small village in the English Lake District, with her husband, their five children and a golden retriever. In addition to writing intensely emotional stories, she loves reading, baking and playing chess with her son—she has yet to win against him, but she continues to try. Learn more about Kate at kate-hewitt.com.

DEFIANT CINDERELLAS

MICHELLE SMART

KATE HEWITT

MILLS & BOON

First published in Great Britain 2024
by Mills & Boon, an imprint of HarperCollins*Publishers* Ltd,
1 London Bridge Street, London, SE1 9GF

www.harpercollins.co.uk

HarperCollins*Publishers*, Macken House, 39/40 Mayor Street Upper,
Dublin 1, D01 C9W8, Ireland

ISBN: 978-0-263-32033-6

11/24

This book contains FSC™ certified paper
and other controlled sources to ensure responsible forest management.

For more information visit www.harpercollins.co.uk/green.

Printed and Bound in the UK using 100% Renewable Electricity
at CPI Group (UK) Ltd, Croydon, CR0 4YY

RESISTING THE BOSSY BILLIONAIRE

MICHELLE SMART

MILLS & BOON

To my wonderful mum. You're one in a million. xxx

CHAPTER ONE

'THE IMPERIAL MARCH' pierced Victoria Cusack's consciousness.

Muttering a curse, she rolled over and flapped her hand on her bedside table, fingers groping for her phone.

Accepting the call, she stuck the phone to her ear and peered through bleary eyes at her bedside alarm clock. It was five a.m.

'What's wrong?' she mumbled as she pulled her lovely warm duvet back up to her chin. It had better be an emergency. Nothing less than broken limbs would count.

'Patrick and Christina are ill.'

She blinked the sleep away. 'What's wrong with them?'

'A virus. They have to isolate and I can't work the coffee machine.'

She groaned. Her boss lived in a loft apartment in one of Manhattan's most exclusive buildings overlooking Central Park. She had no idea why he bothered paying the twenty-four-hour concierge service fees seeing as he never used it. 'I'll get coffee delivered to you.'

'No, I need you to come and make it for me.'

She gritted her teeth tightly before relaxing her mouth into an irritated sigh. 'It's Sunday.'

'You can still take the rest of the day off if you like.'

'How kind.'

Sarcasm was wasted on Marcello Guardiola. 'I'll add a bonus to your salary.'

Victoria didn't want a bonus. She wanted the lie-in she'd been looking forward to.

Friends and family back home in Ireland thought her job was glamorous? Ha!

'I'll throw some clothes on and come over.'

'I've woken you up?'

She rolled her eyes and pulled a face. 'Yes, Marcello, you've woken me up.'

She didn't expect an apology and none was forthcoming. 'More hours of the day to enjoy. See you in ten.'

The line went dead before she could correct him and say she'd be there in twenty minutes, not ten.

Muttering under her breath, she threw her thick duvet off then immediately pulled it back over herself. Good heavens, it was *freezing*.

Only by imagining personally maiming Marcello could she coax her protesting body out of bed and her feet onto the frigid floor. Storm Brigit was due to hit the East Coast that day, and a quick peek out of her curtains proved her suspicions that the expected snow had already started to fall.

A quick brush of her hair, a longer brush of her teeth and then, shivering, she stripped off her flannelette pyjamas and dressed in thick tights covered by fitted black jeans, thermal socks, and a black vest top that she covered with a grey cashmere jumper. Black snow boots, black woolly hat, thick knitted black scarf and then her padded, faux-fur-lined khaki winter coat and leather gloves all donned, phone shoved in coat pocket, and she was ready to go.

Down three flights of stairs and she stepped out into a snow-blanketed Manhattan. The sun hadn't yet risen but everything from the sky to the ground was white. It would have been the most magical of sights if the wind hadn't whipped the thickly falling snowflakes straight into her face.

Cursing her demanding boss, Victoria tightened her coat's hood, hunched over, and set off on the three-block walk to Marcello's. Hopefully a cab would pass any moment for her to hail.

It felt strange walking the streets virtually alone. New York was the city that never slept but this early morning, there was hardly any traffic on the roads and even fewer pedestrians. If she hadn't been a lady on a mission to get to her boss's apartment as quickly as possible, make his blasted coffee, and then get back to her own apartment before the storm really took hold, she'd be creeped out at the vulnerable state she, a young woman walking the streets with hardly anyone about, was in. At least there was plenty of light, and she took comfort too that any predators were likely to get one blast of the wind chill and slam their front door on it.

One block to go and a gust of wind nearly knocked her off her feet. The snow was now coming so thick and fast she could hardly see more than a few feet in front of her. Not that she could really see with the flakes all making a beeline for the exposed parts of her face.

To cheer herself up and make the final block bearable, she imagined maiming Marcello again. Nothing that would incapacitate him, she wasn't evil, just a minor breakage of, say, both his hands, a minor injury that would prevent him using his phone. And while she was at it, maybe a nice dose of laryngitis for him too, so he'd be prevented from speaking until she'd caught up with all the sleep eighteen months working as his executive assistant had deprived her of.

By the time she reached the towering art deco building, Victoria could no longer feel her nose, toes or the tips of her fingers. She had a dreadful feeling the over-enthusiastic forecasters predicting the storm of the century were going to be proved right. She should have known it would be so when they'd named the storm Brigit. Her grandmother was called Brigit and she was the most cantankerous woman to grace God's earth.

When the rest of Victoria's family had reacted with stunned silence at her getting into Columbia in New York to study business, Grandma Brigit's immediate response had been to predict that Victoria would 'get shot because they all have guns there', and then demanded to know what was wrong with Ireland's universities. When the rest of Victoria's family had reacted with the same stunned silence at her being personally headhunted by a billionaire Italian businessman and investor, whose penchant for glamorous girlfriends saw him written about in the press's gossip columns with the same frequency as the business pages, Grandma

Brigit's sharp nose had risen. 'Just you wait, girl,' she'd warned. 'He'll have you running rings for him. You'll be nothing but a glorified dogsbody.'

Victoria frequently thought that Grandma Brigit hadn't been wrong.

Still, for all Grandma Brigit's cantankerousness, she was the only member of Victoria's family who'd not been surprised at either Columbia or the headhunting, mainly because she was the only family member for whom Victoria wasn't a blurred face in the background.

Someone had gritted the building's main entry steps, and when she entered the lobby, its warmth was so welcome that she took a moment to savour it.

The on-duty concierge, who had a slightly frazzled demeanour that early morning, called Marcello's private elevator down while Victoria stamped snow off her boots. Inside the elevator, she pulled her gloves off and used her thumbprint to get it moving. No thumbprint or passcode, no entry into Marcello's private domain. The passcode was changed daily. Christina and Patrick, the currently incapacitated live-in staff, were the only people other than Victoria to have unquestioning access to the Manhattan apartment. Victoria was the only one to have unquestioning access to all Marcello's homes. Even his girlfriends had to make do with the ever-changing passcodes.

She remembered her pride when her thumbprint had been taken. The novelty had worn off by the end of the first month, when he'd woken her to request she arrange the immediate delivery of a crate of champagne. Not just arrange the delivery but supervise its unloading in the apartment. It had been one a.m. Delivery unloaded, she'd politely declined his offer to join the raucous party he'd been hosting. Five hours after she'd left his apartment, she'd arrived at the Guardiola Group's offices and found Marcello at his desk, looking as fresh as a daisy and in his usual upbeat, positive mood.

She stepped out of the elevator leaving a puddle of melted snow on its carpet.

It came as no surprise to find Marcello waiting for her in his reception room—he'd probably watched her through the elevator's security camera—or that he greeted her with, 'Did you get lost?' The only surprise was the stubble on his face. It was rare to see her immaculately groomed boss anything less than immaculately groomed. Sunday morning and he was half dressed for the office. All he needed was to shave, don his tie, waistcoat and suit jacket and he'd be good to step into any board meeting.

She arched an unimpressed eyebrow. 'Have you seen the weather?'

His expression was that of someone who didn't know what *weather* was. 'I have been waiting for you.'

'Well, I'm here now. I'll hang this lot up and then get your coffee made.'

'I need food too.'

Of course he did. Christina or Patrick usually fixed whatever he wanted for breakfast or arranged delivery. In the office, it was Victoria's job to ensure he never went hungry.

'What do you want?'

'Bagels.'

Wet clothes hung in the drying room by the reception, phone secure in the back pocket of her jeans, Victoria entered the vast loft space Marcello considered his home. Of all his properties, this was her favourite. It was just so quirky and interesting.

The main central room was the huge rectangular open-plan living space he hosted his sought-after parties in. Its exposed red brick was cut through with floor-to-ceiling leaded windows that let in an abundance of light and gave a panoramic view of Central Park. High ceilings accommodated galleried overhangs at each end. The overhang above the bottom end was the dining area used for dinner parties, a door off it leading to store rooms and the staff quarters where Christina and Patrick lived. The overhang above the other end was Marcello's home office. A door off the office led to the bedrooms, including his own, the only room Victoria didn't like going into. It wasn't that he'd ever made her feel unsafe or anything—on the contrary, she often got the impression he assumed she was an artificially constructed robot dressed in a woman's skin rather than an actual woman—it was more the feelings evoked when entering his most private domain, the strange queasiness at catching sight of the bed he slept in.

Long used to the magnificence of this most breathtaking bachelor pad, Victoria was too busy ordering bagels via the app of his preferred deli to pay it the slightest bit of attention. At the door under the dining room overhang, she turned her head and found her boss perched on the L-shaped sofa, dark brown leather like the rest of the plentiful seating, now engrossed in his phone.

'I'll show you how to fix the coffee in case Christina and Patrick are laid up for any length of time.'

He didn't look up from his phone. 'I am sure they will be better by tomorrow. Dr Jeffers said sleep is the best medicine for them.'

'You've had your doctor out?'

'He left just before I called you—he didn't know how to work the coffee machine.'

Only Marcello would have the nerve to call his private doctor out in the middle of the night and then expect him to prepare a pot of coffee for him.

Thawing slightly now she knew he'd had the decency to get medical attention for his two most devoted staff, she nonetheless knew to stand her ground. 'There's no guarantee they'll be better by tomorrow.' Manhattan, indeed the whole of New York, was currently plagued by a myriad of debilitating viruses. Marcello, though, was one of those infuriating people who never got ill and had little patience for those who did, expecting instantaneous recoveries from the inconveniently afflicted. 'Let me show you how to fix it for yourself in case you need it tomorrow.'

'I will call you if it becomes necessary.'

'It won't be necessary to call me if you learn to do it yourself.' Just as it wouldn't be necessary for him to call her when he fancied a late-night delivery of food if he'd bother installing the apps he'd insisted she install on *her* phone for the express purpose of ordering delicious goods for him in the hours he thought it unreasonable to wake his live-in staff.

It was the edge in Victoria's voice that made Marcello

look up. Seeing the steel in her eyes, he gave a dramatic sigh. His executive assistant was superb at her job but there were times when she could be a little irritable. He forgave her those touchy episodes only because he didn't want to have to sack her. It wasn't the bother of finding a replacement that was at issue—Manhattan's streets were awash with highly efficient, highly qualified executive assistants—but the bother of having to train someone new. Besides, he liked Victoria's Irish accent. It was one of the reasons he'd poached her after his last assistant selfishly decided not to return after her maternity leave.

So, rather than point out that Victoria was paid generously in money and perks that included her own apartment to be on call whenever he needed her, he decided to humour her. After all, it *was* Sunday. 'Okay, show me how to fix the coffee.'

Marcello's kitchen was a room he only entered if looking for his staff. This was Christina and Patrick's domain, and the domain of the executive chefs he hired…well, who his staff hired on his behalf…when he was playing host. One of the many great things about New York was the abundance of staff for hire. For the right price, they would make themselves available whenever he needed, which meant he only needed two staff living in. Of course, Christina and Patrick hired regular workers to assist with the day-to-day chores but those were generally employed during office hours so he could enjoy his home undisturbed.

His specially imported precious coffee beans were kept in the fridge. It was the one thing he insisted on, a habit picked up from his childhood and his father's insistence that coffee beans remained fresher if kept refrigerated.

His own fridge was a huge triple American one that his mother had gaped in amazement at the first time she'd seen it. From it, Victoria removed the container of beans and carried them over to the coffee pot and placed them on the stainless-steel surface beside it.

Deciding to be a good boy, Marcello stood beside her and pretended to pay attention.

'Fill it with cold water up to the line,' she instructed as she ran water into the pot. She was turning the tap off when her phone buzzed.

Sliding her hand into her back pocket, she read the message whilst carrying the pot back to the machine.

The short puff of air she expelled told him she'd just received unwelcome news.

She looked at him. She wasn't wearing any makeup, he noted. Not that she normally wore much of it but the little she did wear made its absence more noticeable now that he was looking at her face. She hadn't styled her dark red hair into the tidy ponytail she normally wore either. It was much longer than he'd thought, falling halfway down her back.

'The deli can't deliver.'

Assuming she was joking, he laughed.

Not smiling, she held her phone up so he could read the message for himself.

'Staff shortage due to inclement weather? What does that mean?'

'It means you should look out of a window.'

'I know *what* it means but what I want to know is why it should affect my bagel delivery. I am on the same block. Message back and tell them to get someone to walk it over.'

An eyebrow a browner shade than her hair arched. 'It says, quite clearly, that they don't have the staff.'

'Then call the concierge.'

A sharp rise and fall of her shoulders and then she did as he asked whilst simultaneously adding coffee beans to the machine. It was a short conversation.

'The on-duty concierge is waiting for more staff to arrive,' she told him. 'They should be in a position to send someone out for you within the hour.'

That long? Marcello wanted his bagel now, not in an hour. What was wrong with the world that a bit of snow should cause such inconvenience?

'The coffee is prepared, it just needs to drip through,' she added. 'When the red light turns green, it will be ready to pour.'

'Great, then you can go and get me a bagel.'

The steel from earlier returned to her eyes. 'No, Marcello, now I go home.'

'But I am hungry. It will take you five minutes.'

'Ten in this weather. It's my day off and I've got plans.'

'If the weather is as bad as you keep whining about, your plans will have been cancelled.'

Her eyes widened. After a beat, she said, 'Whining?'

'Winter in Manhattan means bad weather,' he explained. 'You need to toughen up.'

While he waited patiently—and people thought he

didn't have patience? Such a misconception!—for her to display some remorse and do as he'd requested, Victoria's now narrowed eyes did not leave his face. It was a long moment before he realised that mutiny rather than remorse had settled in them, a mutiny carried through to the lifting of her chin and the sucking in of her cheeks. 'I tell you what, why don't *you* toughen up? You're not an invalid. You've got a pair of fully functioning legs—if the weather out there's as tropical as you seem to think it is, then go and get your own damned bagel. I'm going home.'

To his astonishment, Victoria finished her tempered outburst by striding across the kitchen, her long red hair swishing behind her.

Incredulous, he took a few beats to realise she was being serious.

'Do I have to remind you the home you refer to comes courtesy of your job for me?' he called out.

'A job that this is my first day off from in eighteen days,' she retorted without looking back.

He strode after her. 'You think I take days off?'

She stepped through the door. 'I am your employee. I have a contract that affords me rights.'

The door almost closed in his face. Almost as put out at her failure to hold it open for him as he was by this bolshy attitude, which, even by Victoria's standards, went beyond minor insubordination, Marcello decided it was time to remind her who the actual boss was and of her obligations to him.

'You cannot say you were not warned of what the job entailed when you agreed to take it,' he said when he caught up with her in the living room. She was already at the door that would take her through to the reception room. 'It is why you are given such a handsome salary and generous perks.'

Instead of going through the door, she came to a stop and turned back round, folding her arms across her breasts. 'Quite honestly, Marcello, the way I'm feeling right now, I'd give the whole lot up for one lie-in. One lousy lie-in. That's all I wanted but you couldn't even afford me that, could you? I tell you what, stuff your *handsome salary and generous perks*—I quit.'

Too astounded to do anything but laugh, he shook his head. 'Now you are being...'

But she'd already disappeared into the reception room, again not holding the door for him. This one being a spring-loaded, reinforced safety door, he came within an inch of having his nose broken by it slamming on him.

His patience close to being fully evaporated, he pushed the door open and loudly said, 'You have to give three months' notice.'

She emerged from the drying room with her outdoor clothing bundled in her arms.

Poker-faced, she eyeballed him as she pressed her thumb to the pad that summoned the elevator. 'Consider this my notice.'

'Are you actively trying to put me off providing you a reference?'

She held her palm up beside her face and gave it a little wave. 'Is this the face of concern?'

The elevator arrived.

'If you leave now, I will sue you for breach of contract,' he threatened.

Still not removing her gaze from his, she gave a defiant smile and stepped backwards into the elevator.

'I mean it, Victoria. I will sue you.'

Still smiling, she wound her scarf around her neck then, the doors closing, waved at him, this time in farewell. *'Ciao, amigo.'*

He wedged his foot in before the doors could fully close and slipped into the elevator with her. *'Amigo* is Spanish.'

'I know.'

'You can't quit over a bagel.'

She punched the button to get the elevator moving. 'I just did.'

'It is not valid until it is in writing.'

'I'll email HR as soon as I get home. Oh, and if you sue me, I'll countersue.'

'You have no grounds and you could not afford it.'

She rammed her woolly hat on her head, covering her ears. 'I think you'll find I can. My handsome salary and generous perks mean I've built quite the nest egg.'

'Then you do not want to lose it.'

'If I lose it, I go home and start again.'

He laughed. 'Home to Ireland? You love living in Manhattan. You would miss the nightlife.'

'My last night out was a date at the theatre. I made sure my boss knew I was going in the hope he'd leave me in peace for one night, and he still thought it acceptable to call me during the performance demanding I return to the office and help him find his Montblanc pen.'

The elevator had reached the ground floor.

Victoria walked out of it putting her coat on.

'The pen was a gift from my father and it was a request, not a demand,' Marcello defended himself as he kept step with her through the empty lobby.

'A request phrased as a demand.'

'You could have said no.' Ignoring the unimpressed face she threw at him, he added, 'You never did tell me who that date was with.'

'Someone who wasn't happy with me cutting and running on them for the sake of a pen.'

'But you are good at finding things.'

They'd reached the door that exited onto the street.

'And you're good at losing them.' Her hand reached for the door. '*Ciao*, Marcello.'

'Come on, Victoria, be reasona—'

A loud bang from outside made them both jump, and cut away Marcello's argument from his tongue.

'What the hell was that?' he muttered, darting to the nearest window.

The gentle fluttering of snow he'd risen to at his usual four a.m. had turned into a blizzard. He had to peer hard to make out the two cars that had collided right outside the entrance door.

CHAPTER TWO

THE SNOW WAS falling so hard that Victoria didn't realise Marcello had yanked open the driver's door of the
first crunched-up car until she walked into him. Her
apology dissolved into the howling wind.

The driver and sole occupant, a middle-aged man
who looked dazed rather than injured, let them help
him out.

'You take him inside,' she shouted at Marcello. The
cold was biting through her thick winter clothing. Marcello didn't even have a suit jacket on to protect him.
'I'll see to the other car.'

'What?' he shouted back.

'Take him inside!'

She then shuffled through what had to be at least
four inches of snow to the driver's side of the other
car, and opened the door. The wind almost pulled it
off its hinges.

Mercifully, there was only one occupant in this car
too, a middle-aged woman who also looked more dazed
than injured. Her airbag had been deployed and, after
she'd fought her way out, she clung to Victoria, shouting
an explanation as to why she was on the roads in such
treacherous conditions that Victoria barely heard a word

of. The wind was just too loud. Supporting the woman's weight, she guided her to the building. Incredibly, the woman was wearing a pair of stilettos, making the going slow and dangerous. Any moment and the woman would lose her footing and they'd both go tumbling. When Marcello emerged before them, she didn't know if she was horrified or grateful that he'd come back out.

'Anyone else?' he yelled close to her ear.

'No, this is it! Go back in! I've got her!'

Ignoring her, he lifted the woman into his arms and disappeared into the whiteness.

Virtually snow-blind, Victoria shuffled one foot in front of the other until she reached the steps. Clinging tightly to the railing, she made it to the top. Shoving the door open, she practically threw herself inside only to collide straight into rock-solid man.

An arm hooked around her back to steady her.

Blinking snow out of her eyes, she looked up and into Marcello's piecing blue stare.

The easy smile that was more familiar than any other spread over his face. 'I know you are cross about a bagel but do you have to keep slamming doors into me?'

His dryness collided with the surging relief that they were both inside and safe. It raced up her throat and expelled from her body as a short burst of laughter. The piercing blue eyes crinkled and then he burst into bemused, disbelieving laughter of his own.

After one quick squeeze of her waist and one dropped kiss on the top of her snow-laden hat, he stepped away from her, shaking his head whilst running his hand through the melting snowflakes in his thick black hair.

Even though she knew intuitively that the squeeze and kiss were Marcello's own relief manifesting, it still made her blink. Marcello was very Italian in his mannerisms, very tactile…but never with her. Everyone who crossed the threshold into his office was greeted with a handshake and a kiss to each cheek. Victoria had sat in on countless interviews kicked off with the same greeting.

It was his charm, Victoria had long ago decided, that along with his smile disarmed people and stopped his tactile manner crossing into unwanted behaviour. It was part of the package that had made an ordinary Roman rise to the top and conquer Manhattan before his thirtieth birthday, when he finalised an audacious takeover of a multi-billion investment group. A strong work ethic, a body that required little sleep and an instinct about people that enabled him to spot a potential troublemaker or a latent genius within two minutes had been the other components in his rise.

Now aged thirty-six, he was the king of his own castle with a devoted workforce. Victoria doubted there were many workers in the Guardiola Group who wouldn't take a bullet for him. It was her own devotion that had held her back from resigning the fifty-odd times she'd considered it before. Because, as selfish and demanding as Marcello was, he was also generous and fun to be around. His bad moods were rare and always followed with an apology. He complained about Victoria's predecessor quitting but he'd been partly to blame for that by giving her an incredibly generous maternity package followed by an eye-watering bonus because, he'd confided with great, if misplaced, authority, 'Babies are not cheap to raise.'

That bonus had been the equivalent of two years' full salary.

When the woman in question, Denise, had brought the baby in for everyone to coo over, Victoria had not long started as her replacement. For all his complaints about Denise leaving him, Marcello had greeted her like a long-lost sister and spent so long cuddling and fussing the baby that the child probably left thinking he was his father. He didn't even complain when the baby brought up milky sick on his Armani suit.

And yet, for all his tactile ways, with Victoria, he was strictly hands off. For her birthday, he'd had their office decorated with balloons and banners, given her tickets to a Broadway show—her last full night off without him bothering her about something inane—she'd longed to watch but couldn't remember mentioning to him, and generally made a great big fuss of the day, all without giving her the smacking kisses to the cheeks everyone else received on their birthdays. The most he'd ever done was shake her hand when they'd got together to discuss the job he'd poached her for.

Shaking off the weird unsettling feeling his brief display of affection had provoked, she cast her attention to the drivers of the collided cars.

Quickly establishing they were both physically fine, she arranged for the concierge, who'd reappeared even more frazzled, to keep them fed and warm until the emergency services arrived, whenever that would be.

With nothing more to be done for them, Victoria rewound her scarf around her neck. 'You should go up and get some dry clothes on,' she advised Marcello. He had to be freezing after his Action Man heroics. If it was anyone else, she'd suggest a hot bath too.

His white shirt was drenched from the melted snow and she was having to make a concerted effort not to let her eyes dip down to the naked chest it now transparently covered. Dark hair that covered much of his ripped torso and brown nipples were clearly visible.

She'd only seen him topless once, around a year ago. Coffee in hand, they'd just left their office for the boardroom when an absent-minded tech guy had walked into him. Coffee had splattered all over his shirt.

Victoria's first boss, the one Marcello had poached her from, would have gone berserk and probably fired the tech guy on the spot. Marcello had reassured him the coffee was cold so no harm had been done, advised him to watch where he was walking in the future, then dived back into his office and through to the mini-dressing room at the far end where his emergency clothing was kept. Victoria had been checking her emails while waiting for him when he came out sticking his arms into a fresh shirt asking her something she'd long forgotten.

What she hadn't forgotten was the fuzzy sensation she'd experienced to see his bare chest. It was much the same sensation as when she imagined him asleep in his bed.

'So should you,' he told her.

'I will.' She set off to the door. 'Go and drink your coffee and get warm.'

'Where are you going?'

'Home,' she answered, surprised he'd asked.

He gave her the look he'd once given a trio of college leavers pitching for an investment in their start-up business of beer brewed with a twist. His expression when he'd actually tasted the beer had been such a picture that she'd barely held it together until they were finally alone and she could let it out. The two of them had laughed so hard tears had been streaming down their faces.

This look was the look given to the initial *We've decided to improve beer by adding strawberries to it* pitch: utter incredulity that someone should think of something so stupid.

'You are not.'

'You've experienced for yourself how bad it is out there and the storm's barely started. Imagine how much worse—'

'You are not walking home in that.' Marcello jabbed a finger in the direction of the window. 'It is too dangerous.' And there was not a chance in hell he would let Victoria step another foot in it.

'I'm not hanging around here waiting for it to pass. They're saying the storm could last a couple of days.'

'I don't care if they are predicting it to last for weeks. You're not going anywhere until it is safe.' He positioned his back against the door, barring her exit. 'You will stay with me.'

'Not necessary.'

He folded his arms across his chest. 'Completely necessary, and it is not an order dressed as a request but an order.'

'You're not my boss so you can't order me to do anything.'

'Your notice has not been given in an official capacity so I am still your boss, and as your boss I am ordering you to stay. You can endanger your life all you want once I have found a replacement for you,' he added.

The glare she threw at him was completely mitigated by the amusement dancing in her eyes and the twitching of her lips. 'Ah, so it isn't concern for me but concern for the management of your life.'

He smiled widely. 'Perfectly put.'

'They're saying everyone needs to stay at home,' the man they'd rescued called out to them. 'Only essential travel as of now. You should take the man up on his offer, lady.'

'See, *lady*?' Marcello said. '*They* agree with me. It is not safe for you to leave.'

She tilted her head and, her Irish lilt musing, said, 'How strange how barely an hour ago you thought it acceptable for me to go out in it and collect your bagel.'

'I wasn't to know the storm had come in so quickly, was I?'

'Of course not. After all, I only mentioned it a dozen times.'

'If I have told you once, I have told you a million times not to exaggerate.'

Her lips twitched again, her chin wobbling, a classic sign that Victoria was suppressing laughter.

Marcello had never met anyone with such similar humour to him before. He'd recognised it the day he'd met her, when she'd been the assistant of the CEO of a firm he'd been considering investing in. During the firm's presentation, anything that could have gone wrong had. Victoria had impressed him with her handling of it all, all grace under fire. It wasn't until the final slide that it had become apparent everything going wrong was due to sabotage. Instead of the usual boring variation of, *Thank you for your consideration* appearing on the screen, someone had replaced it with a still from an old popular musical film where three high school students flashed their bare backsides and 'mooned' to the camera.

The po-faced directors had been outraged. Marcello had thought it hilarious. One look at the curvy redhead's contorted face had only added to his delight. It was seeing the tortured suppression of her laughter that had made his own all the sweeter.

'Your staff must really hate you,' he'd observed once he'd stopped laughing. Then, unable to resist, he'd looked again at the redhead. She'd clamped her hand over her mouth. Her shoulders had been shaking. Tears had been in her eyes. Only the expression in them had betrayed her thoughts. Those eyes had clearly been telling him she couldn't hold it back much longer and implored him not to say another word.

He'd taken pity on her and declined the investment without any further quips.

When Denise had announced she wouldn't return from her maternity leave, he'd known exactly who to appoint as her permanent replacement, and it would be a cold day in hell before he let Victoria leave him…terminate her employment, he corrected himself. It would be a colder day in hell before he let her go back out into that storm.

Unfolding his arms, he held his hands up. 'Okay, I admit it. You were right and I was wrong, and as you were right you must see that walking three blocks in this weather is a suicide mission.'

Eyes narrowing, she lifted her chin. 'Do you take back the part where you accused me of whining?'

He sighed. '*Sì*, I take it back.'

Her eyes now widened as she eyeballed him and non-subtly cleared her throat.

He exaggerated the next sigh. 'I am sorry that I accused you of whining. Now, can we please go up to my apartment before I drop down dead of hypothermia?'

More lip twitching. 'I wouldn't worry about that—you carry enough hot air in you to keep your core temperature up longer than the rest of us mortals.'

He shook his head regretfully. 'More talk like that and I will have to sack you.'

Her twitching lips spread into a wide grin and she shook her head before heading to the elevator, loudly saying, 'You're an idiot.'

He clamped a hand to her shoulder as he fell into step with her. 'You love me really.'

He didn't even have to look at her to know she was rolling her eyes.

Maybe she had a point about him being full of hot air because the warmth in his chest as he rode his elevator back up to his apartment with his favourite person in the whole of New York was enough to take the edge off the chill of his skin.

* * *

With Marcello taking a hot shower to defrost, Victoria curled up on her favourite of his sofas with a mug of his precious and admittedly delicious coffee. She'd thrown her wet jeans in the tumble dryer—she would bet money he didn't know where it was located in his vast apartment—and been astounded to find them dry within minutes. Relieved too. No way did she want to be around Marcello with only tights and socks covering her legs. Her jumper barely skimmed her bum.

She turned the telly on. Storm Brigit and the destruction it was already causing dominated the news.

She flicked through the channels in the hope of finding a forecaster with a better prognosis for it. She'd settled on the most optimistic of them when she head Marcello's footsteps coming down the staircase that connected the ground floor to the overhang behind her.

He refilled his coffee from the pot she'd brought from the kitchen into the living room, and made himself comfortable on the L-shaped sofa to the side of the one she'd taken.

'Jeans?' she gasped with faux horror when she clocked he wasn't wearing a suit.

'Do not tell *Time* Magazine,' he quipped.

'They wouldn't believe me.'

He met her stare and grinned. Along with his faded blue jeans, he'd donned a long-sleeved black top that enhanced his muscular physique. Not that he was over muscly. He didn't aspire to be a bodybuilder or anything, but he liked to take care of himself and made regular use of the apartment building's humungous gym and swimming pool.

'Looks like we are going to be roommates for the next couple of days,' he said, nodding at the telly and the optimistic forecaster still trying to convince New York that the storm was predicted to blow itself out within forty-eight hours when all the other forecasters were predicting three days.

'Don't tell Jenna or she'll scratch my eyes out.' Jenna was Marcello's latest girlfriend. Victoria loathed her more than all the others.

'That's been over for some time,' Marcello admitted, allowing himself a quick side-eye to see her reaction.

'Oh, really?' She took a sip of her coffee. 'I'm sorry to hear that.'

'No, you're not.'

'You're right, I'm not.' Eyes glued to the television, she added, 'When did you end it?'

'The day I walked in on her speaking to you like you were something she had trodden on.' He'd been in one of the rare meetings he didn't need Victoria to accompany him to. He'd returned to the office suite he shared with her to find Jenna with her palms down on Victoria's desk sneering, 'You're just a no one secretary. It's pathetic.'

Her gaze whipped from the television to him. 'That was months ago.'

Three months to be exact. *'Sì.'*

'You never said.'

'It was not important.' He cast her another side-eye. 'You never thought to ask why I stopped scheduling dates with her?'

She fixed her gaze back on the weather report. 'Your romantic life is none of my business.'

'I would not call it romantic.'

'I don't want to know what you call it,' she said sweetly, then drained her coffee. 'Who are you dating now?'

'I thought it was none of your business?'

'It isn't. I'm just being nosy.'

He laughed. 'I am not dating anyone.' Hadn't dated anyone since Jenna.

Victoria faced him with fake alarm. 'Are you ill?'

He'd wondered that himself a few times in recent months. Since Marcello had moved to Manhattan a decade ago, in need of a fresh start and with a determination to put the pain of the past behind him, he'd been as relentless in his pursuit of women as with business, and every bit as successful. It helped that he'd arrived here having already accumulated a modicum of wealth and that he had a face and physique the opposite sex found attractive. It also helped that he wasn't looking for a wife so wasn't seeking a meeting of minds or any of that romantic stuff, which widened his dating pool considerably.

He'd done marriage. He'd done family. What he'd lost could never be replaced.

He knew he'd developed terrible taste in women and he didn't care. It was better that way. If he was to date someone like Victoria for example, someone he greatly respected, who shared the same humour and with whom he could hold an entire conversation without either of them opening their mouths, then it would not be so easy to just send a text message calling things off. Not so easy to remain unmoved and ignore the outraged replies. Dating someone like Victoria would be much less drama in the short term but messier in the long run.

And so he stuck to his wide dating pool filled with shallow beauties whose lives revolved around themselves. Or had because all the shallow beauties he'd met in recent months had left him cold. He could too easily imagine them speaking to Victoria in the same way Jenna had. He could tolerate all forms of behaviour if a warm body was guaranteed but he could not tolerate that.

He hauled himself up from the sofa. 'I am not ill but I *am* hungry.' Now that the drama from earlier was over and he was warm and dry again, his neglected empty stomach was demanding food. 'Would it be unreasonable to ask the agency to send a chef over?' he added tongue in cheek, referring to the agency Christina and Patrick employed the pool of domestic workers who worked their magic keeping his home clean and fresh. Top quality chefs were part of the agency's services.

'Yes,' she stated firmly.

He smiled.

Her eyes narrowed before, half laughing, she shook her head. 'I can't cook!'

'I will add an ever bigger bonus to your salary.'

'I meant it literally. I can't cook.'

'How can you not cook?'

'How can *you* not cook?'

'Because I employ people to do it for me.'

'I don't work for you.'

'You do until you have given and worked your notice.'

'I don't *have* to work my notice.'

'And I don't *have* to sue you for breach of contract.'

Victoria couldn't suppress a snigger. 'Seriously, the only thing I can cook is toast. Oh, and instant noodles. Did you not learn your way around a kitchen before you become a spoilt billionaire?' He hadn't moved to Manhattan until he was twenty-six. His rise since his arrival had been stratospheric but she knew his background was modest and that he came from a family very similar to her own, but with fewer siblings and a less scary grandmother. She knew, too, from the grapevine, that he'd been married before his move to Manhattan, a short-lived marriage that's ending had left him devastated and swearing to never marry again. She'd often wondered what his wife had been like. Had she been an entitled bitch like his succession of lovers or someone normal? What did she have that no other woman had? What had gone so wrong between them that Marcello would become such an avowed bachelor?

All questions she would never learn the answer to. Marcello's marriage was the one subject that had never been discussed between them. As far as she was aware, he didn't even know that she knew he'd been married.

'I have managed to forget the few skills I learnt,' he informed her blithely.

'How convenient.'

'Being a spoilt billionaire is a very convenient excuse,' he agreed. 'What is yours?'

She smiled sweetly. 'Having a slave-driving, spoilt billionaire boss demanding my attention at all hours and leaving me reliant on take-out.'

CHAPTER THREE

VICTORIA STOOD IN Marcello's pantry struggling to keep her jaw from dropping open. This was one part of his apartment she'd never been in before, and *wow*. She had never seen so much food. It was like stepping into a condensed supermarket. The pantry itself was twice the size of her parents' kitchen.

'You could feed the whole of Manhattan with what's in here,' she commented, awed.

'Not quite,' he murmured, standing beside her.

'Close though. At least we won't starve. Can you see the eggs?'

They'd found packets of bacon in the fridge and agreed any idiot could cook that, then agreed that if any idiot could cook bacon, they could cook eggs too. When she'd asked where in the fridge said eggs were, he'd looked at her as if she really was an idiot.

She'd grinned. 'So you're not fully Americanised then?'

'I am afraid of my mother making a surprise visit,' he'd quipped. 'It is one of the few things of my childhood that has stuck with me. Coffee beans kept in the refrigerator, eggs kept at room temperature.'

Eggs and bread located, they went back into the

kitchen. There was a lot of clattering and other noise as they searched the industrially equipped room equal in size to her full apartment for utensils and crockery.

Thirty minutes later and the immaculate kitchen looked like a chimpanzee's party had been hosted in it.

Sitting at the sprawling kitchen island, both looked dubiously at their plates of burnt toast, blackened bacon and rubbery scrambled eggs.

Despite her stomach rumbling whilst they'd been cooking, Victoria's appetite had disappeared and she could only manage half of hers. Marcello, though, ate every last scrap of his bar the pieces of cunningly hidden eggshell, then gazed longingly at her leftovers. She pushed her plate to him with a 'be my guest' gesture, and, feeling suddenly cold, rubbed her left arm for warmth. A mild pounding had formed in her head, and she drained her coffee hoping the caffeine would ease it.

When Marcello put his knife and fork together and slid off his stool, his body aimed at the door, Victoria folded her arms and glared at him. 'Don't even think about leaving me to clear this mess up.'

'The staff will do it when they come in.'

She rolled her eyes. 'There's not going to be any staff, Marcello, not with the stay-at-home mandate.'

His forehead furrowed and he rubbed his fingers through his thick black hair.

'It's a suicide mission to walk out there,' she added, reminding him of his own words.

She could see his clever brain thinking and was not

in the least surprised when he said, 'I will double your salary for the month if you do it.'

'I've quit, remember?'

'You still have to work the notice you haven't given. Triple pay.'

'No.'

If she was going to be stuck in this apartment with him for the next few days then she would not allow herself to be bribed and charmed—suckered—into taking on the domestic chores. She would not allow herself to fall into any kind of domesticity with him, and it wasn't just because she hated housework. All five Cusack girls had been expected to muck in with household jobs. Victoria's job had been to wipe the place mats and clean the table. As she was the second youngest, her designated job had been the second easiest of the lot and still she'd loathed doing it, but she'd had to do it because with a family as large as the Cusacks, everyone was expected to muck in. Having a family as large as theirs meant she could have slipped away unnoticed by everyone except sharp-eyed Kara, the middle sister who would have sat on her if she'd sloped off. If Victoria had wanted to be a domestic goddess she'd have done like her second oldest sister, Mags, and cheerfully offered help with all the undesignated chores too, not hidden in her room and pretended to be deaf on the very rare occasion her parents remembered her existence enough to call her name.

Her main reason, though, was that Marcello would absolutely take advantage if she gave so much as an inch. It would start with cleaning the kitchen and end with him expecting her to do his laundry and pour all his drinks. After all, he hadn't started off as a total slave-driver when she'd first worked for him. He'd made unreasonable demands at all hours of the working week but initially her days off had been Marcello-free.

It had been over a year since she'd gone a whole day without at least talking to him. During her first Christmas in his employ, he'd called her twice during her week back in Ireland, and both calls had been necessary. The Christmas just gone, he'd called her every single day. In fairness, the call on Christmas Day itself had been to wish her a Merry Christmas from his family home in Rome.

It had been the strangest of calls, she remembered. There had been a melancholy in his voice, so faint that if she didn't know him so well she would never have detected it. By the time she'd gone to bed she'd been cursing his name for making her spend her favourite day of the year worrying about what the cause of the melancholy could have been. Their next conversation, the melancholy had been absent and in the two weeks since their return to normal working life, she'd been unable to bring herself to ask about it.

Not liking the reminder of how sick she'd felt for him and the cause of his uncharacteristic melancholy, a reminder that increased the mild burning stabbing sensation in her head, Victoria pulled herself together and made an executive decision. 'You load the dishwasher and I'll clean the surfaces.'

He pulled his most unimpressed face.

She wasn't in the least perturbed. 'It's either that or

we let the mess fester. I'll help but I'm not doing it on my own.'

'Quadruple pay.'

She rubbed her forehead with her palm to try and ease the burny stab. 'Quit the bribes and load the dishwasher.'

Marcello knew when he was beaten.

Giving a theatrical sigh, he picked up his plate. 'How do I do it?'

With a roll of her eyes...ouch, that hurt...she shook her head. 'You're the smartest man I know. You can work it out.'

His ego inflating at the compliment, Marcello went in search of the dishwasher, then watched a video on how to load it and hoped the end result would be better than the video on grilling bacon.

He tried to remember when he'd last performed a domestic chore. Certainly before his short marriage with Livia ended. When they first married, they'd earned enough between them to employ a weekly cleaner. By the time grief drove them apart, Marcello had earned enough on his own for a full-time housekeeper. His mother had half-heartedly tried to domesticate him as an adolescent but he'd been excellent at feigning uselessness at it, so much so that she decided it was easier to just continue doing the chores herself.

Victoria, he thought, watching her lean over to wipe the marble island, would never put up with that. She'd insist the adolescent keep practising until they mastered the art of running a vacuum cleaner around a room...

She stretched right over the island to reach a spot

in the middle. Her sweater had risen and suddenly he had a full display of curvy bottom clad in tight jeans in his eyeline.

Much practice meant he was able to immediately avert his gaze and give his attention back to trying to figure out how to turn the damned dishwasher on.

Experience had taught him the slightly weightier beats of his heart would soon lighten.

He'd headhunted Victoria as Denise's replacement knowing intellectually that she was an attractive woman but never allowing himself to see her as such. There were occasions when he would observe her working on her computer or chatting on the phone or doing some other work-related task, and experience a wave of awareness. Other occasions, usually early mornings, when they shared the back of his car on the way to a meeting or an airport somewhere and she was still so fresh from the shower that he could smell her shampoo and the cleanliness of her skin, and have to block off his senses.

All those things were manageable. He made them manageable. Allowing himself to see her for the beautiful, curvaceously sexy woman she was would only lead to unwanted desires springing to life, which would then lead to a mess that would disrupt the efficiency of his life. And so he didn't allow it. Victoria was his executive assistant, his right-hand woman. She'd become indispensable to him.

'Here,' she said, her musical lilt breaking into his thoughts and the curvaceously sexy body he was trying to tune out breaking into his space to stand beside him and place the grill pan in front of him. 'You missed this.'

'How is that supposed to fit in it?'

'Let me check my guide to loading a dishwasher.'

He turned to face her.

She was staring at her opened palm. Shaking her head ruefully, she met his stare. 'I'm so sorry. The guide's not working. You'll have to figure it out all by yourself like a big boy.'

Ignoring her jest, he leaned his face more closely to hers. Was he imagining that she'd lost colour in her cheeks? Victoria was so naturally pale that it was hard to tell but there was something about her colour that made him ask, 'Are you feeling okay?'

She gave the slightest wince. 'Your whining has given me a headache.'

With any other woman he'd immediately come back with the quip used by men for what was probably millennia. Instead, he said, 'Do you need painkillers?'

'No need for you to take such drastic action on my behalf.'

He grinned. 'Go and sit down. I will finish up in here,' he added magnanimously.

Her eyes widened in alarm. 'Are *you* feeling okay?'

He only just restrained himself from giving her big, beautiful bottom an affectionate slap.

The snow was falling so thickly that Victoria could hardly make out any of Central Park. Manhattan was no longer blanketed in white. It was laden with it. Once the storm cleared, she'd get herself a sled and head to Pilgrim Hill.

One of her fondest childhood memories was of her family all trudging through foot-high snow to the nearest decent slope and sledging on bin bags for what had felt like hours. She'd sat on her mother's lap, she remembered, a treat that had been as rare as having enough snow to sledge on. She remembered, too, how she'd cried when her mother, deciding they were all in danger of turning into popsicles, had made the unilateral decision to return home. The promise of hot chocolate had dried Victoria's tears, and when they'd trooped through the front door and her mother had seen how blue the girls' fingers were, she'd whipped the youngest two, Victoria and Sinead, upstairs and run them a bath, staying to lift them out and dry them, another treat as rare as the snow. Mags had usually supervised Victoria's bath time.

It had been one of the best days of her life, and her already chilled body shivered in remembrance at how wonderfully cold it had been that day and yet how wonderfully warm she'd felt inside under the glow of her mother's attention.

Her brain, though, was still burning, and she pressed her forehead to the cold window pane and dimly wondered if Marcello would like to go sledging with her. As quickly as she thought it, she discarded it. Sheena, her old roommate, would definitely be up for it. That was if she'd forgiven Victoria for abandoning her at the theatre for the sake of a missing Montblanc pen.

Her head was really hurting. And she was still shivering. Marcello's usually tropically heated apartment felt like an igloo.

She was about to climb off the windowsill she'd sat herself on and go to find him for some of the painkillers he'd suggested just fifteen short minutes ago, when he finally came out of the kitchen. Even with her suddenly fuzzy vision, Victoria could see his top was soaked.

'What happened?' Her voice sounded as fuzzy to her ears as Marcello was to her eyes.

'The dishwasher is faulty.'

'How?'

'It made banging noises after I turned it on so I opened it. The top thing that spins around and sprays water was hitting the grill thing.'

That explained why he was wet. From the look on his fuzzy face, Victoria was clearly at fault for not pointing out the danger of this happening.

She scrambled for a quip but nothing came to her. It wasn't just her sight and hearing that had become fuzzy but the whole of her goosebump-flecked body. Her burning brain had become incapable of conjuring even a minor jest.

Marcello, anticipating a witty retort, was disconcerted when nothing came. Surely she must have a riposte for him? 'Is your head still hurting?'

Her answering nod was small, as if it hurt to make too much movement.

Disconcertment turned into concern. Victoria had been his assistant for eighteen months. They worked so closely together that he'd learned to recognise the signs of her cycle, knew that when she spent a couple of days being a touch irritable, in another week she would silently suffer the stomach cramps that had her bring a hot-water bottle to the office and hold it to her abdomen whenever she thought he wasn't paying attention. He wouldn't dream of embarrassing her by asking if she needed anything in those times, but this was different. His brave, stoical executive assistant, who'd never taken a single day off sick, had pain etched on her face.

'You should lie down.'

His concern deepened when, instead of arguing, she gave another small nod.

Concern turned to alarm when she slid off the windowsill and her knees buckled. He had no doubt that if she hadn't gripped the armchair to the side of the sill, she would have collapsed onto the floor.

He strode straight to her.

'I'm fine,' Victoria whispered, holding a palm out to stop Marcello's blurry figure getting any closer. 'Just got a bit dizzy.'

She blinked rapidly to clear her vision but each blink hurt her eyes and hurtled sharp pins into her burning brain. In the deep recesses of her mind was the knowledge that she'd caught one of the viruses debilitating New York, likely the one that had incapacitated Patrick and Christina overnight. She needed to lie down. Needed to get warm.

All she could allow herself to focus on was the long sofa. It was four steps away at the most.

Aware—much too aware—of Marcello standing to her side watching her, aware of his apparent concern, she took the first step, silently begging her legs to keep the rest of her upright. Of all the people in all the world to fall ill in front of, Marcello was the absolute worst.

Fighting through the swimming sensation that had now added itself to the burn in her brain, using legs that seemed to have become detached from the rest of her body, she took the next step...

The room began to spin.

'Victoria?'

She swayed.

The spinning sped up.

His next call of her name came like a distant echo in her ear as the whole world spun around her and then turned to grey.

Marcello caught her mid-fall. Hooking an arm around her waist, he tried to help her stand but Victoria's legs weren't cooperating. With his only other option being dragging her to the sofa, he lifted her into his arms like an injured child and cradled her to his chest.

Her eyes flew open. 'What you doing?' she mumbled.

'Getting you to a bed,' he decided firmly. That was where she needed to be. In bed. He knew because that was what the doctor had said when he'd called him out after Christina and Patrick had been struck down. Christina had deteriorated as quickly as Victoria. Sleep, the doctor had decreed, was the best medicine.

'No,' she protested weakly even as her cheek flopped against his neck. *Dio*, he could feel the elevated heat of her skin. She was burning up.

'Do not argue,' he scolded, heading for the stairs. 'You are not well.'

'Too heavy.'

Tuning out that her breath was hot against his skin and that her breasts were pressed against his chest, he lightly said, 'What did I just say about not arguing?'

Perfectly buxom though Victoria was, she was by no means too heavy for him to carry up the open stairs like a superhero. Through his office he took her and into his sleeping quarters, where he made a split-second decision and carried her into the closest room, which just happened to be his own. It had the most comfort-able mattress and, unlike the guest rooms, had a sofa long enough for his six-foot-two body to sprawl out on while watching over her.

The curtains were still drawn, the duvet still thrown back from when he'd got up that morning, his incapac-itated staff being unable to open the curtains or pro-vide him with the freshly laundered bedding he enjoyed daily. She made hardly any movement as he carefully laid her down, her only word, 'Cold.'

'You are cold?' he clarified, gingerly resting his hand on her burning forehead. Now that she was lying down, there was no need for further physical contact.

'Cold,' she repeated, barely audible, slowly drawing her legs to her chest. Her eyes were closed.

He scratched the back of his head, unsure what to do. Did you put a duvet around someone with a fever? Reasoning she could always throw it off if she over-heated, he covered her before stepping back to con-gratulate himself on a job well done. Superhero that he was, he'd saved his assistant from hurting herself in a faint and selflessly carried her into his own bed. He would remind her of this the next time she implied he was selfish.

'I will get you painkillers,' he said, keen to add more gold stars to his name on the off chance that she really was considering leaving him…quitting her job.

Her, ''K…' came out like a sigh.

This, though, posed its own challenge as, for all his talk about painkillers, Marcello didn't actually possess any. Not wanting to disturb his stricken housekeeper and butler, who must surely have a stash of the stuff, he put a call through to the concierge. It took ten whole minutes for a small tub of ordinary painkillers to be sent up to him in his elevator.

Armed with a glass of water and the means to ease Victoria's temperature and pains, he returned to his bedroom.

She was huddled in the sheets on her side, only the top of her head poking through.

To wake her or not to wake her? That was the question. Crouching down, he lightly pressed his fingers to the inch of exposed forehead. He squeezed his eyes tight and breathed hard. Too hot. Much too hot.

'Victoria?' he whispered loudly. 'You need to wake up and take some painkillers.'

Her eyes didn't open. 'Head hurts,' she mumbled.

'I know. This will make you feel better.'

'Can't.'

'Can't what?'

'Move. Hurts.'

'You want me to help you?'

She made the smallest nod even as she gave a nearly audible, 'No.'

Chuckling softly, he removed two of the tablets from the tub, placed them by the glass, then sat himself beside Victoria and carefully slipped an arm beneath her. 'I am just going to lift you a little so you can take your pills,' he told her.

She gave no protest, verbal or otherwise.

It took only a little effort to raise her so she was semi-upright. Holding her securely to him with his right arm, he reached for the water and pills with his left.

'Open your mouth,' he commanded.

She obeyed. He placed a tablet on her tongue without making any direct contact, then held the glass to her lips. Her hair tickled his throat and chin as she took the water into her mouth and swallowed.

'One more.'

Her lips parted again. This time his precision failed him and his finger brushed against soft, plump bottom lip then soft, plump, wet tongue.

Marcello's chest and airwaves tightened. His grip on the glass when he held it to her mouth a second time was much firmer than his first, reflexively gripping harder still when her hand fluttered up and tentatively covered his in silent encouragement for him to feed her more water.

He didn't know if it was her fever causing it but his own skin heated. The core temperature she'd teased him about only hours ago rose.

It felt like time stood still while he waited for the

signal that she'd had enough, a passage of time where, in an effort to disassociate himself from the soft body leaning against his and the slender hand covering his own, he conjured images of dancing nuns and didn't dare to breathe.

Her hand flopped away from his.

He expelled the breath he'd been holding. 'Done?'

Another tickle of her hair as she nodded and whispered, 'Thank you.'

Putting the glass back on the bedside table, he carefully extricated himself from his role of human support and, doing his utmost to touch her as little as humanly possible, helped her lie back down.

She turned her cheek onto the pillow and gave a tiny whimper.

It was a sound that pierced through him.

A second whimper had him closing his eyes and forcing air into his lungs as he was carried back to the darkest days of his life, a time of unbearable loss and a grief so debilitating he could hardly breathe through it.

CHAPTER FOUR

CHANGED INTO A T-shirt and pair of pyjama bottoms gifted by his brother as a joke birthday present, and which he'd never worn before as he always slept nude, Marcello quietly padded into his room carrying a bundle of bedding taken from a guest bed. Outside, the storm continued to wage its war on the East Coast. The news was reporting half of New York being without power. Guessing it was only a matter of time before his apartment was similarly affected, he'd dug out the scented candles his mother gifted him each year under the delusion they would add a feminine touch to the apartment he'd determined before he'd even bought it would remain a bachelor pad for the rest of his existence.

For the first time in a long time, Marcello thought back to the home he and Livia had created together and the room they'd turned into a nursery. They'd spent hours searching for the best furniture to fill it with, and the best wallpaper and curtains to cover its walls and window. Giraffes. That had been the theme they'd chosen. Cute, cartoon-like giraffes that bore no resemblance to the real-life versions but were close enough that he still couldn't bear to see a giraffe in any shape or form. After moving to Manhattan, he'd deliberately avoided Central Park Zoo until discovering by chance that they didn't house them.

Pushing the memories away, he gave his attention back to the person who needed it most.

The insulation in his bachelor pad was so good that no sound of the raging storm penetrated. In his bed, though, lay Victoria, fighting her own personal storm. He had no thermometer and the concierge service had been unable to assist, so he had only his hands to judge that her temperature was worsening. Had only his eyes to see her struggle to keep warm one moment then to cool down the next.

Once he'd made a bed for himself on the sofa, he braced himself and went back to her with more pain-killers. If he could have given them to her an hour ago he would have but Dr Internet—his own doctor wasn't answering his calls—had been firm that this brand and dose of painkillers could only be taken every six hours. This would be the third lot he'd fed her. She'd been a dead weight in his arms for the second batch, unable to support her own head. He supposed it was some inherent survival instinct that had enabled her to take the water into her mouth to wash the tablets down, and it was the one thing that kept the coldness of fear in his heart at bay and enabled him to leave her for a few minutes at a time.

Gently lifting her upright, his heart stuttered to find her hair wet and plastered to her skull and her sweater drenched. The sheet beneath her was soaked with her perspiration. Fever almost crackled on her skin.

The cold fear broke free and grabbed at his throat.

He took a long breath. Parked the fear. Forced himself to think logically. Panicking did not help anyone. He'd learned that the hard way.

First things first. Painkillers and water.

As docile as a newborn lamb, she let him feed them to her.

Clenching his jaw, he breathed in deeply then said, 'Victoria, you need to take your sweater off.' And everything else. He didn't need Dr Internet to tell him she was overheating.

There was the slightest movement of her head against the crook of his neck.

'Can you lift your arms for me?'

She could barely raise her hands to her elbows.

There was nothing else for it. He would have to do it himself.

'We need to cool you down,' he said in what he hoped was a conversational tone as he manipulated her arms out of the sweater's sleeves whilst keeping her secure against him. 'Lift your head for me.' Her feeble attempt at this fortified him. Somewhere in Victoria's delirious mind she knew he was helping her and was trying to express her consent.

Refusing to let his mind return to the last time he'd held another helpless, overheating human being, he kept a tight hold of her burning body and used his left hand to pull the sweater over her head.

Although he knew to expect it, it still made his chest sharpen to find her fevered skin drenched with perspiration. Her soaked vest top clung to her.

Don't debate it, just do it, he told himself firmly. A minute later, the vest was off and discarded with the sweater. A quick pinch of the fastenings and a skim down her arms and her wet bra was removed too. He didn't even look at it as he threw it on the pile.

Manoeuvring her to the other, dry side, of the bed, resolutely refusing to acknowledge the weighty bare breast pressed against his biceps, he laid her back down, then quickly pulled off his T-shirt and covered her torso with it to protect both her modesty and his eyes.

'Nearly there,' he said. 'Just your jeans now.'

She mumbled something. A hand fluttered to the button and groped ineffectually at it before flopping back to her side.

'It is okay, I've got this,' he assured her.

Mindset fixed on the job in hand, Marcello unbuttoned the jeans, pulled the zip down then tugged at them. He couldn't get them or the tights—tights? Was wearing tights beneath jeans even a thing?—past her hips. 'See, now you know why I work out,' he told her as he slid a hand under her bottom and lifted it so he could ease the jeans and tights down to her thighs. 'It is in case a member of my staff is incapacitated by a virus and needs my superhero strength to undress them.'

He needed to keep talking, for both their sakes, and as he pulled the damp jeans and wet tights down her legs, using every ounce of his resolve not to look at the scrap of black cotton covering her pubis, the one item of clothing he would not under any circumstances touch, he kept the chatter going. He hoped like hell that she could hear him and was comforted and reassured by it.

Her jeans became stuck at the ankles, preventing

him pulling them or the tights over her feet. Damn it, she was wearing socks over the tights! No wonder she was burning like a furnace.

A minute of intense concentration later and the jeans, tights and socks were all removed.

'I am going to get you...'

His intention of telling her he was going to get a cold cloth to wipe her face died on his tongue.

While he'd been removing the last of Victoria's clothing, she'd pulled the T-shirt off her chest. Unprepared, he had nothing to stop his gaze filling with her semi-naked form. Nothing to stop the curvaceous body he'd spent eighteen months pretending was as ordinary as any other body from soaking straight into his retinas.

Victoria opened her eyes. Sharp pain filled them. Her room was in darkness.

Not her room, she remembered through the pneumatic drill pounding in her head. One of Marcello's guest rooms.

She'd dreamed she was in Dante's *Inferno*.

She needed to use the bathroom. She reached through her befuddled brain for where it was. All the rooms in the apartment had an en suite, all situated on the opposite side of the room to the bed. She tried to sit up. A pain lanced her head, so sharp she cried out and flumped back onto her pillow.

'Victoria?'

Marcello?

She heard sheets rustling and then a shape emerged before her. Fingers pressed against her forehead.

She could hardly move her mouth to weakly ask, 'What are you doing?'

'Checking your temperature,' he answered quietly. 'I think your fever has broken.'

'What?'

'That is what Dr Internet calls it. It means the worst is over.'

'My head hurts.' Hurt so much. Everything hurt.

'I am sorry. You need to wait another hour before you can take more painkillers.'

A tear rolled down her cheek. She needed the bathroom but didn't think she had the strength to make it there.

'I need…' Her mouth was too parched to get any more words out.

'The bathroom?' he guessed.

She gave the weakest nod she could physically endure.

A dim light came on, as if he knew brightness would hurt her eyes.

The strange fog she'd been caught in for so long she didn't know if hours or days or weeks had passed reclaimed her. In an almost dreamlike state, she let Marcello lift her into his arms.

A strong sense of comfort in the sureness of his steps and the protective way he cradled her allowed Victoria to close her eyes and relax into him.

Faint light pouring in from the opened blind of the window drenched the dark bathroom in a faint glow.

'Can you take it from here?' he asked as he gently put her on her feet but kept hold of her so she had his strength as support.

Even through the heavy fog and dim memory of Marcello saving her from Dante's *Inferno* by stripping her clothes off her...she had no recollection of him putting the T-shirt she was wearing on her...there was a recoiling of horror at the thought of him watching her use the bathroom. 'Yes.'

He nodded. 'I will be right on the other side of the door.'

She wanted to tell him not to listen but the words wouldn't form.

He smiled, reading her thoughts again. 'I promise to close my ears. Now put your hand on the sink for support.'

Outside the closed bathroom door, Marcello rolled his neck, closed his eyes and concentrated on breathing. It wasn't enough to stop images of Victoria from dancing behind his lids.

It had taken more strength than he'd known he possessed to cool her face with a wet cloth and pat her dry with a towel, superhuman strength to remain dispassionate whilst manipulating her unresponsive body into the T-shirt. Of all the things he'd done for her, that had been the hardest, only the knowledge that she would be deeply embarrassed to wake virtually naked with him in the room spurring him on. When she came back to herself, she would be embarrassed enough to remember what he'd had to do for her.

The faint sound of fingers tapping the bathroom door had his eyes snap open and his chest swell. Opening the door a fraction, he spoke through the crack. 'Are you done?'

Fingers appeared through the crack in answer and gripped the frame surrounding the door.

He opened the door slowly, afraid of knocking it into her too-weak body...had it really been less than a day since she'd taken delight in slamming doors on him?

She was pressed against the wall to the side of the door, her cheek resting against the cool tile. He didn't know if it was a trick of the snow-white light seeping into the room but she was deathly pale.

Dio, even looking as wretched as it was possible for a human to look, she was beautiful.

'Let's get you back to bed,' he said as he cloaked himself with more much needed dispassion and hooked an arm around her. Carefully manoeuvring her so she leaned into him, he added, 'Can you walk?'

Her head rubbed against his shoulder in a nod.

'Hold onto me.'

Fingers slid slowly across the back of his waist then curved to a rest around his hip. Her temperature had dropped considerably since those frightening witching hours yet the burn of her touch cut through the cotton of his pyjama bottoms and seeped into his skin.

Breathing heavily, doing everything he could to block the sensations alive in him, Marcello steered Victoria to the bed and helped her into it, lifting her legs when she didn't have the strength to lift them herself.

'Duvet on?'

The tiniest of nods.

He covered her in it. 'Go back to sleep. I will wake you when it is time for more painkillers.'

When he was about to step away, her eyes fluttered

open and locked onto his. A hand poked out of the duvet and stretched to him. He took hold of it. She gave his fingers the lightest of squeezes before giving the deepest sigh and falling back into sleep.

The first thing Victoria registered was that the pneumatic drill in her head had dimmed to a dull ache. Opening her eyes, she registered that she wasn't in a guest room but in Marcello's bedroom. The guest rooms, though spacious, were smaller, and decorated luxuriously but neutrally. Marcello's room by contrast was huge, and had deep grey panelled walls with splashes of deep, rich colour in the artwork and plentiful soft furnishings. She'd always imagined he'd hired an interior decorator and told them to create the most masculine bedroom possible so as to repel any woman from thinking she could stay more than a night in it.

How many nights had she slept in here? One? Two? Time had slipped away from her. The curtains were open on the floor-to-ceiling window her eyes had opened to, the light diffusing through the thick snow still falling telling her daytime was slipping away.

Bracing herself for pain, she lifted her head. The pain was enough to make her wince but nothing as bad as what she'd suffered before.

The worst really was over. Or had she imagined Marcello saying that?

And there he was, sprawled out on the leather sofa at the far wall opposite the bed, phone in hand, an arm hooked behind his head, hooked-together ankles and bare feet dangling off the end. A heap of bedding had been dumped on the floor beside him.

Blurry memories played like snapshots before her eyes and a swelling like she'd never experienced before released in her chest, gratitude and something indefinable filling her and rising up her throat with force enough to stop her calling out to him.

To see him lying there in…pyjama bottoms? Marcello was wearing pyjama bottoms? She would never have imagined that…and plain black T-shirt, ungroomed thick black hair mussed and sticking out in all directions, strong jaw covered in thick black stubble…

He must have sensed her stare for he turned his face.

Their eyes locked. After a long beat, the smile that had caused a thousand women's hearts to break lit his face. Laughter lines crinkled the corners of his eyes and for the very first time Victoria was unable to stop herself from seeing exactly what it was that other women saw when they looked at Marcello Guardiola.

The swelling in her chest crushed against her ribs.

'How are you feeling?' he asked, swinging his long legs to the floor.

It took a long time before she was able to answer. 'Better.'

'You look better,' he said approvingly. 'I have been worried about you.'

She couldn't take her eyes from him. All the things about him that she'd steadfastly refused to see on anything but a superficial level were right there before her, and she was helpless to stop herself drinking in every inch of the ruggedly handsome face and the hard, lean body he'd used as a pillar and shield to stop her falling.

'Hungry?'

She shook her head, unable to speak through the pulses suddenly raging in her throat.

'Not even for soup?'

Why couldn't she drag her gaze from him?

'I will make you chicken soup,' he decided at her non-answer. 'Dr Internet and my mother—she sends you her best wishes—say it is the best thing for you. If you can't manage it, I will eat it.' He looked at his watch. 'You can have more pain relief soon too.' He rose to his feet and stretched. His T-shirt rose, exposing the flat of his abdomen and the swirls of dark hair around his navel. 'There is water on your bedside table. Do you need my help to drink or need me for anything else before I go downstairs?'

The beats of her heart were racing like a drum in her ears. She gave another shake of her head.

He leaned over to the round table at the head of the sofa, picked up her phone and placed it on the bedside table. 'If you are feeling up to it, you should call your family.'

She stared at him blankly.

'They called to see you were keeping safe from the storm,' he explained.

Did they? she wondered dimly as her gaze remained glued to Marcello's ruggedly handsome face.

'I had to tell them you were ill,' he continued. 'I do not think they are convinced I have been looking after you well, so if you do speak to them, make sure to tell them my skills as a nurse are as exceptional as my skills in business. And please, assure your grandmother that I have not locked you in a basement.' His left eyebrow rose then wriggled. 'Does she breathe fire?'

Not waiting for an answer, he strode out of the room leaving Victoria staring at his retreating figure with the terrifying sensation that she'd caught a secondary virus.

It took more effort to use her hands than she'd have believed possible but somehow Victoria managed to post on the Cusack family messaging group, assuring them she was over the worst of her illness. Marcello must have laid her illness on thick to get them worried. She'd once woken with the most horrendous period cramps, so bad she'd been unable to haul herself out of bed for school, and no one had noticed her failure to make it down to breakfast. The first her parents knew she was still in bed had been via an alert from the school telling them she'd failed to arrive there. Her mum had called the house to see why Victoria hadn't gone to school, then told her to take some painkillers. She hadn't deemed period cramps worthy of popping home in her lunch break to check on her fourth youngest daughter.

Looking back, Victoria understood her mother's blasé attitude—she'd been through it already with the three older girls—but for Victoria, frightened and in pain, her indifference had hurt.

Grandma Brigit immediately responded to her message, and demanded proof it was Victoria who'd written it and not 'that man', which brought the kernel of a smile to her face. Knowing she would otherwise be bombarded with demands of proof in perpetuity, she took a selfie of her face on the pillow and winced at the image taken. Not having the energy to retake it, she pressed send and then used the last of her reserves to delete the image from her files.

She didn't even have the energy to stop herself from thinking about Marcello.

As sleep wound its tentacles back around her, she soothed herself that the swell of feelings for him had been simple gratitude for the simple fact that he'd been her saviour. He'd stepped up when she'd needed him—the first time she'd ever needed him—and got her through the worst illness of her life. That it had felt more than heartfelt gratitude was a mirage caused by her defences being low and her frazzled mind playing tricks on her.

She was sinking back into sleep when the man whose face was lodged behind her closed eyes returned to the room.

Her heart kicked before her eyes opened.

'I bring soup,' he said proudly. He placed a tray on the table by the armchair at the side of the bed, then sat on the edge of the bed beside her. 'You are going to try and eat?'

The look in his eyes…had they always been such a clear shade of blue?…told her that this was a question with only one possible answer. Marcello was determined she should have some sustenance.

See, she assured herself. This was why her heart was racing: a manifestation of her gratitude.

She remembered how her heart had skipped all those many months ago. She hadn't recognised the number flashing on her ringing phone and had braced herself for a scam call. When Marcello had announced himself and then announced why he was calling, her heart had skipped and then raced so hard she'd taken an age to respond. So long had her silence gone on that he'd assumed she wasn't interested and increased the salary offer he'd just made by fifty thousand dollars. He didn't know she'd been too gobsmacked to answer.

She'd remembered him—of *course* she'd remembered him—but it had never occurred to her that he'd remembered her too. That this business titan had remembered her, remembered because he'd *seen* something in her, and gone out of his way to track down her personal number and offer her a job…

For the woman who'd grown up lost in the midst of siblings who all shone brighter than her…

She still didn't know which had meant the most to her, the remembering or the job offer, but, as demanding a boss as Marcello could be, she'd never forgotten how that one call had made her feel. Seen. Special. Things she'd never felt before.

And now, on top of all the care he'd given her, he'd made her soup.

She'd never gone so long without eating before and though she wasn't hungry, she knew she should at least try.

For the first time since she'd fallen ill, she was entirely aware of the muscular strength of Marcello's arm when he slid it beneath her, and wholly aware of the warmth of his hard body when he helped her sit up by resting her against him. Still holding her securely, he leaned over to grab some pillows. In an instant, her senses filled with the scent of faded cologne and warm skin.

She didn't know relief could feel like dejection when, finally satisfied that she was suitably propped up and unlikely to flop back down, he moved away from her. She didn't know, either, if she was imagining how quickly he released his hold on her and got off the bed, or if she was imagining that he spent a long time at the tray before carrying a large steaming mug to her. She didn't know, either, if it was the heat of the mug or the heat of his fingers making sure her hands were wrapped securely around the mug that sent warm sensation through her hands and into her bloodstream.

'You must eat all of it—I made it myself,' he said lightly.

She cleared her throat and tried to convince herself that her racing pulses were due to the virus. 'Really?'

'*Sì*. I have put it in a mug for you so you will find it easier to manage than with a bowl and spoon.' The smile that contained equal dollops of mischief and sexiness flashed at her. 'It would have been ready sooner but I could not find a tin opener.'

Marcello could hardly credit the strength of his relief to see a real smile form on Victoria's pale face at this, and see amusement spark in her eyes.

For the first time he allowed himself to admit that there had been moments during the long night when he'd feared he would never see her smile again. It had been the longest, most frightening night he'd experienced in eleven years.

Moving the armchair to within a foot of the bed so

he was close to hand if she needed him, he parked himself on it and was filled with even more relief when she sipped her way through all the soup. By the time he took the empty mug from her, a hint of her old colour had returned to her cheeks. He didn't kid himself that she was magically better but these little things meant she'd taken the first steps on her road to recovery. They meant that, tonight, he could sleep with his eyes and ears closed.

'You have called your family?' he asked.

She shook her head tiredly. 'I messaged the family group.'

'Good. Put their minds at rest.' He'd only answered her phone because *Mam* had flashed on the screen when it rang. His own mother kept calling too, as he'd stupidly let slip that he'd gained a house guest who'd fallen ill. She seemed as unconvinced as the Cusacks that he was taking proper care of Victoria. 'They have been calling every hour—they are worried about you.'

Her smile was as tired as her head shake. 'You must have told them I was dying.'

That took him aback. 'Why do you say that?'

'They're not ones for making a fuss.'

Seeing she was in no state to argue, he held off from commenting that if that was the Cusacks' definition of not making a fuss, he would hate to see what a real fuss consisted of. 'I told them only that you had a flu-like virus, but you are very far from them. It is natural they would worry more than if you were with them in Ireland and could see you for themselves.' He didn't add that if they had seen Victoria at her worst, worry would easily have turned into the same cold panic that had engulfed him all those years ago, and had come perilously close to engulfing him again.

Doubt clouded her eyes but then she gave another tired smile. 'You think?'

'Trust me. It is the same for me with my family.'

She held his gaze a moment longer then nodded as if reassured, which he found odd but didn't comment on. It would be a while before Victoria was fully herself again.

'Shall I put the television on?'

Her face contorted in a suppressed yawn. 'Only if you want to watch something.'

'You want to lie back down?'

The next yawn refused to be suppressed. She caught it with her hand and gave an apologetic smile that tugged at his heart.

Fortifying himself with the mental blocks needed to get on the bed with her, he put his arm around her and held her steady while removing the pillows he'd propped behind her.

'What's happening with the storm?' she asked sleepily as she lay back down.

Making a heroic effort not to pay any attention to the movement of her breasts as she made herself comfortable, he pulled the duvet up to her shoulders. 'Still doing storm things. They are saying we should expect another two or three days of it.'

'That long?' Her eyes looked troubled. 'I should move to a guest room and let you have your bed back.'

He gave a dismissive shake of his head. 'We can think about that tomorrow. For now, rest and build your strength. The sofa is perfectly adequate for me to sleep on.'

'Don't do that,' she pleaded. 'Take one of the guest beds.'

'If I sleep in a guest room, how will I know if you need me in the night?' He forced a preen into his voice. 'I know I am a superhero but I cannot see through walls.'

He anticipated eyes dancing with amusement at this, hoped too for a quip that would release some of the tension he'd been unable to stop building at the feel of her soft warmth pressed against him. Neither occurred.

The eyes glued to his…for the first time he couldn't prevent his brain recognising what a beautiful hazel colour they were…simply stared. The lips he'd never allowed himself to register as being wide and plump until his finger had brushed against the bottom one pulled in, her cheeks…such high cheekbones she had…sucking in with them.

Her hand slipped out of the duvet and, as it had done all those hours ago, reached for him. 'Thank you,' she whispered.

It was the soft sincerity of her gratitude that made his chest swell all over again and made him swallow before he captured the opened hand in his own. *'Prego.'*

The sensation that seeped through his skin as her fingers wrapped around his…

There was a slight tremor in her lips before she pulled a smile to her face and said, 'Don't think this means I've changed my mind about quitting.'

He brought her hand to his mouth and kissed her fingers before he even knew he was going to do it.

CHAPTER FIVE

'WE NEED TO change the bedsheets,' Marcello declared the next morning. Victoria's recovery was continuing. She'd slept soundly through the night without any spike in temperature and had woken only once for painkillers, for what she'd described as 'a pneumatic drill in my head'. In the hours she'd been awake, she'd eaten two of the croissants he'd found in the freezer, baked for the stated time and only slightly burned for breakfast, drunk two cups of tea from a box the concierge had provided from some hidden stash, brushed her teeth, and taken only half the pain relief allowed. Her colour was steadily improving, the musical lilt of her voice growing stronger too.

She threw him the dubious expression he'd seen many times when she'd been reading through start-up investment pitches. 'Have you ever changed bedsheets before?'

'I have seen it done. Do you need help getting out of bed?'

She'd made a few bathroom breaks with Marcello assisting her to and from the door, but had insisted on doing her last visit solo. In turn, he'd insisted on walking beside her so she could grab him if she felt her legs buckling.

He'd imagined not having to touch her would make the journey from bed to bathroom easier. He'd been wrong. Watching her move across the room was as difficult as having her soft body leaning into him.

'I can manage.' She pulled the duvet off her lap and slowly twisted her legs round until her feet hit the floor.

As with every other occasion that Victoria had left the bed, Marcello did his best to tune out the body clad only in a white T-shirt. It was a feat that was becoming harder with practice, not easier, and he expelled relief that her gait was stronger than the last time, her steps more assured.

She padded slowly past him, her incredible body on full display, the full breasts... God in heaven, he could not stop himself from fantasising about taking them in his mouth...gently moving beneath his T-shirt, the tips jutting out at the perfect angle... And that large, peachy bottom, and those *legs*. Victoria had the hourglass figure of the iconic Italian actress whose films his mother had dieted on in his youth, and as she settled on the sofa and drew her knees up to her belly, he could not stop himself from wondering if the pubis hidden behind the black cotton was the same shade of deep red as her hair or the darker, browner shade of her eyebrows.

His veins, already thick with the awareness alive in him from his waking moment, rose in temperature, and a deep stab of desire burned through his loins.

Turning his face away, he closed his eyes and breathed deeply, swallowing back the moisture filling his mouth.

If she could read his mind she would be furious with him. Sickened.

He was sickened with himself. Sickened that he could not stop his thoughts going to all the forbidden places. Sickened that he was attuned to her in a way he had no right to be. Sickened, too, that it was becoming increasingly hard to control his physical responses around her.

Desire for his executive assistant, the woman who'd become indispensable to him, had grabbed him by the throat and was refusing to let go.

Her phone rang. He picked it up off the bedside table and dropped it on the sofa beside the bottom that the urge to squeeze whenever she was leant against him was becoming intolerable to live with.

'I will get the bedding,' he muttered, already striding to the door.

This couldn't go on. He needed to create some physical distance between them, starting now.

Victoria stared at the door Marcello had just disappeared out of and knew she hadn't imagined the shortness in the way he'd just spoken. Knew too that she hadn't imagined the stiffening in his body when she'd walked past him.

Since she'd woken that morning, she'd felt a lot more with it and much less dopey. More attuned to Marcello's mood. Something was off with him. It was nothing she could put a finger on, more a feeling. There was a tension about him. His attentiveness hadn't dipped but his good humour was starting to feel forced.

Wasn't there a saying about guests being like fish and going off after three days? she thought miserably as she answered her grandmother's call. She didn't know if her family were more worried about her illness or the storm, but at least she could truthfully assure them—her grandmother put her on loud speaker so everyone could join in the conversation whether they wanted to or not—that she was on the mend. There was a weariness in her bones but the exhaustion that had cloaked her these last few days had finally lifted.

The storm, though, had gained a second wind and seemed intent on causing as much destruction as possible. The wind itself had dropped but the blizzard continued unabated. To leave Marcello's apartment, even by car, would be akin to pressing self-destruct.

She was in no position to leave his apartment but she could move to one of the guest rooms, she decided when the call with her family ended. Give Marcello his room back. Give him the space away from her she sensed he needed.

And it would give her needed space away from him too. Because no matter how often she told herself that it was gratitude causing her chest to swell whenever she looked at him, gratitude did not explain why her pulses soared whenever he neared her or why her breaths shortened whenever he touched her, or explain the steady burn deep in her pelvis whenever her shortened breaths inhaled his scent.

She couldn't lie to herself any more. She was attracted to Marcello. Deeply attracted.

She could cry.

Of all the people in the world to experience her first real desire for, Marcello was the worst. No woman with a single brain cell got involved with him expecting it to last longer than five minutes.

And now she could laugh. Why was she thinking such things?

As if she'd be stupid enough to give her virginity to him... Oh, God, why did she just think that?

If he could read her mind, he'd be embarrassed for her. Worse, he'd pity her.

She would never be able to look him in the eye again.

Their working relationship would be ruined.

If he knew the feelings that were bubbling inside her for him, she'd have no choice but to leave his employment for real. They certainly weren't reciprocated. She should be grateful for this. She *was* grateful. In all her imaginings, she'd never considered that the first time she got virtually naked with a man would be through sickness. Marcello's matter-of-fact attitude about it all meant the mortification she would otherwise be experiencing to remember how he'd undressed her, however vague those memories were, never had the chance to take off. She'd spent days in his company wearing nothing but an oversized white T-shirt one glance in a mirror confirmed left little to the imagination, and he'd not given a single sign that he'd noticed.

Facts were facts, and the fact was Marcello never had seen and never would see her as a woman, so more fool her for letting her lowered defences addle her brain enough to finally see him for the drop-dead sexy man he was.

The bedroom door opened.

Her heart kicked against her ribs.

He flashed a smile.

'I couldn't find fresh bedding so I have taken the bedding from the other guest room,' he said as he dumped his haul on the armchair. 'They are all clean.'

Of course they were clean, she told herself, desperately trying to think of something to take her mind from the fact her pulses were going haywire. One of Marcello's little quirks was an insistence of having his bedsheets changed daily. Victoria imagined he'd mentally preened numerous times since finding himself temporarily staff-less at stoically sleeping in the same bedding for longer than a night. She doubted it would have occurred to him to try laundering them himself, a thought that days ago would have made her eyes roll but now filled her chest with an emotion she couldn't begin to understand and made her haywire pulses thrash even louder in her ears.

He gathered all the pillows she'd slept on. 'Now that you are well enough to sleep without supervision, I will move to a guest room.' A brief skim of his eyes to hers and another flash of his teeth. 'This body of a superhero demands a bed to sleep in.'

The swelling in her chest deflated and sank to the pit of her stomach. So she hadn't imagined it. He really was craving space away from her.

Trying to fake amusement so he wouldn't sense the dejection she would hate him to see, she said as lightly as she could manage, 'Superheroes deserve their own beds. *I'll* move to the guest room.'

And be forced to sleep in the bed Victoria had lain over every inch of, and rest his head on pillows her head had rested on? Marcello was trying to drive her out of his senses, not open himself to having her delve deeper into them. He wasn't a masochist. A few nights in the guest room and then the blizzard would be over, Victoria would return to her own apartment and he would return to his bed without fresh memories of her lying in it.

'Victoria, when a man is playing the role of superhero he does not make the recovering heroine move rooms,' he said sternly. 'I need you to stay here so you can fully appreciate my selflessness.'

Thankful for a task that demanded his attention and distracted his gaze from the beautiful, semi-clad woman curled on his sofa, he yanked at the under-sheet until it submitted and pinged free. He imagined his mother's reaction at his feat of separating bedsheet from mattress. His ex-wife too, he thought, would be lost for words. He might message Livia and tell her, but…no. It would only lead to questions and he would be unable to give any answer she wanted to hear.

He'd visited her on Christmas Day. Drank a glass of wine with her and her new husband. Not so new now. Six years and two children together. Beautiful, healthy children. Marcello was happy for her. She deserved the happiness she'd found. Livia had found the courage to put her heart on the line again.

For all his genuine happiness for her though, Marcello could never do the same. There was no coming back from the pain he'd gone through. Not for him.

He still didn't know why he'd woken Christmas morning in his parents' guest bedroom with the urge to see his ex-wife. They'd kept in touch through the years but he hadn't seen her since the divorce was finalised and they'd shared one last meal in a concerted effort to part as friends. He could only assume his grandfather giving him his grandmother's engagement ring on Christmas Eve had set something off in him. He'd known his mother was behind the well-meant gesture so had gracefully accepted the ring, but it had made a difficult time of the year more so.

It was when Livia had been seeing him off from her home and they'd finally been alone that she'd taken his hand and looked him in the eye with a sympathetic smile. 'You are allowed to move on too, Marcello,' she'd said.

'I'm good,' he'd replied, not pretending not to know what she was talking about.

'Then why did you come here?'

He hadn't been able to answer that then and couldn't answer it now. All he'd known as he'd walked back to his car was that he'd needed to hear Victoria's musical lilt and so he'd called her, and for the few minutes they'd spoken, a little of the tightness he'd woken with in his chest had eased. It had been enough to sustain him through a day that always felt more bitter than sweet, a day when the gap in his life and the hole in his heart always felt that much more acute.

He reached for the clean under-sheet and said to the woman whose musical voice had raised a smile on a day his cheek muscles rarely worked without effort, 'Was that your family on the phone?'

'Yes.' It was the first time she'd spoken to any of them other than her grandma since New Year's Day, Victoria realised with a pang. Since she'd moved to Manhattan, the supposed glamour of her life meant things had improved immeasurably when she returned home for visits, her family agog to hear stories about her demanding boss and the city that never slept. But that was only when she was home. Out of sight still meant out of mind. 'I promised Grandma Brigit that you have been superhuman in your care of me.'

The only wonder was that it had taken so long for the man used to having other people cater to his every need to get fed up of playing nursemaid.

He actually caught her eye at this, a look of astonishment on his face. 'The fire-breathing dragon is called Brigit? The same as the storm?'

She grinned. 'Very apt, isn't it?'

'Is she as scary in real life as she is on the phone?'

'Much worse,' she assured him. 'When my sister Mags brought her first boyfriend home, Grandma terrified him so much that he never came back. None of my sisters ever brought a boyfriend home after that, not unless they were certain she'd gone out.'

'She lived with you?'

Watching him wrestle the clean under-sheet with the face of a man wrestling his personal nemesis elicited such a swell of emotion in her that she had to swallow it to answer. 'My granddaddy died when I was a baby. She moved in with us then.'

The way she said *granddaddy*, with the fullness of her Irish brogue, made Marcello grin improbably.

'What?' she asked, noticing.

He shook his head and continued fighting the ridiculous under-sheet. 'Nothing. So you grew up living with the fire-breathing dragon?'

'I did.'

He resisted a quip about Victoria keeping her boy-friends away. This current easy conversation was good. The last thing he wanted was to dip into the dangerous territory of thinking about her romantic life.

Even before he'd developed these disturbing feel-ings for her, Marcello had known he would cheerfully sabotage any kind of romantic life Victoria had until science found a way to clone her for him. He'd only felt compelled to do it once, the one date she'd men-tioned to him: her theatre date. He'd taken great delight in imagining her date as an acne-riddled, pot-bellied bore, then experienced even greater delight that her date must have been as boring as he'd hoped when she left him stranded at the theatre so she could help Marcello find his missing Montblanc.

If he'd known about Grandma Brigit sooner, he'd have offered to pay for her to move in with Victoria as a guard dog to keep suitors away until the scientists had honed their human cloning technique.

'You must have spent your childhood hiding under your bed from her,' he said.

She laughed lightly. 'My sisters would disagree but she wasn't that bad. Saying that, I was always the clos-est to her.'

'She let you get close without burning you to a crisp?' he asked in fake astonishment.

Her smile was wry. 'I suffered my share of singes but…' She was silent a long moment. 'I think it's be-cause I was a baby when she came to live with us. I was a distraction for her grief at losing my granddaddy. Or a comfort. I don't know. I don't remember, what with only being a baby. But she always looked out for me. Stopped me always being swallowed up by my sisters.'

Marcello felt a pang of empathy for the fire-breathing dragon. There was only one lesson in life he would sell his soul to have never experienced, and that was grief.

'What do you mean about being swallowed up?'

She was silent another long moment before quietly saying, 'I'm the second youngest of five girls. I had no clearly defined role in the pack. I wasn't the oldest or the baby—Sinead came eleven months after me—or even the rebellious middle child. I was the one whose name no one could get right first time. If Mum wanted me, she'd always call one of my sisters' names first, which I know is normal but it always felt like I was the only one whose name wasn't on the tip of her tongue, the insignificant one. I could hide in my room for hours and she wouldn't even notice I wasn't there.

'Grandma was terrifying but she knew exactly who I was. She never forgot me or my name.'

An image danced in his mind of a pretty little redhead sitting on a floor, stepped over and unnoticed by the crowd surrounding her.

Blinking the image away, his stare was caught by the grown, beautiful redhead curled on his bedroom sofa, the beautiful redhead whose stifled laughter had stayed at the forefront of his memories like a warm glow for months before he'd grabbed the opportunity to employ her.

'There is nothing forgettable about you, Victoria,' he said with simple honesty.

Her eyes widened.

There was an almost imperceptible rise of her shoulders and then, just as he was about to jerk his stare away, he saw it.

The dark pulsing in her eyes and the creep of colour over her cheeks.

A bolt of electricity exploded in his chest.

Silence chimed loudly.

The hazel eyes widened into orbs. A trembling hand pressed against her breast…

Suddenly fighting for breath, Marcello wrenched his stare to the sheet gripped tightly in his hand. Auto-pilot kicked in and, the room in pitch silence, he fought the under-sheet until it submitted, then worked quickly to place the pillows and duvet from the guest room onto the bed, all the while trying to convince himself that he hadn't just seen what he'd seen. Told himself it had been a trick of the light. A manifestation of his desire in the form of an illusion.

He had to force himself to look at her again. Had to clear his throat to speak. 'I need to make some calls. I won't be far, just in the office.' The office he'd had a second desk added to so Victoria could work from the apartment when needed. 'Do you need anything?'

Even darker colour stained her cheeks and she hastily turned her face away and shook her head.

'Bene.'

He left the room without another word.

Victoria's knees were drawn to her chin, her mouth pressed tight against them.

Her heart was racing.

He'd seen.

Marcello had seen.

Oh, God.

Hot blood was whooshing in her head.

She couldn't think what to do.

He'd *seen*. She knew it.

It had been the starkness in both his expression and voice when he'd said there was nothing forgettable about her. The emotion that had ballooned in her...

In that moment she'd been helpless to stop her burgeoning feelings from showing on her face, and he'd *seen* it. And he'd recognised it for what it was. She knew it. There was no hiding it now. From either of them.

Oh, God, the pained look that had flashed over him.

He'd been unable to get away from her fast enough.

What was she going to do?

More sleep, she decided desperately. Bury herself in oblivion until it was safe to leave the apartment.

The weakness in her legs on her walk to the bed had nothing to do with the virus she'd been fighting.

Whether it was all the sleep she'd had since falling ill or the electrical current zinging in her veins, the oblivion she hankered for refused to come. Even burying her head under the pillow didn't help. All she could see was Marcello's pained expression.

'Victoria?'

She threw the pillow off and whipped her face towards the door.

Marcello was standing on the threshold holding a tray with a bowl and a tall glass of water.

Her heart flew up her throat.

He didn't meet her stare. His shoulders rose, strong, deep olive throat moving. 'Lunch. None of the delis or restaurants are delivering still, so I am afraid you have to put up with my latest attempt at cooking.'

So that was how he was going to play it? By pretending nothing had happened?

A way out of the nightmare opened itself, and she scrambled to sit up, murmuring her thanks. If he could pretend then so could she.

He stepped into the room. 'Where do you want me to put it?'

He hadn't asked that before. He always brought it to her in bed.

'The table. By the armchair. Please.' Pulling the duvet off her lap, she climbed off the bed.

Lips tight, jaw clenched, he turned his face away from her.

For the first time since she'd fallen ill, embarrassment at her lack of clothing seared her, and as mortification engulfed her in a burning flame, she caught a glimpse of her reflection in the full-length mirror and understood why he'd turned his stare away. The light in the room had made the white T-shirt she was wearing semi-translucent.

Wishing something would fall from the sky and snatch her up and take her far away, Victoria hugged her arms across her breasts and padded to the armchair. Marcello visibly stiffened when she passed him, magnifying her awkwardness. When she went to sit, her thigh bashed into the table. In horrified slow motion, she watched the tall glass topple and hit the side of the tray with a loud crack.

The glass shattered.

In the blink of an eye, water flooded the tray, spilling onto the highly polished, expensive side table and dripping onto the Persian rug.

Could the situation be any more excruciating? she wondered despairingly as she crouched down and attempted to gather the broken shards together, mumbling an apology.

'Did any of the glass get you?' he asked tersely.

'No. It's all on the tray.'

'Then leave it. I'll get a cloth.'

His tone accelerated her despair. Marcello was the least precious man when it came to spillages and breakages.

He really was fed up of taking care of her. Probably fed up with her altogether.

'I told you to leave it,' Marcello snapped when he returned moments later with a hand towel from the bathroom and found Victoria putting all the smaller glass fragments into the larger pieces.

'It's my mess, I should clean it.'

'You have done enough.'

Her flinch made his guts clench.

Marcello knew he was being unreasonable but his clenched guts were burning. *He* was burning.

It had been hard enough dealing with and fighting his own erupting attraction when he'd believed it to be one-sided. To see it mirrored in Victoria's eyes…

Dio, he wished he could wipe what he'd seen from his mind.

If that look had come from anyone but Victoria then he'd be welcoming it. *Delighting* in it.

But Victoria wasn't just anyone. She was far from being just *anyone*. She was his Woman Friday. A purely platonic Woman Friday. He'd made damned sure of that.

He could not lose her from his life. To act on their feelings could only lead to disaster.

He had an awful sinking feeling that disaster had already struck.

He'd had to brace himself just to walk back into the bedroom with her lunch, had had to set a clear path in his mind for dealing with it: he would deliver food to wherever she wanted and then, once she was settled and comfortable, he would leave.

If not for the smashed glass he'd already be back at his computer immersing himself in work.

Or trying to.

What was it they said about the best-laid plans? he thought grimly, crouching beside her and doing everything humanly possible to tune out the closeness of the body driving him to distraction.

'I never asked to get ill,' she snapped back, pinching another small shard and dropping it with the others.

He gritted his teeth. 'I never said you did.'

'You just implied it.'

Dio, he should be celebrating that she was enough of herself to argue with him; the memory of that long night when he'd had grips of fear that she'd never argue with him again still fresh, but the sleeve of her T-shirt brushed against his arm as she reached over to pinch another shard and he knew that if he looked down, he'd find the hem had risen higher up her thigh and would be skimming the bottom his fingers wouldn't quit yearning to touch.

'Will you get out of my way and let me clear this up?' he demanded roughly, lifting the tray and running the towel over the table to soak up the spilt water.

'Will you stop talking to me like you think I'm an annoyance?'

'Then stop being annoying.' Feeling her angry… hurt…stare on him, Marcello gritted his teeth even harder. He would swear he heard her grit her teeth too.

'I'm not going to throw myself at you, you know,' she said tautly.

His guts kicked in rhythm with his heart. Breathing heavily, he tightened his grip on the towel. 'Do not go there, Victoria.'

Some things should never be spoken of. Never openly acknowledged.

He felt her shift. Knew without looking that she'd untucked her calves from beneath her and was now sitting on her damnably beautiful bottom.

'Why not when that's what this is all about?' she retorted. 'Because it is, isn't it?' There was a catch in her musical lilt. 'I know you saw it, but I know perfectly well that you don't see me in the same way, so unless you're deliberately trying to hurt me, you don't have to make your revulsion so blindingly obvious.'

CHAPTER SIX

THE CLEAR BLUE eyes Victoria had always been able to read so well suddenly snapped onto hers. They glittered with a darkness that turned her stomach to mush and made the beats of her racing heart thrash.

She forced herself to gaze into the darkness. She didn't have to force the words that came next. 'Do you think I *wanted* to become attracted to you?' Something was building in her chest, a sob or laughter, she didn't know, but she pinched the bridge of her nose in a valiant attempt to stop it escaping. 'Never mind that you're my boss—were my boss—you'd give Casanova a run for his money.' A short bark of laughter escaped at the same moment a tear spilled over. 'Whatever stupid feelings have developed on my part are just a side-effect of the virus, and even if the attraction was returned I would never be stupid enough to act on it, so—'

'For God's sake, Victoria, are you *blind*?' Slamming a hand on the floor beside her thigh, he leaned his taut face down to hers. 'How can you not see it?'

Trembling, trapped in Marcello's stare, she had no choice but to stare even deeper into the darkness that she suddenly saw with a kick in her heart wasn't darkness at all, but a swirling vortex pulsing a mirror of what she was feeling.

The world moved around her. Sensation throbbed in her chest, like he'd squeezed her heart with his bare hand.

As if she were a magnet irresistibly drawn to his hypnotic pull, her face moved closer to his. She could hardly raise her voice above a whisper. 'Then why…?'

The pained look she'd seen earlier flashed over his rugged features. The look she'd interpreted as a mixture of disgust and pity… 'Why do you think?'

But the world was moving too fast around her to think with any coherence. The realisation that her feelings were shared was hitting her in an ever increasing crescendo of waves. Now that she could see it, it was all she could see, right there in the depths of the blue eyes glittering with his desire for her.

He tilted his head. Now he was the one to bring his face closer.

His voice dropped. 'I do not want to hurt you, Victoria, and I do not want to lose you. I want you by my side for the rest of my professional life. To act on our feelings…' He inhaled deeply through his nose. His exhale landed like a whisper against her mouth. 'I have done marriage. You know that, don't you?'

It was a statement rather than a question.

Her chest hitching, she nodded.

The intensity of his stare deepened. 'I will never marry again. I will never live with anyone again. I have committed to being a bachelor for the rest of my life and I date from a pool of shallow vipers precisely for that reason. I can end it with one message and move on without a second of guilt or regret. You deserve so much more than to be treated like that, and your friendship and value as my right-hand woman are worth more to me than any short-lived fling.'

It wasn't just the hoarse delivery of his words compelling her to listen but the demons glimmering in his pulsing eyes. The demons she'd always sensed lived beneath his affable exterior. Marcello's demons, showing themselves to warn her away.

'You've given it a lot of thought,' she said, shaken at the depth of emotion she was seeing.

'I have thought of nothing else since my eyes opened to just how beautiful you are.'

Victoria's shoulders slumped. Her eyes closed. She tried to breathe through the smashing of her heart and the ripples of its beats.

The only people who'd called her beautiful before were drunken, lecherous men. To hear it from Marcello filled her with such an *ache*…

Oh, this was *madness*! It felt like only five minutes ago that all the reasons he'd just laid out to her had already been firmly lodged in her mind. She hadn't needed telling. She'd known only fools let themselves fall for Marcello Guardiola.

And now she was that fool. She'd woken from the worst illness of her life and gazed at him sprawled out on the sofa he'd been keeping watch over her from, and felt something fundamental shift inside her.

But he was right. However deep the longing to press her hand against his stubbly cheek and breathe in the scent of his skin and the undertones of his cologne deep into her lungs, and however deep the burning yearning to fuse herself to him, to act on her feelings would be to press self-destruct on her whole life.

Pride filling her with resolve, she lifted her gaze back to him. 'I think you're forgetting something.'

His shoulders rose. 'What is that?'

'I don't work for you any more.'

For the first time since the glass shattered, the tautness of his features relaxed and, though his eyes didn't lose an ounce of their intensity, the lines around them crinkled. 'Yes, you do. And I will pay any price to keep you.'

And if that meant keeping his desire contained then that was how it had to be. Marcello would not hurt Victoria for anything. He would not lose her for anything.

Victoria sat on the sill staring out of a bedroom window. The wind had picked up again. If she strained her ears she could imagine its howl. The sun had set. Another night under the same roof as Marcello was closing in.

A light tap on the door made her heart thump. She tightened the sash of his robe, taken earlier from the back of the bathroom door, and took a deep breath to compose herself before turning to face him.

He stood at the threshold, arms loosely crossed around his chest. It was the same stance he'd adopted when he'd checked in on her a few hours earlier. As with earlier, he made no comment about her wearing his robe. But he'd noticed. She knew he had. It had been in the flare of his eyes before he'd turned his stare away.

This time he kept his gaze on her. 'I am going to work on my cooking skills. Is there anything you want for dinner?'

'Anything that's readymade works for me,' she managed to jest. Lunch had gone in the bin. Once the broken glass had been cleared, she'd tried the pasta he'd made for her. It had been inedible and not just because it was cold. Her stomach had been too tense and knotted to accept his offer of something else. He hadn't forced the issue. He'd retreated to his office and given them the space they both needed.

He might as well have brought his computer into the bedroom.

He'd kept the bedroom door open so she could call if she needed him. His voice had carried into the room from his office. The words of his conversations had been indistinguishable but the effect of them a torment. She'd never known a distant voice could soak through skin and squeeze a heart.

His laughter was as forced as the bonhomie they were both faking. 'No more pasta?'

She made herself smile. 'Only if you want to kill me off.'

More forced laughter. 'You will be pleased to know the storm is expected to ease soon. I am making arrangements for a snowplough to be sent to collect Bernard in the morning.'

'The chef?'

He nodded. 'And some cleaners.'

'*You're* making the arrangements?'

He preened. 'I know. There is no end to my talents.'

She only had to half force a snigger at this. 'How are Christina and Patrick doing?'

'They are improved but they are not recovering as quickly as you...' A line creased his forehead. 'You *are* still feeling improvement?'

'I'm getting stronger by the hour.'

His head inclined. *'Bene.'* He straightened and made to leave.

'I'm going to take a quick bath if that's okay?' she said quickly, before she lost her nerve. For someone who showered twice daily, Victoria was acutely aware she hadn't bathed since falling ill. While her strength was increasing by the hour, her yearning to feel clean was accelerating by the minute.

There was a slight stiffening of Marcello's shoulders. The air, already laden with tension, thickened. 'You are sure you feel strong enough?'

She nodded.

He lifted his stiff shoulders into a shrug. 'Help yourself to whatever you need. Clean T-shirts are in drawers to the left of the dressing room door. I would offer you jeans to wear too but...'

He didn't need to finish his sentence. They both knew they were both thinking it. There was no way Victoria was going to get a pair of jeans designed for his snake hips past her curves.

His breathing had become heavy. His throat moved before another taut smile curved his cheeks. 'Food in an hour?'

'If I must.'

The smile widened into something more genuine.

He tapped the side of his forehead with two of his fingers. 'Do not drown.'

'I'll try not to.'

Victoria had never been in Marcello's dressing room before. She'd seen glimpses of it but those glimpses had failed to convey its vastness. Stepping into it reminded her of walking into that tailor's shop on Bond Street with him. The difference was in size. Marcello's dressing room had twice the floor space. It smelled crisper too. Unthinkingly, she rubbed her nose into the collar of his robe and breathed in the underlying scent of his cologne. She'd put it on only to cover her flesh and make it easier for the two of them to be with each other. After spending days in his T-shirt, she hadn't expected to feel such intimacy wearing his robe. Hadn't expected it to feel like an embrace.

Expelling the breath, she closed her eyes.

If Marcello was right and the storm did ease overnight, then that meant it should soon be safe for her to leave. If she continued improving as she was then, come the morning, she would dig her clothes out of the laundry pile Marcello had added them to. Get a lift on the snowplough. Return to her apartment. Hope the physical distance from him gave her the head space needed to decide what she should do next.

Resign officially or stay and hope for the best?

She couldn't think clearly in Marcello's home, wearing his clothes and feeling his presence like a vibration in her skin.

Selecting a grey T-shirt, she left the dressing room

for his en suite. Another room stamped as essentially Marcello. As masculine a bathroom as could be imagined. Charcoal tiled walls. Hard black flooring. A huge walk-in shower that could be mistaken for a cave. Even the chaise longue that separated the shower side from the rolltop bath was black leather, and as she poured the citrus-scented bubble bath into the gushing water, it came to her again that he hadn't marked every single part of his apartment with his own stamp for aesthetic reasons, but as a warning to the many women he'd invited into it.

Do not get close.

Marcello tried to focus on the food he'd selected and laid out before him on the kitchen island. Tried not to think that at this exact moment, Victoria was naked in the bath.

In the back of his mind had been the unacknowledged knowledge that at some point Victoria would feel well enough to want to shower. A shower would have been hard enough to handle. A bath was a whole different level of torture.

He'd stayed in his office while she ran it. Had somehow heard over the blood roaring in his ears the sloshing of water as she'd stepped into it. Only when he'd assured himself that she was safely settled did he move downstairs to the kitchen, the furthest point in his apartment from his en suite. With the electricity racing through his veins it could be the other side of the bathroom wall.

He ripped the seal around the steaks with his bare

hands and placed them on the heated pan as the Internet instructed. Washing his hands, he closed his eyes in another effort to eradicate the image of Victoria submerged in the bath. Naked. Fully naked. Water swirling around her breasts and pubis...

He groaned and dragged his wet fingers through his hair.

Earlier, it had taken superhuman control to back away from her but there was no self-control of his mind. Not any more.

The so very erotic images behind his eyelids became suddenly distorted.

Snapping his eyes back open, he found himself in darkness.

Victoria had been trying to summon the strength to get out of the bath when the lights extinguished.

It wasn't physical strength she'd been seeking but the mental strength needed to leave this temporary sanctuary from Marcello and deal with seeing him again. Talking to him. Pretending.

Pretending that when the storm passed and she'd fully recovered, things could go back to how they used to be.

And then she found herself lying in the bath in the pitch black.

The door was closed. No light spilled through the cracks from the bedroom. It must be a full-blown power cut. She'd closed, too, the expertly fitted blinds. No residual light from the outside could penetrate it.

Groping carefully for the rolled sides, she sat up and

called Marcello's name. The bathwater had been cooling and now goosebumps flecked her skin.

She hugged her knees and called his name again. She'd put a towel on the chaise longue but couldn't even make out its shadow.

And then she heard her name.

'I'm still in the bath,' she called back.

'Are you okay?' His voice came from behind the door.

'Yes, but I can't see anything at all.'

The door opened. A circle of orange light filled the doorway. It took a moment for her brain to catch up and see it was the torch from Marcello's phone. Of him, she could see nothing, not even his outline.

'There has been a power cut,' his disembodied voice informed her grimly. 'From what I can see, most of Central Park is down.'

Acutely aware that he could see her, she covered her breasts and tried to speak normally. 'Doesn't the building have a back-up generator?'

'I would assume so. I will check with the concierge once you're out of the bath. Can you see enough to get out safely?'

The orange glow now coming from the doorway was emanating just enough light by the bath to create shadows. 'I think so.'

He must have picked up on her uncertainty. The light moved closer until its source stopped by the double sink. 'Better?'

'Yes…' She swallowed and strove even harder for normality in her voice, as if what she was about to ask were an everyday occurrence. 'Can you pass me the towel please? It's on the chaise longue.'

'Sure.'

The light source moved again. She saw the gleam of an outstretched arm at the same moment she heard the rustle of a bath towel being lifted.

The light moved closer.

She reached for the towel. Once she had it in her clasp, the light source retreated a few steps.

'I will stay close in case you need me,' he said tightly.

She nodded and tried to open her throat to breathe. The light from the phone had put her under a dimly glowing spotlight. The man behind it was still indistinguishable but she could feel him through the vibrations of her naked skin that no longer felt cold. Could hear the long pauses between each of his breaths...

Marcello turned his face from her. He could not turn off the rest of his senses.

Water sloshed and, as much as he tried to think about anything else, all he could see in his mind's eye was the illuminated figure in the bath tub rising slowly to her feet.

He'd had to brace himself before entering the bathroom knowing it would be impossible to avoid Victoria's nakedness. And so it had proved. Her wet hair, part covering her breasts, had contrasted strongly with the luminescence of her skin. A mermaid come to life. A siren leading a man to danger...

'Can I borrow your hand while I step out, please?' she whispered.

Everything inside him contracted sharply then pulsed

in a rush. He had to tighten his grip on the phone before he could force the steps needed to reach her side.

Closing his eyes, he reached out to her and did his damnedest to banish the image of Victoria in full, curvaceous naked bloom. It was futile. One glance had etched in his retinas. Even with only the dim torchlight, that one glance had been enough to see that the soft down of hair between her legs was the same beautiful shade of red as the hair on her head.

Dio, his blood had never pumped so hard.

The tips of their fingers connected. Electricity crackled through his skin and deep into his loins.

The silence as their hands clasped together was so complete he could hear the individual droplets of water run off Victoria's naked skin and splash back into the bath.

The loudest sound, though, came from the drum of his heart beating in his ears.

The heat of the water had opened her pores. His lungs opened to breathe in the scent clinging to her. A scent that should be masculine but on Victoria's skin became something distinctly feminine. Distinctly Victoria.

Awareness and desire had never thrummed so deeply, and he clenched his jaw tighter than he'd ever clenched it before in an effort to control it. Never in his whole life had he fought such a war with his own body.

Never in the entirety of her life had Victoria been so conscious of the skin that wrapped her body, aware that it was a living, breathing organ in its own right. It was breathing in Marcello, her hidden Adonis. Only the hand holding her so securely had emerged from the shadows but she could feel the substance vibrating from his own cloak of flesh.

Pulses thrashing wildly, she lifted her leg over the bath.

The floor was lower than anticipated and the extra depth as her foot searched for hard floor caught her unawares and she wobbled, would have fallen into an ungainly heap if Marcello hadn't wound an arm around her waist to steady her. A moment later he'd lifted her out of the bath.

The phone slipped from his hand at the same moment both her feet made contact with the floor. She had only a dim awareness of the clunk it made because in an instant her thrashing pulses ran out of control and she lost the ability to think coherently.

The towel she'd wrapped around herself had slipped to her waist and she was pressed against Marcello, pressed so tightly her breasts were squashed against his hard chest. His hands were flat against the small of her naked back, the pads of his fingers biting into her flesh.

And she was clinging to him. One hand was holding his shoulder, the other gripping the side of his waist. The pads of her fingers were biting as hard into him as his fingers bit into her.

Blood zoomed through her in a rush, its heat fizzing and throbbing through her skin, deep into her bones and into the places kept secret even from herself. Helpless to do anything else, she lifted her face.

The light from the phone on the floor arched upwards and suffused them both in the spotlight of its glow. Marcello's chiselled jaw was as rigid as his body holding her so securely and yet so stiffly. His eyes, though, locked straight onto hers. If she'd had any air left, the emotion and hunger contained in them would have knocked it out of her.

An age passed before his nostrils flared and he expelled a short but heavy breath. It danced over her forehead like a caress.

'Walk away, Victoria,' he muttered raggedly, his stare continuing to burn into her.

She rose onto her toes without thought.

His eyes became hooded, his breathing even heavier. One hand dragged slowly up her back. 'Walk away. Walk away now.'

Shivers racing down her spine at the pleasure of his touch, unable to tear her stare from his, she slowly slipped her fingers beneath his T-shirt. His warm skin was smooth. Heavenly.

His eyes closed as if in prayer. His other hand moved, fingers sliding beneath the fallen towel to clasp her bottom. His stare fixing back on hers, he made a barely perceptible twist of his hips and clasped her tighter.

She gave a short gasp as the towel fell to the floor and his hardness pressed into her naked abdomen.

'Walk away, Victoria,' he urged hoarsely even as he pressed his thigh between her legs to drive his hardness tighter against her and his taut, pained face inched closer. 'Walk away…' his mouth was so close his hot breath soaked into her lips '…before it's too late.'

Desire pulsed through the very fabric of her being and, her hand now palming the back of Marcello's neck and her fingers tugging at the dark hair at the base of his skull, it was all she could do to stay on her feet. All those long months of pretending to herself…lying…that Marcello meant nothing more to her than the man who paid her salary had been blown away. She'd wanted him from that very first meeting, when he'd walked into her then boss's office with an arrogant swagger she would have hated him for if he hadn't captured her gaze with those blue eyes flashing a twinkle that had made her insides melt.

His procession of lovers…she'd hated them all because deep down she'd been jealous of them. All of them. It had made her *burn* to imagine them in his bed, and, whatever happened now, she would always feel that irrational burn of jealousy. But now she would know it for what it was. Pandora's box had been opened and she could no more keep its contents contained than she could stop the tides from turning.

Whatever happened now, she was going to be hurt. That was her fate. You didn't fall for Marcello Guardiola and expect a happy ending. The most she could hope for was a happy-for-now.

She'd imagined he would be the worst person in the world to fall ill with when he'd turned out to be the best. If just to be held by him like this felt like heaven then…

She sighed against his mouth before staring deep into his eyes and whispering, 'It's already too late.'

CHAPTER SEVEN

IT WAS THE sweetness of Victoria's hot breath falling against his lips and onto his tongue that swamped the last of Marcello's resistance. With a groan of surrender, he pressed his mouth to hers.

If he hadn't already succumbed, the first sweep of her tongue against his would have incinerated his resolve. Wrapping his arms tightly around her, he devoured her pliant softness with hungry kisses that sent thrills licking through his entire being. *Dio*, her lips... soft succulence contrasting headily with the hard, passionate ardour of her responses. He was plundering heaven, and heaven was welcoming the plunder with soft moans and nails scraping into his skull. *Dio*, even her skin when he rubbed his cheek against hers felt like erotic satin.

Biting with barely disguised restraint at her delicate ear lobe, he pulled his head back and gazed at the dimly lit face he'd been blind to the beauty of for so long he wondered how he'd been able to see at all. Exquisitely beautiful, from the mesmerising hazel eyes to the oversized lips and the pretty chin with the faintest cleft in it. Every inch exquisite. Every inch of Victoria exquisite. The need to taste it all...

The second fusion of Marcello's lips to hers was even headier than the first. Sinking into the hard, passionate demands of his mouth and tongue, consumed by his dark taste and the sensations flickering like lightning through her skin, Victoria no longer had thoughts. All she had was Marcello; his taste, his scent, his touch, all seeping through her senses to set her alight. Even his voice when he whispered into her ear, 'Come,' soaked into her skin with the same strength as the feel of his hands sweeping down her back.

Feeling as light as the bubbles in a glass of champagne and as drunk as if she'd consumed a whole bottle of it, she let him take her hand and lead her into the darkened bedroom.

A chink of silvery light from the falling snow seeped through a gap in the heavy curtains, creating a shadowed path to the bed. Hands clasped, they walked it together. By the time they reached the head of the bed, Victoria's heart was thumping so hard that sucking in air to breathe had become impossible. Excitement churned like a sickness in her stomach.

Large hands clasped her cheeks. Marcello's face emerged from the shadows. He pressed his forehead to hers. Eyes intense, his Italian accent more pronounced than she'd ever heard it, his voice was hoarse as he whispered, 'You can still walk away, Victoria.'

Unable to speak, all she could do was shake her head.

His eyes closed. His nostrils flared. And then he moved his hands from her cheeks, straightened, and, in one fluid movement, stripped off his T-shirt and threw it to the floor.

Her heart came close to punching out of her chest. It didn't matter that it was too dark to see clearly. Every inch of his torso had been committed directly into her memory bank that lifetime ago in his office, from the flat brown nipples to the dark hair that swirled around them and snaked over the washboard abdomen and down to the place she always refused to imagine even when a throb pulsed strongly between her legs. That pulse was throbbing stronger than it ever had now, and when he removed the rest of his clothing and stood naked before her and her stare took in the shadowed length of his arousal, the pulse that followed weakened her legs. Weakened all of her…and yet somehow strengthened her.

A hand clasped the back of her head. His smouldering face hovered over hers. 'Last chance,' he whispered savagely.

Something, an instinct that came right from the feminine heart of her, had her cupping his cheeks tightly. Bringing her mouth to his, she whispered with equal savageness, 'No more chances.'

The tiniest beat passed in which time hung by a thread, and then his mouth plundered hers with a kiss so hot and demanding that her weakened legs finally buckled. Wrapping her arms around his neck, revelling in the sensation of his strong arms snaking around her back to hold her tightly to him and the feel of his arousal pressing hard into her abdomen, she moaned into his mouth.

So enraptured was she to be under this sensuous assault that she barely felt her feet leave the ground when he lifted her onto the bed. A fleeting memory came of when he'd first carried her and the embarrassment that she was too heavy to be carried like a child that had broken through the fog of the virus. But there had been safety in his arms too, she remembered with wonder. Even while the virus had been running riot in its quest to infect and incapacitate her, she'd had safety in Marcello's arms, had instinctively known he would never let her fall...

Her head fell onto the pillow. Marcello's weight covered her body, his demanding mouth swooped back on hers, and the memory dissolved as she dissolved into him.

When Marcello covered Victoria's breast with his mouth and felt the scrape of her nails down his back, the thrills of arousal coursing through his loins was strong enough to take him back two decades, to his first time, when the thrill of promised pleasure had almost tipped him over the edge before he'd even started.

That eager adolescent no longer existed. Experience had taught him control. Taught him how to give pleasure for the woman's benefit and not his own. However badly his short-lived affairs ended, he'd never had the worry that they'd left his bed unsatisfied.

The strength of his desire now was beyond anything, even that first time. The urge to make Victoria his, to thrust deep inside her and lose himself in her curvaceous softness was as strong as the hunger to devour every delicious centimetre of her flesh and uncover her every last erotic secret.

Dio, it was like he'd never caressed breasts before. The weight and fullness of Victoria's simply begged to be squeezed, the texture and taste begged to be licked and kissed and nipped…her moans of pleasure… When she cradled his head in a silent plea for more and writhed beneath him, he encircled a large nipple with a groan and gently bit, fighting the very real need to consume her whole. For the first time in his life, Marcello's need to devour had nothing to do with the giving of pleasure to satisfy his ego, but to satisfy his greed, and it was his greed for more, more of Victoria, that had him snake down to the pubis that had haunted his imagination for much longer than the days he'd pretended to himself.

He'd spent eighteen months ruthlessly refusing to think of Victoria as a woman precisely because his subconscious had known what would be unleashed. And now that denial had been unleashed, he was like a child let loose in a chocolate factory without supervision.

He would not deny himself any more. He would not deny her. For this one night he would drown in her.

Spreading her thighs, he pushed them back. Too dark to see with any clarity, he rested his face between her legs and inhaled deeply. He didn't need to see clearly, not when the memory of her naked in the bathroom was still so vivid. He could satisfy his other senses, and, with another greedy inhalation of her erotic musky scent, he laid himself down and feasted.

Victoria had lost her mind. This was beyond good. Beyond pleasure. The sporadic groans from between her legs only added to the heady wonder. Marcello was getting as much from this as she was, and, God, she'd never known it would feel like this. Be like this. Something was building inside her, a thickening beyond any climax she'd brought herself to during the lonely nights she'd tried desperately hard not to picture Marcello touching her…

She moaned loudly as he slid a finger into her heat, and then his tongue found a rhythm that had her writhing and wantonly begging him not to stop until her climax ripped through her and she could speak no more.

The ripples hadn't even begun to subside when he wrenched his face away from the source of her pleasure and crawled back up her body to cover her mouth with a deeply passionate, musky-tasting kiss. Before she could wrap her arms back around him, he was kneeling between her legs and reaching into his bedside table. A short rustling and then he was ripping into a small square foil with his teeth. He'd sheathed himself in moments and then he was pushing her thighs back again, the head of his huge arousal at the entrance of her heat.

Through the dark, she felt his stare on her as he leaned forwards and raggedly muttered, '*Dio*, Victoria, I have never wanted anyone like this.' Without a second of hesitation, he drove deep inside her with a loud, drawn-out groan.

The sharp pain made her gasp. Her right leg reflexively kicked and she came within a breath of telling him to stop.

But he'd already stilled. Breathing heavily, he whispered, 'Are you okay?'

Slowly expelling her own breath, she realised she *was* okay. More than okay. The pain had already faded and as her body stretched to accommodate him and adjusted to the delicious newness of Marcello fully inside her, the magnitude of what was happening hit her.

Marcello was inside her.

Marcello was making love to her.

Cupping the back of his head, she lifted her face for his kiss. The heat of his mouth sent sensation dancing through her and, relaxing, she slid her hand to his shoulder, closed her eyes and trusted him to take her to paradise.

When he started to move, paradise itself moved closer.

This was beyond anything Marcello had ever felt before, ever experienced. Every nerve ending was alive with sensation, every vein threaded with electricity, every sense attuned to Victoria's every touch and every breathless moan. The need to drive deeper and deeper into her tight, slick heat, to fuse himself in his entirety to her...

Her moans deepened.

'*Dio mio*, Victoria, you're incredible,' he groaned before gritting his teeth in an effort to keep control of himself, and increased the tempo of his thrusts; the need to feel and experience her climax with her as strong as the increasing desperation for his own release.

Just as he felt he couldn't hold on any more, the legs wrapped around his waist and the arms around his neck tightened and she spasmed into him and around him, crying out his name as she pulled him over the edge and into an abyss of the most intense pleasure of his life.

Victoria held Marcello tightly and tried to snatch air into her lungs. She could feel the beats of his heart thumping strongly. Hear his own struggles to find air.

He was still inside her. She wanted to keep him there and never let him go…

An impossible dream but with the bliss of her climax still tingling through her veins and skin, and his mouth hot in her hair, a dream it was impossible to deny herself from longing for.

The virus that had debilitated her had weakened her defences and given the space for feelings hidden even from herself to bloom.

They were feelings as impossible as her dream. Feelings that must never be spoken of. This blissful closeness they were sharing was a temporary, fleeting thing. In a minute or an hour or a day or a week or a month, Marcello would call time as he always did.

She'd made love to him knowing he would break her heart. He would have broken her heart even if she'd walked away as he'd urged her to do.

The darkness of the bedroom meant she didn't have to hide her dejection when he finally lifted his head and pulled himself out of her.

'I need to get rid of the condom.'

She sighed and ran her fingers lightly through his hair.

He kissed her gently and then climbed off the bed.

She missed his warmth before his feet even hit the floor.

Snuggling deep under the duvet, she tried to stop herself thinking about the day in her future when an entitled female voice called and demanded to be put straight through to him. Or, worse, the day he casually instructed her to keep an evening in his schedule free.

That he'd been celibate since Jenna was little short of a miracle and a feat unlikely to be repeated. She had to be realistic about these things.

An orange light appeared from the bathroom. Phone guiding him, he strode to the bedroom door without looking at her and distantly said, 'I'm going to find matches to light a candle.'

Irrationally stung, she snuggled deeper, hugged herself tightly and willed the tears not to fall.

Looked like she wouldn't even have an hour to savour what they'd just shared.

He must be regretting it already, and it pained her to remember how many times he'd urged her to walk away before they took things too far.

She had no idea how long she lay there, torturing herself over a future she had no control of, when he padded back into the bedroom, still using his phone as a torch. In silence, he headed to the sideboard in the corner. The angle he placed his phone while unwrapping the candle illuminated him, and she took a crumb of comfort that he hadn't bothered to cover his nakedness. Surely if he was planning to start a big 'We really shouldn't have done that and it must never happen again' conversation, he would put some clothes on?

But then, who knew how Marcello extracted himself from a woman's bed when he had no intention of sharing it with her again? Not Victoria. She'd never asked. Never wanted to know.

There was a click, and then a whoosh of blue and orange flame from what looked like a miniature flamethrower shot out from his hand and the wick of a candle caught light. Another click as he turned the miniature flamethrower off and then he turned, now illuminated by the flickering candle light, and walked towards her.

Holding the duvet tightly to her chest, she sat up.

It wasn't until he'd slid beside her, rested his back against the headboard and taken hold of her hand that she was able to take a proper breath.

It was a breath that stuck in her throat when he said in a voice too casual to be casual, 'Victoria… Tell me that wasn't your first time.'

The freezing of Victoria's hand in his answered Marcello's question.

Biting back a curse, he tipped his head back and forced himself to breathe.

When he'd come back to earth after their lovemaking, it had been the moment he'd first entered her that had rung loudest. Her gasp. The flash of uncertainty that had temporarily gripped him before he'd completely lost his mind in what they were sharing.

Even as he'd been turning the kitchen upside down searching for something to light the candle with, the thought had refused to be shaken off.

And now his worst fears had been confirmed.

Victoria had been a virgin.

This beautiful, witty, confident, highly intelligent twenty-five-year-old woman had been a virgin.

'Why didn't you tell me?' he dragged out. Something dark and acrid was bubbling in his guts.

He heard her swallow. 'Because you would have used it as an excuse to stop.'

'What the hell?' Snapping his gaze to her, he stared intently at the face only a little more discernible under the candle's illumination, but discernible enough for him to catch the defiance on it. 'Did you plan this?'

'Why would I do that?' she asked tremulously. '*How* could I do that?'

Cursing under his breath, he let get of her hand and gripped the back of his neck. 'Why would you give your virginity to a man like me, Victoria?'

Her voice lifted. 'Because you're a professional?'

'This is not the time for jokes.'

'I know but this conversation is excruciating.' She laughed but it sounded more like a sob. 'You kept telling me to walk away, but I couldn't. It was already too late for me. And it was too late for you too—if it wasn't, *you'd* have walked away. If I'd told you I was a virgin then…' She gave another sobbed laugh. 'What I'm currently feeling for you is something I've wanted to feel my entire life.'

The dark acridity in his guts intensified, the impending sense of disaster back with a vengeance. 'I cannot give you anything more than this.'

'I *know*,' she stated vehemently, sitting even straighter. 'I know that better than anyone, but I also know that our working relationship as we've always known it was over the moment this thing between us became impossible to ignore, and to think we could just carry on as if it weren't this enormous white elephant between us is for the fairies. But just because I was a virgin doesn't change anything. You've been straight with me about your feelings on relationships and stuff and I haven't wilfully ignored them. The only reason you're acting the way you are now is because you're afraid my virginity means I'm going to suddenly expect a ring on my finger, so put that out of your mind. I expect nothing, Marcello, and I hope for nothing more than to leave this apartment with some semblance of our old relationship still intact.'

For the longest time their gazes held, her hazel eyes repeating what her lips had just uttered, words that were exactly what he'd needed to hear. Hearing them, though, and seeing them alive in her eyes brought none of the relief he would expect, and it took a long time before he was able to control the beats of doom pounding inside him enough to suck a long breath in.

'I am sorry for making assumptions,' he said heavily. 'I haven't been with a virgin since I was one myself.'

That it had felt like it was his first time with Victoria only added to the weight of doom inside him.

'It really wasn't a big deal for me, Marcello, so please don't make it one for you.'

How could he not make it a big deal when he had so many contrasting emotions thrashing through him? The most unwelcome of them all was the secret thrill that kept punching through the acridity. He'd been Victoria's first. She'd given herself to *him*.

Damn it all to hell, how was he supposed to make sense of any of this?

'I mean it,' she said into the silence, peering at him intently, reading him better than anyone else in the world. 'My virginity is irrelevant.'

'*Was,*' he supplied tautly.

'What?'

'*Was* irrelevant. It is gone. Given to a man who didn't deserve it when there must be hundreds—thousands—of men out there who would be able to give you everything you wish for.'

Her eyes narrowed. 'My virginity wasn't a prize to give, thank you very much, and how do you know what I wish for?'

'You come from a big family. Do you not want that for yourself?'

'I want a family of my own but not yet. Not for a long time.'

But she did want one. In his heart, he'd always known it, had recognised it in the softening of her stare at Denise's baby.

'Then why did you hold on to it for so long?'

'It wasn't a case of holding out. It's just the way life worked out for me.'

He couldn't stop himself asking, 'How?'

Her shrug was almost imperceptible. 'I'm the plainest of five sisters and from a town so small it should really be called a glorified village. There were hardly any boys there and the ones who weren't gay all fancied one or other of my sisters. They never gave me a second glance. Not a single boy asked me out until I arrived in America.'

'Are Irish boys all blind?' he asked incredulously. How anyone could consider Victoria plain was beyond all comprehension. That she should consider herself plain…he made a mental note to drag her to an optician at the soonest opportunity.

Her beautiful features relaxed and she gave a soft laugh. 'My sisters are all stunning. I know I'm not ugly but compared to them I'm nothing. When I started at Columbia, I had hopes of finding a nice boy, but I swear American boys are a different breed from Irish ones—they were all so *confident*, and because I was this duck out of water trying to find her feet in a strange country, I ran a mile from them. By the time I graduated, I'd loosened up a bit but all the decent ones had paired off, and then I started at Hansons and, as you know, it's run and staffed by cretins, and then I was poached by this gorgeous Italian man to work as his executive assistant and any hope of finding someone went out of the window by the constant demands he made on my time outside working hours.'

Something stuck in his throat at the same moment something relaxed in him, just as he'd just seen Victoria visibly relax.

He *was* making too much of her virginity. He was making too much of this whole thing. He'd crossed a Rubicon he'd sworn never to cross and made love to his closest employee, and there was no turning back. What was done was done. He could spend the rest of the night castigating himself for something that couldn't be reversed or...

'This Italian man...' He leaned his face close to hers. 'He sounds like a monster.'

She held his stare a long moment before her lips curved into a smile.

'He is,' she promised solemnly. 'He has no concept of personal time. I've lost count of the times he's woken

me in the middle of the night because he needs something and doesn't want to wake his household staff, and
that's not forgetting the time he basically bullied me
away from a theatre show I'd spent months looking forward to seeing for the sake of finding a Montblanc pen.'

He ran a finger down her delicate jawline. 'Definitely
a monster. How do you put up with him?'

'By putting his photo on a board and throwing darts
at it whenever I have a minute to myself, and by dream-
ing up inventive ways to maim him.'

The darkness curdling inside him finally lifted as
laughter broke free, lifting and floating away completely when the widest smile lit Victoria's face, a moment that felt so good and right that he stamped on the
voice warning him strongly against taking her into his
arms again, and hauled her back to him. The moment
her laughing mouth fused with his, the voice evaporated.

CHAPTER EIGHT

VICTORIA OPENED HER eyes to find Marcello holding a bulging paper bag. The hugest, smuggest smile was on his face.

'Bagels?' she guessed sleepily.

'And coffee. Sit up, breakfast is served.'

Covering a yawn, she held the duvet to her naked breasts and propped her back against the velvet headboard.

'Bacon, cream cheese and avocado,' he said, handing her a wrapped bagel with a flourish.

She blinked her surprise.

He grinned and swooped a kiss on her mouth. 'My powers of observation are limitless.'

'And only slightly lesser than your ego.'

'Impossible.'

Laughing, she unwrapped the still-warm goodie in her hands and took a bite. After days of her only sustenance coming from Marcello's attempts at cooking, it tasted like heaven. That Marcello had ordered it—his plain T-shirt, low-slung shorts and bare feet suggested he hadn't left the apartment to buy them—and that he'd ordered her favourite fillings only made it sweeter. When he stripped those few items and climbed into bed, she thought it might be the single happiest moment of her life.

The talk they'd had after their first time had helped settle Victoria's mind. She'd gone into this with her eyes wide open and she would not close them to reality now. She would take this time with Marcello for exactly what it was: a short but very sweet affair. She would hide away the emotions and think only of the pleasure for as long as it lasted.

'Does this mean Manhattan's back in business?' she asked between bites.

He swallowed the last of his first bagel and dug into the bag for another. 'The bagel shop is.'

'Priorities, eh?'

He winked and took a huge bite of his second bagel. She wasn't in the least surprised when he unwrapped a third for himself or, when she couldn't eat the third one he'd brought for her, that he devoured it too. The meal he'd been going to cook before the power cut had been forgotten by them both. All they'd been hungry for was each other.

'So?' she prompted, determinedly keeping her voice chirpy. 'Is Manhattan back in business?' Meaning, is the Guardiola Group reopening its New York doors?

He shook his head. 'It is still treacherous out there. There are thirty-foot snowdrifts trapping people in their homes, thousands of cars buried… I have given the order to continue working from home until Monday.' He brushed his mouth to her ear, sending delicious shivers lacing her spine. 'It is far too unsafe for you to return to your apartment. You will have to stay here for days longer.'

The purest relief filled her chest.

Days longer to enjoy the bliss of Marcello without the real world intruding.

Eyes gleaming lasciviously, he had a drink of his coffee.

'What?' she asked, noticing the funny way he was staring at her.

He shook his head before his perfect teeth flashed. 'Your hair.'

She put a hand to it. 'What's wrong with it?'

'It looks like a bird's nest.'

'That's because *someone* made mad, passionate love to me while it was still wet from the bath.' And then made love to her again before insisting she get some sleep, only to wake her when daylight filtered into the bedroom for more lovemaking.

It had been the best night of her life and she would cherish the memories for the rest of her life, and make the most of the memories as they made them because it wouldn't be long until the rest of her life opened up. When they next stepped into the skyscraper that homed the Guardiola Group, this brief affair would be over, something they both understood without either having to put it into words.

It couldn't be any other way.

Whether their working relationship could survive it, only time would tell. For now, all she wanted was to live for the moment.

His blue eyes glittered. 'Not that Italian monster you spoke of?'

'I'm afraid so.'

Eyes not leaving her face, he put his coffee cup on the bedside table, then plucked her cup out of her hand and put it down too. The paper bag filled with their wrappings and napkins he threw onto the floor.

Pinching the top of the duvet, Marcello slowly pulled it down, exposing all of Victoria's curvaceous body to his greedy eyes. Bagel crumbs had nestled on the top of her breasts and he dipped his head to lick them off, thrilling at her shivers.

'The Italian monster you speak of needs to make penance,' he murmured as he circled a large, rosy nipple with his tongue.

Her back arched. Fingers laced through his hair. 'Oh?'

Still lavishing attention on her beautifully weighty breasts, he trailed a finger down her rounded belly to her pubis. 'The monster will be your slave for pleasure,' he whispered seductively, sliding a finger inside her and thrilling to find her already hot and sticky for him.

She moaned. 'My slave…?' Her voice broke as he rubbed his thumb over her bud.

'Your slave. Here to cater to all your desires.' Raising his face to hers, he gently bit her bottom lip and increased the friction of his thumb. 'Tell me your desires and fantasies, *bella*. All of them.'

'Just…' She moaned again and writhed into his hand. 'Just…just keep doing that.'

Being Victoria Cusack's sex slave was, Marcello decided a few mornings later whilst trying to catch his breath in her arms, a very fulfilling occupation. She was proving to be an exacting, insatiable mistress, growing bolder with her demands the longer time passed.

The sex between them was out of this world. So incredible was it that he refused to think about the real world that was waiting for them. His household staff were all back and working and had been given strict instructions to keep out of his bedroom. He'd ordered his finance director to run the Guardiola empire in his absence, and given strict company-wide instructions that he wasn't to be disturbed unless a matter of life or death cropped up.

For the first time in over a decade, he forgot about work altogether and lived for the moment... Which was why it came as a shock when a message pinged into his phone from one of only a handful of numbers he'd set to override his phone being on silent.

Cursing to himself, he rolled off Victoria's heavenly body to read it.

She rolled with him and kissed his shoulder blade. 'Is there a problem?'

'It is a message from Benito.'

'Your brother?'

His brother and also the head of the European side of Marcello's empire. 'He has questions about the keynote speech I agreed to make.'

Victoria's lips stilled against his skin. He knew without having to ask that the real world had just penetrated her as it had him.

'That's only a week away.'

'*Sì,*' he agreed heavily. They were scheduled to leave next Friday for it.

'You should call him back.'

'Later.' Firing a message to his brother saying just that, he put his phone down and turned onto his back. Immediately, Victoria slung her arm over his waist and cuddled into him.

'Everything's already organised for the conference, and all the travel to and from it,' she told him quietly.

He kissed the top of her head. 'I know.' Victoria would have organised everything with her usual forensic efficiency.

He still couldn't understand why he'd agreed to it. Marcello avoided Rome as much as possible. It had been during his latest Christmas visit, over a game of pool in their parents' games room, that Benito had asked Marcello to make the keynote speech at a conference he was organising. He didn't know which of them had been more surprised at his acceptance.

He'd called Victoria straight away to inform her. He remembered the noise in the background. She'd been playing charades with her family. There had been a huge smile in her voice. He'd suspected she might have been a little tipsy, something that had made *him* smile.

'I've done the first draft of the speech for you too.'

He kissed her again and held his mouth to the hair he'd combed conditioner through when they'd shared a bath. Victoria was the only person he'd ever trusted to write a speech for him. She had an unerring ability to put herself in his head and write as if she were speaking from his mouth. He rarely made alterations to them.

Damn it, he couldn't lose her.

It was impossible that they could return to the status quo of their working life but he had to find a way to ensure this affair between them didn't have the repercussions he'd feared before it had even started. He would do whatever it took to keep her by his side as his right-hand woman. Whatever was necessary.

'Let's take a walk into Central Park,' he impulsively suggested. Get some fresh air into their lungs and into his head. Prove to himself that he could go more than a few hours without having to make love to her.

She lifted her head and rested her chin on his chest, bemused doubt in her stare. 'You? Walk?'

'Why not? We only have two days left before we return to the office.'

There was a flicker in her eyes but her bemused smile didn't falter. 'Are you seriously telling me you have suitable clothes to go trekking through feet-high snow in?'

'All the roads and paths have been cleared.'

'You wear handstitched shoes. They will be ruined.'

'I am sure there is an outdoor clothing shop that will deliver stuff to me…' A thought occurred to him, a thought that was, to his mind, a most excellent idea.

'What?' she asked.

He smiled. Truly, no one knew him or could read him better than Victoria Cusack. 'I have just thought of the perfect surprise for my favourite redhead.'

'Which is?'

'It will not be a surprise if I tell you, will it?'

'Please?'

'No.'

Her fingers slid down his abdomen and she kissed his nipple. 'Please?'

He sprang to immediate attention. 'No.'

Wrapping her fingers around his arousal, she gripped it with just the right pressure and lazily moved her hand up and down the shaft. 'Please?'

'No.'

Keeping hold of him, she lifted herself so her face was over his. Still masturbating him, she hooked her thigh between his legs and kissed him deeply, parting his lips with her tongue and moaning into his mouth.

Threading his fingers into her hair, Marcello closed his eyes and submitted to the eroticism of Victoria's hand pleasuring him, her pubis grinding into his thigh, the weight of her breasts pressed against his skin, and her hot mouth devouring him.

'Please?' she breathed into his ear, now masturbating him with the vigour he craved.

'You are not playing fair,' he groaned.

'I know.' And with that, she released his arousal and twisted around so her back was to him.

'Why, you little tease…' Moving quicker than he'd done since childhood, he ignored her kicks and squeals of laughter as he tussled with her and pinned her onto her back.

They were both still laughing when, fully sheathed, he drove himself inside her.

Victoria thought the best thing about being a billionaire had to be the way it made mere mortals bow to your requests. Two hours after Marcello suggested a walk in Central Park, they were both dressed for an Arctic expedition and crossing the slushy, gritted road, heading towards the most magical of winter wonderlands. Fresh snow had settled overnight and covered it all afresh, and it seemed that the whole of Manhattan had come out to experience it, families building snowmen, children being pulled along on sleds by hardy parents, even hardier joggers making the most of their freedom and ploughing their own trail.

'Shall we skate?' he suggested when they spotted an ice rink through the trees ahead.

'I don't know how.'

'Then I shall teach you.'

'You know how to skate?' she asked, amazed.

'My grandparents lived in Milan near the Bagni Misteriosi. It is the most beautiful outdoor swimming pool and in the winter it is turned into an ice rink. When we were children, Benito and I spent much of our Christmas holidays skating on it.'

Once upon a time, Victoria would have changed the subject at such a personal turn to a conversation. It had been a part of the rhythm of their lives. Talk about anything and everything so long as it didn't have real meaning. Now, though, everything was different. She was different. They were different. And it was his use of the past tense that made her carefully ask, 'Are they still with us?'

'My grandfather is. He moved back to Rome after my grandmother died. That was a few months before I poached you.'

'Oh, I'm sorry. I didn't know.'

Victoria had met his parents during their last two visits to Manhattan and thought them lovely, warm people. She wouldn't have guessed they'd been suffering a recent bereavement.

He squeezed her hand. 'No need to be sorry. She was very ill and now she is at peace.'

They'd reached the queue waiting their turn on the rink.

'Shall we?' he invited.

'You're sure you can teach me?'

He raised his eyebrows. 'You doubt me?'

Laughing, she shook her head. 'If I know you, you were probably good enough to turn professional.'

'It was suggested,' he said without an ounce of fake modesty that only made her laugh harder.

'What stopped you?'

'It was a winter hobby. I cannot help that I am naturally talented at everything.'

She'd only just stopped the tears rolling down her cheeks when he used his magic charm to wangle them to the front of the queue without a pre-booked ticket, and without anyone trying to kill them.

Marcello could not remember a better day. Watching Victoria attempt to ice skate would go down in his annals of history. If he lived to be a hundred he would never forget the day his super-professional right-hand woman was laughed at by small children zooming past her. If he lived to be one hundred he would never forget his pride at the moment she finally dared let go of his hand and skated three feet on her own. Afterwards, they'd shared a giant box of churros dipped in chocolate and drank mulled wine, then taken a carriage ride back to his apartment with the sun setting behind them. Her joy at this had lit her face into something that transcended beauty.

The best part came when they returned to his apartment and she found a pile of boxes laid on the freshly laundered and made bed.

The large hazel eyes landed on him with a question. He adored that her cheeks were still rosy from the cold.

He sat on the armchair. 'Open the Genevieve box first.'

Excitement thrumming—Genevieve was the current go-to designer of New York's elite—Victoria removed the lid and carefully parted the tissue paper to lift out a red velvet dress. Shaking it out, she fingered the soft texture with amazement then looked back at Marcello. Expectation was alive on his face.

'This is for me?'

'Unless you know another Victoria who wears the same size dress as you. Take another look in the box.'

At the bottom lay an envelope with her name on it. Her heart thumping, she opened it and gasped to find two tickets to the Broadway show she'd abandoned Sheena at. Peering closer, she saw they were for the next night and in what had to be the centre front of the mezzanine.

'I have been assured that they are the best seats possible for this show,' he said. 'We will be able to see the whole ensemble perform without any restrictions, and the acoustics are supposed to be incredible.'

She just gaped at him.

'I can easily change them for orchestra seating if you would prefer?'

And he would. She saw that. The Lord alone knew how he'd managed to get these spectacular seats at this short notice—she imagined a large amount of money had been exchanged in bribes and sweeteners—and the royal *we* he'd used...

Marcello would be going with her. Marcello who, when she'd first told him she was going to watch this particular musical, had asked why on earth she wanted to waste hours watching people prance around singing and dancing on stage dressed as witches.

And now he would be taking her.

This was his surprise for her and just as he'd used sweeteners to procure the tickets, the show itself was a sweetener. His last gift before he said goodbye to her as a lover.

'Do you want me to change them?' he asked, doubt creasing his forehead.

She swallowed to loosen her throat, and shook her head. 'These are perfect, thank you. And so is the dress.'

The doubt remained. 'You are sure?'

Not wanting to spoil what for Marcello was the most thoughtful and unselfish gift he could have given her, she smiled through the pain lacing her veins. 'When I went with Sheena, we were so far back in the gods that the cast were like ants.'

The crease in his forehead changed. 'Sheena?'

'My old roommate.'

Understanding dawned. 'You went to see the show with a girl friend?'

She nodded.

To her amazement, he burst out laughing. The sound rumbled through the vast bedroom and soothed her despondency enough for her to straddle his lap and rest her hands on his chest.

'What's so funny?'

His grin was as wide as she'd ever seen it. 'I thought you had gone on a real date.'

'That's what I wanted you to think.' Leaning her face into his, she eyeballed him and added, 'I stupidly thought you'd give me some peace for the night if you thought it was a proper date.'

His hand slipped under her jumper and flattened against her naked back. 'You should have told me the truth. If I had known you were with *Sheena*, I would have waited until the next day to get you to help me find that pen.'

Her mouth dropped open. 'You sabotaged my night out on purpose?'

'*Sì,*' he agreed without an ounce of shame. 'I didn't want you doing what Denise did to me.'

'That's a blatant abuse of power. There are laws against things like that, you know.'

He slid his hand around and cupped her breast. Voice thickening, he said, 'We have already established that I am a monster and that monsters need to perform penance.'

Capturing the hand on her breast and squeezing it, Victoria shifted herself forward so his hardness pressed between her legs. She ground down on him. There it was. That dilation in his eyes. She would never, ever get enough of seeing that and knowing she was the reason for it, not even if they had all the time in the world…

The despondency at what the dress and theatre tickets represented suddenly lifted.

Marcello had feelings for her. She knew it as well as she knew him. He'd deliberately sabotaged what he thought was a real date. Not even he usually stooped that low: he didn't have to. It was a rare member of his vast staff who left for pastures new. Denise leaving had been an anomaly. From the few conversations Victoria had had with her predecessor, Marcello hadn't been a fraction as demanding of her personal time as he was of Victoria's.

Her chest contracted and then bloomed open, and, though she tried her best to temper it, hope rushed to fill the gap.

Frightened at the direction of her thoughts and feelings, Victoria yanked her jumper off and then kissed him hard, infusing her senses with his dark taste and driving out everything else. Dragging at his bottom lip with her teeth, she huskily whispered, 'Sabotage means serious penance.'

Marcello cupped the back of her head and pulled her mouth back to his. 'Punish me however you see fit,' he said between savage kisses.

Hazel eyes flashing their desire, she tugged at his sweater. Between them they lifted it off him before she slipped an arm behind her back and released her bra. Beautiful, bountiful breasts jutted before him, and he took one into his mouth and sucked greedily, his hands already working on the button and zip of her jeans.

With the barrier of two sets of denim between them, Marcello clasped her bottom and got to his feet, carrying her with him, then practically threw her onto the bed.

When he yanked her jeans and knickers down her legs, he had a brief memory of the first time he'd performed this same act. Then, he'd been determined to avoid letting his gaze focus on any aspect of Victoria's body. Now, he shamelessly soaked in every perfect inch.

How the hell was he supposed to return to their normal working life after this? he wondered for the hundredth time as he kissed her perfect toes and, working his way out of his own clothing, kissed his way up her perfect leg. Just to imagine being back in the office they shared...

His arousal grew even stronger as he inhaled the heat of her excitement at the same moment an image flashed in his mind of bending Victoria over his desk...

Burying his face between her legs, glorying in her moans and pleas, he submitted to his imagination and let it run riot into all the directions he'd expressly forbidden it from running before.

He didn't see how they could end it. Not yet. It was too soon.

But end it they must.

Somehow, he would have to find a way for them to work as they'd done before with this chemistry still blazing so brightly between them, but it was impossible to imagine catching a glimpse of Victoria absently chewing on her bottom lip and not wanting to replace her teeth with his own. Impossible to imagine sharing the back of the car or the cabin of his private jet and not having the need to pull her onto his lap, bunch her smart skirt around her waist, pull her knickers aside and thrust up into her, and as he imagined that, she arched her back and cried out loudly.

Crawling up to kiss her, he groped in his bedside table drawer for a condom with something bordering on fury. Finally grabbing hold of one, he yanked it out with such impatience that he knocked the drawer off its hinges. It fell to the floor with a loud clatter.

'Clumsy,' she breathed heavily as she snatched the foil from him and, with a growl, used her teeth to rip it open. 'On your back, slave.'

The fury abated as he did as commanded.

Heaven was Victoria rolling the condom over his arousal.

Nirvana was Victoria climbing on top of him and sinking down on his length, and as she grabbed his hands and placed them on her breasts then pressed her hands tightly into his chest, cheeks ablaze with the colour of her passion, he realised true nirvana would only come the day he entered her bare...

The thought was swept aside as the pleasure took control and the glory that was Victoria riding him with her head thrown back before she threw herself forward and, her lips entwined with his, ground herself down on him hard enough to bring them both to an earth-shattering climax.

Such was the force of Victoria's orgasm that she fell into the most delicious passion-induced coma in which her brain switched off but every nerve ending buzzed with pure post-coital bliss.

This was her favourite time, the silent moments when they lay replete in each other's arms, as close as it was possible for two humans to be.

Marcello's sigh brought her out of the coma. She sighed too, because she knew what it meant. Time to break the fusion.

With a kiss tender enough to make a grown woman cry, he climbed off the bed and padded to the bathroom.

Stretching, she sighed again and rolled onto her side. The bedside table loomed in her vision and she smiled, remembering why its drawer was on the floor, then peered over the side of the bed to see the mess it had made, smiling even wider to see the scattering of the restocked condoms he'd had delivered and…

The smile froze on her face.

For the longest time she stared at the photo that had fallen onto the floor with the rest of the drawer's contents before she plucked up the courage to pick it up.

It was a photo of a much younger Marcello in jeans and an open-necked navy shirt. He was cuddled next to a beautiful brunette wearing a long towelling robe. They were sitting on a hospital bed together, beaming smiles on their faces. In Marcello's arms was a tiny newborn baby.

CHAPTER NINE

THE FIRST THING Marcello saw when he came back into the bedroom was Victoria, seemingly frozen, half hanging off the bed.

'What are you doing?' he asked, amused.

That brought her to life, and she scrambled back onto the bed…but not before he saw the photo fall from her fingers.

Their eyes met.

What he saw in her stare made his heart freeze.

She hugged the duvet around herself and whispered, 'I'm sorry. I didn't mean to look. I wasn't snooping, I swear.'

It took him a long moment to be able to breathe again, and even then it was through a throat that had tightened into rock.

For the first time in a decade, the past and the present collided.

His core knocked off balance and on legs that felt like they belonged to someone else, Marcello walked to the mess on the floor made by the drawer he'd knocked out, and picked up the photo. It was the original of the photo he carried in his wallet so it could always be kept close to him.

It was his most treasured possession.

It would be the easiest thing in the world to put the drawer back in place, tuck the photo back into its place inside it, and dredge up a meaningless conversation to skip over the whole thing.

If he was with anyone but Victoria he would do just that, but the starkness in her stare…the compassion and the fear…

His heart heavier than it had been for many years, he sank on the bed and reached for her hand. She shuffled closer to him and, with a quiet sigh, rested her cheek on his shoulder. He could sense her stare boring into the photo and was grateful that she didn't ask any questions. Grateful for the space she gave for him to compose his thoughts.

He cleared his throat and placed a kiss into her hair. 'You have not done anything wrong so there is no need to apologise.'

Finally she spoke. Whispered. 'You're a father?'

He expelled a long breath and closed his eyes. 'Yes.'

He could hear her breathing. Could hear the questions whirling in her head.

Releasing her hand, he lightly touched his son's face. 'This is my son, Tommaso. He was born eleven years, three months and two days ago. He died when he was three days old.'

Although her heart had already known the child had passed away, Victoria still covered her mouth to stop her horror escaping.

'He had what is known as newborn meningitis. They believe it was caused by a bacteria he caught from Livia during the birth. Completely harmless to the mother but to the newborn child...' His shoulder rose against her cheek. 'The first symptoms developed ten or so hours after this picture was taken. He did not want to wake to feed. From there...' His shoulder rose again, his accent becoming more pronounced. 'He went downhill very quickly. They did everything they could for him but he was too little. Too vulnerable. His immune system was not strong enough.'

Hot tears swimming, Victoria swallowed them back as hard and as silently as she could, utterly devastated for Marcello's loss and wretched that her curiosity over a photograph fallen on the floor had compelled him to relate what must be the most soul-wrenching period of his life.

And she'd had no idea. She didn't think anyone in America had.

He'd carried this loss for all these years...

The tears finally choked her and spilled out in a flood.

Marcello felt the heave of Victoria's sobs and, fighting back the burn in his eyes, wrapped his arms around her. Holding her tight, he kissed the top of her head and breathed in the scent of her shampoo.

'I'm sorry,' she wept into his chest, her fingers digging and clinging into his side. 'So sorry. He was so beautiful and perfect and... God, Marcello, I'm so sorry.'

'It is okay,' he whispered. It had been many years since he'd told anyone about his son. Anyone who mattered had been there at the time and had grieved with them.

Victoria mattered. Mattered far more than she should. Than he should allow.

That she should feel it so deeply…

He closed his eyes again to his own tears and breathed in more of her soothing scent.

She disentangled herself from his hold and stared at him with tears still falling over her blotchy face. 'You shouldn't be having to comfort *me*.'

He brushed a tear away with his thumb. 'The death of any child is never easy to hear about.' He wiped another tear with a sad smile and pressed a kiss to her forehead before reaching over for the box of tissues on the bedside table. He thrust them under her nose. With a grateful smile, she grabbed a handful and blew her nose while Marcello climbed off the bed and headed to the bureau he kept a bottle of his preferred eighteen-year-old single malt in. Taking the bottle and two crystal glasses, he re-joined her on the bed and poured them both a glass.

Visibly calmer, she took a small sip of hers then fixed her red-rimmed eyes back on him. 'I'm sorry you felt boxed in and compelled to tell me.'

'I'm not.'

Her eyebrows drew together.

'You *should* know that about me.' They were far beyond keeping things from each other. Their time together as lovers was coming to an end but Victoria was the most important person in his life. The last few days had taught him that much. He could envisage a future where they were both old and wrinkled and she would walk to his car with the aid of a stick and climb in next to him, and the pair of them would wheezily laugh together over the latest of life's absurdities.

She deserved to know the truth about why that future could only be as friends.

She took another drink of her whisky and, her eyes on his, held a long breath before slowly letting it out. 'Is Tommaso the reason you came to America?'

He inclined his head and drained his glass. Filling it back up, he explained, 'When Livia fell pregnant we had been having problems. The pregnancy pulled us back together and papered over the cracks in our marriage, but Tommaso's death broke us, as people and as a couple. We tried… God knows, we tried, but we could not find a way through. Not together. The old problems came back and magnified—I worked too hard, she preferred being with her sister and her mother to me. We argued over everything. Silly things. If I said something was blue she would say it was green, if she said it was pink I would insist it was black.'

He took a long sip and swirled the whisky in his mouth before swallowing it.

What he was about to say was the hardest thing to admit to. 'I wanted out. I wanted to escape it all. We had both built a whole life in our minds of us and Tommaso, and it was taken from us, and the reminders were everywhere. Every street I walked, I had pictured walking it with him, holding his hand.

'I wanted a fresh start, not to forget him because that would be a betrayal of his life, but to breathe again. I was suffocating. Manhattan was the perfect place to relocate to. I had always enjoyed my time there and the cut and thrust of doing business there, and it was big enough and busy enough for me to immerse myself into a brand-new life. Livia did not want to come with me and I didn't try hard to convince her. We both knew we were over.'

'That's just so incredibly sad,' she said softly.

'It is,' he agreed. 'But it was the only way I could live with it. We managed to part as friends and if I am proud of anything, it is that. Livia is a wonderful woman but we were never right for each other. She has a family now with a husband who *is* right for her, and she is happy, and I built the new life I wanted for myself and have found a different kind of happiness.' He raised his glass with a wry smile. 'Even if it is happiness of a shallower kind.'

She raised a wry smile of her own. 'You came to Manhattan and conquered all before you.'

'I would trade every dollar to have my son back.' Trade his very soul.

Tears filling her eyes again, she nodded to convey that she understood.

Taking the glass from her hand, he placed it with his glass and the bottle on the bedside table then ran his fingers through her glorious hair. Strangely, the weight that had formed to see Victoria with the photo of his precious boy had lifted.

'Do not cry any more, *bella*,' he urged. 'The past cannot be changed. I have had to learn to live without him and I take each day as it comes because life is too fragile and uncertain to do anything else. Live for the moment and let the moment be this.'

Victoria parted her lips to Marcello's gently probing mouth and wound her arms around his neck, deepening the kiss, deepening the connection.

Even as she responded to his lovemaking she had to fight more tears.

Any hopes of even a tentative future with him had been dashed before they'd had the chance to fully form.

Marcello's demons went far beyond a marriage turned sour.

Grief had broken his heart beyond repair.

Somehow she would have to find a way through her own, different, grief because the physical pain of hearing his story had brought the truth home to her.

She'd fallen completely and irrevocably in love with him.

The first thing Victoria did when she woke the next morning was look out of the bedroom window. There had been another flurry of snow overnight but nothing to write home about. Nothing that promised another shutdown of Manhattan.

This time tomorrow, they would be in their office on the sixtieth floor of the skyscraper the Guardiola Group occupied, preparing for the scheduled board meeting.

Their short but beautifully hedonistic and sweet affair would be over.

She couldn't even begin to think about how she was going to cope.

Slipping her arms into Marcello's robe, she set off to find him.

She didn't have far to go. Her early bird was in his home office answering emails, wearing only a pair of boxer shorts.

His face turned to hers and lit into the dazzling smile he always greeted her with. She'd never noticed how heartbreaking it was before.

Pulling her onto his lap, he kissed her deeply, hands already breaking through the sash of the robe to roam over her body.

'*Dio*, I thought you would never wake up,' he murmured, burying his face between her breasts and manipulating her so she straddled him. His hardness pressed right at the centre point of her own arousal, feeding a hunger that had sprung from nothing but his first touch. If he didn't have the barrier of his boxers, he'd be inside her already.

'Did you bring a condom?' he asked with a groan, sucking deeply on her nipple and thrusting upwards.

Holding his head to keep him exactly where he was, rocking against him, she managed to gasp a, 'No…' at the exact moment movement from the main living area below caught her attention.

In utter horror, Victoria watched a member of the cleaning crew drag a vacuum cleaner across the room, but it took seconds before what her eyes were seeing connected with her body, and she scrambled off his lap, frantically tying the robe back together to cover her nakedness.

Marcello followed Victoria's flame-faced stare,

laughed a curse and muttered, 'I need to buy a new apartment.'

Oblivious to what she'd disturbed on the overhang above her, the cleaner plugged the vacuum in just as Christina joined her from the kitchen door. She, too, was oblivious to them. That didn't stop Victoria shrinking even further back.

'They wouldn't have seen us,' he assured her.

'Yes, they would. Your balustrade is glass.'

'Tempered glass,' he corrected.

'Well, that makes all the difference.'

Amused at her unnecessary embarrassment, he reached for her hand. She dodged out of his reach.

'I don't want Christina to see me like this,' she hissed.

'Like what?'

She patted the robe. 'Like *this*.'

'Victoria, you spoke to her just last night.' The two women had had a long discussion about their respective illnesses.

'I was wearing my own clothes then—'

'Clothes she laundered for you,' he pointed out.

'Because she knows I've been ill!'

'She knows we are currently lovers.'

If he'd thought she was embarrassed before, that was nothing to the colour her face turned now.

'She's not blind, *bella*.' Or deaf, something he failed to add in case Victoria took it on herself to dive out of the window and into the snowdrift still piled high against the side of the building to cool her flaming face off in.

'That doesn't mean I want her to see me wearing

your robe!' she spluttered, before turning on her bare heel and fleeing back to the bedroom.

Following her, Marcello closed the door firmly behind him. 'There,' he said. 'Now no one can see or disturb us.'

'How do you live like this?' she asked, shaking her head with bewilderment.

'It has never been a problem before.' And it never would be again. The few women he'd allowed to stay the whole night before Victoria had been dispatched back to their own homes first thing in the morning. He could not even imagine allowing them to do that much in the future.

Coldness filled his chest to imagine allowing another woman into his bedroom at all.

It was the intensity of what he and Victoria were sharing, he assured himself as he shook off the unsettling feeling. The closeness. Opening up to her about his son and his marriage.

He stepped to her and ran his finger in the dip where the robe joined together from her neck to her cleavage. Then he pulled it apart, exposing her to him. 'Where were we?'

Victoria sat at the desk Marcello had long ago designated as hers in his home office and, for the first time in—how long? A week…? Time had flown—turned on the desktop he'd also long ago designated as hers, and opened her emails. Over four hundred new messages.

The cleaning staff had all gone. Christina and Patrick were in their own quarters. The only person who was going to disturb her was Marcello and he'd fallen asleep. She was taking no chances though, and had put her jeans and vest top on. A quick glance in the mirror had made her put her bra on too.

Back to the real office tomorrow. Back to the real world.

The real world had already found its way back to her though, and she stared at her mammoth inbox without seeing.

She'd been too caught up in the bliss of everything she was experiencing to realise Christina had figured out that they'd become lovers, and it made her cheeks burn with humiliation to imagine what the older woman must think of her. Made them burn harder to imagine what it would be like dealing with her in the future.

She knew Marcello wasn't any more ready than she was to say goodbye as lovers yet, but the unspoken deadline of their return to the office marking the end of them would not change.

The grief that had brought Marcello to Manhattan had cut too deep for him to ever dare open his heart in the same way again. He'd let her in as much as he could and tomorrow he would let her go. For him, life would return to how he needed it to be.

She'd let him so far into her heart that he'd nestled inside it with no means of release.

She closed her eyes to the swelling tears and took a long breath.

How long until he re-joined his usual dating pool? She no longer believed he would ask her to keep evenings free for him or do any of the old stuff he used to do when he had a lover on the scene—she might tease him for being a monster but he wasn't. Marcello was often thoughtless but he was never cruel—but the tabloids took a keen interest in his sex life. His shallow lovers saw to that, many using their affair as a springboard to craved fame. Victoria would once again find herself reading about his sexploits and fielding calls from disgruntled women cast aside without a thought, and know that they'd shared the bed she'd found such joy in.

All the things she'd known lay in her future and known would hurt her…

And now she knew she could not endure any of it. Because she hadn't known just how deeply in love with him she would fall.

Putting a hand to her pounding heart, she took another deep breath and blinked away the tears until she could see more clearly.

She knew what she needed to do.

Another deep breath and then she composed an email to the head of HR. She would send it in the morning, after she'd told Marcello that it would be impossible for her to go back to how things used to be.

Marcello straightened his black bow tie, flicked a speck of dust off the lapel of his black dinner jacket, then patted cologne into his shaven cheeks and neck. He was ready.

In the bedroom, Victoria stood before the full-length mirror putting on the diamond teardrop earrings he'd had delivered as a surprise for her only an hour before.

If he hadn't wasted an hour of the day sleeping, he'd have snuck out and chosen them from the real-life versions and not the online versions.

He still struggled to believe he'd fallen asleep in the afternoon. His mother still regaled family and friends with stories of how, even as a toddler, Marcello had refused to nap. Since moving to Manhattan, his body's need for sleep had diminished to such an extent that he rarely slept more than five hours a night. He could only assume the copious amount of sex he'd been enjoying with Victoria was the cause of his unintended snooze. He'd woken from it, rolled over to cuddle into her and coax her into more lovemaking, only to find the bed empty. She'd returned to the room inconveniently clothed before he could seek her out. Her face had coloured when she'd explained that she'd been sorting out work stuff.

'Never mind that,' he'd said thickly, throwing off the duvet. 'Come back to bed.'

And so she had, and this time she'd been the one to doze off afterwards. When she'd woken, she'd been the one to instigate more lovemaking.

Just as he struggled to believe he'd had an afternoon snooze, he struggled to understand why his mind kept substituting the word sex for lovemaking. And why his mind flatly refused to imagine a time without Victoria in his bed.

Tomorrow they would part as lovers and return to the rhythms of their old working lives. There would be a period of adjustment but he was confident they would get through it. He was sure that throwing himself back into his pool of shallow vipers would take off the edge of his craving for his executive assistant. He would just have to be discreet, and throw himself back into the pool away from his apartment until Victoria's imprint had faded to nothing.

Back to the bland, vaguely satisfactory couplings that demanded nothing of him but his body.

Damn it, if he could keep this affair with Victoria going until it was naturally spent then he would, but this was as much as he could allow, and he had to think, too, of what it would be like for her if they did continue things a little longer. Offices could be febrile places filled with gossip and innuendo. He would not have her humiliated. He needed her as his assistant. Needed her in his life.

His hopes for them to be old and wrinkled and wheezing together would never die. Maybe he should add the grandchildren she would surely have to the mix. Imagine them pushing the pair of them around in wheelchairs.

But where would her future husband be? he wondered, his mood dipping. To have grandchildren, she would need children first, and it was inconceivable that Victoria would choose to have children without a man by her side. A husband. A man she would pledge her life to.

His guts filled with acid.

He could provide a crèche and childcare staff in the office so she could bring her imaginary future children to work, but what if she met the father on one of her visits home and decided to move back to Ireland for real, and not just as a threat to Marcello to pull him back a peg?

She caught his stare in the mirror's reflection.

After the longest time passed, she smiled. 'You look beautiful.'

Pulling himself together, he straightened and strode over to her.

They still had this one last night together.

'Beautiful?' he said, feigning outrage. 'I think the word you are looking for is handsome.'

She turned around and gently tugged at his bow tie. Eyes on his, she said with simple sincerity, 'No. The word is beautiful.'

Her words touched something in him that made him close his eyes before taking a step back so he could drink the whole of her in. The red velvet dress fitted as if it had been tailored especially for her. Long sleeved, it dipped in a V to her breasts, giving the most tantalising glimpse of her generous cleavage, then hugged her curvy waist before cascading like drapes to her feet. Only the heels of the black knee-high boots she was wearing, a sop to the wintry weather, stopped the hem trailing on the ground. Her red hair, the perfect complementary shade to the colour of the dress, had been parted in the centre but then gathered together to fall over her right shoulder. It gleamed like the finest gold.

'No. You're the beautiful one.'

Rosy colour flushed her cheeks. 'It's the expensive makeup you bought me.'

Expensive makeup subtly but strikingly applied. 'It

only enhances what God has blessed you with. You are a beautiful woman, Victoria Cusack.'

The flush deepened. 'I keep telling you, you should see my sisters. They really are beautiful. No enhancement needed,' she quipped.

He captured her chin and rubbed his thumb over the faint cleft in it. 'Stop comparing yourself to your sisters. You are perfect exactly as you are.'

The hazel eyes softened. 'You mean that, don't you?'

He brushed a kiss over her lips and breathed her in. 'Yes. And it is time you started believing it.'

CHAPTER TEN

VICTORIA WAS SPELLBOUND. When she'd watched this musical all those months ago, her vision had been obscured and she'd been sat so high up and so far back the cast really had seemed as small as ants. She'd also kept her phone clutched in her hand, surreptitiously checking it every five minutes. When Marcello had asked her back to the office, she'd told herself she was furious with him for calling her away on something so whimsical, but now she could admit the truth to herself—she'd been waiting for it. Hoping for it. By the time her phone had silently vibrated with his call, she'd already planned her escape route to take it without disturbing the other theatregoers.

This time, she kept her phone in the gold clutch bag that had been in another of the gold boxes Marcello had surprised her with, and watched on a seat so good it was as if she could reach out and touch the stage. Maybe if her hand weren't so tightly clasped in Marcello's she would have tried.

To Marcello's surprise, he thoroughly enjoyed the show. Victoria's joy would have made it worthwhile for its own sake, but the songs were catchy and the plot good enough to keep his interest.

When things had settled between them and they'd slipped back into the old rhythm of their lives, he would take her to another Broadway show. They would go as the friends they'd been from the start. He knew it would take time to find that old rhythm but they would find it. They had to.

But not yet. Tonight they were enjoying Broadway as lovers.

Outside, the snow was falling again, and when they climbed into the back of his waiting car for the short drive to the restaurant he'd booked them to dine at, fat flakes clung like sparkling diamonds in her hair before melting into a glisten and vanishing.

Palming her cold cheek, he leaned his face into hers and thought he would never be able to endure seeing the sparkle in her eyes vanish, not when they shone with such brilliance as they did now. 'Go on, tell me, how many times have you already seen it?' he murmured.

She grinned. 'Four times. How did you guess?'

'Your singing along to every word was the giveaway.'

Both laughing, they kissed, a short kiss because their short drive had ended.

Marcello watched for a reaction when she recognised the name of the restaurant, and experienced a surge of gratification when the sparkle in her eyes intensified. Famed for its fresh atmosphere and even fresher sea-food, something he knew she had a deep and abiding love for, he'd selected this place with Victoria's desires at the forefront of his mind.

Thinking there was a very real danger she could burst from happiness, Victoria felt like a celebrity when they were whisked up the steps and welcomed into what she could only describe as a sophisticatedly funky interior. Evening coats taken—her Merino wool coat had been another surprise from Marcello—they were swept off to a corner table. Water poured, drink order taken, a limoncello vodka martini for Victoria, a dirty vodka, whatever that was, for Marcello, and then they were left alone with their menus.

Immediately, she leaned her face over her menu to confide, 'I looked at bringing Sheena here for her birthday last summer but couldn't get a reservation for love nor money.' She'd been snootily informed the restaurant had a fourteen-month waiting list. 'She is going to be *green* when I tell her I've been.'

'You should have told me—I could have got the two of you in.'

'Don't *ever* tell Sheena that.' Not that he would ever meet her. Not now. Marcello didn't know it but this wasn't just their last night together. This was the beginning of their end, something she was resolutely not allowing herself to think about. He'd gone to so much effort that it would be cruel to ruin the evening by letting her emotions get the better of her. There would be plenty of time for that when she broke the news to him. Let them have this one last night and part with the best memories of each other.

He grinned. 'How do you know Sheena? Did you meet at Columbia?'

'No, after Columbia. We lived together for a while. I

was looking for a new place to live and she was looking for a new roommate. Mutual friends facilitated it and introduced us. They were convinced that as we're both Irish we were bound to know each other because obviously everyone from Ireland knows each other.'

His grin widened. 'I used to get that when I first moved here. Anyone with a first-generation Italian friend was certain we must have spent our childhoods together.'

'Do you know what the best bit is?'

His eyes gleamed. 'Tell me.'

'It turned out that Sheena and I *did* kind of know each other. Our mothers used to work for the same accountancy firm!'

Oh, how she loved Marcello's laughter at this, loved how when their drinks arrived he held his aloft so she could clink hers to it, loved how he urged her to try his and loved even more his laughter when she pulled a disgusted face—who put *olive juice* in a vodka, for heaven's sake?—at its offensive taste.

'Your tastebuds are warped,' she informed him.

'So you don't want to share the seafood platter, then?' he teased.

It was after they'd finished their first course, were on their third round of drinks and helping themselves to the enormous tray heaped with clams, oysters, tuna crudo, jumbo shrimps and lobster that had been delivered to their table, that he said, 'Do you know, I have never asked what brought you to America?'

She looked up at him, startled by the observation. 'Haven't you?'

He shook his head. 'I just assumed you had followed the American dream like most other people who emigrate here.'

The look that passed between them conveyed perfectly well that it didn't need to be said that Marcello had turned his back on a nightmare rather than follow a dream.

'I did have that dream,' she admitted, squeezing lemon juice over the seafood she'd piled onto her plate. 'But it wasn't the dream of making a pot of money. It was the freedom New York promised that drew me.'

'What kind of freedom were you seeking?'

'All kinds. I'm from a small town with a small high street where all the shops close at five and the only night life are pubs where the only activities are games of darts and table skittles, and the music comes from twenty-year-old jukeboxes. New York seemed to promise everything I thought I was missing out on. The city that never sleeps? I wanted that, thank you very much.'

Marcello laughed and plucked a fat chip from the metal basket piled with them. 'That aspect drew me too. Did you not consider moving to an Irish city or to England?'

'All my favourite films were set in New York so for me it was a no-brainer. I couldn't believe it when I was accepted into Columbia. I only chose business on a whim because I couldn't think of anything else.'

'You were eighteen?'

'I'd just turned nineteen.'

He thought of himself at nineteen. He'd gone to university in Bologna, a four-hour drive from his family home in Rome. His parents had visited every other weekend armed with cases of freshly laundered clothes, which they'd swapped for the mounds of dirty clothes he'd piled all over his cramped room.

Where he'd been happily spoilt and cosseted by adoring parents, Victoria had fought to be seen by hers. Moving to New York meant Victoria had been on her own. In the eighteen months she'd worked for him, not a single member of her family had flown out to visit her.

'That must have been daunting.'

'It was *terrifying*,' she agreed gleefully.

'And your family? What did they think of you leaving? Were they proud?' He hoped as hard as he'd ever hoped for anything that they were.

'They were delighted for me. I became the golden Cusack they could all brag about to their friends and casually drop into conversation about my life in The Big Apple.' The gleefulness in her voice faded. 'It took me leaving to make them actually remember my name.'

That was one thing he would never understand. He supposed in big families like the Cusacks, it was all too easy for one of them to feel lost within it. Marcello's extended family was big, but when he was growing up, his immediate family had been just the four of them, their parents spoiling and cosseting Benito as much as they'd done him.

He found himself having to swallow a sudden lump in his throat. 'Do you miss them?'

'Not as much as I would without the technology we have. I'm in all the family group chats and stuff but...' She gave a small shrug. 'It's silly but I still feel excluded. It's my own fault, I know. I chose to move across the Atlantic and live in a different time zone from them. But they answer each other's posts within minutes, sometimes seconds whereas mine are often left hanging. The only one who always responds to mine is Grandma.'

Victoria gave a wistful shake of her head and tried to pull herself together and not let the despondency she'd worked so hard to smother that evening leach out. 'I told you I'm being silly. It's always great when I go home and we have such a lovely time together. I guess I just wish it didn't feel like they forget me the minute I'm out of their sight.'

But as she said this, she realised that since working for Marcello, the sting of it had lost its needle precision. Her visits home had been happier occasions for her, not just because she no longer felt lost in the crowd of Cusacks but because she was happier and more confident in her own skin. And all because one man had seen something in her that had left a lasting impression.

Marcello had remembered her.

'I can tell you this much, *bella*,' he said. 'When you were ill, I nearly suffered a burst eardrum from all the calls I kept receiving from them.'

She spluttered a short burst of laughter at the imagery.

His smile was soft. 'I cannot pretend to understand the dynamics of your family but I know they love you.'

She returned the smile. 'I know they do. I guess it's all a continuation of how things were for me growing up. My voice always got lost.' She wrinkled her nose.

'I probably should have shouted louder to make myself heard. That's what the others did.'

'If you did not have your voice there, I would say that you have found it here.'

'Do you think?'

'There is not a person in the Guardiola Group who would dare ignore your voice.'

'You make me sound like a dragon!'

Laughing, he shook his head and cut into his tuna. 'No one thinks that. People listen to you because you have proven that you're worth listening to. You organise your thinking the same way you organise my life.'

'Thank you… I think.'

'*Bella*, it is not just me who values and respects you. The whole workforce does.'

The tears she'd been fighting so hard to hold back suddenly brimmed as the life she'd enjoyed since arriving in New York flashed through her. The good friends she'd made. The great social life she'd enjoyed even if it had ground to a halt since working for Marcello. But that was her own fault too. She saw that now. She'd let him make outrageous demands on her personal time because, even when she was miffed with him, there was no one in the world in whose company she'd rather be.

Because of Marcello, she'd found a career to thrive in and was paid generously for it. For all that she'd often thought of herself as his glorified dogsbody, he'd taught her more about business than any number of degrees could have. He'd made it no secret that he was grooming her to one day take a seat on his board, a seat in her own right and not just as his Woman Friday.

At twenty-five, she'd built the life her bored, insecure teenage self would have thrilled for.

Tomorrow, she would take a sledgehammer to it.

Today she had everything. A great career. Disposable income. A decent apartment to live in. A love affair more fulfilling and consuming than she could ever have dreamed possible.

Tomorrow it would all be gone.

'*Bella?* What is wrong?'

She looked back into the eyes she loved more than anyone's in the whole world and knew that in the morning she would be taking a sledgehammer to Marcello's world too, even if it was a much smaller one.

But tomorrow hadn't arrived yet. They still had these last few hours together and she wouldn't spoil them for anything.

With a soft sigh, she said, 'I was just thinking my teenage self would approve of how my life has turned out.'

Shoulders relaxing, he raised his glass. 'We should drink to that.'

'As long as I don't have to drink that evil stuff in your glass,' she managed to quip.

His answering laugh helped smother the despondency back to where she could keep it hidden and contained from them both for their last few hours together.

Marcello's eyes were wide open in the early morning darkness. He wasn't sure if he'd slept at all. Too many thoughts crowding his head in the lulls between lovemaking.

Nestled beside him, her hand a deadweight on his abdomen, a strand of her long hair tickling his arm, Victoria.

The dream-like bubble of the past week was coming to an end. Soon, he would have to wake her. They needed to shower and then head to her apartment so she could change into her work clothes before they went into the office and reminded the staff of what they looked like.

He hadn't had so much time off work since Tommaso.

It had been a difficult birth. Livia had suffered. But then their perfect baby had been born and happiness had suffused her. Suffused them both. The purest kind of love. The three of them, his little family. A whole life together to be lived.

In the blink of an eye it had all gone and the purity of his love had turned into a grief so unbearable the pain had made him want to die.

Work had been his salvation. He'd returned to the small building that had homed his then small empire the day after they'd laid Tommaso to rest. He'd taken only rare days off since. His annual visit to his parents' home for Christmas was always calculated to last no more than four days, including travelling. Work hard. Play hard. Exhaust the mind and body. Leave no time for thoughts or feelings.

His thoughts now refused to switch off but, without any forethought, he slipped out of bed and headed silently to his dressing room, closing the door before switching the light on so the brightness didn't wake Victoria.

Behind his rails of shirts, he unlocked the hidden safe he kept his more expensive valuables in. He didn't possess many of them. He'd never been one for status symbols. A handful of ridiculously expensive watches, a signet ring he always felt like a mafia boss wearing, a few pairs of diamond cufflinks too expensive to go into the cufflink drawer, and his grandmother's engagement ring.

'You're the only one left who can use it,' his grandfather had said when he'd given it to him over Christmas. Meaning Marcello was the only one of his grandchildren unmarried, something his mother, who'd abandoned any subtlety of her hope that Marcello remarry this past year, had no doubt put in his mind.

If he hadn't respected his grandfather so greatly, and if he hadn't understood his well-meant intention, Marcello would have reminded him that he was unmarried because he was divorced and that the scars from what he and Livia had been through meant he would never marry again.

The ghost of Livia's voice echoed through the walls from the last time he'd seen her.

Then why did you come here?

He was still no closer to an answer. No closer, either, to understanding why he'd agreed to the keynote speech in Rome. He'd refused his brother's four previous requests so why accept this one? Why put himself through the pain of returning to the city of his darkest days when he didn't need to?

And why was he standing in his dressing room staring at a ring? He didn't know why he'd felt compelled to look at it. Didn't understand the hollowness of his mood or the brooding nature of his thoughts.

Exhaling through his nose, he locked the safe back up and moved his shirts back into place to cover it, then turned out the dressing room light and gazed at Victoria through the dim moonlight pouring through the windows. She'd turned over and huddled deeper into the duvet.

His next exhale was a fight against his own airwaves.

He'd let her sleep a little longer.

Showered, still trying to make sense of his thoughts and feelings, Marcello selected his suit, then rifled through his ties. The hot water had done him the world of good and washed away much of the strange mood that had clung to him. He'd figured out, too, what had caused it. It was all the talk and thoughts about Tommaso. The grief he usually kept compartmentalised had risen these last few days. Longer really. He'd thought about his son more in recent times than he usually ever allowed himself.

Victoria was still asleep.

He watched her from the bedroom door as he'd done a short while earlier from his dressing room, a fresh weight forming in his guts.

This would be the last time he saw her like this.

He closed his eyes and breathed out the pain.

It had to be this way.

CHAPTER ELEVEN

DREAD LAY HEAVY in Victoria from the moment consciousness pulled her from sleep.

This was it. The day she destroyed her own happiness and threw away everything she'd worked for.

Stifling a whimper, she rolled over, seeking out Marcello. His side of the bed was empty.

Cuddling into his pillow, she squeezed her eyes shut and breathed in the remnants of his scent. She wanted desperately to make love to him one last time, before she detonated the bomb. Experience the blissful closeness one last time.

His robe was slung on the back of the armchair, and she wrapped herself in it before searching for him. His office and the living space below were both empty.

She tried to draw air into her tight lungs.

The dread spread into her limbs. She had to drag her legs back to the bedroom.

With still no sign of Marcello, she took a quick shower and tried her hardest not to think of standing under this very shower only hours ago with him, when they'd returned from the restaurant. Brushed her teeth trying not to remember how, only hours ago, Marcello had stood at the adjoining sink brushing his own teeth.

Christina had laundered her clothes for her again, and when Victoria tugged her grey cashmere sweater over her head and then straightened it over her stomach, there was a beat when she thought she glimpsed the pounding of her heart pushing through her chest.

The door opened.

Marcello strode into the bedroom carrying two cups of coffee. He was already dressed for the office in a white shirt, navy trousers and a matching waistcoat.

'Good morning, Victoria,' he said in greeting, as if he were already back in the work office and had beaten her in by ten minutes. He put her coffee on the table by the armchair, and stood with his own close to the door. Already creating a distance between them. Already showing that this was the point they returned to how things should have stayed.

Her heart twisted to see his tie. Its knot was too big. Marcello was always precise with his knots.

'You are ready?' he asked.

Somehow she managed to form a nod.

He gave a sharper nod of his own. '*Bene.* The car will be here in fifteen minutes.' He flashed his heartbreaking smile. 'Bagels will be delivered momentarily.'

Bagels? In that moment, she couldn't even conjure the image of one. The world was swimming around her and it was taking every ounce of her strength to keep hold of the emotions battering her into a bruise.

She thought she might be sick.

Gripping the cup tightly, she lifted it to her lips.

There was no comfort in the warm, familiar bittersweetness.

His tone became even lighter. 'How did I do?'

He was unshaved, she realised with another twist of her heart. Unshaved for the office. It was a sight that made her want to cry. 'You made it?'

Another dazzling smile. It didn't meet his eyes. 'My first attempt at making coffee in a decade. Marks out of ten?'

'A definite nine,' she croaked through her splintering heart.

'It appears I am as naturally talented at making coffee as everything else,' he said with a deadpan modesty that would normally make her laugh but now made her eyes fill with tears. 'Other than cooking, that is. But do not think this means I will be taking on coffee-making duties in the office—this is strictly a one-time event.'

He continued talking as he reached for the door handle, his accent becoming more pronounced with every word. 'We will stop at your apartment on our way to the office so you can change before the board meeting. I have already—'

'Marcello, stop,' she interrupted softly, unable to bear the faux normality a second longer.

His hand tightened around the door handle but his light expression didn't change.

She shook her head whilst frantically blinking the tears away, and tried her hardest to control her wobbling chin. 'I'm sorry but I can't do this.'

Marcello's grip on the door handle was so tight he could feel the bones of his knuckles press against his skin.

He could no longer ignore Victoria's pallor. She was paler than she'd been since her illness. More than pale.

The weight he'd woken to in his guts spread and clamped his heart in a vice.

Her eyes shining with tears, she shook her head again.

He cleared his throat. 'What can't you do?'

But he knew. His weighted guts had known it the moment their eyes had locked together when he'd come back into the bedroom with their coffee. The misery contained in her stare.

Her grip on her cup was as tight as his hold on the door handle. 'I can't go back to the office and pretend that nothing happened between us.'

'It will be difficult,' he admitted evenly, in what he knew was the understatement of the century. They'd both known it would be difficult to return to how things had been. 'But we are both professionals, and—'

'I can't go back to how we were. Not now.'

His heart was thumping so hard it was a struggle to hear his own voice over it. 'Would you like to take a few days' paid leave? That might be the best thing for both of us—a short reset and then we…'

But she was shaking her head.

A tear rolled down her cheek. 'A few days is not going to reset my feelings. I'm sorry.'

'Okay, paid leave for the week, until our trip to Rome on…'

But she was still shaking her head. More tears spilled down her distressed face. 'It can never work, Marcello. Not for me. Not now.'

'Don't be so defeatist,' he chided through the scratching in his throat and the hot pulse raging in his head as his planned route to a dotage with Victoria in his life and her grandchildren pushing them around on wheelchairs began evaporating before his eyes.

'Marcello, *please*.' Victoria put the coffee cup on the table and wiped the tears away, wishing with all her splintering heart that she could turn back time a week and a day, to the morning her phone had woken her at five a.m. Wished she could put herself back in her bed and ignore his call.

But she'd never been able to ignore him. The pull of hearing his voice or seeing a written message from him had always been too powerful to resist. Marcello had become her whole world long before she'd even realised it.

And now she had to walk away from it.

A pulse was throbbing on his unshaven jaw. 'Victoria, we will make it work as we said we would. Whatever you need to readjust, I will provide it, and then—'

'But there is no way, don't you see?' she implored. 'I can't spend twelve hours a day every day by your side feeling the way I do. I just can't. It would kill me.'

His head reared as if she'd slapped it.

'What…?' His voice trailed off, and he stared at her as if looking at her for the very first time.

As much as she wanted to turn her stare away, she forced herself to hold the lock of their eyes. Forced him to read what was in hers.

Shocked understanding flared.

He shook his head slowly, as if in disbelief.

She simply held his gaze until, without uttering a word, he staggered over to the bed and sank onto it, cradling his head in his hands.

'Now do you understand?' she whispered.

The silence was so total that when he dragged his hands down his cheeks she could hear the scratching of his fingers against the stubble.

He tilted his head back slowly. Blew out an equally slow breath.

Feeling sicker than she'd ever done in her life, Victoria sank onto her knees before him and captured his stubbly cheeks in her hands. She could feel the barely suppressed tension breathing out from his pores.

'You don't have to leave,' he said raggedly, turning his mouth into her palm. 'We can find a way to make it work.'

'The only way it can work for me is if you love me—'

His eyes squeezed shut as he let out a long groan. 'No, Victoria, don't say it.'

'But I do love you,' she told him quietly. 'I think a part of me has always loved you.'

The strong throat she loved nothing more than burying her face into and breathing in the scent from moved, but nothing came out. It made her broken heart splinter a little more to know she would never breathe in his scent again.

'Do you think I wanted this to happen?' she choked into the silence. 'I spent eighteen months pretending to myself that you weren't the sexiest man alive and that my feelings for you were strictly platonic, but the way you took care of me during my illness...' She closed her eyes to hold back another wave of tears and tried with all her might to stop her voice from breaking. 'How could I not have fallen in love with you after that? And loving you has changed everything for me. A family of my own has always been a distant thing and now I find myself longing for it, and I'm longing for it with *you*. I want to spend the rest of my life with you and have your children and raise a family...'

Pain flaring in his eyes, he snatched hold of her wrists and pressed his forehead to hers. 'Bella, if I could give it to anyone it would be you. But I can't.'

She'd known it, but to hear it from his own mouth hurt more than she could ever have believed.

The nugget of hope her heart had held onto even when her brain had been telling it not to be so foolish shattered, and she finally crumbled.

Marcello could never allow himself to love her.

'I know you can't, and that's why I have to go,' she sobbed.

He shook his head despairingly. 'You *don't* have to go. We can—'

'I *do*. I don't want to leave you, Marcello, you must know that. Working for you has been the most infuriating but fulfilling time of my entire life and if I could stay by your side as your right-hand woman for ever then I would, but I *can't*. I can't be around you with these foolish dreams. I can't work by your side waiting for the day you start dating again and have my heart broken all over again.'

He palmed her cheeks and caught her tears in his

thumbs, then pressed his forehead to hers again. 'I never wanted to break your heart, *bella*.'

'You're not breaking it, Marcello—I'm breaking it all by myself. You gave me every warning and I tried to listen but there was nothing I could do to stop it. I know you care for me and I know this is hurting you too, and I'm so sorry, and I'm sorry but I can't go to Rome with you.'

The scratching in Marcello's throat had spread to his chest. She could have been ripping at them with her nails.

The disaster he'd sensed coming when he'd recognised the attraction in her stare had detonated around him, and for the second time in his life, the solid foundations of his world were cracking around him.

'You want to leave me now?' he asked, still hardly believing. Not wanting to believe. Still half waiting for Victoria to break into a smile and tell him this was all one big joke.

'I don't want to leave you at all but I have to. Please try to understand. I will work until the end of the week to get everything in order but I can't do Rome. I just don't think I could bear to watch you act normally when I know the memories will be ripping you to pieces and the comfort I'll want to give you… It's just too much. Please understand. Please.'

The thick weight in his guts was pulling him under, a darkness in his bloodstream steadily creeping through his pores and deepening with every passing second. His nightmare a reality.

The best person in his life. He was losing her.

He was losing Victoria. And it was all his own fault. He'd sensed the danger. Not just sensed it. Known it.

He could make threats. Legal threats. Financial threats. Deploy all the weapons in his arsenal to make her stay and keep her by his side for ever.

'I understand,' he whispered hoarsely.

And that, for him, was the worst part. He *did* understand. He'd fled Rome and made Manhattan his home to escape his own pain, and because he understood it, he had no choice but to let her go.

He could never give her what she needed. What she deserved.

He should have walked away when he still had the chance.

'I will not make you work any of your notice period. We can say goodbye to each other now.'

Her face contorted. 'Thank you.'

The bleakness in his stare felt like a knife in Victoria's heart, and she tightened her hold on his cheeks and pressed her lips wet with tears to his.

His hands burrowed into her hair and his lips parted as they shared a kiss of such tender passion the anguished scream from her heart that this would be their last had her clinging tightly to him and scraping her fingers through his hair, imprinting his taste and scent into her memories to see her through a lifetime.

Letting him go was a physical wrench but it had to be done. Every minute longer that she stayed only prolonged the agony.

In silence, she gathered the last of her possessions and walked to the door.

He made no effort to follow her. Neither of them needed to say it was better that way.

'I'll email Audrey when I get back to the apartment,' she said quietly. She didn't add that her resignation was already written. Only that now-smashed nugget of hope had stopped her pressing send before.

What a foolish, foolish thing to hope for.

He closed his eyes and nodded.

She swallowed. 'Thank you for taking such good care of me and for everything you've taught me.' She had to catch a breath to continue. 'Thank you for being the best person in the world... I will carry you in my heart for ever.' The tears almost blinding her, she wiped them away so she could look at Marcello's beautiful face one last time and give the thanks that meant the most. 'And thank you for remembering my name.'

The smile he conjured was only a ghost of the heart-breaking smile she loved so much but it shattered her heart into a thousand pieces.

Hoarsely, he said, 'As if I could ever have forgotten it.'

CHAPTER TWELVE

MARCELLO ATE THE last of his surprisingly bland break-fast bagel, screwed the wrapping into a ball, and aimed it at the wastebin he kept in the corner of his office for this express purpose. 'In one,' he preened with a fist-pump.

But there was no droll, 'Congratulations,' to follow.

There hadn't been for four days.

There was only him.

Only him, and he had an investment pitch to pre-pare for.

About to buzz Ryan into his office, there was a knock on the door and Ryan walked in.

Ryan was Victoria's trial replacement, recommended by Victoria in her official resignation letter. Marcello was prepared to give him a chance at filling Victoria's shoes but was not yet ready to have him occupy her desk.

He didn't think he would ever be ready to see some-one else occupying the space she'd made her own.

'Excellent timing,' he said. 'I was about to call you. Can you prepare a report on Symon Tech for me?'

'It's already done, sir.'

'Good work,' he said, impressed.

Ryan looked sheepish. 'I didn't do it.'

He swallowed against the automatic tightening of his throat. 'Victoria?'

Four days on and saying her name hadn't got any easier.

The younger man nodded. 'I'll email it to you.'

'Thank you.' He let a beat of silence pass. When that wasn't filled, said, 'I presume there was something you wanted from me?'

'Yes. Err… A few of us have, err, been, err…'

He had to fight his eyes from rolling. Victoria *never* prevaricated. 'Get to the point.'

'We've organised a whip-round to buy Victoria a leaving gift,' Ryan blurted out.

This time the whole of Marcello's body tightened.

'And you are wanting me to contribute?' He was already pulling his wallet out of his suit jacket pocket. In a digital world, Marcello never felt comfortable unless he had a wedge of cash on him. He pulled out five one-hundred-dollar bills.

Ryan's eyes widened.

'Anything else?' Marcello asked when the man who wished to fill the indispensable Victoria's shoes continued hovering.

'Would it be okay for me and Cate to finish early today so we can buy her the gift? We were going to buy it over the weekend but we've just learned she'll be gone by then.'

'Gone where?' he asked casually.

'Back to Ireland. Dani called her. She's flying home

tomorrow evening. Ideally we want to drop the gift to her apartment tonight.'

His heart contracted then pulsed with ice that spread into his every crevice.

Fingers digging into the mahogany of his desk, Marcello inclined his head and, through a smile he had to use imaginary marionette strings to pull off, said, 'Do you know what you are going to buy her?'

'We did but her leaving means we need to rethink it.'

'She likes to wear rose-gold jewellery. Do you have a card for her?' he added in case Ryan was tempted to ask how Marcello knew the kind of jewellery Victoria liked to wear. He wouldn't have been able to answer. It was just something he knew.

'Yes, sir.'

'Good. Bring it to me to sign and send me the report, and then you and Cate can leave. Take the day.'

Ryan's eyes widened again.

'And, Ryan?'

'Yes, sir?'

'If I have to tell you one more time not to address me as sir, I will open up recruitment for the role. *Capisce?*'

Ryan gave an uncertain smile and nod.

'*Bene.* If you ever meet my father you can address *him* as sir. Now get me the card and the Symon Tech report.'

Alone again in his office, Marcello blinked sharply, breathed deeply, and pulled his schedule up on his computer. He had a flight of his own tomorrow evening, to Rome, but there would be no chance of bumping into

Victoria at the airport. Flying privately was a whole different experience from flying commercial.

The schedule before him had been inputted entirely by Victoria, who always thought and worked ahead. Her efficiency meant he was yet to let Ryan loose on it. Her efficiency meant that only her physical presence had been missed. He noted that meetings that had been arranged for the week the storm had shut Manhattan down had all been rearranged. She must have done it the afternoon he'd fallen asleep.

He took a deep breath to loosen the painful tightening in his chest. He was having to do that a lot.

A message pinged. The Symon Tech file.

Usually he would get Victoria to print off two copies, one for each of them to read through. Get her to write her thoughts in the margins. Compare notes. By the time they met with the company seeking his investment, he would have a good idea if he wished to go ahead with it. He was always open to changing his mind— you needed to meet the people behind the company before solidifying if you wished to invest with them. After all, he'd gone to the Hansons pitch two years ago thinking he would likely invest, but the directors had proved themselves to be such terrible people that their staff had deliberately sabotaged the pitch.

Cretins was what Victoria often referred to the directors of Hansons as. Cretins. Delivered in that Irish lilt that always put a smile on his face.

He was quite sure that in another week or so he'd be able to smile again without having to use imaginary marionette strings. One day soon, he hoped to remember her smile without having to struggle for breath.

Victoria hurried up the stairs to her apartment being careful not to squeeze her coffee cup too tightly and have the hot fluid spill over her hand.

Catching her breath, she unlocked the door and put her pastrami wrap and coffee on the small kitchen table. The washing had finished. She chucked the contents into the dryer then put her towels into the washing machine. That would be her last load. If she hadn't overslept, it would already be done. But she had overslept, mainly because she'd still been awake at three a.m. willing her body to go to damned sleep.

She estimated she had just enough time for the towels to dry and for her to lob them in the suitcase before the car came to take her to the airport.

A car Marcello had arranged for her.

Not that he'd told her of it himself. Audrey had done that when Victoria had gone to the office the day before to hand in her company credit card and complete the company exit form. She'd timed it for when she knew Marcello would be in a meeting. She was functioning with what felt like all her limbs missing and a heart that had forgotten how to beat a normal rhythm. Just to imagine entering the skyscraper knowing he was under the same roof as her made blood pound in her head. Made it pound everywhere. She was holding up well enough, just focussing on tying up everything that needed tying up before she flew home to her family. To see him again would destroy that. She only had so much strength. Getting through each day was as much as she could cope with.

Before she'd left though, Audrey had asked what time she needed to be at the airport because 'the boss' had instructed Audrey to arrange for a Guardiola Group car and driver to transport her.

Victoria had no idea how she'd kept her legs upright or how she'd managed to answer without breaking down.

One day at a time had become a mantra, and she repeated it now while she forced her stomach to accept food it recoiled from. She managed half the wrap before binning the rest and dragging herself to the bedroom to clean the windows. She would give the apartment keys to the driver. If—and this was a big if—Ryan proved himself to Marcello and was given the job permanently, the keys would be passed to him.

On the bed lay her opened suitcases. Already packed in one was the Tiffany box containing a rose-gold bracelet that she'd been gifted from her colleagues. It was exquisite. It must have cost a fortune. Ryan, Cate and Dani had come to the apartment the night before with takeout and given it to her then, along with a giant leaving card. It had been a wonderful gesture and a wonderful evening, even if she'd had to deflect as to why she'd resigned and was moving back to Ireland. Missing her home was the excuse she'd used. She had the impression none of them believed her.

Was she doing the right thing? Running from her life and back to the home where she'd always felt like the cuckoo in the nest? Adapting to life in America had been hard but once she had adapted, it had been wonderful. New York was home.

But it had taken Marcello to feel like that. Taken Marcello to make her feel wanted. Needed. Remembered. To bring her to life and step into being the woman her teenage self had so longed to be, all long before they'd become lovers. And he hadn't even tried.

And now he was tied to everything. There was not a single aspect of her life he hadn't weaved his way into.

Although she'd promised herself to leave it until she was back in her childhood bedroom, she sat on the bed and reached into the case for the leaving card. She'd opened it in front of her expectant ex-colleagues but had only skimmed the hundreds of messages and signatures crammed into the white space. Now, she pored over it, searching, searching...

And then she found it. No bigger or smaller than any of the others it was nestled amongst.

Best wishes in wherever life takes you. Marcello.

A tear rolled down her cheek and landed with a plop on the card. It was the first tear she'd shed since leaving his apartment... Horror gripped her to realise the tear had landed on his name, and she dabbed frantically at it with her sleeve. Her efforts only made it worse. She'd smudged his name and his message. Smudged the one thing created by his hand that she had to take with her.

With a howl of anguish, she rolled into a ball and sobbed.

Marcello paced his office. Could not stop pacing. Kept looking out of the window over the Manhattan skyline.

The fresh snow that had been falling on his drive to the office had stopped. The skies were clearing. Soon he would be up there in it. In two hours he would be on his way to the airport, on his way to Rome. In one hour and thirty minutes, Victoria would step into a company car and be taken to the same airport for a flight to the same continent but to a different country and for purposes that were the reverse of the same coin.

She was flying from pain. He was flying to it. And he wouldn't even have her by his side to…

He stopped pacing abruptly.

A wave of revulsion at the direction his thoughts had tried to take washed through him.

Dio, he was despicable.

Was he seriously trying to suggest to himself that he'd only agreed to Benito's request because he'd subconsciously thought having Victoria there would make it bearable?

There was a knock on his door quickly followed by it opening and Ryan stepping in.

'It is customary to wait for an affirmative response before entering a room,' Marcello snarled.

The shock on Ryan's face brought him up short.

Running his fingers through his hair, he took a deep breath. 'I apologise.'

'No, my fault,' Ryan said, backing out of the office.

A sudden image of Victoria backing into his apartment's elevator flashed before him. The smiling wave she'd given him.

'Ciao, amigo.'

'Amigo is Spanish.'

'I know.'

'You can't quit over a bagel.'

'I just did.'

Suddenly he found himself unable to draw breath. The walls of his office were closing in on him, perspiration breaking out over his skin.

'Sir?'

Ryan's voice broke through.

Marcello looked at the young man doing everything he could to impress and prove he could replace Victoria.

But no one could replace her. No one could even come close. Not in any aspect of his life.

Head spinning, the walls crowding ever closer, he headed to the door. He needed air.

Travelling the elevator to the ground floor with no memory of getting in it, he stepped from the lobby into the crisp winter daylight of the pedestrian plaza his building faced. People going about their business at the end of the working day. Workers with their heads down. Tourists with their phones out snapping photos. A young father in unsuitable winter clothes holding the hand of a toddler dressed in a snowsuit…

'You can't quit over a bagel.'

'I just did.'

He put a hand to his chest and tried to pull air into his uncooperative lungs.

The child stumbled. The father scooped him up. Marcello couldn't tear his gaze from them.

Livia floated in his vision.

'You are allowed to move on too, Marcello.'

'I'm good.'

He closed his eyes. Opened them. The father was still carrying his toddler. He stared after them until they disappeared from sight.

He'd not been *good* since he'd touched his son's forehead and panicked to feel the heat coming from it.

He'd run from the pain but had never run from Tommaso. He carried his child with him. A piece of him. He'd given the whole of his heart to his son and would never betray his memory and the purity of his love by letting anyone else in to share it. Would never open himself to pain again.

But pain had found its way back to him.

Pain and loss. Deeper than he could have believed he was still capable of feeling after Tommaso.

Work hard and play hard, that was what he'd dedicated himself to. Because life was fragile. Fleeting. You could close your eyes to the night and never see another sunrise, and all that would be left of you was an emptiness in the souls of those who'd loved you that nothing could fill.

Or so he'd believed.

It hadn't been his office walls closing in on him, it had been the world. His world. His world without Victoria.

She was his world. His everything.

He raised his head, closed his eyes and spoke a prayer to his son.

And then he went back into the lobby and spoke to the nearest doorman. 'I need a car. Now.'

At Marcello's second stop, he jumped out of the car and slid through the slush to the door. On the side of it a list of apartment numbers but no names.

He'd never visited the apartment before. Had no idea what number it was.

Swearing loudly, he called Ryan. The car for Victoria would be arriving at any moment.

The tumble dryer beeped at the same moment Victoria's intercom rang.

She closed her eyes.

So this was it, then.

Dully, she pressed the button to open the entrance door. She'd been told the driver would carry her cases to the car. Her life, all packed away. All except three towels. She could only hope they'd actually dried.

She supposed the towels being a little damp wouldn't matter. It wasn't like her parents didn't have a washing machine or anything.

She wouldn't stay with them for long. That much she'd decided. She had her nest egg plus the extra three months' salary unexpectedly credited to her bank account only that morning. Marcello generous to the very end, and now she could easily afford to put down a deposit on a home of her own. Maybe afford to buy a home for herself outright. Maybe ask Grandma Brigit if she'd like to move in with her. At least her dragon breath would keep Victoria warm and her sharp tongue keep her on her toes. Stop her falling into the pit of despair she was so close to the edge of. The tears she'd wept earlier had been a temporary stem on the pain but she was barely clinging on.

Her decision had never felt so real as it did in that moment.

In a few hours she would no longer share the same sky as Marcello and she was going to have to find a way to live with that.

Although expected, the knock on her door made her jump. She hadn't moved from the intercom.

Pulling herself together, she yanked the door open, took one look at the man standing there and, with a whimper, reflexively closed it.

Adrenaline shooting through her, hand over her mouth, she staggered backwards.

The voice she loved was faint through the reinforced safety door.

'Please, *bella*, let me in.'

She shook her head frantically as if he could see her, the only word in her head an echoing *no*.

Not now. Not when she'd spent the whole week fighting the craving to seek him out and tell him she'd changed her mind, that she would rather suffer twelve-hour days by his side knowing he would never love her than spend another second without him.

She'd never understood what it felt like to miss some-one before. Truly miss them, as an ache in her very soul.

She understood it now.

'I know this is terrible timing but there are things I need to say to you, and I want to say them to *you*, not to a door. Please let me in.'

Shaking inside and out, she stared through the blind-ing tears at the door.

After she'd wiped the tears, it took a burst of impe-tus to make her body move and open it.

Bright but dull blue eyes captured hers. Broad shoul-ders rose. 'Thank you.'

It hurt to even look at him.

Turning her face, she whispered, 'I'm leaving in a few minutes.'

He closed the door.

She heard him take a deep breath. 'I know, and I'm here to beg you not to go.'

The howl that echoed in the room came from her own throat.

'Please, *bella*, come back to me,' he begged. 'Don't go. Come back. I can't function without you.'

Her heart and stomach plummeted to her toes. Ryan had confided that he was finding it hard to gel with Marcello and that he believed it obvious Marcello thought him a poor replacement for her.

Stumbling to the tumble dryer, she groped for the towels and hugged them tight to her chest. She had no idea how she made her mouth work. 'Look, Marcello, I know Ryan can be a little earnest but he has great—'

'Not as my EA,' he interrupted.

She blinked hard.

He stepped over to her and gently took the towels she was using as a shield from her arms, and placed them on the edge of the table. Then he gazed down at her and, with a long sigh, stroked her cheek. 'Victoria, I want you to stay with me as my wife. I want to marry you.'

His words were such a shock that it took a long moment to fully absorb them.

Absorbing them only added to the distress.

Swiping at his hands, she backed away from him so quickly that she bashed into the table.

'I never thought you were capable of such cruelty,'

she cried. 'To play on my feelings like this, just because you can't adjust to having—'

The precariously placed towels fell to the floor. With them fell a glittering ring.

Marcello watched Victoria's gaze fall on the ring he'd raced back to his apartment to get and had held tightly the whole way to her, the ring he'd forgotten he was holding the moment he'd looked at her for the first time in what felt like a whole life. He must have let go of it when he'd taken the pile of towels from her without even realising.

Crouching down in the stunned silence, he picked it up then slid onto his knees before her and gazed at her until her wide eyes slowly turned back to him.

It killed him to see the misery contained in them. The redness ringing them. The dullness of her complexion.

He took hold of her hand. It was cold.

'I love you, *bella*,' he said quietly. 'That is why I want you to stay. I want you to come back to *me* because I cannot live without you.'

Her chin was wobbling. Her beautiful little chin with the faint little cleft.

He tightened his hold on her hand. 'I never forgot you because you caught me spellbound the moment I saw the look on your face at the final piece of sabotage your old colleagues did for that pitch. I carried that look with me for months. I carried your name. I gave Denise a maternity package my finance team told me I was mad to give but I did not care, and do you know why?'

She gave the smallest shake of her head.

'I did not care because deep down I knew it meant

she would never come back and that I could bring you in as her replacement.'

She sucked in a small breath.

He smiled wanly and kissed her fingers. 'All this time, Victoria. I have loved you all this time and I was too damned blind and too damned scared to see it. I let you go and sabotaged my own happiness because I thought there was no room left in my heart, but you are in there with him, and I swear to you, there is room in there for all the children you want to have with me. I want them too.' Tears filled his eyes, and he shook his head, still hardly able to believe the truth and the depth of his feelings. 'It has taken me eleven years to learn that although the past cannot be changed, the future does not have to be stuck there. You…' He sighed and kissed her fingers again. Was he imagining that they were warming…?

Keeping hold of her hand, he spread her fingers out and slid the ring on her wedding finger. 'This belonged to my grandmother. My grandfather gave it to me over Christmas. He knew—my whole damn family knew—that my heart had opened for someone…you…but that I needed the push to open my eyes.'

He smiled again at the widening of *her* eyes. 'I needed the push. All the pushes. My heart knew but the rest of me refused to see, and now it is all I can see and all I can feel. I have run from pain before but I cannot run from this…there is nowhere for me to run to. I do not know what the spell is you have cast on me but you have brought me back to life. I can get through anything if I have you with me. You are in my heart and my soul—you *are* my soul. My soul mate. You make each day a joy to live. Stay with me, please. Forgive me for being so blind, and stay with me for ever and let me love you the way you deserve to be loved, which is entirely for yourself because you are the best person in the world and just to see your face is enough to make my heart sing. Please, Victoria, stay with me. Marry me.'

Warm fingers tentatively touched his head and then slid down his cheek as she sank to her knees. 'Say it again,' she whispered.

'Which part?'

'The part about loving me.'

He gazed deep into the hazel eyes he would love for ever. 'I love you.'

A tentative smile. 'Again.'

'I love you.'

A wider smile. 'One for luck.'

Laughter broke free and he kissed her. 'I love you.'

Victoria wound her arms around Marcello's neck and stared in wonder at the face that had become the most beloved face in the whole of her world. 'I thought I would never see you again.'

'Forgive me. I never wanted to cause you pain.'

'I know,' she said softly. She'd always known what she meant to him but had never dared believe he would allow his heart to open enough to embrace it.

To feel the embrace of his love… She expelled the happiest sigh of her life. 'I love you, Marcello.'

'And I love you.'

'Say it again.'

'I love you.' He cupped her cheek and kissed her

deeply. 'Marry me and I will show it and say it every day for the rest of my life. Marry me and let us spend every day of the rest of our lives together.'

'I like the sound of that.'

'Then you will marry me?'

'As soon as we can.'

She didn't just see his smile but felt it right in her heart.

'I like the sound of *that*.' He kissed her again. 'Victoria Guardiola. My wife and business partner.'

'Business partner?'

A slow nod and smile, all without the tip of his nose leaving hers. 'Everything I have is yours. Let us take on the world together.'

Their next kiss was so deep and passionate, and the joy bursting from Victoria's heart so loud, that she failed to hear the intercom buzz, announcing the driver's arrival.

It didn't matter. She was exactly where she was meant to be.

EPILOGUE

JESSICA PUSHED HER great-grandfather's wheelchair onto the back lawn of the sprawling garden. Keeping pace with them, her sprightly great-grandmother.

The snow had fallen hard overnight. To Jessica's mind, snow like this, rare though it was, was no playground for the elderly. Her great-grandparents, though, were no one's idea of elderly. At the first hint of snow, they insisted on getting out there and enjoying it like children. According to Jessica's grandmother, they had always been like this. Ninety-four and eighty-three respectively, they wore their ages loosely.

Wheelchair parked, Jessica helped her great-grandfather to his feet. She always had the sneaking feeling he got a kick out of getting her or one of her siblings or cousins to push him around as he was actually pretty nimble on his feet. The one time she'd suggested he might be faking his occasional lack of agility, his blue eyes had emitted such a twinkle that she'd understood why her great-grandmother had fallen in love with him all those decades ago.

Her great-grandmother, from whom Jessica had inherited her red hair, smiled at her husband as she slipped her arm into his. Her hair now pure white, the lines etched on her aged face suited her. You didn't have to look hard at her great-grandmother to see the young woman who'd captured her great-grandfather's heart.

With a wistful ache in her belly and chest, Jessica watched them walk companionably to the bench in the section of the garden they'd created to remember those they'd loved and lost through the years, including the baby who would have been her great-uncle. They both kicked the snow as they walked. She watched them sit together, gloved hands clasped tightly, her great-grand-mother's cheek resting on the side of her great-grand-father's shoulder, chatting in that easy way they always did that often sounded like it was in their own particular language. So taken was she by the strange yet beautiful sight of a love that had lasted for generations that she didn't notice the snowball hurtling towards her until it smacked into her shoulder.

It was impossible to tell which of her great-grandpar-ents had thrown it—they were both doubled over with the familiar shared laughter Jessica knew she would never settle for anything less than when she found her own soul mate.

* * * * *

SPANIARD'S
WAITRESS WIFE

KATE HEWITT

MILLS & BOON

CHAPTER ONE

TECHNO MUSIC PULSED in time with the beat of his heart as Santos Aguila's narrowed gaze surveyed the crowded bar, his arms folded across his powerful chest. He didn't want to be here. Moreover, he didn't want Mia to be here. His wife—his *wayward* wife.

A frown settled between Santos's dark brows as his gaze continued to move over the young, enthusiastic crowd partying it up—a tiresome and expected mix of trust-fund babies and inebriated gap-year students, along with the odd socialite who had decided to slum it at this rooftop bar in Ibiza Town. He had it on good authority—that of the world-class private detective he'd hired ten days ago—that Mia would be here tonight.

Raucous music continued to blare from the speakers, mixing with the shrill shrieks of feminine laughter, as well as the clink and clatter of glasses and trays. Tension banded Santos's temples as he felt the unfortunate start of a migraine that he did his best to stave off. He needed to find Mia before he succumbed to any such infirmity. He needed to find her—and bring her home, for good. *Why* he needed to do this, considering she'd left him without so much as a word, was a question Santos chose not to examine too closely. She was his wife, she belonged with him… and that was all that mattered.

They had first met at a bar much like this one—full of the young, hip and trendy, with eye-wateringly expensive cocktails—in Portugal's Algarve just seven short months ago. She'd been behind the bar, her auburn hair messily piled on top of her head, her blue-green eyes alight with humour and mischief as she'd shaken cocktails with sinuous, elegant ease. Just as with this bar tonight, Santos hadn't wanted to be there. His oldest friend Emiliano had insisted on a wild stag night, even though Santos didn't *do* wild, or even parties; but, when his gaze had snagged on Mia, he'd found himself caught, transfixed.

There had been something about the way she'd moved with such easy, lithe grace, and he'd become mesmerised by every flip of her wrist and the way she tilted her head back when she laughed, a generous, open sound that had floated through him like a warm breeze. She had a small space between her front teeth that somehow just added to her enchantment. She wasn't classically beautiful, certainly not in the way of the women he'd usually had on his arm—elegant, entitled women suitable for a man of his standing—like his almost-fiancée, Isabella. Mia had been something more, something real and warm…or so he'd believed at the time.

Her gaze had skimmed over him, resting on his form for barely a millisecond before moving on, and it had somehow felt like both a challenge and an invitation. He'd decided he simply had to say hello to her—a compulsion that, a bit uneasily, he had acknowledged was very unlike him—and they'd ended up talking until the bar had closed at three a.m. And then afterwards as well… Oh, he certainly remembered the *afterwards*.

With effort, Santos pushed such thoughts and the ensuing recriminations out of his mind. No point dwelling on the past and how it had all gone so very wrong. Right now, he just wanted to find Mia…and bring her home.

He shouldered his way through the crowd, continuing to scan the faces that were starting to blur a little as pain tightened on his temples. He hadn't had a migraine in over a year, he thought in irritation. Why now? And where was Mia?

A sweaty, red-faced twenty-something guy holding two cocktails aloft knocked into his shoulder, sloshing the lurid red liquid over the rim of the glasses and almost onto Santos's expensively tailored jacket. Santos stepped quickly out of the way, causing a blaze of pain through his head as the guy slurred his apologies and moved on. What on earth was Mia doing in a place like this? It was a question Santos didn't want to think about too closely because, the more he considered it, the more he feared he'd never known his wife at all.

And yet they were married, and would stay married, because an Aguila kept his vows. Even here, amidst the pounding music of the bar, Santos could recall his father's voice, deep and certain, telling him again and again what it meant to be an Aguila. He could see his aristocratic face crumpled in pain…

But he couldn't think about that now. That memory was buried far too deeply. What he knew, what he was absolutely certain of, was that as an Aguila he would keep his word. He would keep his *vow*…no matter what happened.

Santos stepped out of the crowded indoor space onto the rooftop terrace. The air was soft, the harbour glinting under the moonlight dotted with fishing boats and private yachts. It was quieter out here, at least, and he felt he could breathe. The pain in his head eased a little…and then he saw her.

The pain flashed again like a blaze of lightning, and he had to put one hand on the doorframe to steady himself. He blinked to clear his blurred vision and there she was: leaning against the low wall that surrounded the terrace, the silver-limned harbour the perfect backdrop for her long, lithe figure. Her auburn hair blew in tangled waves in the sea breeze, and she pushed it back with both hands as she laughed at the man standing next to her. A man, Santos noted grimly, who was looking at her in frank and unabashed admiration.

She was wearing a dress—and, oh, what a dress. It was made of a shimmery emerald satin with a halter top, and it covered her from collar bone to ankle, yet clung to every curve and dip of her figure so lovingly that Santos thought she might as well be naked.

His head continued to pulse with pain. What the hell was his wife doing in a place like this, wearing a dress like that, and with a man next to her, ogling her all the way? None of it boded well. All of it made him coldly furious. Slowly, each move lethal, he stalked towards his wife.

She was so busy talking to the Lothario in tight leather jeans, with his shirt unbuttoned nearly to his navel, that she didn't notice her husband standing a few feet away—not until her companion threw Santos a startled glance.

'Umm…do you need something?' he asked in heavily accented English.

'Si,' Santos replied curtly. 'Mi esposa.' My wife.

He looked pointedly at Mia, while the man's jaw dropped, and then Mia finally looked at him. Her face drained of colour so the freckles on her nose stood out in bold relief, her eyes widening to aquamarine pools and her lips—those lush lips he'd kissed and tasted—parting slightly.

'Santos…' His name was no more than a breath.

'Mia.' His voice was flat and hard. They stared at each other for what could only have been a second but felt endless. In that brief flicker of time, Santos felt as if he could recall every moment of their marriage: the early rapture; the ensuing cold silences; a chasm neither of them had been able to cross; the deep, deep disappointment and the lancing pain. And now this.

'I think I'll leave you two alone,' the man murmured, slipping away while Mia simply stared at Santos, her face still deathly pale.

He folded his arms across his chest and waited for her to speak. Surely, she would say *something*—apologise, explain? Stammer something, at least, even if he already knew nothing she could say would make much of a difference. She'd left him without a single word six weeks ago, slipping away in the night like a thief. She'd never let him know where or how she was or if she was even alive. She had a *lot* of explaining to do, Santos thought with a cold fury that he feared masked a far worse hurt.

And yet she didn't say a word. After a second, her gaze flicked away from him, almost as if he'd been dismissed. The fury he'd been keeping on a tight rein burst into flame and made the pain in his head a thousand times worse. After six weeks of silence, this was what he got—absolutely nothing? He reached for her arm, her skin soft and cool beneath his touch.

Mia tensed as his fingers curled around her wrist. 'Let go of me, Santos,' she said in a low voice that trembled. She wasn't looking at him.

'Let's get out of here,' he replied grimly, and she jerked her arm away from him.

'I'm not going anywhere with you.'

She cradled her arm to her chest as if he'd hurt her, but Santos knew he hadn't. He'd barely touched her, and yet she was acting as though he was a bully, a threat, a danger. How had *that* happened? She was the one at fault in this scenario. She was the one who had run away without a word…and he wanted to know why.

'Mia, you're my wife,' he told her. 'You're coming with me.'

'We might be married, but you don't own me,' she fired back, and he took a slow, steadying breath. Responding in anger—as much as he was tempted to—wasn't going to help things, and it would make his head blaze all the more.

'We need to talk at least,' he stated. 'In private. Surely you owe me that much?'

She hesitated, and he saw the shadow of something in her eyes—something like regret, or maybe just guilt. 'Please,' he said quietly, and, with a slump of her slender shoulders she finally relented.

'All right,' she said, her tone both wary and defeated, and then she glanced around in furtive apprehension. Who was she looking for—the man she'd been talking to? Jealousy wasn't an emotion Santos was used to feeling. He certainly didn't like it, but damn it, they were *married*. Hadn't their vows meant anything to her?

'Where should we go?' she asked and once again he swallowed down the anger and the hurt.

'My yacht is moored in the harbour.'

Her eyes widened and she hesitated, clearly not liking the idea of going there with him. Why not? Was she actually afraid of him? He'd never, ever given her reason to be.

'I'm not going to kidnap you, Mia, if that's what kind of nonsense you're thinking,' he told her tersely. 'But my yacht is private and comfortable and not too far away.'

And he needed the quiet as much as the privacy to keep the pain in his head at bay.

She bit her lip and then nodded. 'All right,' she said for a second time, a concession, and she reached down to grab a bag which she slung over one shoulder. Santos realised it was the same beat-up backpack she'd had back when they'd first met. It looked incongruous against her emerald satin dress. She hesitated and then she glanced around again.

'Who are you looking for?' Santos demanded. 'That chancer who was chatting you up?'

'What? No.' She shook her head, tumbled waves flying. 'No, the owner of the bar. I was here for a job.'

A *job*? He could buy this whole bar with his pocket change. Why on earth would she be looking for a job here? He decided they could talk about that later. There were more pressing matters to deal with first.

'You can send him your apologies,' he told her, and put his hand on the small of her back, guiding her forward with firm decision. 'Now, let's go.'

Mia's mind was reeling, the space on the small of her back where Santos had pressed his palm burning as if she'd been singed. He'd always had that effect on her, right from the first night they'd met, when she'd handed him his whiskey sour and her fingers had brushed his, sending an electric current all the way up her arm and straight to her heart.

If you're going to play with fire...prepare to get burned.

A shudder went through her that she tried to suppress, not wanting Santos to see how his presence *still* affected her. She'd never expected to see him again. She'd thought him too proud a man to go chasing after her and, in any case, he'd been *tired* of her, hadn't he? Exhausted and utterly fed up—at least, he'd certainly acted as if he had

been. The last six weeks of their marriage had been interminable, unbearable, each day more difficult than the one
before, until she'd felt she couldn't stand another moment,
not without losing some essential part of herself. Running
away had felt like the only option.

And it's what you've always done before.

They made their way through the crowded bar, Santos's
hand on her back the whole time, guiding her forward. Mia
wasn't actually being frog-marched, but she felt as if she
was. The pressure of his hand was firm, insistent, and she
could feel each individual long and lean finger against her
spine like a brand. What did he actually *want* with her?
She'd genuinely believed he would be relieved to see the
back of her. He'd surely regretted their brief whirlwind of
a marriage; he'd certainly acted as if he had.

So why was he here? Mia supposed she'd find out soon
enough.

They made it through the bar and down the stairs, out
into the street facing the promenade. A balmy, brine-tinged
breeze blew over them, cooling Mia's heated cheeks as she
gazed out at the port with its flotilla of super-yachts. She'd
never actually been on Santos's yacht. She'd never even
known he had one, although she supposed she shouldn't be
surprised that he did. He was a man who had just about everything. Except the one thing he'd really wanted: a *child*.
A child of their own…and she hadn't given it to him.

Guilt, regret and grief burned like acid in her throat,
forming a lump that made it hard to swallow. *Forget about
that*, she told herself. They weren't going to talk about it.
They certainly never had before.

'So, where is this yacht of yours?' she asked, and he
nodded towards one of the more streamlined of them, two
stripes of grey and gold on its hull—the Aguila colours,

after their eagle crest. Mia squared her shoulders, trying to suppress the fizz of nerves in her stomach. She had no real reason to think Santos would kidnap her; he'd said he wouldn't. In fact, she thought quite the opposite—he'd be more likely to heave her overboard than kidnap her, although she didn't really think he'd do that either. So, what exactly was she afraid of?

The answer came immediately: *him*. She was afraid of the man himself: of his powerful charisma; of the way he just had to look at her to make her feel all mixed up inside, a tangle of fear and yearning, hope and aching disappointment.

His hand was still on the small of her back, and it still burned. Her whole body did.

Feeling as if she were facing her doom, even as she told herself not to be so melodramatic, Mia slowly started to walk towards the yacht. Santos matched her steps, stride for measured stride. A security guard stood at the gangway—Ronaldo, Mia recalled. He'd been kind to her, but the look he gave her now was like granite.

Did everyone hate her now? And yet, why shouldn't they? She'd been the worst wife ever, running away the way she had. And, even before that, she had not performed as the Aguila heiress and future matriarch should. Not at *all*…but, really, was that a surprise? She was the illegitimate daughter of a single mother who had never stayed in one place for long. She hadn't gone to college, had barely completed school and had never held down a job for more than a few months at a time; she'd skipped from place to place, because not planting roots was what she knew, how she'd always lived. None of it had been befitting of an *Aguila*.

She swallowed the smile she'd been about to give Ronaldo and started up the gangway. Santos guided her towards a lounge with leather sofas and glass coffee-tables, everything the epitome of luxury. With a firm click, he closed the double wood-panelled doors, enclosing them in total privacy. It felt a little bit like a tomb.

Mia swallowed hard. She wasn't ready for this. She wasn't ready to face the man she'd married, the man she'd fallen in love with—or at least had started to; in the six weeks since she'd left him, she'd wondered if any of it had been real. Could she really fall in love with someone that fast, that hard? Had Santos loved her, or had he just been caught up in it all? Mia had never been able to answer that question. The longer she'd lived with Santos, the unhappier they'd both become; she'd decided it couldn't have been love, no matter how much they might have convinced themselves. They could call it infatuation—obsession, even—but it hadn't been *real*… It certainly hadn't lasted.

And yet, now he was here.

'Drink?' he asked tersely and headed over to a well-stocked mahogany bar. Mia watched with more than a little trepidation as her husband poured himself a double whisky. He took a packet of pills out of his jacket pocket and broke the foil on three, tossing them back with a gulp of the amber liquid, before he returned the empty glass to the bar.

'What are those for?' she asked, and he turned around, leaning against the bar, his arms folded across his chest.

'Headache.'

For a second, Mia wondered if he was being sarcastic, implying that *she* was the headache. It must have taken some doing to find her, she supposed. She'd made sure only to use cash as she'd made her way across Spain so she couldn't be traced. Then she saw him flinch, and re-alised he really did have a headache.

She gazed at him uneasily as he stared her down, seem-ingly willing to let the silence spin out. His darkly hand-some looks still made her stomach contract with both longing and memory: the ebony hair and those golden-brown eyes the colour of the whisky he'd just tossed back; the trimmed beard on his lean cheeks and sculpted jaw glinting in the dim lighting of the room; the broad shoul-ders and powerful chest; the same well-muscled body en-cased in hand-tailored linen. In the six weeks since she'd last seen him, nothing about him had changed at all, except he looked wearier, maybe a bit more cynical. That had to be because of her.

Mia swallowed again and made herself lift her chin and look him right in his golden-brown eyes. 'So,' she asked with a poor attempt at insouciance, 'What do you want to talk about?'

He let out a huff of hard laughter. 'You haven't changed, I see.'

Actually, she thought, unable to keep a corrosive edge of bitterness from sharpening her insides, *I've changed a lot. And not for the better.*

'Neither have you,' she replied, tilting her chin up just that little bit higher. He was as coldly arrogant and assured as ever. 'Why did you find me, Santos?'

'Because you're my wife.'

'I'm not a possession,' she reminded him although, to be fair, he'd never truly treated her like one. *That* hadn't been their problem, at least.

'I didn't say you were,' he returned evenly, *so* evenly... The man never raised his voice, never got angry, a fact which had come to infuriate Mia. She'd wanted a *fight*, had wanted to get all the ugly emotions out, and he'd refused to give her one. He'd always spoken with that even, measured voice, revealing nothing, feeling nothing except judgment…so much judgment. She saw it in his eyes now, in the way his lips tightened, and she remembered all over again why she'd had to leave.

'Well,' she asked, unable to keep from sounding sarcastic, 'Is there another reason, then, why you came looking for me besides the fact that we made a very silly mistake in marrying each other?'

'*Don't* say that,' he ordered with quiet lethality, enough to make Mia blink.

'Say what?'

'That our marriage was a mistake.' His golden-brown eyes gleamed into hers. 'We made vows, Mia. As an Aguila, I take those seriously.'

'As an Aguila,' she repeated. She'd known that Santos had a thing about being the patriarch of one of Spain's oldest aristocratic families. Their titles had been lost a long time ago, but the pedigree remained. Aguilas were men of their word, who took their vows seriously—of course they were.

'As a man,' he qualified, and Mia wondered if that meant anything different. She knew what it *didn't* mean, anyway—he didn't love her, didn't respect her. He *couldn't*, she'd decided, when he'd treated her the way he had—with glowering looks and simmering, accusatory silences. If he'd decided he wanted to stay married to her now just to be a man of his word, well, it would end up being hell for them both…just as it had been before.

So, if Santos had found her simply to bring her back to Seville so that he could remain a person of integrity or some such, well, Mia would simply have to convince him that that was not a good idea for either of them.

Because Santos Aguila might be a man of his word, but Mia was a woman of hers. And she'd made a promise too—a promise to herself—never again to let Santos make her feel the way he had before.

CHAPTER TWO

SANTOS STARED AT MIA, his jaw clenched, his head pounding. He really needed those pills to kick in, if just to take the edge off, but so far his head just felt worse. He hadn't had a migraine this severe in years; he'd learned to deal with them when he felt the first symptoms—the pain, the blurred sight and the dark spots dancing in his vision. But he could hardly take a breather and go and lie down in a dark room with Mia here. And he needed answers, even if, with the way she was coolly gazing at him, it didn't seem likely she'd give them.

'Why were you in Ibiza?' he asked abruptly.

He wasn't in the right frame of mind, physically or emotionally, to ask the big questions.

Why did you leave me?

Why did you cut me off so completely?

Why did you not want our baby?

No, he definitely wouldn't ask any of those. Not yet, and maybe not ever.

Mia shrugged one bare shoulder, the slippery satin of her dress tightening over her breasts as she moved, drawing his attention to the curves he knew so well, had *loved* so well. 'Why not?' she asked, her tone almost flippant.

It was no answer at all, of course, and he shouldn't be surprised. She'd always been good at deflecting. At the start, he had found it charmingly insouciant; with something that actually mattered, much less so.

'I'm serious, Mia.' He closed his eyes briefly, willing back the pain throbbing in his temples.

'So am I,' she returned, and now she sounded cool. 'It seemed as good a place as any. I'm a cocktail waitress, Santos, so I went where people drink cocktails.' She paused and then added indifferently, 'And it's crowded and easy to lose yourself. I didn't think you'd be able to find me there.'

He gritted his teeth so hard his jaw ached. 'And you didn't want me to find you.'

'Obviously.' She smiled wryly then, her eyes lightening to the blue-green of sea foam, reminding him how he'd once felt…as if he could drown in them. When he'd first met her, she'd seemed like such an enigma, and yet at the same time so warm, open and uncomplicated, so different from him, which had been enchanting. He hadn't expected not just to be charmed by her, but fascinated. When she'd laughed, he'd felt something lighten in him that he hadn't realised was so heavy. All the responsibilities that had weighed him down, the memories that had been even worse, had fallen away when he'd been with Mia.

How that had changed once they'd made painful memories of their own.

'And the dress?' he asked, nodding towards what could only be considered a sexy evening gown. She looked amazing in it, and perversely that made his blood boil. Why was she wearing it? Obviously, it wasn't for him. 'Is that part of your *job*?'

The wry smile that had lightened her features flickered and died. She crossed her arms across her body. 'What are you implying, Santos?'

'I'm just asking,' he returned evenly. 'You don't normally need to wear an evening gown to mix cocktails.'

She sighed, a gust of breath escaping her as her shoulders slumped and she looked down at the floor. 'Yeah, well, that might have been a mistake,' she admitted in a low voice. 'I applied to be a bartender but Ernesto—the guy who runs the place—asked me to try being a hostess and gave me this dress to wear. I'll need to give it back to him at some point.'

'A hostess,' Santos repeated evenly. One step up from a paid escort...and maybe not even that. 'Seriously, Mia?'

'I didn't realise.' She glanced up, her eyes sparkling with anger or tears; he couldn't tell. 'He gave me the dress when I arrived tonight and I thought... Well, I don't know what I thought. I was running out of money, and I really wanted a job. But of course, I wasn't going to do something like you're obviously thinking.'

Why would she be running out of money, he thought, when she had access to his? He'd given her a bank card, credit cards, plenty of cash. They hadn't even signed a pre-nuptial agreement, much to the dismay of his lawyer, but most of the Aguila fortune was tied up in the estate and investments, anyway, and was out of reach. At that point, he'd felt so recklessly heady with what he'd felt with Mia, so certain that being with her was right, that he hadn't given himself time to think, to be sensible, to be *himself*. That was the last thing he'd wanted to be. He'd been himself, dutiful and dour, for his entire life. With Mia, he'd been able to be—to feel—different, and it had felt thrilling.

But Mia should not have had to take sketchy bar jobs for a few euros. He took a step towards her, even though it made the room tilt as his head blazed. 'And what,' he asked, 'Do you think am I thinking?'

'I don't even know,' she cried, flinging her slender arms out wide. 'I never know what you're thinking because you never tell me. You just *look* at me like—like your dog just died or something.' The words hovered in the air for a sizzling moment and then fell to the ground like ash.

'Not my dog,' Santos said quietly, and Mia's face crumpled.

'Don't, Santos,' she whispered. *'Don't.'*

Was there any point to this discussion? Santos wondered wearily. He was a reasonable man; he prided himself on it. But he did not know how to reason with Mia. Not when there were so many unsaid things between them, things neither of them could bear to talk about, because he didn't think either of them could handle the answers.

And yet…she was *wife*. He'd meant what he'd said about taking his vows seriously. He wasn't going to walk away from their marriage, and he wasn't going to let her walk away either. Yet what did that mean for their future? How could they possibly work this out when he couldn't trust her and obviously, for whatever reason, she didn't trust him?

Everything felt impossible. Part of him wanted to go back to that moment in the bar when he'd met her and re-live that enchantment, the way she'd wound around his soul. Another part of him wanted to go back to that moment and walk away—turn in the other direction and never slide onto that bar stool, never ask her what she'd recommend he drink. Never watch the way her hair flew about her face, the way her freckles seemed to dance across her nose when she laughed.

A whole lot of nevers, and it was all too late now. They were married. They'd married on a beach in Lagos Old Town, the waves glinting behind them as they'd held hands and said their vows. They'd known each other for a little less than two weeks.

In hindsight, it had been utter insanity. It was the kind of thing he'd never, ever done, which was why he'd done it. All he could remember now was always wanting to feel the way Mia had made him feel—happy and light, as if anything was possible, as if freedom and joy were the very air he breathed. For a little while, a very little while, he had felt like that and it had been wonderful.

That felt like a long time ago now, and he didn't know if he would ever get it back—if *they* would—but they certainly wouldn't if he Mia didn't come back with him. They wouldn't even have a chance.

'Fine,' he told her. 'I won't talk about all that. But you're coming back with me to Seville, Mia.' That much was non-negotiable. He was not going to have his wife running around Europe, bar-tending in dives.

Her mouth twisted into something like a smile. 'I thought you said you weren't going to kidnap me.'

'I'm not.' Even though part of him was actually tempted. He could give the order to sail right now, and there'd be nothing she could do about it, but that was not the way he operated. 'You'll come willingly, I hope, for the sake of our marriage.'

Slowly, despairingly, she shook her head. 'Why, Santos? You know we weren't happy together. We made each other miserable—'

'Don't.' Now he was the one begging her to stop the reminders, because they *hurt*. Yes, they'd been miserable—neither of them could deny it—but they *had* been happy once. Maybe they couldn't be again—heaven knew there was a lot of surging, muddy water beneath that particular bridge—but they still belonged together. At least, they could. It wasn't just about being a man of his word, he realised. He and Mia had shared something special and important. He didn't want to walk away from their marriage…even if Mia had already tried.

But what if it's the smartest, safest, most sensible option?

The possibility felt like a betrayal—and not just of his vows, but of himself. He was an Aguila: he was a man of his word. It had been instilled and drilled into him since he'd been a small boy, looking up adoringly at his father, a man who had spoken with such grave intent.

Never forgot you're an Aguila. Never forget what it means.

The Aguila family had always been known for its loyalty and integrity. They'd never broken their word, never been questionable in business. All through Spain, the name Aguila *meant* something, his father had reminded him again and again—something both powerful and good. And, now that he was the only male left, the weight of that responsibility was all the heavier and more important.

'Mia…' he began, and then had to stop, because as he moved the pain in his head suddenly reached a shrieking crescendo. He blinked as the room swayed and blurred. With a hazy sensation of unreality, Santos realised he was about to pass out.

'Santos?'

Mia stared at her husband in concern as his face leached of colour and he swayed where he stood. He blinked several times, but his gaze was unseeing, vacant. His jaw slackened and then, with obvious effort, tightened again.

'I…' he began, only to start slumping forward, one hand flung out to steady himself on the bar.

Mia rushed forward to try to catch him in her arms. She

wrapped them around him, breathing in the familiar, pine scent of his cologne and feeling the warmth of his body that still managed to cause a treacherous tendril of desire to wind right through her, even though he was practically unconscious. What on earth was happening? She'd never seen him like this.

'Ronaldo!' she called, her voice hoarse and panicked as she attempted to keep him upright, his powerfully muscled chest pressed against her, his head lolling downward. *'Ronaldo!'*

Santos had passed out now, his body a dead weight on hers as she staggered back. He wasn't overly tall, just a hair's breadth over six feet, but he was powerfully built, and he was heavy.

'Ronaldo!'

The security guard burst into the room, flinging the doors back so hard, they hit the wall with a bang. Santos let out a groan.

'Madre mia!' Ronaldo exclaimed as he rushed towards her. 'What has happened to the *señor*?'

'I… I don't know.' Mia's arms ached with the effort of holding Santos up, and her knees trembled with fear. Was he deathly ill? Was *that* why he'd come and found her? 'He just…collapsed.'

'Ronaldo,' Santos mumbled, his voice slurred, as if he'd been drinking. *'Migrena.'*

Ronaldo nodded and heaved Santos up with one powerful arm underneath his shoulders. 'I'll take him to his room,' he told Mia, and it sounded cutting, like a dismissal.

'I'll come with you,' Mia said.

Ronaldo frowned. 'It is not—'

'I'm his *wife*,' she reminded him. Even if she'd been trying to forget that fact for the last six weeks. 'I'm coming.'

Mia wasn't even sure why she insisted. Surely this was the perfect opportunity to leave the yacht and hightail it out of Ibiza so Santos couldn't find her again? Except he would, because he'd found her once already; she had absolutely zero doubt that he would do it again. That didn't mean she had to follow him into his cabin and act as his nurse maid, yet that was exactly what she was doing.

Ronaldo deposited Santos on the wide double bed and Mia found herself taking over.

'He has a migraine,' she surmised, from what Santos had said. Even she, with her very limited Spanish, had been able to understand that much.

Ronaldo nodded. 'He gets them sometimes. Not usually this bad.'

Something she hadn't known about him. Mia supposed there were a lot of things she didn't know about her husband, considering how they'd only met seven months ago. 'I can manage from here,' she told Ronaldo. 'I'll take care of him.'

The security guard frowned. 'I don't…'

'I'm his wife,' she reminded him—or maybe herself. 'I'll take care of him.'

'*Señor* does not like people to see him like this,' Ronaldo protested quietly, just as Santos let out a groan. He flung out one hand.

'Mia…'

The sound of her name on his lips, like an entreaty, made something in her both soften and ache.

'See?' she remarked to Ronaldo. 'He wants me here.' She wasn't sure about that, but she decided to go with it.

Slowly, reluctantly, the security guard nodded his assent. 'All right. But you must come for me if he needs anything more. If he gets worse.'

'I will,' Mia promised. Ronaldo nodded once and then left, closing the door behind him.

Mia let out a long, low breath as she wondered what on earth she'd done—and why. She wasn't very good with sickness. Her mother hadn't been either, which was probably why Mia struggled.

"Pull yourself together, because I can't handle any inconvenience." That had more or less been her mother's motto, said in a briskly practical way.

More than once—*when* Mia had gone to school—she'd gone with a high fever or a stomach bug. More than once the school receptionist had phoned her mother to come and get her because she'd been too ill to manage her classes, and her mother had come, annoyed that Mia had made a fuss, as if getting sick had been her fault.

She'd learned to act being well even when she wasn't, to hide anything that could be seen as weakness. It was a lesson that, for better or worse, had become deeply embedded in her psyche, thanks to a mother who resented her very presence. There had never been anyone else to depend on—no father, no friends, no kindly neighbours. It had been a lonely existence, but it had made Mia independent and strong—she hoped.

Now Mia turned to gaze at Santos, stretched out on the bed. His midnight-dark hair was rumpled, his breathing coming in ragged gasps, his eyes fluttering open and closed. Even in pain and sickness he looked eminently handsome, desirable. She remembered how his eyes had gleamed gold when he'd looked at her, before they'd darkened to bronze as he'd bent his head to kiss her. She remembered how his lips had felt on hers, soft yet firm, moving over her mouth with such tender intention, making both heat and hope flare deep inside her—hope that she'd finally found someone who saw and understood her, who loved her for who she was, because no one ever had before.

A shudder rippled through her and Mia shook herself, doing her best to banish the tempting, taunting memories. Why on earth was she thinking about all that now? Santos hadn't touched her for weeks before she'd left. But then, she hadn't touched him either. She hadn't dared.

Gingerly she perched on the edge of Santos's bed. He groaned and flung out one hand, and she gently caught it with her own, drawing it back to his side. His fingers clenched on hers, trapping her hand, and she let him hold it. She remembered how much she'd once loved him holding her hand, and how loved she'd felt when he had, his strong fingers twining with hers.

Loved. She hadn't had a lot of love in her life; she had learned to make do without it, in as briskly practical way as her mother had. Why crave something she could never have? Learning to do without it had been a much better way to live her life.

Except, it didn't actually stop the craving, Mia reflected. She hadn't realised that until she'd met Santos and his attention—what she'd believed had been his love—had revealed the big, gaping emptiness inside her and filled it…for a time. Only for a time, until she'd wrecked it all and his blame had made her feel even worse than if she'd never known his attention and kindness at all. Whoever thought it was better to have loved and lost than never to have loved at all had no idea what they were talking about, Mia thought grimly.

A sigh escaped her as Santos moaned again, his eyelids flickering once more. 'Mia…'

'I'm here,' she said softly, as those yearnings she was desperate to push away came rushing back. He might have treated her terribly for a time, but he was a kind man at heart. She'd always known that, which had made his anger and blame so much harder to bear. 'Rest, Santos. You have a migraine. You need sleep.'

'Hurts…' he mumbled, his eyes closing once more.

Her heart ached in a way that surprised her. How had she not known this about her husband? He'd always appeared so strong and invincible, as immovable as a mountain. It had been both incredibly reassuring and, especially towards the end, impossibly frustrating. How could she love a mountain? How could a mountain love *her*?

'Let me get you a cold cloth for your head,' she said, and she extricated her hand from his as she went to the sumptuous *en suite* bathroom to wet a facecloth and wring it out. Back at the bed, she gently laid it on his forehead as a groan of something like satisfaction escaped him.

'Thanks…' he mumbled.

She smiled—ever the gentleman. He'd been so kind to her at the start. No one had ever treated her with such sensitivity, such gentleness. It hadn't just been the basic chivalry of opening doors, pulling out chairs or standing when she came into a room, although all that *had* made her feel like a cherished princess. It was the way he'd listened when she'd spoken, the way he'd always enquired after her comfort and her happiness. It was the look of wonder on his face when, just two weeks after they'd married, she'd told him she was pregnant…

No. She wasn't going to go there. It hurt far, far too much.

Carefully, Mia rose from the bed. She needed just a little distance from this man who made her feel so much, even if it was just from the other side of the room. But, before she could move, Santos's arm shot out and his fingers circled her wrist, just as they had back at the bar. It hadn't hurt then, and it didn't now. It felt like temptation, causing a sweet ache of longing to reverberate through her as she remembered just how his skin felt on hers, his body felt on hers…

'Don't go,' he said, his eyes still closed, his voice a slurred whisper. 'Mia…please don't go.'

Her heart ached at the pleading note in his voice, and yet she couldn't help but wonder if Santos would have made such a request if he'd been in his right mind. He might say he wanted her back, but she didn't believe he did. Or at least, she didn't believe he wanted her back for the right reasons. Pride, reputation or integrity might all have something to do with his insistence that she return to Seville with him as his wife, but love? As much as she'd wanted to believe he loved her when they'd first married, she'd come to realise he couldn't have. Love took time to grow and strengthen. Whatever they'd felt had been no more than facsimile of it.

And yet, with his fingers still circling her wrist, that jagged plea still reverberating through her, she found herself sinking back onto the bed against her instincts. He drew her closer to him, and she came, at first cautiously, but somehow she ended up lying nestled next to him, her head on his shoulder, her legs curled into his. She breathed in the scent of him and remembered the nights she'd lain just like this, feeling ridiculously, incredulously happy. Now she only felt sad.

Santos's breathing evened out and his fingers relaxed on her wrist, his hand falling limply to his side. Mia could have got up then and crept away, let him sleep. It would have been the smart, sensible thing to do, but somehow she couldn't make herself do it.

She told herself it was because she didn't want to risk disturbing him, but she knew that was a lie. The truth was, it simply felt too good to lie there, her head on his shoulder, the steady and reassuring thud of his heart under her cheek and the solid warmth of him making her feel safe, protected. His breathing deepened and his body relaxed but still Mia stayed.

Santos might not be aware she was there, but *she* certainly was. And it offered her battered, wounded heart a comfort she knew she needed…more than Santos would ever know or believe.

CHAPTER THREE

SANTOS BLINKED IN the bright morning light as he looked around his cabin in sleep-fuddled surprise. *What on earth....?* What had happened?

Fragmented memories came back to him in jagged pieces: Mia at the bar; that evening gown, that stupid guy; the haughty way she'd looked him... And then, back at the yacht, the sadness he'd seen her in face; the things they hadn't said; the crushing sense of impossibility...and then the blazing pain.

How had he got to his cabin? He couldn't remember. What he did know was he was nearly naked, wearing only boxers, and the yacht was creaking and swaying beneath him. They weren't moored in Puerto de Ibiza any more. Why not? How long had he been asleep?

Groaning a little, Santos eased himself up. His head still hurt, but it was an echo of the blinding pain from... when?...last night? Surely no longer? His mouth was dry and his tongue felt thick. He glanced at the table by the bed and saw a jug of water, with a glass already poured, and next to it a sticky note with Mia's familiar, loopy scrawl.

Drink some water! You are probably dehydrated.

He smiled at that, and then felt the ensuing flash of loss. At the start of their brief marriage, she used to leave sticky notes for him everywhere. Nothing too mushy or saccharine; often they'd been practical reminders such as this one, to drink some water. But they'd made him feel loved, and he'd enjoyed the sight of her rounded letters; even her handwriting had seemed carefree and insouciant, just like her. She'd stopped leaving those notes weeks before she'd left. Right after…

But, no; they hadn't talked about that last night. They'd never talked about it because, Santos suspected, it was simply too painful; there were too many things they didn't want to voice out loud. And yet it had been at the root of all their problems…hadn't it?

Or was it really simpler than that— were they just incompatible? Mia wasn't the woman he'd thought she was, back at that bar. Or maybe he wasn't who she'd thought he was. Either way, they'd run into trouble pretty soon after they'd said the vows. But they'd said them, and he'd meant them: to have and to hold, for better or worse… He couldn't go back even if he wanted to, and he wasn't sure that he did. But what did Mia want?

Santos's head was starting to ache again. He didn't want to stir all those memories up like slimy, dead leaves at the bottom of a pond swirling up into an unpleasant, opaque muck, muddying every truth he'd known. He didn't want to…but maybe he had to. The only way he and Mia could possibly have a future was if they faced the past—as difficult a prospect as that was.

The door creaked open and Santos looked up to see the blue-green of Mia's eyes gleaming through the crack.

'Hello,' he said, his voice coming out in a rusty croak.

'Hey.' She opened the door wider and slipped through, then closed it behind her and leaned against it. Her hair was in a loose French plait, a few curly wisps framing her heart-shaped face, and she wore a well-worn T-shirt with some faded logo on it and a pair of cut-off jean shorts. She looked just like she had when he'd first met her: young and free. It made him realise how she hadn't looked like that for most of their marriage. For most of their marriage, she'd looked pale, tired and worn down. The realisation was an uncomfortable one.

'How are you feeling?' she asked, and he gave a small, rueful smile.

'Better than before, at any rate. I'm sorry to have subjected you to such a sight.' He didn't want to think about last night and how he must have collapsed, or as good as, in her presence. He despised such shows of weakness and had hid his incapacitating migraines as much as he could. It was definitely not the way he'd wanted to begin their reconciliation…if such a thing was even possible.

Mia came to perch on the edge of the bed. Her legs in the cut-off shorts were long and golden, lightly freckled, and the end of her plait hung over one slender shoulder. She rested one hand on the bedspread, her fingers spread out. She was still wearing her wedding ring, Santos saw with a pang—a simple platinum band. He was glad.

'I didn't know you got migraine headaches,' she said quietly.

Santos managed a wry grimace. 'It's not something I spread about,' he admitted. 'And I don't get them very frequently—maybe once a year, if that. I hadn't had one for quite a while.'

'Still.' She fell silent, gazing down at the bedspread, at her outspread hand…at her wedding ring? He wondered what she was thinking or feeling. Then he registered the purring movement of the yacht beneath them once more.

'Why have we put out to sea?'

She glanced up at him, her blue-green eyes wide and

clear. He could count every freckle on her nose. 'You'd only reserved the mooring in Ibiza for twenty-four hours.'

'Surely it hasn't been more than twenty-four hours?' he protested in surprised alarm. 'I arrived last night.'

Mia shook her head, the end of her plait swinging. 'No, Santos. You've been asleep for almost thirty-six hours.'

'What?' He tried to sit upright, but it caused his head to hurt again, and he was forced to sink back against the pillows as he stared at her in shock. 'How can that even be possible?'

'You were out for the count.' She smiled. 'I don't even think a tropical storm would have woken you.'

The painkillers he had taken had been strong, Santos allowed, and had been mixed with alcohol. Plus, he'd already been exhausted from looking for, and worrying about, Mia. Still, *thirty-six hours*—a whole day and a night—and he couldn't remember any of it. What had Mia done for all that time?

'I can't believe it,' he murmured, and then he glanced at Mia, registering what her presence meant. 'You're here,' he said, stating the obvious. She smiled wryly in acknowledgement. 'I mean…you could have gone, left.'

'I know.' The wry smile flickered at its edges, but she kept his gaze.

'Why?' Santos asked baldly. 'Why didn't you go?'

'Well, I have to say it's pretty cushy here, and I've never been on a yacht before. You know how I'm always up for new experiences.' She tilted the smile up again at its corners, but there was something shadowed and sad about her face, and in her eyes, and it tugged at him.

'I'm serious, Mia.'

She paused, glancing down again, and then admitted,

'I don't know why, Santos. I suppose because it felt wrong to leave you when you were sleeping.'

'You left when I was sleeping last time,' he reminded her, unable to keep from saying it, and hearing the bitterness in his voice. He'd woken up and felt the emptiness of their bedroom, the whole house, like a wind blowing through him.

'Maybe,' she stated quietly, 'I didn't want to do that a second time.'

He sifted through that statement, looking for truth, unsure if he could find it. 'What about your things back in Ibiza?' he asked, deciding to focus on practicalities. 'Do we need to go back and get them?'

The smile she gave him was genuine, then full of rueful amusement. 'We're about twelve hours out from Ibiza, so I'm not sure that's practical. But, in any case, I had everything with me.'

'Just that one back pack?' he asked in surprise, although really, why should he be shocked? He'd seen the wardrobe full of designer clothes she'd left back in Seville, the velvet cases of diamonds, sapphires and emeralds that she hadn't taken.

She shrugged, her T-shirt sliding off her golden shoulder. 'You know I always travel light. I'll need to give back the dress at some point, but I don't suppose it's a matter of urgency.'

Santos stared at her, trying to make sense of what she'd said and what he felt. For the first time since his wife had sneaked out in the night without a word of explanation, he didn't wonder why she'd gone—something that had confounded, infuriated and hurt him—but why she'd felt she had to, and with only one small, battered back pack.

It was a question that he needed to ask her, he realised…
even if he wasn't sure he wanted to hear the answer.

Why *had* she stayed?

It was a question Mia had asked herself many times in
the thirty-six hours that Santos had been asleep. She had
yet to come up with an answer that satisfied her. She'd left
him once, after all, so she could surely do it again. It was
what she did, what her mother had taught her to do.

'You always know when it's time to move on,' her
mother used to say.

How many times had Mia come back to whatever
shabby flat or bedsit in which they'd been staying to find
her mother chucking things in a bag, barely looking at
her? Usually there had been a man involved, a man her
mother had to avoid, whether landlord, lover or both. Mia
had learned to sense when the sea change was coming;
she'd felt it in the air and had braced herself accordingly
for the inevitable detachment from the little life she had
built for herself.

Maybe that was it, Mia reflected. This time she *hadn't*
known. Santos's insistence that she was his wife, that their
vows mattered—as well as the fact that he'd wanted her
there, in his sleep-fuddled pain— had somehow made a
difference. It had made her stay even though, as ever, her
instinct had been to run.

But, she'd reflected, maybe they needed to have a reck-
oning, if not a reconciliation. Mia still couldn't see a way
forward for their marriage, not when at heart she felt it had
been a mistake. At the time, she'd been desperate to believe
in it, in them. She'd been swept away on a tide of feeling,
loving the way Santos made her feel—how he looked at

her so wonderingly, as though he couldn't believe she was real. How he'd *touched* her…

But since those first heady days they'd both said, done and *felt* things they couldn't come back from: hard, hurtful things. Moving on had been the easier choice, but maybe not the right one. Not yet, anyway…until they'd made peace with their past.

Santos dropped his gaze, scrubbing his hands over his face. 'I think I need a shower,' he said, and Mia managed a light laugh, even though inside she felt heavy.

'I think you probably do.'

He dropped his hands from his face and there was no mistaking the sudden, yearning heat in his eyes. Was he remembering the times they'd showered together back at the beginning of their short-lived romance? They'd soaped each other's bodies, slippery flesh sliding and colliding with the water streaming down, all laughter and kisses until passion had overtaken them.

Mia swallowed. If he didn't remember that, then she certainly did. She stood up from the bed. 'Shall I leave you to it?'

'All right,' Santos answered after a moment. 'But, after that, we'll talk.'

There could be no mistaking the intent in his words—talk with a capital 'T', clearly. What did that even mean, though, when they hadn't talked about the most important things? They hadn't been able to for weeks and weeks.

'Okay,' Mia replied, keeping her voice as light as she could. 'We'll talk.' Her talk was definitely with a 't'.

She slipped from his room, walking out to the sun deck at the stern of the yacht, the aquamarine waters of the Mediterranean rippling out behind the boat flecked with white. They'd been hugging the coast of Spain since they'd left

Ibiza, presumably going back to the Aguila estate on the outskirts of Seville.

Mia pictured the high, mustard-yellow walls surrounding the Aguila hacienda with its many porticoed porches, the groves of Seville oranges and manzanilla olives stretching out all around in orderly rows of orange and green, and shuddered. She *couldn't* go back there. It had far too many painful memories—stilted, awkward encounters as well as heart-rending, blood-soaked ones she had done her best to forget, even though she knew she never, ever would. Not that Santos would ever believe that.

She thought of his mother looking so elegant and remote, trying to be friendly but with an icy hauteur that had never thawed and probably never would. Mia really couldn't blame her. She was not the expected choice of wife for the heir of one of Spain's oldest families. She had no pedigree, no breeding, no style or class—far from it.

With a sigh, she rested her hands on the burnished wood of the yacht's railing. She didn't have to go back, she told herself. She might be married, but she was still in control of her own destiny. And she and Santos might need to talk—even with a capital T—but she didn't know if she could believe it might change anything between them. That, perhaps, was why she'd stayed—to convince him to let her go. Surely it wouldn't be too hard?

'Señora Aguila?' The voice of one of the yacht's cabin crew, Gabriela, came softly from behind her. 'May I get you something to eat or drink?'

Mia turned from the railing, managing a smile for the young, round-faced woman. 'Señor Aguila is waking up,' she said. 'And after sleeping for so long I'm sure he's hungry. Could you please prepare something for him to eat?

Maybe just some fruit and tapas—I don't know how much he'll want.'

Gabriela nodded her assent. 'Of course, *señora*.'

'Thank you.' It still boggled Mia's mind that Santos's staff had to cater to her whims. She'd been earning her living waitressing or housekeeping in a variety of low-brow places since she'd been sixteen. The idea that someone would have to serve *her*, and in such elegant, extravagant surroundings, had seemed ludicrous. In her three months living with Santos at his estate, she'd never really got used to it. She had always felt like an interloper, an intruder.

No one, not even Santos, had made her feel any different. Santos had been too busy, having to make up for the time he'd taken off work when they'd married. His mother had not known what to do with her; maybe she'd been hoping Mia wouldn't last. The staff had been scrupulously polite without actually being friendly. Mia knew she couldn't really have expected anything else. Santos had completely shocked everyone by bringing home a wife—a wife he barely knew, a footloose and fancy-free American who was nothing like what they must have been expecting.

Mia straightened, steeling her spine. She was going to convince Santos that they were better off apart—an amicable divorce, maybe even an annulment, if a lawyer could make it stick. There had to be some sort of grounds, considering how brief their marriage was. Then he could go on to marry someone far more suitable—some Spanish heiress, perhaps. And what would she do? Move on, Mia supposed, fighting a sense of desolation at the thought—as usual.

'Here you are.'

She turned to see Santos standing in the doorway of the lounge, its louvre doors open to the deck. He was wearing a cream linen shirt and loose dark trousers. He looked refreshed and frankly wonderful, his dark hair still damp from the shower, the smell of his cologne spicy and clean. For a second, no more, Mia had an urge to rush into his arms and let them enfold her. She smiled instead, one hand still resting on the railing to anchor her.

'Here I am,' she agreed cheerfully. 'Gabriela was going to put some food out in the dining area. What is that called on a yacht—a galley?'

'A galley is the kitchen.' He smiled, strolling towards her. He seemed far more relaxed than he had back in his cabin when he'd been lying in bed, still recovering from the aftereffects of his migraine, as well as purposeful. 'I think I'd just call it the dining room.'

'Right. I thought ships had special names for all the rooms, but I guess they don't.' How stupid could she sound? Mia cursed herself for feeling so unsteady in his presence. He was standing right in front of her and it was taking all her strength not to step close and curl into him. She wanted to rest her head on his solid chest, wrap her arms his waist, press close and feel both subsumed and safe.

She recalled how safe she'd felt lying next to him that first night, her head on his shoulder as he'd slept. He hadn't even been aware she was there, but they'd slept the whole night together before she'd slipped away in the morning, not wanting anyone to know, trying to convince herself that she didn't really miss him.

Santos leaned forward to lift the end of her plait from her shoulder, his fingers brushing her collar bone as he gently placed it behind her back, his fingers sliding along the knobs of her spine. 'Thank you, Mia,' he said quietly.

'Thank you?' Mia's voice was unsteady as she stared at him, conscious of the way his fingers had trailed up her spine as he'd removed his hand, trailing sparks of heat wherever he touched. 'For...for what?'

His golden-brown gaze rested on hers, as molten as a pool of honey. 'For staying. For being willing to talk things through.'

She was only doing that so he'd let her go, Mia reminded herself. This was about convincing him they should divorce, nothing else, even if she could still feel the brush of his fingertips along her spine, never mind that he was no longer touching her. Even if her head was starting to feel as if it were full of cotton wool, and all she could think about was how he'd touched her, how he looked and even how he smelled—like trees and sunshine with a hint of leather. She wanted to bury her nose in the hollow of his neck and just breathe him in. Once, she'd had that right, but no longer. She wouldn't let herself.

'We have unfinished business, Santos,' she forced herself to state, thankful her voice came out strong...stronger, anyway. 'If we talk, maybe then we can both move on.'

A frown settled between his dark, straight brows. 'Is that why you stayed—simply to convince me to *move on*?'

'For both of us to move on,' Mia amended. 'It's for the best, and I think you'll realise that eventually, if you don't already. Maybe we both need closure.'

His frown deepened, although when he spoke his voice was mild. 'So, you still think our marriage was a mistake.'

Mia shook her head slowly, not in denial of what he'd said, but rather in disbelief that he could act as if she was the only one with that notion. 'Be honest,' she told him. 'Never mind what you've said about vows and all that— don't *you* think it was a mistake?' How could he not? They'd known each other for just two crazy, passion-filled weeks before they'd married. Admittedly, they'd spent just about every second of those two weeks together, but it had still just been a fling, an infatuation.

The best thing that had ever happened to her.

'Señor? Señora?' Gabriela appeared in the doorway. 'Your meal is ready.'

'*Gracias*, Gabriela,' Santos murmured before turning back to Mia, his forehead still furrowed. 'I'm going to answer that question you just asked,' he promised. 'And we're really going to talk—properly—about everything.'

A shiver of apprehension and even fear rippled through Mia. *Everything?* She wasn't remotely ready for that, and she didn't think Santos was either.

With trepidation bordering on terror, she followed him back into the yacht to a meal that was starting to feel like her last.

CHAPTER FOUR

GABRIELA HAD OUTDONE HERSELF, Mia thought, as she came into the dining room with its cherry-wood table that seated twelve and matching chairs with cushions of cream leather. Built-in cabinets of glossy wood housed a set of expensive-looking porcelain, with Aguila's eagle crest and trademark stripes of gold and grey.

On one end of the long table, several dishes had been laid out—the typical tapas of Seville including Iberian ham, manzanilla olives, spinach and chickpea tapenade and pork in whiskey sauce. There was also a bowl of ripe, succulent fruit, as well as freshly baked bread and a round of Manchego cheese. Two place settings had been laid, complete with crystal glasses and linen napkins, the chairs perpendicular to each other.

It was a cosy, inviting spot. Santos, chivalrous as ever, pulled out the chair at the end of the table for her. With murmured thanks, Mia sat down. She was trying not to freak out about the thought of talking about everything. Surely he hadn't actually meant it? He'd never wanted to before...and neither had she.

He sat down in the seat perpendicular to her, close enough that his knee nudged hers, and the warmth of his leg against hers was enough to send her heart rate skittering as awareness rippled along her skin. Had he done it deliberately? He didn't seem bothered by the contact, but Mia was. Everything about this experience was making her feel uneasy and anxious, as well as hyper-sensitive, as if her nerves were being scraped raw. She couldn't handle being so close to this man, not with so many memories between them—the beautiful, bittersweet ones, and the painful ones that still caused her shudders of agony. The sooner they agreed to go their separate ways, the better. She wasn't sure she could survive much more.

Santos, as relaxed as ever, held up the platter of pork. 'May I serve you?'

Mia hadn't eaten all that much since she'd boarded the yacht and, while she was hungry, she wasn't sure she could manage so much as a mouthful right now. But she forced a nod. 'Just a little, please.'

She watched as Santos loaded up both their plates with various delicacies. There was a bottle of white Rioja chilling in a bucket of ice next to the table, and he took it and poured them both a glass. It was all so very civilised, she thought as he lifted his glass.

'Arriba, abajo, al centro y pa' dentro!' he proclaimed, reciting the old Spanish toast. *You are never above me, never below me, never away from me and always with me.*

Was that a warning, Mia wondered as she drank, or a promise?

'So,' Santos said after he'd set down his glass and leaned back in his chair, steepling his fingers together like a professor. 'In answer to your question, do I think our marriage was a mistake…?'

He paused and Mia tensed. She realised, in that moment, she didn't actually want him to think that at all, which had to be phenomenally stupid. *She* thought it was a mistake and of course he should as well. It would make everything easier if he did.

'The answer is twofold,' he continued in that calm voice, as smooth as a river of honey rolling right over her. 'First, I *don't* think that, but second, it doesn't matter—even if I did, we are still married, and should therefore honour our vows.'

Mia carefully set down her glass. 'Putting the second point aside for the moment,' she replied as mildly as she could, 'Why don't you think that?'

Santos gazed at her thoughtfully, his head cocked to the side. It felt as if he were trying to plumb the depths of her soul, and it took all of Mia's strength simply to sit there, a faint, enquiring smile on her face, and wait. 'I suppose,' he answered after a moment, 'The question really is, why do you?'

She let out a small, hollow laugh. He was deflecting, the way she often did, another aspect of her mother's 'don't let anyone close' philosophy, don't actually ever admit what she was thinking or what she cared about—who she *was*. And yet, what was the point of this conversation, its discomfort, if she didn't tell the truth—or at least a bit of it?

'I suppose,' she answered slowly, toying with the fragile stem of her wine glass, 'Because we're so different. And we want different things out life.'

'I can certainly agree with the first point,' Santos replied with a smile, his teeth gleaming whitely in his tanned face. After the carefully leashed fury of that first night, he seemed remarkably at ease now. Why? What had changed? 'As to the second…what do you want out of life, Mia? Truly?'

Startled, she lifted her glass and took a sip of wine as she attempted to organise her thoughts. What did she want out of life? 'Safety' was the first word that came to mind, but she discarded it because she already knew Santos would insist he could make her safe—more than anyone else, with his money, his power and his high-walled estate locking everything and everyone out if he so chose.

But that wasn't the kind of safety she meant. Physical safety and emotional safety were two very different things. As a child, she'd known far too well what it was like to have neither—she'd hid under her covers, listening to her mother and her drunken friends in the next room. The two of them would have to run from yet another commune, farm or shabby flat because once again it had all gone wrong... Her childhood had been a tempestuous sea of instability, and she'd been tossed on its waves over and over again.

Santos *had* made her feel safe, back at the beginning, in both ways. It was what had compelled her to agree to his unexpected and reckless proposal of marriage. She'd trusted him at the start, and she wasn't someone who gave her trust away easily. How had it all gone so wrong, so quickly? And was there any way to make it right again? Santos seemed to think there was, but Mia felt too jaded to share that hope.

'Freedom,' she finally said, because hadn't she learned that was what emotional safety essentially was—never letting anyone close enough to hurt her? Going her own way as a choice rather than default or rejection?

'Freedom,' he repeated slowly. His eyes had narrowed, but his tone was mild. 'What kind of freedom, exactly?'

Mia shrugged restively, not wanting to give much more away. 'Just...being free. Making my own choices, being able to do what I want.' Which made her sound a bit selfish, she realised, and it wasn't really about that at all. It was about not being hurt—not *able* to be hurt. But she didn't know how to explain that and, even if she did, she wasn't sure she wanted to. Actually, she *knew* she didn't want to…but then maybe this conversation was pointless.

A sigh escaped her at the thought, and she reached for an olive from her plate, nibbling its tart saltiness. 'Anyway, it's the first point that's more relevant, Santos,' she replied with clear deflection. 'We're simply too different.'

He leaned back, steepling his fingers together again. 'Don't they say opposites attract?' He smiled faintly as he cocked his head and waited for her reply.

'Attract, yes,' she allowed. They'd certainly been attracted to each other They'd left the bar the first night they'd met and gone right to Santos's five-star hotel. There had been no discussion, no question about any of it. Mia remembered soaring up in the lift to dizzying heights, her heart racing in time with it. Santos's slow, sure smile as he'd reached for her hand… And, when he'd kissed her for the first time, it had felt as if fireworks had gone off inside her head, her heart.

She'd never been one for flings, and had never had a one-night stand, because she hadn't wanted to give that much of herself away so cheaply. Yet she'd had no doubts about being with Santos, about it feeling and being right. At least, not until much later.

'Whether opposites can stay together is another matter,' she finished, and then popped the olive into her mouth, forcing herself to swallow, for her throat suddenly felt dry as Santos's eyes narrowed in speculation.

'I suppose it takes more effort,' he remarked slowly. 'To understand where the other person is coming from.'

Effort, Mia supposed, that neither of them had really made. Their attraction had been so wonderfully easy, and she'd assumed—maybe they both had—that the rest would be too. The first bump in the road that they'd come to—and admittedly it had been a big one, very early on—had utterly derailed the whole thing. It had been hard, if not impossible, to recover from that.

'I suppose any marriage is hard work,' she replied, meaning it to be more of a generic observation than an assessment of their own unfortunate nuptial state.

Santos leaned forward, his eyes firing to bronze. 'Then let's put in the work, Mia.'

She'd walked right into that one, Mia realised, but even so she was surprised. Santos certainly hadn't seemed to want to put in the work before. Did she even want him to now? Did *he*, really? Was it worth it? She didn't think could take any more heartbreak, any more *guilt*.

She definitely knew she couldn't stand Santos looking at her the way he had in the hospital, when their baby had bled out of her, as if she'd committed a crime.

'What would the point be, Santos?' she asked finally, her tone weary. 'We've already seen we don't work together.' For six excruciating weeks after her miscarriage.

'We worked very well together at the beginning.' His voice had dropped to a husky murmur, laced with meaningful innuendo, his gaze darkening as his eyes bored into hers, forcing her to remember. And in truth, it didn't take much to catapult Mia right back to those first few, heady days and weeks—to the joy and pleasure of discovering each other's bodies, revelling in the way they'd seemed to connect not just physically, but emotionally, utterly at ease in each other's company in a way she'd never experienced before. But none of it had lasted.

'Yes, at the beginning,' she agreed, her voice wavering as heat flooded her body along with the memories—Santos, his lips on her throat, his hands anchoring her hips as he trailed kisses down her body. Memories of her head thrown back, her body thrumming with pleasure, never having known it could be like that between a man and a woman.

'Plenty of people have that, Santos,' she continued, managing to make her voice stronger. 'It's called infatuation.' She forced herself to face him down, quailing at the blaze in his eyes, a potent mix of fury and desire, as she basically reduced their relationship to something shallow and tawdry. But she had to, to make him let her go. She finished as she reached for another olive, 'It was just a fling.'

Just a fling? *Just a fling?*

Santos felt a righteous rage roar through him, a tidal wave that hid the underlying surge of hurt. Was she reducing the most important relationship he'd ever had to schoolboy emotion, a sordid affair? Yes, it had been swift, intense and overwhelming—he could certainly grant all that—but it hadn't been a *fling*. He didn't even have flings; he knew plenty of men did, especially ones with money and power, but he'd always seen casual sexual relationships as a distasteful abuse of his position. He'd been selective with his partners, and had made sure they meant something.

Even though Mia had been different—and, yes, it had all happened so fast—he had never, not even in the first wild, heady throes of passion, thought that what they had wasn't real. Even later, when he'd had cause, so much cause, to doubt, he'd done his best to keep himself from it. He'd done his best to believe that Mia was a good person, the woman he'd thought she was, even when it had been damned near impossible. Even when she'd left. Even when he'd found her in a bar, looking as if she was living it up in his absence.

And he was here now, wasn't he? Still trying to believe the best of her against all odds. He took a deep breath and let it out slowly. He eased back in his chair and took a sip of wine to calm the raging emotion he normally didn't let himself feel.

An Aguila must always be master of his mind and his heart. He could hear his father saying that in his steady, commanding voice, and it gave him the level-headedness he needed. 'So, why did you marry me, then, out of curiosity?' he asked.

Mia looked startled by the question, then pensive as she considered her answer. 'I suppose I got caught up in it all,' she replied after a moment, her tone cautious as she nibbled her olive. 'It was exciting, new…overwhelming. And you made me feel…' She stopped suddenly and gave a little shrug. 'I believed in it, in *us*, for a little while.'

Us. A concept that for her no longer seemed to exist. What had she been about to say? Santos wondered. What had he made her feel? He decided not to ask her now, when she seemed so reluctant to part with any information. 'So you didn't think it was just infatuation at the start,' he stated.

Mia frowned, finishing her olive, and then she shook her head, her plait flying over her shoulder. 'Well, it wasn't love.'

She sounded so certain, he was perhaps more stung than he should have been. Could a person even love someone after just two weeks? And yet he'd felt as if he had, or something close to it. Maybe not *love*…but happiness, excitement, wonder… Yes.

'Why not?' he asked. The two words came out like bullets, fast and hard. He was glad he was challenging her.

Maybe *this* was the conversation they'd needed to have all along. 'Why wasn't it love, Mia?'

She stared at him, her lips parting soundlessly for a few seconds before she replied. 'Santos, real love is something that roots down and grows. It's not a spark that suddenly bursts into flame. You're a reasonable man; you must know this. I'm sure you actually believe it yourself.' She stared at him, her eyes wide and blue-green, as clear as the crystalline sea. 'We didn't know each other well enough to truly be in love.'

She was right, of course. They hadn't. He *did* know that. He believed it; he'd even say so himself. So what exactly was he trying to prove now? Why did her telling him they'd never been in love annoy and, yes, hurt so much?

'That's where the work part comes in, doesn't it?' he remarked after a moment, feeling his way through the idea. 'Love isn't necessarily easy, Mia. Growing something takes time, effort, commitment. Making a marriage work is the same.' But she had chosen not to put in the effort. She'd made that abundantly clear when she'd left.

'What exactly are you saying?' she asked. 'You *want* to make this marriage work?' She sounded so incredulous that he almost laughed, although in truth he was irritated by her disbelief.

'Why do you think I came halfway across Spain and found you?'

'Honestly, I don't know. I'm not sure you do either.' She gave him a shrewd look before she shook her head and sighed. 'I didn't think you would. I thought… I thought you'd be glad to see me gone, frankly.'

'Well, I wasn't,' he replied shortly. He stayed tight-lipped after that, because he wasn't going to go into how hurt and humiliated he'd felt, how rejected and lost when he'd seen the empty space next to him in the bed. He'd felt it in his soul when he'd realised she'd sneaked away without leaving so much as a note. She'd cared about him that little.

Yes, things had become hard between them, damnably hard. And they hadn't dealt with any of it, not in a way that was helpful or reasonable. But he'd still thought they would get through it. He'd trusted her…at least, he'd *tried*…but when she'd left the doubts had come like a flock of crows, nesting inside him, cawing their lies. He was here because he wanted to face down those doubts, prove that Mia was the woman he'd always thought she was. Prove that their marriage *could* work…if they just committed to it.

'I suppose,' Mia said slowly, sounding out the words as they came, 'I thought that if you came and found me it would just be because of your reputation—the "an Aguila is a man of his word" thing—not because you actually wanted our marriage to work.'

So did she think he cared more for appearances than realities or relationships? All right, he supposed he could understand why she might think that, at least a little. He'd made it sound as if the only reason he'd come after her was because he was a man of his word, not because of any *feelings*. But surely he'd showed her that wasn't the case, at least not entirely? Although in truth his feelings were as tangled up as hers seemed to be.

Santos slowly shook his head. 'Mia, what's the point of a marriage if it doesn't work?'

'What's the point,' Mia countered, sounding weary and despairing, 'Of trying to make a marriage work that *can't*?'

Santos absorbed that proposition with a slow blink. 'Why are you so sure ours can't?' he asked levelly. Part of him wanted to prove just how well they'd *worked* right there and then. It would be easy: he'd take her by the hand

and draw her onto his lap; fasten his hands to her hips and let her feel how much he wanted her. And he would feel it in her as well—the shudder of her breath, the widening of her eyes, the way her lips would part as her gaze dropped to his mouth…

Desire fired through his blood, making his heart race and certain parts of him tighten. It would be so easy…but it would be wrong. This wasn't about physical desire or sexual conquest. That was the one part of their relationship that *had* definitely worked all right. It was everything else that had been the problem.

Belatedly, his mind still fogged with desire, Santos realised how silent Mia had gone, how stricken she looked. The only sound was the purr of the yacht's motor, the lap of the waves against its hull. Mia's face was pale, her eyes dark and wide.

'Mia?' he pressed.

She shook her head and then rose from the table in one abrupt movement. Santos half-rose himself as he watched her walk to the corner of the room, her back to him and her head bowed as she wrapped her arms around herself, as if she had to hold herself together. He felt as if he'd missed a crucial moment of their conversation, an emotional turning point that had happened in a beat of silence when he'd been imagining her naked.

'Mia,' he said again, quietly.

'I can't do this,' she whispered, her narrow back to him practically vibrating with tension. 'I'm sorry. I just… I can't. I can't do this.' She let out a gulping sound that, with a ripple of shock, Santos realised was her holding back a sob.

He straightened and took a step towards her. He wanted

to take her in his arms, hold her, *comfort* her, but he had no idea what had just happened and, more importantly, *why*.

He'd asked her why she thought their marriage couldn't work. She'd responded by having to hold back sobs. An unease rippled over his skin, clenching his gut. There could only be one reason why Mia was reacting like this, and it was the thing they'd done their utmost not to talk about, backing away every time they'd come close because it hurt too damned much. At least, it had hurt him. He had no idea how Mia felt about it; he didn't want to know. It was the raw wound that still pulsed with pain and which he'd done his best to ignore. Stupid, really, but sometimes it was the only way to survive…even as he bled out.

'Mia,' he said again, and he took another step towards her, close enough so he could rest his hands on her shoulders, feel the warmth of her skin seep through his palms. She tensed beneath his touch but she didn't move away. Another shudder went through her, and another gulping sob came out before she pressed her fist to her mouth. 'Mia, talk to me,' Santos said.

Mia was silent for a long moment, her whole body quivering. Then she shrugged off Santos's hands, jerking away from him in one abrupt movement. He was still absorbing that as she whirled round and faced him with fury in her eyes.

'All right, Santos,' she said in a voice of cold, controlled anger. 'Why are you so keen to make our marriage work when you believe I murdered our baby?'

CHAPTER FIVE

THE LOOK OF blatant shock on Santos's face would have been comical if it hadn't hurt so much. He was *surprised—* really? After everything that had—and hadn't—happened between them? She still remembered the agonising moment he'd walked out of her hospital room without a single word and left her there alone to deal with the aftermath, blood, pain and grief. It was something she wasn't sure she could forgive...just as he couldn't forgive her for what he'd thought she'd done. What he knew she'd felt.

'Don't deny it,' she told him in a low voice that thrummed with both anger and pain. She felt dangerous all of a sudden, ready to strike, lash, *wound*. She'd been holding back this anger for months; she hadn't believed she had the right to be angry, because she'd felt so guilty for what had happened. But now the guilt was gone and all she felt was pure, clean rage.

'Mia...' Santos shook his head slowly, spreading his hands wide. 'I never believed you murdered our baby. Of course I didn't.'

She let out a hollow laugh. 'Oh, it's that obvious to you, is it? Well, trust me, Santos, it wasn't to me.' The words came out of her in jagged bursts, splinters that drew blood with every syllable.

Santos frowned, his straight, dark brows drawing together, his eyes flashing darkly with concern and confusion. Even though he seemed disturbed by her accusation, she couldn't quite assess his response. Was he pretending to be so surprised that she'd thought that? Or had he actually convinced himself that he hadn't blamed her back then? 'I never accused you—' he began.

'Santos, you didn't need to.' The anger was gone, as quick as it had come—just like their infatuation—a spark that had turned into a fire then died out, leaving her only cold and weary. 'You showed me,' she told him quietly, 'With everything you said and did. And with everything you *didn't* say or do.' She'd not forgotten the silences, the accusing looks. The way he'd averted his head whenever she'd come into a room, as if he couldn't bear to look at her. Those two months had been the longest she'd ever known, every day an endurance test, until she'd finally broken—and run.

He was silent for a long moment, his forehead still furrowed. 'So you are condemning me for thinking something I never even said?'

'Do you deny it?' She met his concerned gaze with a challenging one of her own. They'd never, ever spoken about this, as she had backed away from it every single time, but she was actually glad they were having it out now, whatever the result of their conversation. 'Do you deny it?' she said again, a statement as well as a demand. 'Surely now is the time for truth, Santos. If we're going to talk about what happened, then let's talk about it—*all* of it.'

Pain flashed across his face and his gaze briefly dropped from hers before he resolutely returned it to stare her down. 'All right, we will. But not in anger.'

Of course he would be so level-headed about it all, so emotionless. A memory crashed through her brain of her screaming at him to feel something. He'd replied coolly, 'You don't know what I feel.' And that, Mia thought, had been the problem exactly: he'd never told her. He'd never let her in. She hadn't been much better; she could acknowledge that now, and would have even then.

But if he'd held her…if he'd made her feel safe…maybe she would have admitted how guilty she felt, how grief-stricken, yet how she feared she didn't have the right to the emotion. She would have confessed everything she'd buried deep inside, but his chilly silences had possessed the power to hurt her, so she'd shut down, just as he had.

'I'm not angry,' she stated as calmly as she could. And she wasn't, at least not in this moment; she felt too tired for that level of emotional engagement now. 'But if you're going to deny basic reality then I'm not sure how far we'll get.' All right, maybe she was still a little angry after all, Mia thought. She could feel her hands curling into fists before she wilfully unclenched them. 'You blamed me, Santos. At least, you acted as if you blamed me, for two whole months.'

He fell silent again, clearly considering his response, staying so even-tempered while she felt as if she could fly apart into a million pieces, scattering to the four winds. 'I did not blame you for the death of our child,' he stated finally. He sounded like a lawyer, being so careful with his words. 'You had a miscarriage, Mia. It could happen to any woman. It wasn't your fault.'

The words sounded, and felt, robotic and rote. She didn't believe he meant them, even though it was what the doctor had told them both when they'd been in hospital, having seen the still, lifeless form on the ultrasound—such a little peanut! It had been tiny and curled up, yet with arms, legs, fingers and toes. She'd only been eleven weeks' pregnant.

She hadn't realised that a baby looked like, well, a *baby* so early on. She hadn't let herself think that way; in that moment, with that tiny form so still on the screen, she had.

'I know I had a miscarriage,' she replied, trying to keep her tone as even as his. 'But that doesn't mean you don't blame me. Maybe you think I willed the baby to die somehow.'

He made a scoffing sound. 'Superstition. No, I'd never think something like that. I *didn't*.'

'Or maybe you think I didn't do enough to keep it heathy—taken pre-natal vitamins, or rested the way I should have, or cut out caffeine.' She hadn't done any of those things. She'd still been adjusting to the utter shock of her pregnancy and Santos's delight. She'd been afraid, but that wasn't what Santos had seemed to assume. He'd seemed to think she was selfish, shallow, for not wanting their child, but it had been so much deeper than that.

The tiny, electric pause that followed her statement was all the confirmation she needed to know he *had* thought something like that. He'd blamed her for not doing enough. 'The doctor said those things wouldn't have made a difference,' he finally said, his tone cautious, as if he didn't want to admit it.

'Did he?' Mia thought back to that dazed conversation, sitting across from the desk, feeling so *empty*. She recalled the pamphlet the doctor had pushed across to her that she'd been unable to bear reading. 'I don't remember him saying anything like that,' she said.

The guarded look on Santos's face, quickly veiled, made understanding flash through Mia like a lightning storm. 'You asked him, didn't you?' she realised aloud. 'When you were by yourself, after you'd left me. You asked him if the things I did or didn't do would have made a difference.' Her words rang out in accusation. Before he spoke, she already knew.

'I was trying to make sense of what happened, Mia,' he admitted quietly. 'As I imagine you were. Or,' he added, his tone suddenly turning quietly lethal, his eyes narrowing just the way they'd used to, 'Maybe you were just relieved.'

Mia went completely still and taut, her face like a blank mask, while Santos wished he could bite back the words. He hadn't meant to say them, or hadn't wanted to feel them, yet...*yes*; part of him did feel them and mean them. It was a truth he hated to acknowledge, but there could be no doubting it. She hadn't wanted their baby. They both knew that unequivocally. She'd told him so, when she'd found out she was pregnant, in a conversation that had shocked and hurt him unbearably. Whatever happened after, *that* had been a basic reality neither of them could deny.

'I always knew you felt that,' she said quietly, too quietly. Her voice was small and sad, and it made him long to hold her, although neither of them moved. 'Why did you deny it?'

'Why are you denying it?' he countered. 'Mia, you didn't want our child. You told me so in no uncertain terms. And me acknowledging that truth is a far, *far* cry from acting as if you killed our baby.' His voice caught and he felt the sting of tears behind his lids. *Their baby*—so tiny, so perfect. The grief he hadn't let himself feel since that day in hospital, when he'd been so horribly numb, now felt like a tidal wave poised to pull him under.

An Aguila is master of his own heart.

He forced himself to push it all back.

'But you blamed me,' she said softly. 'You wouldn't have

asked the doctor those questions if you hadn't, at least on some level.'

Briefly Santos closed his eyes, his thumb and forefinger bracing his temple. He felt the flicker of his migraine, like a ghostly reminder of the pain. 'I didn't blame you,' he stated again. 'Please believe that.' *He* wanted to believe it, but Mia's stark certainty was making him question himself. Had he blamed her? He'd been angry, certainly, as well as hurt. And there had been the grief he'd felt that he'd feared, and felt, she hadn't. So he had retreated into a silence that had probably felt cold to Mia, like a rejection.

But she'd been the same, hadn't she? She'd shut him out in so many ways, refusing to answer his questions, closing in on herself so he felt he had no access. They'd both been as bad as the other…or almost.

'I can't believe that, Santos,' Mia said quietly. 'I'm sorry, but I just can't.' She straightened, tilting her chin up a notch, her expression bleak. 'So, where does that leave us?'

He stared at her for a moment, trying to sift through what she was saying. 'You think we should divorce, then— just because you refuse to believe I didn't blame you for the miscarriage?'

'And you refuse to believe that you acted as you did, that you made me feel…' She drew a shuddering breath. 'It just feels like too much to get over. Maybe it was a mercy that things happened that way—me getting pregnant so quickly and…and then losing the baby.' She gulped and then continued, 'It made us see how incompatible we were…before it was too late.'

There was so much wrong with that theory that Santos didn't even know where to begin. His jaw clenched as he fought down a wave of fury and did his best to keep his voice even. 'Mia, we went through something hard—really hard. It doesn't mean we're incompatible. And it *is* too late, anyway, because we're married.' He took a step towards her. 'Did those vows mean anything to you?' he demanded. 'For better or for worse? In sickness and in health?'

'Did they mean anything to *you*?' she tossed back at him. Their conversation had become a tennis match, each slinging accusations back and forth, a volley of words that left them both bereft. 'You left me alone in hospital,' she told him. 'Right after I'd had the procedure. You turned and walked out of the room without a single word.'

Her voice throbbed with pain, shocking him. He'd completely forgotten about that and, remembering it now, he felt a flicker of shame. He *had* left her, slumped on the edge of the bed, refusing to look at him or even to speak to him. He'd been in a fog of grief, dazed and reeling, painful memories mixing with the terrible present. He'd walked away because he hadn't known what else to do. In truth, he couldn't even remember doing it.

'I suppose I thought you wanted to be alone,' he told her. 'You didn't say a single word to me. But maybe I should have tried harder. At the time, I was just…reeling, really.' He paused and then, the words feeling awkward even though he meant them, said, 'I'm sorry.'

'Oh, Santos.' Mia let out a jagged laugh. 'Don't you see? We isolated ourselves from each other every single time. When things got hard, we did everything wrong. We never, ever turned towards each other in our grief and pain. I know you don't think I felt any,' she added, her tone turning spiky, 'And maybe you'll never be able to believe me about that, just like I can't believe you about the blame. But I did feel it. I was sad about the loss of our baby, even if I wasn't thrilled when I found out I was pregnant.'

'I believe you,' he said after a moment, and he did. It

didn't negate the other fact, of course—that she hadn't wanted their baby—but he could see how those two sentiments could co-exist…sort of.

'Do you?' she asked despairingly, shaking her head.

A flash of irritation went through him, although he did his best to tamp it down. 'What can I do to convince you, Mia?' he asked. 'You seem remarkably determined to believe the worst of me.'

'And you seem determined to believe the worst of *me*,' she retorted, and then threw her hands up in the air. 'Listen to us! We just never get anywhere. This is why we should divorce. You won't ever see my perspective, and you won't ever even let me know yours. How can we possibly make a marriage work?'

He stilled at this new accusation. 'Wait…what is that supposed to mean?'

She took a deep breath and let it out slowly. 'You shut me out, Santos, at every turn. You wouldn't talk about how you felt sad, or angry, or anything. Maybe I should have tried harder to get you to open up, but when I did it felt as if you just shut down even more. I ended up screaming at you like—like a fishwife and feeling worse about myself than I already did.

'Do you know why I left?' she demanded, her voice raw and throbbing with pain. 'Because I couldn't take it any more, feeling that way. Having you make me feel like the worst person in the world. I left because I couldn't bear it. Sometimes…sometimes I thought I'd rather be dead, than feel the way I did, like our baby.' She pressed her fist to her trembling lips as she choked back a sob, turning away from him to hide her face.

Santos stared at her in stunned disbelief. She'd rather have been *dead*? He didn't think she was being melodramatic; Mia wasn't prone to theatrics. But had he made her feel that way? He wanted to deny it, *needed* to, and yet he saw it there in her face—saw the way she was curling into herself, trying to hold back the sobs—and it felt as if the knowledge was tearing him to shreds.

Dear heaven. What had happened to them? How had they got to this forsaken place?

'Mia…' he began, reaching one hand out to her, even though she was too far away to touch. It was a paltry gesture, and he had no words. He felt utterly unequipped to deal with this moment and its fraught emotions. 'Mia, please. When we get back to Seville we can—'

'I can't go back to Seville,' she said suddenly, the words coming on a ragged gasp. 'I can't face that house—your mother, the *silverware*…' She let out a high, semi-hysterical laugh that ended on something between a shriek and a sob. 'I won't go back there, Santos. Don't make me.' She whirled around, her face pale and streaked with tears, her voice turning shrill, as if she was gripped by panic. 'Don't make me! Don't make me, *please*!'

He'd never seen her as distraught as this, not even after the miscarriage. What on earth was going on? The *silverware*…? Santos realised there was a lot more going on than he'd ever understood, or tried to understand, but maybe he needed to now. He closed the space between her in two long strides. She was crying silently, tears slipping down her cheeks as she stared at him helplessly, and he took her by the shoulders.

'Mia, please. It's all right. It will be all right. I won't make you. We…we don't have to go back to Seville.'

She gave a shuddering gulp as she stared at him, tears still trickling down her face. 'We…don't?'

'No,' he said firmly, although he was thinking on his

feet. He had at least a dozen meetings scheduled for next week in Madrid and Rome, as well as estate business to see to back in Seville. Every moment of every day was accounted for, as it always was, but just then none of it mattered. 'We don't. We'll go somewhere else.'

The idea unfurled inside him, blooming into something both cautious and wonderful. 'We'll go somewhere just the two of us together. I have a villa in Greece, on a little island.' It was a place where he'd dreamed of staying for weeks at a time, but he'd never managed it. Not yet. 'We could go there for a little while. We never had a honeymoon, after all. Maybe now is the time.'

'A *honeymoon*…?'

The look of blatant scepticism on her face would have hurt him once, but now it just made him more determined. He'd come to Ibiza to find his wife and he'd go to Greece— he'd move heaven and earth—to win her back. Whatever had happened in the past, they could get over it…together. He'd make sure of it; he'd put in the work that he'd said every marriage needed. He'd put in the work for Mia, because this wasn't just about keeping his word or being an Aguila—it was about what they'd shared, and what they could share again. It was, he decided, time to woo his wayward wife.

CHAPTER SIX

MIA WOKE SLOWLY to sunlight, her whole body aching as
if she'd taken a physical battering. She felt as if she had,
emotionally at least. Yesterday had been…intense. She
closed her eyes as the memories washed over her of their
blazing argument; the sobs she'd tried to keep in; the guilt
she still felt that she hadn't been able to bear explaining to
Santos. All of it together felt like too much to process, and
she had no idea at all where they stood with each other.
Yet somehow they were going to Greece.

When Santos had suggested heading to his villa—something else she hadn't known about—Mia had agreed in a
moment of weakness or maybe strength; she wasn't actually sure which. She was tired of fighting, of running, and
she had no money, no energy or no hope. Maybe a few days
in a private villa, away from all the stresses and strains,
would be a good thing. She hadn't let herself hope it could
actually repair their marriage, although Santos seemed to
think it would.

'This will be good for us,' he'd told her, his hands still
resting on her shoulders. 'This could be exactly what we
need.'

As if a holiday would sort everything out. Well, at least
it would be a rest, Mia thought wearily. But she wasn't
ready for round two of picking apart the past. Talking

about her miscarriage as much as they had had been hard enough, and there was still so much that hadn't been said. She feared Santos would never truly understand how she could both have not wanted the baby and been saddened by the loss. Mia falling pregnant just two weeks after their wedding had not been in either of their plans. But birth control had failed, as it did sometimes and, improbably, Santos had been delighted—Mia very much less so.

'But Mia…' He'd looked confused, even hurt, when she'd seemed decidedly less than thrilled with the results of the test, staring at the two blazing pink lines. 'It's a baby. A *niño*! Or *niña*. Either way…' The smile he'd given her had been endearingly crooked, his eyes warm with excitement and love—or what she'd thought was love. How could it have been love, considering what had happened later and how quick he'd been to blame her? 'Our child.' He'd taken her hands in his. 'I know it's soon, very soon, but I am pleased. And excited. I've always wanted a family.'

And then he'd registered the look of misery on her face, perhaps had felt how icy her hands were in his, and he'd frowned. 'What's…what's wrong?'

'Santos, I…' Even then she hadn't wanted to admit it, but why hadn't he been able to understand? They'd known each other for a *month*. 'I'm not… I'm not ready to have a baby.'

He'd grinned at a problem easily solved. 'It's a good thing then that it takes nine months for one to grow! You'll be ready by then.'

'No, I won't be.' Her voice had been flat, and his grin had vanished, replaced by something far worse than a frown. That had been the first time of many she'd seen his narrow-eyed look, the way his mouth both pursed up and turned down.

'So…what are you saying?' His voice had been danger-ously soft.

'I… I don't know,' she'd admitted helplessly. 'I'm just… I'm not ready.' Although in truth she hadn't known if she'd ever be ready. What could she possibly know about being a good mother, considering her own upbringing? Yet she hadn't wanted to explain that to Santos. He wouldn't have understood; he'd have dismissed her concerns and insisted it would all be fine. She'd known that already. 'This wasn't in our plan…' she'd tried again. Not that they'd had much of a plan, getting married so precipitously. They'd both just been carried along on a tide of feeling, of desire and joy. But she'd been only twenty-six years old, and they'd been married for a matter of *weeks*. It surely hadn't been what either of them wanted.

He'd stared at her for a long moment while she'd looked back miserably, the pregnancy test still held in her hand. She'd only taken it because her period was usually like clockwork but she hadn't actually *thought*…

'I hope,' he'd told her in that same ominous voice, 'That you are not suggesting what it sounds like you are suggest-ing. Because this is my baby as much as it is yours, Mia. No matter what you think about such things, I do not be-lieve you have the right to take away my child, my flesh and blood.' His voice had thrummed with anger, his body with tension.

'If you're talking about me having an abortion,' Mia had replied, her voice trembling, 'Then, no; I'm not think-ing that.' She'd still been reeling from shock. 'I don't… I don't know what I want, Santos. I just… I didn't want this.'

If she'd hoped he would be understanding of her un-easy ambivalence, he hadn't been. His tone had been flat as he'd turned away from her. 'Well, *this* is a child we cre-

ated together,' he'd said. 'And *this* is what we are dealing
with now.'

It had been the end of the conversation.

With a sigh, Mia swung her legs over the edge of the bed
and gazed out through the porthole at the aquamarine sea,
its surface dancing with sunlight. She was so lucky, she
told herself. She was on a multi-million-pound yacht with
a man who wanted to be married to her, who had professed
to being committed to making their marriage work. If she
stayed with him, she'd never want for anything materially
again. Emotionally it would be another matter, but even so,
maybe she needed to start counting her blessings—think
about what she did have, rather than what she didn't.

The need to protect herself was deeply ingrained; she'd
had too many years of her mother's determined indifference and sometimes wilful neglect not to be cautious with
her own battered heart. Mia had long ago learned to be
wary and guarded with strangers; it came with the territory of a wandering lifestyle, first with her mother, and
then chosen as an adult because it was all she'd been ever
known. Her own guardedness had made her initial response to Santos all the more surprising. She'd trusted
him from the start—against her better judgement, perhaps,
but not against her instinct. She truly believed Santos was
a good man at his core. Yes, he could be intractable, in-
transigent, *stubborn*. He could also be arrogant, autocratic
and bossy. But she had her own faults that he'd had to deal
with. If they really were both committed, maybe they could
make their marriage work. At least, they could try.

And yet Mia wasn't even sure where to begin…or if she
could. Did she really have that emotional resilience after
everything? Running—and keeping on running—felt safer.
Maybe stronger too, even if she knew it really wasn't.

With a sigh, she rose from the bed and went to shower and dress. All she could do, she told herself, was take this—*them*—one day at a time.

Twenty minutes later she left her cabin below deck and headed up to find Santos. It was a beautiful summer's day, the air soft and balmy, the sky a hazy blue fleeced with puffy white clouds. She found Santos at the helm of the yacht, the breeze ruffling his dark hair, his eyes hidden by a pair of aviator sunglasses. He was wearing white linen trousers and a loose button-down shirt in navy, his skin like burnished bronze against the fabric, his whole body seeming both relaxed and in control. He smiled when he saw her, his teeth gleaming in his tanned face.

'Sleep well?'

'Yes, I think so.' She'd been so exhausted by everything that had happened that she'd practically fallen into a coma the second her head had touched the pillow. She pulled her thin cardigan around herself as the breeze buffeted her. 'What's the plan now, exactly?'

'We're on track to sail to Amorgos, where I have the villa.'

'I didn't know you owned a Greek villa.'

He shrugged easily. 'I don't suppose I ever had occasion to mention it.'

'How many properties do you have, besides the estate in Seville?' she asked out of simple curiosity. As someone who had never owned any property at all, never mind a villa or an entire estate, the idea of having several was utterly alien to her. Sometimes, when she was with Santos, she forgot how wealthy he was…until something like this reminded her. They were worlds apart—galaxies.

Santos frowned in thought as he considered her question. 'Hmm…let's see. The villa on Amorgos, an apartment in Madrid—mainly for work and my mother's shopping trips—a place in the Caribbean and a ski chalet in Klosters.' He smiled and spread his hands. 'That's it.'

'That's it.' Mia let out a little laugh as she shook her head. 'I can't imagine having that many houses. I can't even imagine having one.'

He frowned. 'Not even one?'

That had slipped out without her meaning it to. In their five months together, Mia hadn't told him very much at all about her tempestuous childhood and upbringing. She'd kept the details vague, simply saying she'd grown up with a single mum and that they'd 'moved around a bit'. Such an innocuous term for a childhood that had been at best unsettling and at worse truly dangerous…something she tried not to think about too much. It had been hard enough never to have known her father, to feel her mother hadn't wanted her, but to feel as though everyone else was out to get her as well… Mia hadn't wanted to dwell on it.

Neither had she wanted Santos feeling sorry for her, and she still didn't now. But if this whole 'let's work on our marriage' thing was indeed going to work, then maybe she needed to be honest. At least, a *little* honest. She wasn't ready to tell him everything; she already knew that for sure.

'We never owned a house or an apartment or anything like that,' she told him. 'My mother liked to move around a lot.'

'Yes, I remember you saying something like that,' he replied thoughtfully. He left the helm, putting his hand on the small of her back to guide her to an L-shaped sofa in the shade of a pergola. Someone had left a jug of fruit punch and several glasses on the coffee table, and he poured them both some. 'How much is a lot?' he asked as he handed her a glass.

Mia took it with a murmured thanks and curled up in one corner of the sofa. So, they were going to do this 'let's get to know each other for real' thing now. Why did it make her feel so edgy? This was what she'd wanted, or at least what she'd *said* she'd wanted—them opening up to each other. Or at least, Santos opening up to her. Truth be told, she wasn't sure she felt like reciprocating. She wasn't used to it, because keeping her emotions close to her chest was a way of staying safe. But surely she could talk about the ancient history of her childhood without it hurting too much?

'A lot was a lot,' she told him frankly. 'Sometimes every few months.' Or even every few weeks, depending on what events had led them to leave...again. 'My mum didn't let any moss grow on her rolling stone, shall we say.' *To put it mildly.*

'Still, that sounds rather disruptive.' Santos cocked his head, his gaze sweeping over her. 'Did you enjoy that much moving around?'

Mia shrugged. 'I didn't know anything different, I guess.' And it was what she'd chosen for herself as an adult—moving from place to place, never getting close or caring too much. As much as she longed for something more, she wasn't sure she knew how to be any different. Maybe that was another reason why their marriage hadn't worked.

And yet, with Santos she'd felt safe for the very first time in her life. She'd felt as if she'd found somewhere— and with *someone*—she wanted to stay.

'Still.' Santos took a sip of his punch, his dark gaze tracking her over the rim of his glass. 'I imagine it must have been quite difficult to have to make new friends so often.'

Mia let out a hollow little laugh. 'Well, after a while you stop trying. Good thing I've always liked my own company.'

He was silent for a moment, absorbing that. Mia felt she was revealing more than she'd meant to, and she didn't even know what it was. What did Santos think about her unorthodox childhood, about the way it had shaped her? What did *she*?

'Where is your mother now?' he asked and she felt a little splinter of shock that he didn't even know this about her. How was it that in their admittedly brief marriage they hadn't covered this stuff?

Because you didn't want to talk about it. You still don't.

'She died when I was seventeen,' Mia told him. 'Cancer. She never went to the doctor, so it wasn't caught in time. In the end, it was pretty quick.'

'I'm sorry,' Santos said quietly. 'I know how hard it is to lose a parent.'

Mia knew he'd lost his father when he'd been just a bit older, although, like her, he hadn't seemed to want to talk about it…and she hadn't asked. When someone didn't want to be asked many questions, they tended not to ask questions of others.

'I think you were probably closer to your father than I was to my mother. It didn't hurt as much as you might think.' Her mother had never really been interested in her as a person, never mind as a daughter.

He frowned. 'Even so, a parent is still a formative person in your life. My father was in mine.' The slight pause he gave was the perfect opportunity for Mia to jump in and ask a question, but he continued before she could think of what exactly she wanted to say—or summon the courage to say it. 'Still, that's very young to be left all on your own. What did you do? Did you have any relatives to take you in, support you?'

Mia took a sip of her drink, mainly to stall for time. She

really didn't want his pity, and yet she feared she would get it when she told him, which was probably why she never had. 'No, there wasn't anyone like that,' she replied, trying to keep her tone brisk and matter of fact. 'But you know, it was fine. I was working by then, anyway. I left school when my mum got sick. I was able to support myself.'

She'd waitressed in a diner and rented a room in a shabby house outside New York City. It had been a lonely existence, sordid and small, and she'd moved on as soon as she'd saved enough for a plane ticket. She hadn't looked back—had never looked back.

Santos, predictably, looked horrified. 'But you were only seventeen! A child…'

'Did you think of yourself as a child at that age?' Mia challenged, and Santos fell silent. 'Besides, a hundred years ago, or even fifty, sixteen-year-olds got married and had babies,' Mia replied, and then wished she hadn't brought it all up. 'All I'm saying is,' she said quickly, 'Sometimes you have to grow up fast, and that can be okay. I was fine.' Her voice came out a little too stridently, and she feared he didn't actually believe her. There was the pity in the softening of his eyes, the downturn of his mouth.

Mia gritted her teeth. She didn't want anyone feeling sorry for herself, and especially not Santos. Yes, her childhood had been hard, harder even than she'd told him, and she hadn't grown up with the kind of privilege and wealth he had, but she'd been *fine*, darn it. She'd made her way; she'd had friends in every place she'd lived, she'd never truly suffered and, in the end, she'd come out all the stronger. Hadn't she?

'I'm not saying it wasn't tough sometimes,' she admitted. 'But I survived—thrived, even,' she added, in something of a challenge. 'Anyway, enough about me. Let's talk about you.'

* * *

Santos kept his body relaxed as he leaned back against the sofa. 'All right,' he said easily. 'Let's talk about me.'

Mia looked surprised by his instant acquiescence and he supposed she would be. It wasn't his usual way, but he was trying to be different, better. And, he realised, she needed a break from the deep dive into her childhood. No matter how much Mia insisted she was absolutely fine, Santos suspected that kind of turbulent upbringing had to have left scars.

Besides, he could talk about himself now, because he'd had a lot of time last night to think about all the things she'd said, about how he hadn't shared his feelings, and he'd acknowledged the truth of that—he hadn't. He'd been taught not to; taught that a strong man, an Aguila, kept control over those flimsy, ephemeral emotions. And he wasn't about to start emoting big-time now, but he could at least be a little honest. He could try.

'What is it you want to know?' he asked pleasantly while Mia tried not to gape at him. He almost smiled; he found he enjoyed confounding her. She'd put him in something of a box and he was breaking out. He was *trying*…and maybe it wasn't going to be as hard as he'd thought it would be.

'I don't know,' she admitted. 'I know you grew up on the Aguila estate, and that you went to boarding school in Barcelona, and your father died when you were twenty-one.' Yes, he'd told her all that, with very sparing details. 'But I guess I don't know how you *felt* about any of it,' she continued slowly. 'Were you close to your father?'

'Yes,' Santos replied quickly, automatically, before he'd even thought about it. He pictured his father's autocratic features—those heavy eyebrows, hooded eyes, the Roman nose and tense jaw. Whenever he pictured his father, it was with his characteristically stern expression. He'd admired his father, revered him, even, but had they actually been *close*?

It was, Santos realised, a question he wasn't sure he could answer and that made him feel...uneasy, wrongfooted. One question in, and already this was starting to feel harder than he'd hoped.

'He was a man of incredible strength and integrity,' he continued after a moment. 'I always hoped to follow in his footsteps.'

'Hoped?' Mia repeated. She'd tucked her legs up under her and she was resting her chin in her hand, her hair loose and wavy about her shoulders, its auburn strands glinting in the sunlight, her freckles standing out on her nose. 'Do you not think you have?'

'I suppose the verdict is still out,' Santos replied with a small smile. He was thirty-four, fifteen years younger than his father when he'd died. He'd done his best to live as a man of his word. He'd improved the Aguila estates and managed its many investments and property interests with honesty and integrity. But did he feel as good, as strong, a man as his father? No, he realised, he did not. He didn't think he ever would, and he wasn't sure he could even say why...only that it was deep-seated, ingrained and certain.

'You've been in charge of the Aguila estate for, what, thirteen years?' Mia raised her golden eyebrows. 'Why is the verdict still out?'

Santos shrugged, discomfited. 'I don't know. I suppose because I still don't feel like I've lived up to his standard.' This was far more honest than he'd ever been before with anyone, and it was harder than he'd thought—a lot harder. 'Maybe I'll always feel that way,' he said lightly. 'Maybe every child feels that way about a parent who was...a large presence in their life. It doesn't necessarily mean anything.' For some reason, he felt as if this meant-to-be careless remark revealed even more about him. Maybe they should stop talking about their pasts.

'Do you *like* managing the estate?' Mia asked. 'I mean, do you enjoy it?'

'Yes,' Santos said again, just as quickly as before. 'It's… in my blood. I can't imagine not doing it.' Which was true enough. As the only Aguila son, he'd been born to it, brought up to it and instructed every day about what it meant.

'That doesn't really answer the question,' Mia pointed out with a small, wry smile.

He nodded in acknowledgement, conceding her point. 'I do enjoy it,' he replied after a moment. 'Not every bit, every minute—because a lot of management work is nothing more than tedious administration—but safeguarding something, nurturing it, watching it grow…'

He thought of the estate: the main house nearly six hundred years old; its walls steeped in history; the orange and olive groves that stretched almost all the way to the Sierra de las Nievas… But he didn't always like thinking about that: the tragic scene he hadn't been able to prevent happening in that shadowy space; the tart smell of Seville orange sharpening the air as his father had gasped for breath, his arms outstretched towards Santos as he'd begged him to help him live…

Santos pushed the thought away, as he always did, because he could not bear to remember.

'All that, I love,' he told Mia firmly. 'And the estate workers…from the families who have harvested the oranges and olives for generations to the staff who work in the house…feel like my family. I have a responsibility to them…one I take very seriously.'

Mia was silent for a moment, her expression pensive. 'We're even more different than I thought we were,' she finally said, reflectively. Santos's heart sank even as irritation spiked through him. *That* was her take-away?

'You've had all these people surround you, people who you view as family,' she elaborated, her gaze still pensive and distant. 'And you've been rooted in one place, so much so that it's become an integral part of you. Whereas I've never been in a place long enough to call it home, and I don't have any family at all.' She spoke matter-of-factly, without any self-pity, and Santos was pretty sure she didn't want him feeling sorry for her. The differences in their backgrounds were indeed stark, but that didn't mean they were insurmountable. He hoped that wasn't what she was implying.

'I suppose,' he said after a moment, 'There are advantages and disadvantages to both. You had a kind of freedom I could never even dream of.'

She smiled faintly, her eyebrows lifting. 'Would you dream of it?'

It was an intrusive question, and one that made him stiffen defensively, although he kept his voice mild. 'Yes, on occasion, as I imagine most people do.'

She nodded, still looking thoughtful. 'So, if I had freedom…what did you have?'

'Security, I suppose,' he replied. 'And…a sense of belonging. Of knowing who you are.' He'd certainly always known that. He was an Aguila, a man of his word, in control of his destiny and his world. A man who did not succumb to emotion or weakness, who shouldered responsibility with ease as a glad burden.

And yet he'd thrown that all away, recklessly but also with joy, when he'd married Mia. He'd enjoyed it, a fact which brought him shame and confusion, but which he still didn't regret. He might be an Aguila, but he wanted Mia. And somehow both of those things had to work together. He would make sure that they did.

An emotion flickered across her face, but Santos couldn't tell what it was. She drained her drink and placed the empty glass on the coffee table. 'Yes, I suppose you're right,' she said as she leaned back against the sofa. The closed-off look on her face made him decide not to press. They'd shared a lot already, and maybe it was enough for now.

'So,' she asked after a moment, her tone turning determinedly bright, 'When do we get to Amorgos?'

'We're just off the coast of Barcelona now,' he told her. 'And it's another two days' sailing to the Cyclades. But before then…'

He paused, feeling hesitant, although he wasn't sure why. Maybe it was because last night, whether she'd wanted to or not, Mia had shown him how fragile she truly was. Fragile, and yet also wonderfully strong. But he felt the need as well as the desire to treat her tenderly, as well as giving her agency and choice, even in matters as small as this.

'I thought perhaps we could stop in Barcelona,' he suggested. 'And do some shopping. You've only got that back pack you brought with you, and as it happens I didn't pack for a significant time away. We could stay in the city for a few days and then head to Amorgos after, if that's agreeable to you?'

Mia considered the matter, her head tilted thoughtfully to one side. 'I feel bad, buying more clothes when I have a whole wardrobe back in Seville.'

None of which she'd taken with her. He'd bought them for her gladly, wanting to shower her with presents, but she'd barely worn any of the clothes or jewels. He hadn't quite clocked that until now. Why hadn't she? Santos decided it wasn't a question for just then.

'Unfortunately, your clothes are in Seville and not here,' he replied lightly. 'And I imagine you could do with a few more items, as could I. Besides…' He kept his voice light, even a little suggestive. 'It could be fun.'

Their gazes met and held, memory unspooling between them in a long, lovely, golden thread. Memories of all they'd shared together, physically and, yes, emotionally, because making love with Mia had felt emotional. Spiritual, even, if it wasn't too crazy to think that way, their bodies joined, their hearts and minds as well.

And two nights in a five-star hotel in Barcelona sharing a bedroom…a *bed*…well, yes, Santos thought that could be very *fun* indeed. It had been a long time since they'd so much as kissed—months…since before the miscarriage, even. Things had become tense when Mia had clearly been less than pleased about her pregnancy. Santos had hoped she'd come round, but the pregnancy had ended before she'd got the chance…and made everything worse between them.

Looking at Mia now, seeing the way her eyes darkened and her lips parted, her breath coming out in a soft, unsteady sigh, Santos wanted that part of their marriage back again—badly. Because that part had always worked exceedingly well…and maybe it would even help to heal the other parts too.

Mia kept his gaze as she answered, forming the words slowly, with clear deliberation. 'Yes,' she agreed, a small smile curving her lips, and Santos's blood surged. 'That would be…fun.'

CHAPTER SEVEN

IN ALL HER travels Mia had never been to Barcelona. The city stretched before her now in a sea of terracotta buildings and stretches of vivid green grass punctuated with the electrifying and elaborate architecture the city was known for. Before her lay the prow-like Natural History Museum, the rumpled roof of the Santa Caterina market and, of course, the wedding-cake spires of Gaudi's Sagrada Familia cathedral, still unfinished after nearly one hundred and fifty years. All of it was a feast for the eyes, the senses, and Mia could scarcely take everything in as she and Santos left the confines of the yacht for the city.

They'd moored the yacht at the exclusive Marina Port Vell right in the centre of town. Santos had arranged for a car to be waiting for them to whisk them away to the penthouse suite of the Mandarin Hotel on Passeig de Gràcia, in the beating heart of the city's luxury shopping district.

Even though Mia had lived with Santos in some style for several months, the wealth and luxury had never quite felt real; she'd never felt as if such things could be trusted. In the imposing rooms and galleries of the Aguila hacienda, with its ancient oil paintings and ornate woodwork, Mia had felt like a gawking visitor, and sometimes an unwanted one at that. Certainly his mother, although doing her best to be gracious, had been unenthused by her only son's choice, and in truth Mia could hardly blame her. If she'd been in a similar situation, she would probably have been horrified.

During their short time at the estate, she and Santos had never ventured far, save for a few dinners out in Seville, and the days had often been long and empty because he'd been so busy with his work. She remembered wandering the rooms of the hacienda, feeling entirely out of place, his mother eyeing her narrowly, no doubt wondering how long she'd last. Well, not very long, as it had turned out. She hadn't even met Santos's sister Marina, who lived in Madrid.

Now, strolling into the elegant foyer of the hotel as the porter sprang to attention to take their bags, Mia felt as if she was experiencing something else entirely—truly the honeymoon they'd never had.

'I've never actually been in a penthouse,' she remarked when they'd taken the lift up and she walked through the stylised rooms of the hotel's best suite on the top floor. Everything was sleek and sharp, with lots of streamlined angles and modern art. A set of sliding glass doors led to their own private rooftop terrace overlooking the old town. There were two bedrooms, including a stunning master suite with its own sumptuous bathroom, its gold-plated fixtures gleaming; a kitchen, a living room, dining room and a study. They had a butler at their beck and call and the use of a private car for their entire stay. It felt extraordinary…decadent.

Admittedly, she'd had similar privilege back in Seville. The staff at the Aguila estate numbered in the dozens, and everything had been the height of old-world luxury. Yet somehow this felt different—more personal, perhaps— because it was just the two of them. There were no sober-faced staff standing by to intimidate her, no censorious mother-in-law to impress or avoid.

Until she'd fled, she hadn't realised just how oppressive she'd found the whole experience, Mia reflected—such as her mother-in-law's careful yet pointed reminders of which fork to use for which course at the elaborate family dinners, while Mia had fumbled and dropped a spoon. Such as her remarks about how Mia would have to educate herself on Spanish customs and manners, making her feel like an absolute yokel. She recalled how *busy* Santos had always been so busy, managing a massive estate. And how extraneous she'd seemed to everyone, wandering around the empty rooms, trying not to feel lost, homesick for… what?…a place she'd never even known.

Yes, thankfully this was all different. She could breathe more easily here…except when she thought of what might happen later that night, and then her breathing hitched as her heart started to race with anticipation. She didn't think she'd imagined the look of blatant intent simmering in Santos's eyes when he'd suggested coming to Barcelona. Was he expecting her to share his bed tonight? Did she want to?

Part of her, a very large part, ached to be in his arms again. Ached to feel loved, even if she knew she still couldn't trust that it was real. Another part told her to be cautious, to guard her body along with her heart. They hadn't so much as brushed lips since before the miscarriage. There had been a reason for that.

'Why don't you relax?' Santos suggested as he strolled through the penthouse as if he owned it. He was a man totally at ease in this world in a way that Mia doubted she ever would be. Yet another difference between them— she was mentally chalking them up, trying not to let the sheer number dispirit her. They were there, though, and they mattered. She had convinced herself they didn't when she'd been swept away in the first whirlwind of their romance, but over the difficult months of their marriage she had come to realise just how much they did...whether Santos was willing to acknowledge it or not.

'When are we going to go shopping?' she asked.

'I called a few boutiques and arranged for them to stay open for us privately,' Santos told her, as if it was a small matter to arrange such a thing. 'So, we can suit ourselves with the timings, but we do have a dinner reservation for eight. I thought we'd appreciate not having to deal with the crowds.'

'The *hoi polloi*?' Mia replied wryly, and he shrugged.

'Yes, if you like. Do you feel differently?'

She knew he was doing his best to be thoughtful and considerate, and she appreciated it; she *did*. And yet... 'No, not really, but... *I'm* the *hoi polloi*, Santos.' It simply had to be said. 'The great unwashed, as it were.' She was not even half-joking although she kept her tone light. 'I hope you don't mind rubbing elbows with *me*.'

He frowned before deliberately turning the corners of his mouth up into a smile. 'You know I don't, Mia.'

'I know, it's just...' Heaven knew, she wasn't trying to pick a fight, but these things had to be pointed out. They *mattered*. 'Another way in which we're different,' she finished before adding resolutely, because perhaps this needed to be said too, 'Maybe too different.'

Santos folded his arms, his expression turning obdurate in a way she remembered all too well. He really could be the most stubborn man. 'You seem determined to believe that such things are insurmountable.'

'I'm just trying to be a realist.'

'Which is what all pessimists say,' he teased, unfolding

his arms and walking towards her with them held out, as if he was going to catch her up into an embrace, although he stopped short of that as he came to stand in front of her. 'No, you're not of some ancient, aristocratic lineage. So what? I don't care.'

'Maybe you should,' Mia returned, feeling compelled now to an honesty to which she'd never dared give voice before. Once she started, it felt hard to stop. 'Your mother does, I imagine, and don't you think your father would have as well? Maybe your sister, too?'

As soon as she asked the question, Mia realised she'd struck a nerve, a painful one. Santos stilled, the teasing smile dropping from his face like the mask it clearly had been, his arms falling to his sides. 'This isn't about my mother,' he said after a moment, his tone repressive, hinting at a latent anger underneath. 'Or my father. And my sister definitely wouldn't care about anything like that. She lives her own life as a textile designer in Madrid.' His expression softened briefly. 'I hope you meet her one day. I'm sorry you didn't before.'

Mia suspected she hadn't because his mother hadn't wanted her to. She'd wanted to keep Mia apart, to wait and see if she lasted.

'Isn't it about them, at least a little bit?' Mia challenged quietly. 'You told me yourself you wanted to follow in your father's footsteps, and that you feared you never could. Marrying me… Isn't that part of all that fear? Your father must have wanted you to marry some—some blueblood, someone of your social standing and pedigree.'

Not an illegitimate American waif who had never had a home to call her own. In light of all that, Mia supposed his mother had been as welcoming as she possibly could have been. Her frostiness had to have been expected; at least she hadn't been outright cruel, even if Mia had longed for so much more. She'd wanted a home, a family, and she'd found neither.

Santos swung away from her. 'Let's not talk about all that, Mia,' he said gruffly. 'I don't want to be mired in the past. We're here now. Let's enjoy ourselves.'

Which was a pretty effective way to shut down the whole conversation without addressing any of the issues, but Mia accepted it…for now. She was as weary as he was of raking over the past, and they only planned to be in Barcelona for a few nights. She wanted to enjoy herself just as much as he did.

'Okay,' she said, and then, wanting to be as honest as she could, added, 'I'm not trying to pick a fight, Santos, or make things more difficult than they need to be. It's just… I'm afraid that this stuff matters.'

He turned back to her with a smile that seemed forced, his eyes still shadowed. 'I know,' he said, coming up to her and resting his hands on her shoulders. 'I know.' He gazed down at her for a moment and then slowly he drew her towards him. Mia came in a few faltering steps, her heart starting to beat rather hard. Was he going to kiss her? His expression looked too sorrowful for that.

He drew her right up to him, so her breasts were brushing his chest, making them ache with both memory and desire. Every time he'd touched her, she'd come alive. She'd had no idea a man could make her feel that way, like little sparks setting off all over her skin. *That* hadn't changed, she acknowledged as she felt the warmth of his palms through the thin cotton of her T-shirt.

His breath fanned her hair and his hands were warm

and solid on her shoulders. For a few seconds, they simply stood there, breathing each other in. The ache of desire inside Mia was spreading, taking her over and making her sway. She wanted him to touch her, to kiss her. He must feel how much she wanted him to.

Then slowly, deliberately, he pressed his lips to her forehead. Mia closed her eyes. There was something infinitely sweet and tender about the gesture; it felt like a seal as well as a promise. His lips lingered on his skin and then he eased back with a smile, although his eyes still looked sad.

'We'll get through all this,' he told her. 'We will. But today…tonight…let's just have fun. We haven't done that for quite a while.'

Not since those first heady days in Portugal, when everything had felt electric. 'I know,' she whispered, and for the first time since he'd come back into her life she felt a pang of genuine sorrow for the loss of all they'd once shared. She *missed* the way they'd been together.

Once she'd made the decision to leave, she'd been so determined to convince herself it hadn't been real. She'd been so desperate to write her feelings off as foolish infatuation, as a dreaded fling, that she hadn't let herself think about just how sweet, how powerful and poignant things had truly been between them…at least at first. Now, for a few achingly sweet moments, she let herself remember. She let herself *feel*…and want.

Gently, Santos squeezed her shoulders. 'The shops should be opening for us in about an hour, if you want to get ready.'

'All right,' she whispered, and she slipped from beneath his hands, her whole body aching with remembered and reawakened desire.

* * *

As Mia disappeared into the bedroom, Santos swung away from her, fighting a rising tide of sexual frustration as well as alarm and even fear at what she'd brought up.

Don't you think your father would have as well?

The question had been painfully pointed, more than Mia could possibly know, because he absolutely knew, one hundred percent, that his father would have wanted him to marry elsewhere. His father had picked out his bride when he'd been just seventeen years old—Isabella Ruiz, the daughter of an old business associate with a lineage as esteemed as his own. Santos had nothing against the girl. He'd met her on various occasions and found her meek and willing, obedient and hopeful. He'd told himself he would be willing to marry her eventually, and yet as the months and then years had passed, and his reluctance hadn't faded, he'd realised the only thing to do was put them both of their misery.

He'd asked her to meet him for dinner and explained that he didn't feel they were suited. He hadn't gone deeper than that, and in the end he hadn't needed to, because Isabella had been relieved. She'd fallen in love with someone else and, while she would have married Santos out of duty, she was glad to be free…and so was he.

His mother had been disappointed, but Santos had assured her that he would find a suitable bride. And so he had, although he acknowledged Mia was hardly what his mother had expected. Still, with time, he'd believed she would come round.

'I'm ready.'

He turned to see Mia come out of the bedroom; she'd changed into a pale-pink sundress with straps that tied on her shoulders, and made Santos instantly, overwhelmingly, want to release the bows and watch the dress slither down her body, revealing the perfect, golden flesh underneath he remembered so well.

Later, he told himself. He hoped…

'Wonderful.' He kept his gaze on her face even though he ached to let it rove over her curves, slender yet lush. 'Shall we go?'

Almost shyly, she nodded. This was new for both of them, he realised—the seeming normality of it. They were moving on, not just from the pain surrounding the miscarriage, but the novel, heady passion of those first few weeks together.

Real love is something that roots down and grows, Mia had said. Santos hoped that was what was happening right here. He hadn't let himself think about love when he'd first gone to find Mia; he'd just known that he wanted her back in his life. He'd told himself he was being a man of his word…yet already he knew his feelings for Mia were so much than that. Maybe they really were love, or at least the start of it.

He took her arm as they strolled into the lift, and she let him, resting her hand on his forearm. 'So, what boutiques do you have this private arrangement with?' she asked a bit teasingly.

'Only a few, but we can go in any shop that takes your fancy. I don't mind. Trust me, I will enjoy buying you whatever you like.'

He'd bought her so many clothes and jewels when they'd first married. He'd showered her with designer gowns, and diamond necklaces she hadn't worn, but in hindsight Santos realised he hadn't actually had her choose any of it. Such a notion hadn't even occurred to him. He'd simply ordered everything in her size from the most elite and expensive designers and had them delivered to the estate.

She must have worn some of those clothes at the formal dinners his mother still insisted on, he acknowledged—five interminable courses, eaten mostly in silence—yet he found he couldn't picture her in one. All he could remember, he realised with a pang, was the look of strain on her pale face as she'd studied the five rows of cutlery on either side of her plate. Knowing now what he did about her upbringing, he realised just how strange and overwhelming coming to the Aguila estate must have been for her...and he hadn't made it any easier.

He let out a startled, 'Oof!' as Mia poked him in the ribs. 'You've gone quiet,' she told him with a small smile. '*And* you're scowling. What's wrong?'

'Nothing's wrong,' he said quickly, more unsettled by that memory and all it could signify than he wanted to be. 'I'm just looking forward to seeing you try on all these clothes.' He allowed himself a wolfish smile. 'Maybe you'll need help with some of the zips.'

To his delight, Mia blushed. 'Maybe I will,' she murmured, looking away, her cheeks still washed with colour.

The first boutique they went to on the Passeig de Gràcia was one of those insufferable places with bony, sharp-faced women swarming them as soon as they crossed the threshold, all face lifts and haute couture.

'Señor Aguila,' one of them purred. 'Always a pleasure to do business with your esteemed family. How is your dear mother?' Her gaze flicked to Mia, with the most cursory glance, and back again. 'And who is this? A...friend?'

'My *wife*,' Santos replied rather tersely, seeing how stricken Mia looked by the whole, awful experience.

Like a flock of crows flapping their wings, the women immediately gave him their congratulations, and assured them both they would like nothing better than to dress the new Señora Aguila.

Santos glanced again at Mia, who still looked pale and a bit sick, and found himself shaking his head. 'I believe we'll go elsewhere,' he stated firmly and, taking Mia by the arm, he exited the shop without a word.

Mia let out a trembling laugh as they emerged onto the pavement flanking the wide, tree-lined boulevard.

'What was that all about?' she asked. 'Why did you leave?'

'I didn't like them—sanctimonious, snobbish busybodies.' He was surprised by how much he meant it. He didn't think he would ever have noticed such things before, or maybe even cared, but he'd felt acutely conscious of it today. He hated the way they'd looked at Mia, as if dismissing her, before he'd told them who she was.

Mia glanced at him, wide-eyed but also sceptical. 'You don't need to do that just for my sake, Santos. I mean, I appreciate it, but I should be able to handle this world. I'll have to learn, anyway, if you want me to be part of it.'

'Maybe *I* don't want to be part of it,' Santos countered.

Her eyes widened further. 'The world that's in your blood?' she returned. 'That's so much a part of you? You can't mean that.'

'It's not all of a piece,' he argued. 'The Aguila estate is in my blood, yes—oranges and olives and history—but that doesn't mean some skinny, supercilious clothes horse in Barcelona has to be.'

To his surprise and delight, she let out a laugh of such genuine amusement—that open, easy sound of joy he remembered—that several passers by turned their heads, curious and charmed. He liked making her laugh, he realised. He liked the fact that he was starting to understand her more than he ever had before, when he'd first been so fascinated. Already their relationship felt deeper, more important and *real*, and he was glad.

'Fair enough,' she conceded, smiling wider still, her eyes sparkling. She looked so much like she used to back when he'd first met her that he had the urge to catch her up in his arms and kiss her senseless. 'Fair enough,' she said again, and then, still smiling up at him, she slipped her arm through his as they walked to the next boutique.

Fortunately, the sales associates of that establishment were far more amenable, seeming genuinely friendly, and whisking Mia away to a dressing room to try on various outfits while Santos made himself comfortable on a velvet sofa outside the curtain. He slid his phone out of his pocket, intending to check his messages, realising he hadn't so much as looked at them in over twenty-four hours, something that was incredibly unlike him.

He started scrolling through them, glimpsing several from his mother as well as his estate manager, along with a few from other business interests. He texted a quick message to his estate manager, and another to the manager of the head office in Madrid, asking them both to handle anything pressing. He found himself swiping to close the messaging app, and then put his phone back in his pocket with something like relief. He didn't want to deal with all that now; he didn't want it to interfere with what was developing between Mia and him.

'Anything I'm allowed to see?' he called out, and a moment later Mia pulled back the curtain, smiling at him shyly. She was wearing a gown and, oh, what a gown. It was the aquamarine of her eyes, with twisted, Grecian-style straps and a plunging neckline that somehow still managed to seem modest yet so very intoxicating. The dress clung to her hips and then fell in a swirl of shimmering fabric to below her ankles.

'I don't know that I'll ever have an occasion to wear something like this,' she told him, 'But the sales assistants both insisted. They said it matched my eyes.'

'It does and we'll take it,' Santos replied immediately. His blood felt as if it were on fire; it took all his strength simply to sit there on the sofa rather than sweep Mia into his arms and slip the straps from her shoulders. 'As for an occasion to wear it, you already do. Tonight, for dinner with me.' And later, he very much hoped he'd have the occasion to take it *off* her.

Mia must have seen something of that in his eyes, for her smile faltered for a second before returning in force, curling slowly as her gaze swept over him, lingering in a way that made his blood heat all the more. His palms positively itched to touch her and caress her.

'I guess it's a winner, then,' she said and, with that smile promising all sorts of wonderful things, she slowly drew the curtain closed again.

Santos leaned back against the sofa, his breath coming out in a rush as he shifted where he sat to ease the undeniable ache in his groin. He was very much looking forward to dinner, he decided, and, more importantly, *afterwards*.

CHAPTER EIGHT

MIA WAS UNDENIABLY OVERDRESSED, even for dinner in the Michelin-starred restaurant Santos had chosen for their evening meal, but she didn't care because she felt beautiful and, more importantly, desirable. Together it was a very potent and heady mix. Hours later, she was still tingling from the heated look Santos had given her in the boutique when she'd come out of the dressing room wearing this gown. It was a look that had seemed to sizzle the air between them and remind her of just how good they'd been together.

One of the sales assistants had murmured laughingly as she'd helped Mia out of the dress, '*Señor* clearly only has eyes for his wife. *Oh, la la!*' She'd clucked her tongue, smiling and shaking her head, while Mia had blushed.

And Mia only had eyes for him, she thought. Whatever else was going on in their marriage, whatever else was out-and-out wrong, and maybe even impossible to fix, they still had that. And maybe *that* wasn't a small thing. Maybe it was actually quite important, a way of connecting that didn't require words that could be misconstrued, silences that felt oppressive and accusing. It was certainly exciting, anyway, and just now it felt just about all she could think about.

But first dinner, and in one of the most expensive and

exclusive restaurants in all of Barcelona. Santos had reserved a table for two in its own private alcove on a rooftop terrace overlooking the city, sheltered from the other diners by velvet-draped partitions.

As the *maître d'* guided them to their table, Mia noticed other diners glancing at them in curiosity, which was understandable, considering she was dressed as if she were attending the Oscars. She didn't care that she might appear a little ridiculous, though. She just liked the way Santos looked at her, with both heat and admiration in his eyes, every gaze lingering on her as if he were savouring the sight.

Still, the gown *was* a bit much… 'I think I am a bit overdressed,' she remarked wryly as she sat down.

'I think you look perfect,' Santos replied. He looked pretty perfect himself, in an expensively tailored navy suit jacket and trousers, his white shirt, unbuttoned at the throat, the perfect foil for his bronze skin. His dark hair was brushed back from his face, the silver and gold links of his expensive watch glinting on his wrist. 'As beautiful as you did the first time I saw you,' he added, and Mia couldn't help but let out a little laugh.

'Really? Because, if I recall correctly, back then I was wearing a T-shirt and cut-off jeans.'

'I know. And you looked beautiful to me.'

Mia shook her head slowly. She wasn't quite sure what to do with these compliments; there'd been months of icy silences, of disapproval, hurt and guilt, so that she no longer felt as though she could trust the kind words that were coming out of Santos's mouth. Yet maybe, for the first time since he'd come back into her life, she wanted to.

'Why did you come up and talk to me that night, anyway?' she asked. The more she had come to know Santos, the more she realised how utterly out of character for him it had been. He was as sensible and strait-laced as they came, considering every angle before he made a move, thinking through all the options, making sure he picked the wisest one.

And, as for marrying her after just two weeks, he might as well have had a personality transplant. Why had he done it? Did she really want to know? What if it wasn't the reason she hoped it was?

'I'm not really sure,' he admitted. 'A moment of…of madness, I suppose. Very unlike me, as I'm sure you've gathered.'

A moment of madness? Mia wasn't sure how she felt about that. And yet, what had it been for her? A sense of slotting into place, of belonging in a way she never had before, right from the beginning. She'd jumped in with both feet and hadn't let herself think about any repercussions because she'd wanted that—him—so badly.

Except it hadn't turned out to be real…

'I couldn't help myself,' Santos admitted, drawing Mia back into their conversation. 'There was something about you, Mia…there still is. I was…utterly compelled.' He let out a little laugh, shaking his head. 'As fanciful as I know that sounds.'

'And completely out of character,' Mia added. 'Of course, I didn't know that at the time.'

'It was out of character,' Santos agreed with a nod. 'But it felt right.'

But did it still feel right, Mia wondered, nearly six months on? And, even if something *felt* right, did that mean it actually was? Those differences between them were still there, and stark. Whether they were insurmountable remained to be seen.

A waiter came with their menus and, as Mia opened hers, she almost laughed. It was full of incomprehensible-sounding dishes, things she'd never heard of, never mind had: what was arepa, agrodolce, mochi or gurnard? She'd never heard of any of them, and it was a salient reminder of how different they really were.

Santos seemed to be taking the menu in his stride, perusing the offerings with lively interest while she just felt lost…and that was before she'd counted the forks. Six, in total, even more than his mother had had for those interminable dinners, along with knives and spoons. She hadn't noticed them when they'd first sat down, but now she saw the table was covered in cutlery and it filled her with dread.

They're just forks and knives, she told herself. They didn't have to mean anything. And anyway, she thought she knew which one to use. Santos's mother, Evalina, had murmured to her to start from the outside and work her way in. It had been a kindness, Mia realised, even if it had embarrassed her at the time, and Evalina's tone had seemed a bit too pointed.

'What is it?' Santos asked, looking up from his menu with a frown. He seemed attuned to her moods in a way that was both gratifying and a little alarming. How could he sense what she was feeling about cutlery, for heaven's sake, when he'd misunderstood so completely about something as important as their own child?

But she didn't want to think that way, Mia reminded herself, not tonight. 'I'm just wondering what to order,' she admitted. 'All of it looks incomprehensible.'

'Yes, I have no idea what onglet is, and I can't decide if it sounds tasty or not.'

'You don't know what it is?' Mia asked in surprise, and Santos raised his eyebrows.

'Is there a reason why I should?'

She shook her head slowly, bemused at how confounded she felt that her assumption about this very small thing had been wrong. 'I don't know… I just assumed you knew everything on the menu—that you'd had it all a million times before. Just like you know which fork to use.' She glanced wryly down at the full array of silverware.

'I just follow the golden rule,' Santos told her. 'Start from the outside and work your way in.'

Mia let out a little laugh. 'That's what your mother told me.'

'That's what she told me as well, so it must be right.' He smiled at her, his face full of warmth, and her heart felt as if it were turning over. It was such a small thing—a matter of *forks*—and yet it felt much bigger. It felt as though the wryly wagging finger of providence was reminding her that they weren't as different as she feared they might be.

Of course he knew what onglet was, just another word for a certain cut of steak, but Mia clearly didn't know that, and Santos was desperate to put her at her ease. To reassure her that she belonged in this world, she belonged with *him*. A little white lie was certainly understandable, permissible, and he had been telling the truth when he'd said his mother had told him about the forks. It was sound advice and, with a pang, it had made him remember how lost Mia had looked at the dining-room table in Seville.

A bit, like how she looked now, he worried. He was acutely conscious of the way worry chased across her features like shadows. She kept trying to banish it but it kept coming back. What would it take to convince her they belonged together?

If you really do?

No, he didn't want those doubts to settle in his mind, his heart, again. He'd banish that flock of cawing crows every time if he had to. They'd already addressed some of the issues, he reminded himself. They were working through things; they were getting there.

It doesn't change the truth that she didn't want your baby.

No, he wasn't going to go there, Santos told himself. Not tonight, when Mia was looking so beautiful and, despite the worry flickering across her face, so happy. Not when all he wanted to do—*still*—was take her in his arms and kiss those softly parted lips. He would not let the doubts in. He certainly wouldn't let them win, not tonight.

'So,' Mia asked, 'Are you ordering the onglet then? Give it a try?'

Santos smiled, doing his best to banish the worries, the doubts, that maybe Mia was right and they were too different. Those differences could be overcome; they were *being* overcome already, tonight. 'Yes,' he told her. 'I think I will.'

They ate all five courses, washed down with wine, as the moon rose over the Mediterranean, washing the placid waters in silver. As the evening spooled out like a golden thread, Santos found himself relaxing, and he could tell that Mia was too from the way she tilted her head back as she laughed and the smiles that came far more often, and with ready ease. Several times she reached over and touched his hand—which he treasured—her fingers brushing his in a way that made every nerve tingle with anticipation.

As the hours passed, he found the easy languor of his

mood being replaced by a far tauter, and more wonderful, expectation. *Tonight*... Tonight, they would be together.

It was nearing midnight by the time they left the restaurant; in typical Spanish style, the night seemed young, and many people were still dining. The streets were full of tourists and Spaniards alike as they headed out into the Old Town, everyone enjoying the sultry evening, the electric sense of possibility that buzzed through Barcelona. That buzzed through him.

As they strolled down the street back to the hotel, Santos took Mia's hand, carelessly enough, twining his fingers through hers in a way that he hoped felt casual, natural. It certainly did to him, even if it also felt as if he'd put his fingers into an electrical socket, though pleasurably. Everything came pulsatingly alive. They didn't speak as they walked along, but Santos felt that sense of expectation building inside him, a towering wave of need and desire.

He hoped Mia felt it too. He hoped she remembered, as he did, just how wonderful they'd been together physically right from the first; it had felt like the purest form of communication, needing no words. He wanted that again. He wanted it *tonight*—not just for the pleasure and satisfaction he was definitely anticipating, but for *them*, for their relationship. There were so many ways for them to connect, to solidify the closeness that was growing between them, including what he hoped would happen between them tonight.

They went into the hotel and took the private lift to the penthouse, neither of them speaking, their fingers still twined. As the lift soared higher, Santos felt everything in him tauten all the more with expectation, with hope as well as desire. This was going to happen. It needed to...

As the doors of the lift opened, Mia slipped her hand

from his, strolling into the penthouse ahead of him. Santos followed, shedding his suit jacket, wanting to gauge her mood correctly. As much as he wanted her right now, as fiercely as the desire was roaring through his veins, he still needed Mia to feel what he was feeling. He didn't want to have to convince her. Too much had happened between them already for that.

The rooms of the penthouse were lost in shadow as Mia walked through them, no more than a moonlit silhouette in the darkness. Santos could make out the tumble of her hair, the curve of her cheek, the swell of her breasts underneath the shimmering silk of her gown. She paused in front of the doors to the master bedroom, one slender hand resting on the frame, her back to him, revealing a golden expanse of flesh barely visible in the shadows.

Santos stood there, waiting, hoping... Should he say something, or should he wait for her to say it? If she said goodnight and closed the door, he thought it might just about kill him.

Mia turned so she was in profile, her lashes dropping down to her cheeks. She drew a breath. The very air between them seemed to quiver.

'I think,' she said softly, 'I need help with my zip.'

Santos's breath came out in a rugged shudder. 'I believe I can manage that,' he told her, his voice little more than a rasp. He came towards her slowly, his palms tingling in anticipation of touching her. He saw a small smile curve her lips and heat bloomed within him.

He stood behind her, close enough so he could feel the warmth of body, breathe in the scent that was uniquely, exquisitely her—almond and roses, sweetness and sunshine. The gown delved in a vee over her shoulder blades, the zip starting halfway down her spine. Santos's fingers whispered over her skin as he reached for the zip. He heard and felt a shudder go through her as gently, languorously, he tugged the zip down, enjoying every protracted second of the experience.

It came easily, the soft fabric of her dress parting to reveal more smooth, golden flesh. He tugged the zip down to the small of her back, pausing while she waited, her body practically quivering in anticipation, and then tugged it the rest of the way down over the curve of her bottom. The straps slipped from her shoulders so the dress slid from her hips and barely covered her breasts.

Santos took another step towards her so he was right behind her, close enough that her bottom was brushing his thighs, causing an almost unbearable ache of desire to go through him. He rested his hands on her shoulders, keeping the gown in place…for now.

'Do you need any more help?' he asked, his voice barely a breath of sound that stirred the tendril of hair on the nape of her neck. He longed to press his lips there and savour the feel of her skin.

She swallowed, and he felt her tremble. When she spoke, her voice was soft, no more than a whisper. 'I think I do.'

Slowly he pulled the dress down further so that it pooled about her waist. He bent his head to do what he'd been aching to do and pressed his lips to the warm, soft skin on the nape of her neck. A moan escaped her, soft and mewling.

Santos slipped his hands round her front and cupped her bare breasts. They felt exactly as he remembered, filling his hands with their warm, perfect weight. She let out a shuddering breath as she leaned back against him, arching her back to give him greater access, his thumbs tracing her nipples as she arched even further.

Then he slipped his hands from her breasts to her waist,

pressing her even more firmly against him. She rocked her hips back against his, and now he was the one groaning with both need and pleasure. They'd barely begun and he didn't know if he could take any more.

'Santos…' she murmured, and then she twisted to face him, her arms fumbling as they came around him. Then her lips found his and the kiss felt like a punch to the heart, a firework exploding in his brain, the first stars coming out in the night sky, shining in the darkness, reminding him of all that had been good about how they'd been together.

He deepened the kiss, his hands still on her hips, fastening her to him. Then they were stumbling backwards, laughing even as they continued to kiss, as what had been tender and intense became a blaze of passion and need.

Mia kicked the dress away, another breathless laugh escaping her as the gown lay crumpled and discarded on the floor.

'That's haute couture,' she murmured as Santos filled his hands with her breasts again. 'I should hang it up.'

'All I wanted to do with that dress was take it off,' he muttered as they fell back on the bed in a tangle of limbs. He swallowed Mia's gurgle of laughter with another consuming kiss.

This, he thought as his mind hazed with both happiness and pleasure, was all he'd ever wanted. All he'd ever need.

CHAPTER NINE

MIA LAY SPRAWLED supine on the bed as Santos knelt above her, his eyes blazing, his cheeks slashed with colour. It was both thrilling and humbling, to see and know how much he wanted her. To *feel* so wanted rocked her to her core…again.

With fingers that trembled, Santos began to unbutton his shirt. Mia raised herself onto her elbows. She was naked save for a scrap of lace, and she felt completely unashamed, unafraid.

'Let me do it,' she said, and reached for him.

Santos gazed down at her, his expression serious and intent, his eyes still blazing as she slipped the buttons from their holes. Now it was her fingers that were trembling. They'd been together more times than they could count, and yet it had never felt as intense as this; as momentous, as *sacred*. The past still lay behind them, littered with their mistakes, and yet the future felt endless and shimmering with possibility as it stretched ahead.

Mia slipped his shirt from his shoulders, revelling in the feel of his bronzed, burnished skin, the muscles taut and hard beneath her questing hands. Then she went to his belt buckle, working it from the loops. It slithered out and she tossed it to the floor as Santos chuckled softly.

The button came next, and then she eased his trousers

from his lean hips, conscious of the proud, straining length of him brushing the back of her hand as she pulled the fabric free. Santos kicked off the trousers and then divested himself of his boxer shorts as well. Mia's breath came out in an unsteady rush as she took in the full, glorious sight of him, so utterly, potently male.

'I think,' he said softly, his fingers skimming up her thigh, 'You have too many clothes on.'

She let out a choked laugh. 'Too many clothes?' She was wearing only a thong.

'Yes, too many clothes.' He hooked his finger underneath the scrap of lace and slowly, with a smile curving his mouth, tugged it downwards. Something in Mia trembled as he divested her of her last bit of armour. She was naked, utterly open and vulnerable to him, and in that moment she felt it.

Santos must have sensed something of this, for he eased down beside her, pillowing her head beneath his arm, his other hand resting on her bare midriff, bronzed fingers splayed and his thumb brushing her pubic bone. For a few seconds they simply lay there, both of them already breathing hard, yet also finding a surprising sweetness and peace in the moment. That sense of vulnerability eased, and as Mia twisted to look up at him he cupped his hand with her cheek, his thumb brushing her lips.

'I've missed you, *querida.*'

Tears stung her eyes, and she blinked them back as she pressed a kiss to the pad of his thumb. 'I've missed you too.'

He bent his head to brush a soft kiss across her mouth that started out tenderly and then deepened, the passion they'd just felt for each other blazing high and hot once more. Her legs tangled with his as she wrapped her arms around him, pressing closer. Santos slid his hand down to cup her bottom, bringing her into achingly exquisite contact with the most male part of him. She pressed even closer and he groaned.

'I want to go slowly with you,' he muttered against her mouth, and she let out a shaky laugh.

'Maybe slow is overrated.' She pushed up against him, thrilled to feel him press back as pleasure flared deep within her. 'We can do slow later.'

He slid his hand down towards her legs, cupping his hand between them, feeling how ready she already was for him.

'Are you sure?'

'*Yes*, Santos.' She pushed against his fingers, desperate now for the feel of him inside her. 'I am very sure.'

With a throaty chuckle, he rolled on top of her and braced on his forearms. He paused to glance down at her, his expression serious. Even though everything in her was aching, straining, for him to join their bodies, in that space of a second she felt that something even more important was happening.

'I love you, Mia,' he said, his voice low and sure. Her heart stuttered and for a second she could only blink up at him as he slid inside her in one sinuous movement. Out of both instinct and need she wrapped her arms around his shoulders and her legs around his waist, drawing him even more deeply into herself. Her mind was reeling from what he'd said, but her body's response to and need for him felt even more overwhelming. As he began to move in slow, sliding strokes, she matched his rhythm, the words he'd just said pulsing inside her in beat with their bodies.

I love you, Mia. I love you, Mia. I love you, Mia...

Santos's breath came out in a ragged gasp and Mia let

out a cry as their bodies moved in sync, reaching higher and higher until her climax exploded through her, her body convulsing around his as a rip tide of pleasure carried her away for a few heavenly minutes.

Santos pressed his lips to the side of her neck as the last shudders of his climax went through him. Mia's head flopped back on the pillow as she closed her eyes, feeling incredibly sated, her limbs boneless and relaxed.

I love you, Mia...

Had he meant it? He'd never actually said it before. He'd said, 'I think I'm falling in love with you,' in a voice full of wonder in those first few crazy weeks, but it had felt like a 'maybe' or an 'if'. Then she'd got pregnant so quickly and it had all started to unravel...

There had been no 'I love you's after that.

Slowly Santos rolled off her, pressing a soft, smiling kiss to her mouth before he left the bed, slipping into the bathroom. Mia pushed her hair out of her face as she took a steadying breath. How much had what they'd just done changed things? What would Santos expect now? Should she have said 'I love you' back? *Did* she?

A low breath shuddered through her and she rolled up from the bed. She grabbed one of the hotel's towelling robes from the wardrobe and slipped her arms into its velvety-soft sleeves. Then she took her crumpled dress from the floor and hung it up because, no matter how much passion had overtaken them—and it certainly had—it was too beautiful, not to mention expensive, to be treated like that.

Santos was still in the bathroom, and Mia was starting to feel a tiny bit apprehensive. Was he regretting what they'd done, what he'd said in the heat of the moment? The words had seemed to come from somewhere deep inside him, but that didn't mean they were real.

She went to the kitchen and took a bottle of sparkling water from the sub-zero fridge, then slipped outside to the terrace. It was into the early hours now, but Barcelona was still buzzing with people, parties, music and lights, an ant-hill of activity far below the penthouse suite. The sultry breeze slid over her still-heated skin like silk as she stood at the railing and gazed down at the world below.

Mia wasn't quite sure how she felt—a mixture of bit-tersweet joy and sorrow, apprehension and hope. She re-alised she wasn't sure if she'd just made a big mistake, giving her body and a big piece of her heart to Santos, or if she'd taken a flying leap into love—and what could be better than that?

What was she still so afraid of?

Getting hurt, she supposed, having it not work out. Needing someone and finding out they didn't need you, that she wasn't enough. If her own mother hadn't been able to love her, why should anyone else?

A sigh escaped her, and she closed her eyes. All the old fears and doubts…would they ever let her go?

'How are you feeling?'

Santos's voice was quiet and concerned as he stepped out onto the terrace. He sounded as if he wanted to do a post mortem on their passion, and Mia knew she wasn't ready for that. She needed to work out how she felt first before she dealt with any of Santos's emotions. She took a quick breath and then turned around with a bright smile.

'I feel frankly wonderful,' she told him, her tone deliber-ately flippant. 'That was amazing. How do *you* feel?' She waggled her eyebrows just in case he didn't get the memo that she was keeping this light.

Santos cocked his head, his gaze turning thoughtful as it moved over her. He'd clearly got the memo and more, judging from his lack of response as well as the pensive expression on his face, but whether he was going to play along was another matter entirely.

'I feel amazing too.' He started to stroll towards her; he was wearing a pair of loose trousers and no shirt, his chest gloriously muscled and bare, crisp dark hair veeing down towards his trousers. It made desire start to wind its tendrils through Mia all over again, pulling her closer towards him even though she hadn't meant to move. 'You were amazing,' he added, reaching out one hand to loosely link his fingers with hers, drawing her even nearer. 'You *are*.'

'Well, it takes two to tango,' Mia replied teasingly.

She was going into deflection mode as a matter of instinct, a way to protect herself even as she wondered if she really needed protecting. Santos wouldn't hurt her… would he? Maybe he wouldn't mean to, but he certainly had before. She told herself she was right to be cautious.

'Mia…' His voice was low and concerned. She tensed, their hands still linked, as she wondered what he was going to say. 'We didn't use birth control.'

Relief flooded through her and she smiled, shaking her head, so her hair was sent flying. 'It's all right. I'm on the pill.'

Santos frowned, his fingers tensing on hers before he tugged them away. 'You *are*?'

She was on the *pill*? Why? And why had she never told him? They'd used condoms when they'd first got together, condoms that admittedly hadn't worked. There had been no need for birth control after the miscarriage because they hadn't slept together. They hadn't even touched.

So why the *hell* was she on the pill now?

Mia let out an uncertain little laugh, her gaze scanning his face. 'Why do you sound so…disapproving?'

He folded his arms across his chest, hating how vulnerable he felt. He'd just told her he *loved* her, for heaven's sake, the words having slipped out of their own accord, but he'd meant them…even if she hadn't said them back. And now she was telling him she was on birth control… *Why?* 'I just don't understand why you would be on the pill.'

'Um…to prevent pregnancy?' Her eyebrows drew together as she cocked her head. 'So we don't have to panic on a night like this?'

'I'd wouldn't have thought you'd be expecting "a night like this",' Santos pointed out in what he hoped was a reasonable tone, although his jaw was clenched tight. Was he overreacting to this bit of news, simply because he felt vulnerable and he didn't like that feeling? He thought they'd been on a journey together, that they'd been feeling the same sorts of things, but now he wondered. 'Considering you ran away from me *weeks* ago,' he continued, 'And you obviously had no idea I would come and find you.

'How long have you been on the pill?' It had to have been for a while; there had been no time for her to get a prescription since he'd found her on Ibiza; and, in any case, didn't a woman have to take it for a week or so before it worked reliably? Why on earth would she have needed birth control when they'd been apart?

In a blinding flash, he recalled the sexy emerald evening gown she'd worn, together with the man lounging next to her, and his initial surprise hardened into a terrible suspicion. Had more been going on there than he'd realised? Heaven knew, he'd wanted to give her the benefit of the doubt, but just now he found it hard—*very* hard.

Mia must have seen his thought process reflected on

his face, for she folded her arms, her hands lost in the voluminous sleeves of the bath robe she wore, her eyes narrowed to blue-green slits.

'Just what are you suggesting, Santos?'

What *was* he suggesting? The suspicion he'd been feeling, bordering on certainty, now teetered on the precipice of doubt. Surely he wasn't actually accusing Mia—his wife, whom he'd only just held in his arms and made sweet love to—of being *unfaithful*?

'Well?' she demanded, her voice ringing out loud and hard.

Irritation flickered through him. It wasn't unreasonable of him to wonder why his wife would be on birth control when they'd been apart for so long. 'I just asked a question,' he replied coolly. 'One that, for some reason, you haven't seemed willing to answer.'

For a second, he saw hurt flash through her eyes and her face started to crumple. A sudden, crippling guilt assailed him. What was he saying, thinking, about *Mia*?

'Mia…'

Her chin came up as her expression ironed out into something hard and unyielding. 'I believe your question was, how long have I been on the pill? I'd be *delighted* to answer you, Santos. I've been on the pill since the obstetrician who delivered our dead baby offered it to me after the procedure. You weren't there for the conversation, you see, because you'd walked out of the room.'

And then she did exactly that, storming past him back into the penthouse. He heard the slam of the bedroom door and bowed his head. He felt like an utter ass, an idiot, a *brute*. He hadn't really thought… And yet, for a few damning seconds, he'd acted as if he had. He knew it, and it made guilt and regret churn acidly inside him.

He turned to go after Mia and then decided to give her—and himself—a few moments to cool down. He needed to work out what had been going on in his mind and, more importantly, why.

Slowly, frowning in thought, Santos walked to the bar and poured himself a large whisky. Why, he wondered, had he jumped to such conclusions, and so quickly? And had Mia really faced that alone? She'd said he'd walked out of the room back at the hospital.

Those grief-stricken hours felt like a blur. She'd barely spoken to him, and he'd felt so helpless in the face of their loss—a loss he hadn't been sure she felt, at least not the way he had. The loss of their baby had brought up so many memories, stirring to life the old grief for his father that he'd thought long buried. He'd never explained any of that to Mia, had never even tried to tell her how his father had died or how guilty he'd felt. The burden of carrying on his father's name had sometimes been too heavy to bear. But surely they both had enough to be going on with without having to think about all that now?

And yet…what if it was all related—the assumptions he'd made about Mia now as well as then? *Why?* Because, Santos acknowledged starkly, on some level he felt he hadn't really known her. How could he have after just a few weeks? It was a point she'd made herself, and he hadn't been truly honest with her about his own doubts. Not that their marriage was a *mistake*, precisely, because he still meant what he'd said about taking his vows seriously. But maybe it had been precipitous, a point his mother had made with both acerbity and alarm. It had also been so utterly out of character for him; afterwards, he'd half-wondered if he'd been possessed not just by passion but by some deeper, driving need to be happy…to be *free*.

Maybe these were some of the thoughts he needed to share with Mia, instead of stubbornly insisting he hadn't had any doubts. Santos drained his whisky and then set the empty glass on the bar. Slowly he walked towards the bedroom, pausing before the closed door before he tapped once and then opened it.

Mia was curled up on the bed, her knees hugged to her chest, her tangled hair spread across the pillow and covering her face. It made pain lance through him, the regret he felt, before sharpening to an agonising point.

'Mia, I'm sorry,' he stated quietly.

She took a hitched breath, the sound making him ache. 'What,' she asked, her voice muffled and clogged with tears, 'Are you sorry for exactly, Santos? I'm just curious.'

He perched on the edge of the bed, close to her tucked-up legs. He wanted to touch her, but he decided to wait.

'For making assumptions. Not just about the birth control thing, but before, about…about the baby.' The words came stiltedly, but he still meant them, and he hoped Mia knew it. 'I know you said you weren't ready to have a baby,' he continued, 'But that didn't mean you weren't sad when you miscarried. I do realise that, even if I didn't show it or say it.'

Mia pushed her hair away from her tear-streaked face as she scooted up against the pillows. 'Why didn't you say it, Santos?' she asked quietly. 'It would have made such a difference to me.' A single tear slipped down her cheek, and she brushed it away, sniffing.

'I…don't know,' he admitted, although that felt like a cop-out. It *was*.

'I thought you blamed me,' she whispered. 'I *still* think you blame me, at least a little bit, for not wanting the baby in the first place. But we'd been married for two weeks,

Santos!' She blinked at him through her tears as she shook her head slowly. 'We'd known each other for little over a *month*. It all felt like it was happening way too fast.'

'I know.' He'd felt that too, even if he'd been pleased. He'd always wanted a family, and in all fairness he'd supposed having a baby together would cement their marriage—legitimise it in a way a barefoot ceremony on the beach in Portugal hadn't; not entirely, anyway. Perhaps he'd felt a baby would bind Mia to him more than a piece of paper did. On some level he'd been thinking that way without even fully realising it.

But he hadn't fully realised a lot of things back then, Santos acknowledged, and maybe he still didn't. He hadn't realised how Mia had struggled with so much, including adjusting to life in Seville. He hadn't considered how having a baby in that new environment might make her feel even more uncertain and afraid. And he wasn't entirely sure what was going through her mind now…but he wanted to know. He wanted her to tell him.

'Sometimes,' Mia whispered, 'I wonder why you married me. I wonder why you don't seem to regret it. Maybe you do, and the whole "vow" thing is a millstone around your neck; I don't know.' She paused and then met his gaze directly, seeming to summon her courage before she asked bluntly, 'You told me you loved me, but I… I don't know if I believe you. I believe you think you love me—'

'Mia—' he protested, although he wasn't sure what he was going to say. Did he want to double down on saying he loved her now, when she clearly wasn't going to say she loved him? Surely love wasn't a tit-for-tat thing? And yet…he felt vulnerable enough already.

A sigh escaped Mia, long and low. 'Why did you marry me, Santos? Really?'

Santos stared back at her, knowing she needed his honesty, yet not quite sure how to give it. Did he even know himself? 'Mia, if I had an easy answer, I'd give it to you,' he said slowly. 'The truth is, I… I don't even know. All I can say is, when we met, when we spent time together, I felt happier than I had in a long time—maybe ever. And I wanted that to continue.' He paused, his throat working as he continued raggedly, 'I *needed* it to.'

To his surprise, she reached for his hand, threading her fingers through his. 'Why?' she asked softly. 'Weren't you happy before?'

The questions were becoming even harder to answer. They felt more painful, more revealing.

An Aguila must always be master of his own mind and heart.

To him that had meant not admitting his weakness, his need. And yet maybe that was what Mia needed. Maybe it was what he needed too. There was a positive side to this sort of vulnerability, opening up, as well as giving. 'Not like that,' he confessed in a low voice as he gazed down at their twined fingers. 'Never like that.'

Gently Mia squeezed his fingers. When he risked a glance at her, he saw her smiling softly through her tears, and he felt a sudden pressure in his chest, a lump in his throat. Somehow, in that moment, neither of them seemed to need any more words.

CHAPTER TEN

THE BLUE-GREEN WATERS of the Aegean broke across the bow of the yacht in lacy curls of white foam as Santos stood at the helm and guided it towards the private dock at his villa on Amorgos. It had been three days since they'd left Barcelona, three glorious, sun-soaked, lazy, languorous, lovely and *loving* days.

Mia was doing her best not to over-analyse anything; simply to take every day, every moment, as it came and enjoy it for what it was. Something had shifted between Santos and her during that tumultuous evening when they'd made love, and then made up as well. They'd *had* to make up because of the hurtful things said—and thought—on both sides. Mia was very grateful for Santos's understanding, as well as his humility. He was a proud man, maybe even an arrogant one, but he'd still been able to say sorry when he'd felt the need to. Love wasn't never having to say sorry, Mia had thought ruefully, but rather the reverse: love was being willing to, however many times.

That was if Santos loved her all. She still had her doubts; saying something in the passion of a moment was different from living it out day by day.

I love you, Mia.

The memory of those words, and the thrum of his voice as he'd huskily said them, still had the power to rock Mia to the very marrow of her bones. She still didn't know how she felt about it, and more importantly how to respond. After their heart-to-heart that evening, which felt as though it had changed everything, they'd both mutually, silently, agreed on something like a truce. Or at least *silence*, but not a tense and accusing one like before. This one felt both healing, good and, more importantly, necessary. They needed simply to be with each other, rather than analysing every word that came out of their mouths.

And so, in three days, they hadn't had any 'talks with a capital T' at all. There'd been no raking over the past, remembering the loss, grief, sorrow or pain. There'd been no talking about it. No thinking about it, even—at least, Mia had tried not to. And now they were here, about to spend a week at Santos's private island on a sun-soaked Greek island in the middle of the Aegean. It looked like paradise. Mia hoped it really would be.

'Welcome to Villa Paraiso, Señora Aguila,' Santos said with a glinting smile as he stretched out one hand to help her from the yacht while a staff member secured it. Smiling, Mia flicked back her hair as she took his hand, his warm, dry palm sliding confidently across hers as she stepped onto the dock.

The villa was barely visible through a hillside grove of fig and pomegranate trees, with oleander and frangipani growing in rampant, beautiful abandon. Mia could only glimpse a wall of gleaming white stucco and several pairs of bright blue painted shutters. She felt a leap of anticipation inside at the prospect of exploring everything.

She'd always loved going to new places—wandering down cobblestone streets simply to soak in the sights, or sitting in a café and watching the world go by. Whenever her lifestyle had made her lonely—and it had, more often than she cared to admit, even to herself—she'd reminded herself of all the adventures she'd had, all the beautiful and remarkable places she'd seen…including Villa Paraiso on the island of Amorgos.

'I want the grand tour,' she told Santos with a smile. 'Of everything.'

'And I'll give it to you, I promise.' His golden-brown gaze was warm and approving as it rested on her and made her feel as if she were melting inside. The last three days had been really, really good. If only they could always be like this—escaping reality, never having to dig deeper…

But that wasn't how life worked, was it? Unfortunately, Mia couldn't keep the practical, pragmatic side of her brain from piping up. At some point they'd have to face reality… and whatever that meant…but not yet. Thankfully, not yet.

'Come, let me show you,' Santos said, drawing her along the dock by the hand. Laughing a little, Mia let him lead her up the winding path through the garden, the bright-yellow and pink frangipani flowers releasing their soft, peachy scent as their waxy petals brushed against her. At the top of the garden, a wrought-iron gate opened to a wide terrace that overlooked the sea, with three sets of French doors open to the sultry breeze.

For a second Mia simply stood there and let herself soak in the view: the undulating, flower-strewn hillside down to the deep-blue sea that stretched untroubled to the horizon. She turned slowly to take in the rest of the view: the olive grove to the side of the villa; the gnarled trunks and twisted branches of the trees looking as old as time itself. Then the villa: three sets of doors led into a huge lounge with a terracotta-tiled floor and comfortable sofas in varying shades of cream scattered across the huge, relaxed space.

Still holding her by the hand, Santos drew her inside.

A smiling, round-faced woman came from the kitchen to greet them, her dark hair pulled back into a neat bun.

'Señor Aguila.' She turned to give Mia a warm smile. 'Señora Aguila. It is so lovely to meet you at last.'

'This is Rosita.' Santos introduced them. 'She's housekeeper here, and her husband Alvaro manages the grounds.'

'It's lovely to meet you, as well,' Mia replied. Santos was still holding her hand in a way that Mia found she liked. Back at the Aguila estate in Seville, they'd kept their gestures of physical affection—even the barest of handholds—to private moments. Although she and Santos had never actually discussed it, Mia had had the sense that physical affection was frowned upon by his mother, not seen as the appropriate behaviour for the head of such an august family or his wife.

Apparently it wasn't that way here, and she was glad. It was just one more way that this felt like a time out of reality. But she wasn't going to think too much about that, she reminded herself. She was just going to enjoy this time together…however long it lasted.

'Rosita,' Santos was saying, 'My wife wants a tour of the villa. Where should I start?'

'Upstairs?' Rosita suggested with a rather ribald wink that made Mia choke on a laugh. The housekeeper turned to her with an unabashed grin. 'We have quite the honeymoon suite here.'

'Do you?' Mia murmured as Santos tugged on her hand to lead her up the curving staircase from the foyer. 'And why is that?'

'I designed this place to be my bolt hole,' he explained as they climbed the stairs. 'A hideaway…and one that I hoped, one day, to share with my wife.'

'So, were you planning on taking me here?' Mia asked,

genuinely curious. 'I mean, before…' She stopped, wishing she hadn't started down that bumpy road.

Before we lost our baby. Before life felt unendurable. Before I left. There were far too many ways to finish that sad sentence.

'I certainly hoped to,' Santos replied easily enough, neatly sidestepping any potential recriminations, which was a relief. Like her, he seemed to want to ride this pleasurable wave for as long as it lasted.

And, Mia told herself, maybe that would be a long time, longer than either of them expected.

For ever…?

She pushed the thought away, determined to stay in the moment and revel in it.

'Here it is,' Santos said, pushing open a door before he stepped aside so Mia could go in first.

Shooting him a quick smile of gratitude, she walked into the bedroom, drawing her breath in sharply with appreciation. She'd been in a lot of beautiful rooms since she'd met Santos, far more than her ragtag childhood and wandering adulthood had ever allowed her. She'd been in his five-star hotel suite in Portugal, as well as the one they'd shared in Barcelona, both the epitome of luxurious living; and of course she'd spent several months at the Aguila estate in Seville, with its wood-panelled rooms, the walls lined with oil paintings and the floors of cold tile. They'd been elegant in their own way, steeped in history and importance.

But she'd never been in a room like this. It was built out over the hill with floor-to-ceiling windows opening onto a balcony that hung out over the hillside, practically over the sea itself. In every direction she could see the Aegean shining as brightly as a jewel. Until she'd come to this vantage point, she hadn't realised the villa was built on a peninsula; they were surrounded by sea on every side, and it made her feel as if she were floating, flying.

Slowly Mia turned in a circle, taking in and savouring the view. Then her gaze caught on the main piece of furniture in the room—a king-sized bed on its own dais, giving it all the benefits of the room's amazing view. A canopy of near-transparent linen blew in the sea breeze, seeming to beckon her forward. The only other furniture in the room was a pair of discreet bedside tables and a cream velvet *chaise longe* on the opposite side of the room, positioned towards the balcony. Doors led to a sumptuous *en suite* bathroom, as well as a massive walk-in wardrobe.

'I know it's all rather bare,' Santos said with a wry grimace, 'But I didn't want anything to take away from the view, which really is the centrepiece of the place.'

'It's perfect,' Mia told him, her tone heartfelt as she turned to face him. 'Like…an eagle's nest. I wouldn't want to be anywhere else.'

And, Santos thought, he didn't want to be anywhere else either. His heart felt full as he walked towards Mia, catching her hands in his. She smiled as he drew her gently towards him, brushing his lips against hers and then settling there. Their hips bumped and heat flared deep within.

The last few days had been wonderful, filled with both desire and joy. It had reminded him of how they'd been together back at the beginning, lost in wonder and love. Yes, he thought almost fiercely, *love*—or at least a version of it. Maybe they hadn't known each other well enough then, but they knew each other now, or at least were getting to know. He hoped what they'd been building over the last few days was strong enough to last…but they didn't have to test it just yet.

'That bed is very comfortable,' he murmured against her lips as he steered her towards it until the back of her legs hit the dais, and then he hoisted her onto the bed, falling onto the mattress next to her as she let out a breathless laugh.

'It's broad daylight and Rosita is right downstairs...'

'Trust me, she won't come up to check on us.' He ran his hand up her calf and thigh, revelling in the feel of her smooth, golden skin. She was wearing a sundress in pale green cotton, and it was wonderfully easy to slide his hand under the thin material, right between her legs.

Mia let out a gasp. 'Santos!'

He pressed his palm against her and she let out a groan, offering her hips up to him as her eyes fluttered close. He loved how he only had to touch her to make her come apart. And he loved how she only had to look at him to accomplish the same thing.

Sure enough, Mia's eyes fluttered open again and she gazed at him with blatant hunger that made Santos feel as if he were about to explode. He captured her mouth in another kiss as Mia twined her legs around his, pulling him closer to her as his fingers slipped inside her underwear to feel the damp heat beneath.

'Santos...'

He loved how she said his name—both as a plea and demand, her body arching up against him, giving and receiving. And he loved how he could answer both—with his lips, with his hands, with his body. They'd never had any trouble talking like this, he thought as he lost himself in her. It was the purest form of communication, of bliss...

Later, as the sun slanted lazily over their twined bodies, the sheets rumpled about them, Mia finally stirred, brushing her tangled hair out of her face.

'Rosita will wonder where we went to,' she remarked wryly.

Santos stroked her side from breast to hip. Even sated as he was, he still felt the need to touch her and memorise the feel of her. 'I think she might have guessed.'

Mia's face went pink with embarrassment, which he found rather adorable. 'Really? But you just came up to show me the bedroom…'

'We are newlyweds,' Santos reminded her. 'And this is, in effect, our honeymoon.'

Mia's embarrassed expression dropped away, replaced by something far more pensive. She rolled over on her side to face him, tucking one hand under her cheek.

'Can it be that simple?' she asked quietly. 'A reset is all we need?'

Santos was jolted by the stark honesty of that question. It was the closest either of them had come to addressing what this time in Greece was, what it could be, as well as all that had painfully gone before.

'Why shouldn't it be that simple?' he countered, his gaze steady on hers. He wanted it to be that simple. He *needed* it to be, because having Mia in his life again reminded him of why he'd married her in the first place. When he was with her, he was the man he wanted to be—light, laughing, with an ease and joy inside him he'd never experienced anywhere, or with anyone, else.

'I don't know,' Mia replied slowly. 'I suppose because we ran into problems before. Because we're still so different.'

'And, like I said before, differences don't have to be deal-breakers, Mia. We can work through them. We *are* working through them…don't you think?' He caught her free hand and brought it to his lips, pressing a kiss to each of the tips of her fingers. 'Haven't these last few days been pretty good?' he asked, a hint of playfulness in his voice, although he meant the question with utter seriousness.

She let out a shaky laugh as her face softened and she brushed his lips with her fingers, a kind of kiss in return. 'They've been wonderful,' she told him quietly, her tone heartfelt. 'Some of the best days of my life, Santos.'

'Some of?' He pretended to be affronted, if just a little, wanting to keep the mood light for her sake as much as his own 'And what were some of the others?'

'Those first few days in Portugal with you,' she replied with simple honesty. 'It was everything in between then and now that was hard, Santos…for *both* of us.'

It took him a few seconds to realise the allowance she was making. She was acknowledging that it had been hard for him, too, and yet, in a flash of insight, Santos realised it hadn't been nearly as hard for him as it must have been for Mia. She'd had to come to an entirely new place, a house full of strangers who didn't speak her language and seemed suspicious of her, and try to fit in. And within weeks of that she'd found out she was pregnant with a baby she hadn't envisioned having for years.

He hadn't had to deal with any of that, and yet he'd resented her—or acted as if he had—because she'd struggled with all the adjustments. How had he not realised any of that before? How had he not told her so?

'What is it?' Mia asked unsteadily. 'You're looking at me in a funny way.'

'I'm just realising how incredible you are,' Santos replied. 'And how amazingly strong.'

'What?' Mia looked surprised as well as relieved, and Santos realised she must have been bracing herself for some sort of criticism. Why? Had he really been that negative before, that ungenerous?

'I should have told you before,' he said, 'Back in Seville, at the estate. You took on a lot, Mia, coming home with me. Trying to work out a whole new way of life.'

'I don't think I did a very good job of it,' Mia replied, biting her lip. 'I suppose I could have tried harder.'

'I could have tried harder too.'

She stared at him, her brow furrowed, as if she couldn't quite believe or trust what he was saying, but she didn't ask any more questions, and Santos was relieved. He still needed to untangle his own thoughts…as well as his own feelings. And just now he wanted simply to enjoy what they had.

Mia must have felt the same, because a smile entered her voice as her hand slipped tantalisingly down his chest. 'We've talked enough for now, I think,' she murmured. 'This is our honeymoon, remember?' She rolled on top of him, and now the smile was on her lips and in her eyes too, her hair brushing his bare chest as her body moved against his. 'Let's make the most of it,' she whispered.

And that, Santos decided as his mind hazed with desire, seemed like a very good idea indeed.

CHAPTER ELEVEN

'I CANNOT *BELIEVE* you haven't done this before.'

They were standing on the dock, under the hard, hot light of the summer sun, as Santos loaded the snorkelling equipment into the sail-boat and Mia watched him, hands on her slender hips. She was wearing a white bikini top and a pair of cut-off denim shorts. Thanks to the sun, the freckles on her nose stood out in golden relief, making her look all the more enticing.

They'd been on Amorgos for three days, and those days had been just as wonderful as Barcelona, if not more so…or even the first heady days of their romance. They'd walked into the nearby village and bought feta swimming in brine, fresh olives, tomatoes and crusty bread for a picnic they'd had on the rocky shoreline, washed down with a bottle of Agiorgitiko as they'd basked and kissed in the sun.

They'd hiked up to the top of the nearby mountain, visited a beautiful old monastery clinging to the hillside and had drunk retsina and eaten rosewater jellies with the smiling monks who'd given their marriage a blessing, chanting prayers over them before they'd left. They'd wandered through ancient ruins, following the footsteps of those who lived long ago, imagining who might have once lived there and the experiences they might have had, while wild goats had daintily plucked their way through the strewn rocks.

Everything he did with Mia made him feel as if the volume had been turned up, the intensity and brightness too. He was experiencing life as he never had before, and he loved it.

And as for at *night*… At night, they'd rediscovered each other's bodies again and again, finding passion and joy in each other's arms that Santos thought he would never, ever tire of. This was the life he wanted—not one of stultifying duty or relentless work, but one of love and laughter, light, life and joy, amidst all the necessary travails.

Chasing on the heels of such happiness, the thought gave him a sinking sense of guilt and despair that he struggled to shed. They might not have said as much to each other, but this week at Villa Paraiso was a step out of time, of reality. In a few days, maybe a week, he would have to return to Seville. They both would. And, silently, they'd agreed not to talk about it.

And they wouldn't today, Santos told himself as he gave Mia a smiling shrug. 'I haven't snorkelled because I've barely been here. I only had the place built a few years ago.'

'Years,' Mia repeated, cocking one eyebrow. 'That's a long time, Santos.'

He shrugged again, the smile slipping from his face. 'There have been many demands on my time.'

'I know.' Her face softened. 'I'm amazed you've been able to take this much time off, frankly, with all the responsibilities you have.'

They were skirting dangerously close to what they weren't supposed to talk about. Santos held up a mask. 'Have you ever snorkelled before?'

'Yes, a few times. Nowhere as amazing as here, though.' The smile she gave him was easy and wide. 'I'm looking forward to it. I bet the view under the water is amazing.'

'The view from here is pretty good already,' Santos replied, with a waggle of his eyebrows at her bikini top.

'I'd have to agree,' she replied, waggling her eyebrows back at him and making him laugh. He'd never laughed so much as when he was with Mia. How had he forgotten that, in the midst of all their troubles? Why had he not worked harder to recapture it?

'All right, I think we're ready,' he told her as he loaded the last of the equipment into the boat and then reached one hand out to help her in.

'So why *did* you build this place?' Mia asked as she settled herself in the boat and Santos hoisted the sail. Soon they were skimming over the blue-green waters, the villa and the dock receding behind them. 'That is, if you were never really going to have the time off to come here. Does your mother come here, or your sister?'

He didn't miss the slightly diffident tone she took when she mentioned his family, which he suspected was without even realising it. His mother had been as welcoming as she knew how to be, considering the state of appalled shock she'd been in that her only son, the heir to the Aguila fortune, had married a no-name American after two weeks' acquaintance. Santos had believed—and still did—that his mother would warm to Mia in time. And when his sister finally made it back to Seville—something she didn't do all that often—Santos hoped Mia would find a kindred spirit in her.

'No, my mother never did,' he told Mia. 'I'm not sure she'd be interested. My mother prefers shopping and skiing to lazing about in Greece. And my sister would probably love it, but she's often busy with work…as I am.' He acknowledged this with a rueful grimace. 'But in any case, I built this place for me. For my family: the family I hoped to have one day, not so much for them.'

The family I hoped to have one day. For once, those words didn't reverberate with loss, but rather with hope. Yes, Mia's miscarriage had been hard for both of them, but it was in the past, and they had a future to look forward to.

'And then I never ended up going,' Santos finished on a sigh. 'More fool me, I suppose.'

'Well, you're here now,' Mia reminded him. 'And I'm glad.'

'So am I.'

They shared a lingering look that made Santos's insides warm. Yes, the future *was* something to look forward to. With that happy thought in mind, Santos went to adjust the sail.

When he returned, Mia continued with the questions, leaning back on her elbows, her hair flying in the wind. 'You still haven't said *why* you built it,' she pressed. Her voice was light enough but there was an insistence underneath Santos both heard and felt. 'For you and your family, yes, but why, when you have the estate, the apartment in Madrid, the Caribbean whatever, the ski chalet and I can't remember where else?'

'I think those are all of them,' Santos said with a smile. 'But this place is different. It's…mine. And I wanted an escape.' It sounded like an innocuous remark, he'd meant it to be, but he knew right away that he hadn't fooled Mia by the way she narrowed her eyes and cocked her head.

'An escape?' she repeated slowly. 'From what, exactly?'

Santos was silent for a moment as he turned to squint out at the sea, its surface shimmering with sunlight as if some giant, benevolent hand had strewn it with diamonds. He could breathe so much more easily out here, under the sun and on the sea…and with Mia by his side.

'An escape from everything,' he stated simply. 'From

being an Aguila. From being *the* Aguila—the head of the family and all that it means. From the responsibilities of work and managing an estate with over a thousand staff, and that's not even including the Aguila offices in Madrid and Rome, which employ hundreds. From…from being me, but not really me—being the me I need to be in order to be the head of the Aguila family.' The words had come out of him in a staccato rush and, he realised, were some of the most honest and revealing he'd ever said.

Mia stared at him for a long moment, her expression thoughtful, her eyes soft with sympathy which Santos couldn't quite bear. He didn't want to be pitied, of all things. He was an *Aguila*, the head of one of Spain's oldest and most aristocratic families. And yet wasn't that the problem in the first place?

He glanced back at the water, not trusting the expression on his face, not wanting to see the pity on Mia's. Then he felt her reach over and cover his hand with her own.

'I'm glad you have this place,' she said softly. 'For your sake, but also for mine—for *ours*.'

Santos nodded jerkily, still not trusting himself. They didn't speak for a few moments, but as he let himself relax into the silence he realised it wasn't as bad as he'd feared. Mia's understanding wasn't actually pity; it didn't weaken him in her eyes, or in his own. To his own surprise, he realised that he was actually glad he'd told her.

Mia tucked up her knees to her chest, wrapping her arms around them as she tilted her face to the warm sun. Santos was focused on steering the boat into the cove of a small, uninhabited island, little more than an outcrop of rock with a stretch of sand.

His handsome face was drawn into lines of concentration, his hands resting on the tiller, his broad shoulders gleaming under the summer sun. He looked a little bit like she imagined Apollo should look, Mia thought fancifully—bronzed, powerful, perfect. Every time she looked at him, she marvelled that he wanted to be with her. And yet, against all odds, he did…and, slowly and cautiously, she was starting to trust in that.

They hadn't spoken for a little while, and Mia had been okay with that, because she'd sensed Santos had probably said more than he'd wanted to or was comfortable with, and he needed time to recover his equilibrium. She was still very glad he'd said all he'd had. Grateful that he'd been willing to share so much with her, because it helped her to understand him so much better.

If only she'd understood that before…

But no—no more recriminations or regrets. No more looking back at all. The future was shimmering all around them, just like the sunlit sea, and that was what Mia wanted to focus on.

'So, if you've never been snorkelling, how did you know where to go?' she asked teasingly.

'Alvaro told me. He said this was a particularly good spot—not too rocky.'

It looked like a good spot, Mia acknowledged, the water crystal-clear, with a sandy shore all along the postage-stamp-sized island.

Tossing her a quick smile, Santos heaved himself off the side of the boat and waded through the water. He was a breath-taking sight, dressed only in a pair of board shorts, the sun glinting off his dark hair and the neatly trimmed stubble on his jaw, his burnished, olive skin taut over sleek muscle. He certainly stole her breath, anyway, Mia thought wryly. She felt as if she could watch him for ever.

'Aren't you coming in?' he called to her, and she didn't need to be asked twice. She slipped over the side of the boat and into the water, which was lovely and warm and came up to her thighs. Santos secured the boat and then handed her snorkelling gear—mask, breathing tube and fins.

'I always feel a little ridiculous with all this on,' Mia admitted, and Santos grinned at her.

'You look ridiculous too,' he said, before pulling her in for a quick kiss before she put in her breathing tube. Mia laughed and shook her head, enjoying how happy he seemed. It was an unsettling thought, because it made her realise Santos hadn't seemed happy back in Seville…and neither had she been. Had that been the cause of the problems, rather than any of their differences—rather their surprising and unspoken *similarity*?

It was a thought she couldn't quite her head around, not yet anyway. She needed to consider the idea more, let it settle and seep through her. Santos had talked about needing this escape and how heavily duty seemed to weigh on him…she'd had no idea about any of that. No idea that any part of him resented or at least felt burdened by the responsibility he carried so squarely on his shoulders.

Did the fact that she now knew that change anything? Mia wondered. She thought it did, or at least it could. She felt as if she knew and understood Santos more with him away from the estate and everything it represented, or at least this version of him. She felt the same way she had when they'd met in Portugal. But in Seville he had changed; he'd become taciturn, remote…and no more so when she'd told him she wasn't happy to be pregnant. But even before then she'd felt his disapproval, his disappointment, and it had played on every doubt she'd ever had from a childhood of living with a mother who had resented her at every turn.

You're not good enough... You'll never be good enough... Nothing you ever do will win anyone's love.

Those thoughts had circled relentlessly through her head in the awful weeks before she'd finally worked up the courage to leave, or, really, given in to the desperation to.

Being here in Greece reminded her of how different Santos could be...and how different she could be with him. With him like this, she didn't doubt him or herself. She didn't let herself get sucked into those old, toxic thought patterns of feeling inadequate or unlovable. She didn't want to get sucked back into it once—*if*—they returned to Seville.

Would knowing this about him make enough of a difference?

'Ready to snorkel?' Santos asked and Mia nodded with something like relief. She didn't want to think like this. She just wanted to *be*...with Santos.

Taking a deep breath, she dived down under the crystalline water and kicked her fins to glide ahead, with Santos swimming easily by her side. She turned to smile at him and he grinned back, his lips curving around the mouthpiece of his breathing tube. Then he pointed, and she looked ahead to see a school of tiny blue fish moving like a cloud through the water, and she gave a gurgle of underwater laughter.

They continued to swim side by side, pointing out various fish and sea creatures to each other. At one point Santos saw an octopus in the distance, its tentacles almost seeming to move balletically as it propelled itself forward through the sea. After about an hour, Mia started feeling tired, and Santos suggested they swim back for a rest and their picnic, which sounded like heaven to her.

'I forgot how tiring swimming is,' she remarked as she

waded through the water towards the beach of their little island, her mask and fins in her hand. Santos was at the boat, lifting a picnic basket Rosita had packed for them from its interior. He'd already tossed his snorkelling things onto the beach. Mia smiled in anticipation of a few hours eating and lazing—and who knew what else?—on the beach under the sun on this private slice of paradise.

If only they could stay here for ever...

But no, she reminded herself, she wasn't going to think that way.

'Hungry?' Santos asked, turning to her with a smile, the picnic basket looped around one arm. His chest was beaded with droplets of water, his dark hair slicked back from his forehead. He looked utterly delicious, never mind what was packed in their picnic.

'Ye—*ouch*!' Mia let out a gasp of pain as she grabbed her right foot. 'I think I stepped on something!' Already her foot was starting to throb.

Santos's forehead furrowed with concern as he chucked the picnic basket back into the boat and hurried towards her.

'Let me see.' He grabbed hold of her arm to steady her as Mia winced in pain. Whatever she'd stepped on, it had really hurt. She supposed she shouldn't have taken off her fins before she'd got out of the water. 'Can you walk?' he asked.

'I think so,' she said after a second's hesitation, because she hated feeling feeble, and she was certainly used to doing things for herself, but her foot really *hurt*.

Santos must have heard her uncertainty because without another word he swept her into his arms and carried her to the beach himself.

'Santos, I'm sure I'll be fine,' Mia protested, struggling a bit feebly to get down. Santos's arms merely tightened around her. 'It was probably just a jagged rock or something.'

'Well, let's check it out.' He lay her on the blanket he'd already spread out and then knelt in front of her, taking her foot into his hands. Mia bit her lip hard because, now that she was sitting on the ground, her foot started to feel hot and swollen, throbbing in time to the beat of her blood, which couldn't be good.

'I think you were stung by a sea urchin,' Santos told her. 'It can hurt quite a bit, but it's generally not very serious— a bit more than a bee sting, but that's all. Still, there are some spines embedded in your foot, which is causing you the pain. I can get them out, if you can hold still.'

'Okay,' Mia replied, her voice wobbling a little even though she wanted to sound brave. Her mother had never tolerated any weakness or whining, and Mia had always tried to take care of herself and stay strong. It was an instinct she struggled to shed, and yet right then it felt almost unbearably comforting and poignant to have Santos looking after her so tenderly.

He removed four spines, each one causing both a sharp pain which was followed by an abrupt relief, and when he was finished Mia sagged back onto the blanket. 'Goodness, I don't want to go through that again,' she said faintly with an attempt at a laugh that didn't quite work.

'Your foot is quite swollen and hot to the touch.' Santos frowned. 'Maybe we should head back. We could have a doctor look at it.'

'You said it was only a little worse than a bee sting,' Mia protested. As much as she liked Santos taking care of her, she realised she did not want to be made a fuss of. She never had.

'Still…' His frown deepened as he glanced down at her foot. 'It looks worse than I'd expect for a sea urchin sting.'

A frisson of alarm went through Mia at that, but she

kept her voice light. 'Well, have you ever been stung by a sea urchin?' she asked.

'No,' he admitted, frowning. 'But I don't like the look of it.'

Mia shrugged. 'I'm sure it's fine. By the time we've eaten lunch and dried off, I'll be ready to snorkel again.' Even if it was hurting like the dickens just then.

'All right,' Santos agreed reluctantly. 'I suppose we might as well eat. But if it's still hurting after that, we'll go back.'

He went back to fetch the picnic basket from the boat, and that was when Mia felt the first wave of dizziness sweep over her and start to pull her under. She blinked and the whole world seemed to waver as though she were in a dream. Nausea surged in her stomach, and she blinked rapidly in an attempt to clear her head.

Santos turned from the boat and was heading back to shore, the basket over his arm, but it looked as if he was rippling...that the whole world was rippling...and everything was happening in slow motion. Her foot felt both icy and hot, numb yet throbbing with pain. How was that even possible? What was going on?

The rippling version of Santos came closer, everything about him distorted and blurry, but even then Mia could see the alarm on his face as he dropped the basket, sending strawberries and olives rolling across the sand. She opened her mouth to say something, but nothing came out. A strawberry rolled towards her and she kept her gaze fixed on it, trying to anchor herself in reality, except reality was fading in and out and she felt so very *strange*...

'Mia!' Santos cried, reaching for her.

It was the last thing she heard before she slumped to the ground, unconscious.

CHAPTER TWELVE

MIA BLINKED THE world slowly into focus. Her head felt as if it were full of cotton wool, her limbs immovable and as heavy as lead. Where was she? In a bed of some sort, but the sheets felt scratchy, and she could hear a persistent beeping. And she couldn't remember anything...

Blink... Blink...

Like the twirl of a kaleidoscope, the blurry shapes and colours of the world around her slowly clarified into a whole: a room— a hospital room, by the looks of it—the bright-blue sky visible out of the window. The beeping was from a machine next to her bed. And next to the machine, in a vinyl-covered arm chair, was Santos.

His head was pillowed by his hand, slumping forward, as though he'd fallen asleep without realising. He looked exhausted—his clothes creased, his hair rumpled, his close-cropped beard not as neatly trimmed as it usually was.

What on earth had happened?

Mia must have made some sound, because Santos stirred, lifting his head and looking around blearily before he suddenly lurched forward.

'Mia...'

'What?' Her voice came out in a dry rasp. 'What happened?'

'Oh, my goodness, Mia.' To her shock, his eyes filled

with tears and he covered her hand that lay on the bed sheet with both of his own as he bowed his head over her, almost as if he was in prayer.

It wasn't until his shoulders shook that Mia realised he was actually crying. For her; when, she wondered, had anyone shed a tear for her? It was a humbling and yet also strangely gratifying thought, and yet she hated seeing him look sad.

'Santos.' She felt a lump form in her own throat, simply at the sight of all that emotion. 'Santos, it's okay. I'm okay.' At least, she hoped she was. 'What happened? What's going on?' Her voice sounded like a rusty saw being scraped across an old board. 'And may I please have some water?'

'Of course.' He jumped up, wiping his eyes, shocking her further, and then went to pour her a glass of water from the jug by her bed. Mia tried to reach for it but realised she was too weak; she could barely lift her arm from the bed. What in heaven's name was wrong with her? She couldn't remember anything.

Santos held the cup to her lips, and she drank as best as she could, grateful for the cool liquid that wet her lips and trickled down her throat. After a couple of sips, she eased back and Santos returned the water glass to the bedside table before sitting in the chair he'd been in before, his hands clasped between his knees.

'I was afraid you were going to die,' he said in a low voice, like a confession.

Die? Surely he was exaggerating? Now that she'd had a few moments to think, along with some water, Mia felt her mind clearing as the memories started to slot back into place. They'd been snorkelling, she'd been stung by a sea urchin and then she must have had some kind of allergic reaction. She remembered Santos removing the spines and saying her foot looked swollen, and she even remembered starting to feel woozy, the world turning all weird and waving. She must have passed out and Santos had brought her here to the island hospital. But surely, she hadn't been in any danger of *dying*?

She managed a smile, although her lips were cracked and the effort hurt just a little. 'And I thought you said a sea urchin was just a little worse than a bee sting.'

'*Mia.*' He looked up at her, his expression anguished. 'I'm serious.'

Taking in the torment on his face, she knew he was, utterly. 'Santos,' she whispered. 'What happened?'

He gave a gulping sort of swallow as he slowly shook his head. 'They think you had a severe allergic reaction to the sea urchin sting. It's very rare, but it can happen, and when it does it can be incredibly serious. You lost consciousness, right there on the beach. I carried you to the boat and then sailed to Katapola, where an ambulance from the hospital met us—I'd called 112.'

The Greek emergency number. A ripple of shock went through Mia, icy and incredulous. Had it really been that bad? She couldn't remember any of it.

'I...' She found she had no words.

'You didn't regain consciousness *once*, Mia, in forty-eight hours.' Santos's voice was ragged, his eyes wide and dark as he stared at her as if he could imbue her with the strength of his feeling and his fear. 'At one point, they weren't sure you ever would. They told me that sometimes allergic reactions to sea urchin stings can be fatal.' His voice choked. '*Fatal.*'

'Santos, I'm so sorry.' She spoke the words helplessly because she had no others. He must have been through hell in the last two days, not knowing if she would live or die. She twined her fingers through his. 'I'm so sorry,' she whispered again.

Abruptly he rose from his chair, the legs scraping against the tiled floor, his back to her as he stalked to the window, raking one hand through his hair. Mia eyed him in fearful uncertainly. He was clearly in the grip of some powerful emotion. Was he angry...with her? Or with himself, for caring about her in the first place?

It reminded her of her mother, in an entirely visceral way. Blaming her for being sick, for *being* at all. Without Mia, her mother would have been unencumbered, free, *happy*. She'd always made that abundantly clear, even when she'd showed her affection, doled out in miniscule amounts, as if she was reluctant to feel anything for her; yet at times, as her mother, she just couldn't help herself.

The sense of guilt and inadequacy Mia had felt as a child came rushing back, worse than ever. Somehow, and it really didn't matter how, this was all her fault—again, as always. Santos's pain was her problem, not his. She was to blame...just like she had been for the miscarriage.

'I'm sorry,' she whispered, her voice choking. 'I'm so sorry.'

Santos whirled round, his hand dropping from his hair. 'Mia, what on earth do you have to be sorry for?' he demanded, his voice sounding as if it had been scraped raw. '*I'm* the one who is sorry—me. I'm...' Now his voice was choking. 'I'm so damned sorry.'

Mia stared at him in shock, speechless for a few seconds as she registered the utter anguish in Santos's eyes. 'You're sorry?' she whispered, not understanding. 'Why?'

'Because...! I should have checked for sea urchins. I should have called the emergency number sooner. I should have kept this from happening. I should have *protected* you.' He gave a gulping sound that was halfway to a sob and filled Mia with wonder.

She had not expected this reaction at all. This was so far from her experience, her expectation, that she needed to cringe and apologise for being any kind of trouble…

The way she'd been made to feel in the hospital, after the miscarriage.

But maybe *she'd* made herself feel that way, and not Santos. It was an extraordinary thought, unsettling and hopeful all at once.

Santos stared at Mia as he shook his head. For two days he'd been wracked with guilt, wishing he could turn back time, do things differently. He thought of watching her slump forward on that beach, her skin blazing to the touch, her head lolling back as he'd lightly slapped her cheeks and begged her to wake up…

That it was happening at all had been terrifying and terrible, a blur of fear, guilt and horror. Santos had been reminded of his father's heart attack, out in the orange groves; he'd been the only one there to perform mouth-to-mouth and attempt to save him. He'd failed. And, there on the beach, he'd feared he would fail Mia…

So many memories had come rushing back, tangling with the present, just as they had when Mia had miscarried… remembered grief as well as fear for the future. Knowing, absolutely knowing, that he could not survive losing another person in his life—losing Mia.

'Santos,' she said softly, 'It wasn't your fault.'

'I could have prevented it,' he insisted with staunch swiftness.

Mia let out an exasperated breath. 'How?'

'Checked the shore. Told you to keep your fins on. Chosen somewhere else to snorkel. *Warned* you, at least. I knew there were sea urchins in these waters and I never even told you so.'

His stomach churned with acid at the thought. How could he have been so *careless*? He knew the answer: because he'd been so *happy*. He'd let his usually innate sense of diligence and responsibility slip away because he hadn't wanted to bother with it, hadn't wanted to feel its heaviness, but he should have. How he should have...

'It was an accident, Santos,' Mia said quietly. 'It could have happened to anyone. And what are the chances that I'd have an allergic reaction? You said yourself that it's very rare. This is just one of those things, and I'm okay.' She stretched out one slender arm in supplication. 'I'm *okay*.'

'Yes, but...' His voice wavered and he found he had to look down, blinking hard, his throat working in order to compose himself. Something was breaking apart inside him and he wasn't sure he could keep it together much longer. This was something he hadn't even realised he could *feel*, until Mia had been lying lifeless in his arms. He'd told her he loved her, but he realised then that those had just been words. When Mia had been in his arms, her head lolling back, he'd realised what it *felt* like to love someone that much, to fear losing them.

'Santos, please.' Her voice was a soft, pleading caress. 'Please, come sit by me and tell me what's going on—because this is about more than a sea urchin sting, isn't it?'

Yes, it was. Slowly, reluctantly, he came and sat down next to her. She reached for his hand and he let her take it, craving her touch even as he dreaded this confession. He didn't *do* this kind of stuff.

An Aguila must always be in control of his heart and his mind...

But just now he wasn't in control…of either.

'Santos,' Mia whispered. 'Tell me.'

'I shouldn't have left you in the hospital room,' he blurted in a low voice, his gaze on their clasped hands. 'Before…after the miscarriage. I shouldn't have left you to deal with all of that alone. I can't believe that I did, that I could have been so cruel.'

She was silent for a long moment, and he made himself look up at her. Was she angry at him? Did remembering those old wounds hurt her the way it did him?

'You were upset,' she said at last. 'And angry.'

'Mia, I wasn't angry.' He hated that she thought he had been, that he'd acted as if he was, and that he'd let her think that for so long because on some level it had felt safer, stronger.

'Santos…' There was a note of sorrowful exasperation in her voice that tore at him. 'You were. On some level, you were. You must have been. I mean, when I said I didn't want… I wasn't ready…' She trailed off, not seeming to want to put it into the starkness of actual words.

'I was hurt,' he confessed quietly, the words coming out stiltedly because he still wasn't used to being so honest or so emotional. It didn't come easily, and it made him feel as if he was covered in prickles or open sores—maybe both. He felt desperately uncomfortable, that was for certain, as if he were in pain—and maybe he was. 'I wanted you to want my baby,' he told her in a raw voice. 'And,' he added, compelled to complete honesty now he'd started, no matter how much it hurt, 'I wanted you to want what I wanted: a family…with me.'

Mia stared at him for a long moment, her brow still furrowed, although her expression had turned thoughtful. 'I can understand that,' she said quietly. 'And I know my re-

sponse shocked you and we had to work through our different reactions. We didn't really get time to, I suppose, but…'
She paused, drawing a breath before she pressed on, 'You
don't blame me for what happened—for the miscarriage?'

Clearly that was a deep-seated fear of hers, and it made
him feel even more horribly guilty. 'Mia, I never blamed
you,' he assured her, his voice a low throb of feeling. 'I
know you think I did, and I acknowledge that it may have
seemed as if I did, and also that I might have acted like
I did. But deep down, in my heart, in my soul, I didn't. I
promise you that, on my life.'

'Not even some small part of you, Santos?' she asked in
little more than a whisper. 'You barely spoke to me after
the miscarriage. You barely *looked* at me. I know you said
you shouldn't have acted that way, and I understand that
now, but *then*?'

The hurt in her voice reminded him of broken glass, and
it cut him as if it were, splintering his soul. How could he
have hurt her so dreadfully and not even realised at the
time? Maybe not even cared, because the truth was he'd
been hurting so much himself…and that was something
he'd never explained to her.

He gazed down at their clasped hands once more, and
then back at her. Her eyes were wide, with a sheen of tears
that made him hurt all the more. 'I'm so sorry,' he said in
a low voice, 'For the way I treated you. Maybe some small
part of me did blame you in that moment, Mia. A *very*
small part; I can be honest enough to admit that. But, if
I did, it was only because it felt easier than what I really
felt—which was that I should blame myself.'

'You…' The word slid from her lips on a soft gasp.
'Why?'

Because he was an Aguila, the man of the family who

took responsibility for everything. Because he should have been able to protect his wife, his *child*. Because if he'd been a better man, husband or father, this would never have happened.

He knew, in his head at least, that none of that really made sense. The doctor had been abundantly clear that it was just one of those things; some babies died before they were born, before they'd barely had a chance to grow. It was sad, it was hard, but it was also a simple reality of life. He *knew* that…and yet he'd felt something else. And it made him realise afresh how different emotions, different ideas, could co-exist. How Mia could have not wanted the baby and still grieved its loss. How he could have known it was an accident of providence or fate but still blame himself. Human beings were contrary. Life—and love—was complicated.

'So,' she said slowly, 'Like with the sea urchin, you blamed yourself?'

'Yes, but more than that.' He swallowed, trying to ease the aching tightness in his throat. 'There's something else—I didn't tell you how my father died.' He'd mentioned it in passing, consigned it to distant memory and assured her, and himself, that he'd moved on. It was what he did with everyone.

'You said he had a heart attack,' Mia murmured, a gently questioning lilt in her voice.

'He did,' Santos confirmed. 'It was all very sudden. We were walking in the orange groves. He was showing me some of the trees. He was worried about a disease, a tree-killing bacteria—it had wiped out ninety percent of some growers' harvest in different parts of the country.'

Even now he could picture the furrow in his father's forehead, the sombre way he spoke. Santos had been concerned, but he hadn't felt the weight of it the way his father had. 'We could have survived that,' he continued, wanting, needing, to explain. 'Our financial interests are mainly in investments and property—but the orange and olives groves were my father's heart. The family estate was his soul. He was terribly anxious, and when he saw a sign of the bacteria he clutched his chest and keeled over. It happened in a matter of seconds.'

Mia's voice was soft and sad. 'Oh, Santos...'

'We were too far from anywhere for me to go for help,' he continued bleakly. 'I knew I had only seconds. I tried to give him mouth-to-mouth. For a second, I thought he might respond. His eyes flickered...he looked as if he wanted to say something...but he couldn't.'

He paused, reliving those awful moments even though he didn't want to: the icy panic, the terrible dread and somehow, even worse, that treacherous flicker of hope. 'He didn't recover, though, obviously,' he finished flatly. 'He died in my arms a few minutes later.'

'Santos.' Mia clasped his hand with both of hers. 'I'm so, so sorry.'

'When you lost the baby,' he continued, knowing this part was even more important to say, 'I remembered all that. It came back to me like a...' He shook his head slowly in wonder. 'Like an avalanche. I felt like I couldn't think, couldn't breathe. I'd suppressed the memories on some level, you see, for years...decades. I'd refused to think of it, to...to process it. Emotionally.

'But when you started bleeding... When we saw the baby on the ultrasound and for a second, just like my father, I thought it was going to be okay and then I realised it wasn't, that there was no heartbeat... Our tiny little baby was so very still.' He gazed at her, blinking back the haze of tears in his eyes, only to see her own slipping down her cheeks.

'I shut down,' he confessed. 'In that moment. Truth be told, I can't remember much of it—the procedure, I mean, or afterwards. I just felt as if I were existing in some… some empty space. It doesn't excuse me; I know it doesn't, not for a single second. But that was what was going on with me, Mia. Not anger, but sorrow. Not blame, but grief.'

'Oh, Santos.' She shook her head as more tears spilled down her cheeks. 'Thank you for telling me all this. But I wish… I wish you'd told me before.' She swiped at her cheeks as she shook her head again. 'In all those weeks after when it felt as if you were freezing me out…as if you couldn't stand the sight of me…why didn't you explain then?'

He hated, absolutely *hated*, the thought that she'd suffered for so long and, worse, that it was all his fault. 'I'm sorry,' he said helplessly. 'I know I should have. But I felt as if I were frozen inside. And you are right—I was angry at you, in some small way,' he added, knowing he needed to be completely honest. 'But only because it felt easier than dealing with my own emotions. And after you left, well, then it became even easier to be angry with you.'

She let out a trembling laugh. 'So why did you ever come and find me? Was it just pride?'

'No, not pride.' His voice was a thrum in his chest. 'Desperation. I missed you, Mia. And… I missed who I was when I was with you. I wanted that back and I wanted *you* back.' He remembered the ache in his chest when she'd left him, as if an essential piece of him had been ripped out. 'I was angry at first, yes, and—and I was hurt. More hurt than I wanted to admit to anyone. It took me two weeks before I decided to start looking. I hired a private investigator, one of the best in the world.'

Mia let out a shaky laugh. 'I had no idea someone was on my tail for that long.'

'You're good at running,' he remarked wryly. He'd been surprised at how long it had taken the investigator to find her—nearly three weeks. It had felt like for ever.

She shrugged, her gaze sliding away from his, her mouth drawing down as, for a few seconds, a sorrowful wistfulness slipped over her like a dark cloak. 'Well,' she said quietly. 'I've been running for most of my life.'

He frowned, trying to untangle that statement. He knew she'd grown up with a mother who had moved all over the world, but *running*...? They were two different things, surely?

'It doesn't matter now,' she said a little too quickly. 'What matters is you found me. And I found you, in a way. I understand so much more now, Santos, and for that I'm glad. I'm even glad that stupid sea urchin stung me!' She smiled, but he couldn't quite manage it. She'd come too close to death for him ever to laugh or even smile about that.

Mia reached for his hand once more. 'It's the future we need to think about now,' she said, but Santos had a feeling it was the past she did not want to talk about. Still, he decided to let it go—whatever 'it' was.

They'd shared so much already and, while it had been healing, it had also been hard. Truth be told, he didn't know if he had the words—or the strength—for anything more, at least not then.

'The future,' he agreed, and leaned forward to seal that promise with a tender kiss.

CHAPTER THIRTEEN

MIA STARED OUT of the window as a soft sigh escaped her. They'd been at Villa Paraiso for ten days, ten *glorious* days she didn't want to end, and yet she felt in her bones that it was time to go home. Santos hadn't said as much, and neither had she, but it was as if there'd been a change in the air, a shifting of seasons, as inexorable as the waning of the moon or the pull of the tide.

The sun still shone brightly, the days were long and lazy and full of love, but still Mia heard a whisper of the future, and it felt like the threat of a storm, despite the blue skies.

One morning while she sat in the garden, soaking in the sunshine and reading a paper-back she'd found in the library, Santos disappeared to his study to answer some emails. Three long hours later, he came to find her, managing to look both sheepish and obdurate, his shoulders thrown back, his dark brows drawn together.

'Did you get done what you needed to?' she asked lightly, and he let out a small sigh as he sank into a deck chair next to her. All around them oleander and frangipani grew in unruly abandon, and in the distance the sea sparkled under the sunlight, as bright as a diamond. Still, despite the peaceful beauty of the scene, Mia braced herself for what might come next.

'More or less, yes.'

'Which is it?' she asked, striving to keep her voice light. 'More…or less?'

Santos didn't answer for a moment, his lips pursed and his gaze on the ground. Mia put down her book. It definitely seemed like less…which meant Santos needed to return to Seville. She'd known it was coming; had felt it in herself, in the changing mood, a sense of time running through their fingers like sand. And yet still she experienced a sense of wrenching loss, almost like a tearing inside. She didn't want to go. She didn't want to return to Seville and the painful memories they'd made there.

'I've been absent from work for over two weeks,' he said at last. 'I haven't been gone from work for that long since we first met…' He glanced up at her, and she was heartened to see his expression soften. 'And, even then, I was back at my desk on the fourteenth day.'

She smiled in memory. 'Were we crazy, do you think, to get married after such a short time?'

He smiled back as he reached for her hand, twining his fingers though hers. 'Most likely, but I don't regret it for a second.'

'I don't either,' she replied honestly. And yet…the future loomed in front of them. It was easy, Mia thought, to feel as if she was in love when she was on a Greek-island paradise, without any problems or other people around. But, back in Seville, she feared the old issues would come to haunt them. They'd revert to their former and maybe even truer selves—who was to say otherwise? Santos would become cold and stand-offish, and she'd become both rebellious and despairing, longing to run, to escape.

'What are you thinking about?' he asked softly. 'You suddenly have the bleakest look in your eyes.'

'I'm worried,' Mia admitted. 'About going back to Seville.'

His fingers tightened on hers. 'It will be different this time, Mia, I promise.'

'You don't need to take all the responsibility, Santos,' she said. 'All the blame. What happened before was down to both of us. How we reacted when the pressure hit... It became the perfect storm that took both of us.'

His forehead creased, his eyes narrowing. 'What do you mean?'

What *did* she mean? 'I suppose we're both products of our backgrounds,' she replied slowly. 'You, with the weighty history of your family, as well as your father's death...'

His frown deepened. 'And you?' he asked after a moment.

Mia shrugged. She was the one who had opened this particular can of worms, and yet now she was reluctant to let any of them wriggle out. She hated talking about her past, the pity it inevitably incurred. She'd told Santos a little about it when they'd first met, and more on the yacht, but she had always done her best to act dismissive, as if none of it mattered any more. Did she really want to go into it all now? And yet maybe she needed to, for both their sakes.

'Mia?' he prompted gently.

'I just mean,' she said, knowing she was hedging a little, 'That I've been similarly affected. You remember I told you that I moved around a lot as a kid? Well, that affected me—as you would expect it to.'

That was the very much condensed version, she thought with an inward sigh.

'Ye...s,' Santos agreed slowly. 'But you never talked

about *how*. In fact, you assured me it hadn't actually affected you all that much. Something I didn't really believe at the time, but I didn't press the point, because it felt as if we had so much other stuff to deal with. Maybe I should have…although I suspect you would have given me the run-around. But I hope you're not going to do that now?' He quirked an eyebrow, and she had to smile. He knew her so well.

'No, I'm not going to,' she replied wryly. Despite her deliberately light tone, her heart was starting to thud rather hard. She really didn't like talking about this. She didn't even like thinking about it, or remembering…

'You told me,' Santos began, glancing down at their clasped hands, 'That you moved around a lot, sometimes every few months, and that it got lonely. You also said your mother died when you were seventeen and you started working then, on your own.' He shook his head slowly. 'I knew that must have affected you, but you turned the tables on me so neatly, and made me talk about myself, that I let it go. I shouldn't have. I realise that now.'

Mia rolled her eyes. 'Santos, are you going to blame yourself for this too?'

He gave a small smile of acknowledgement, his eyes crinkling at the corners. 'No, not if you tell me what you didn't want to before.'

'It's not a big secret or something,' Mia said quickly. 'I just don't like talking about it. As you haven't liked talking about, well, about stuff.' She didn't want to dredge anything else up, not now.

Santos gave a brief nod, his warm, golden-brown gaze steady on her. 'Okay,' he said, his voice level, accepting, as if he was ready for whatever she threw at him.

'Well…' She hesitated, not knowing how to begin; not wanting to. 'It was a pretty unstable childhood, as you can imagine,' she said slowly. 'Not just the moving around, but the places we moved to. My mother was something of a free spirit, so we ended up in a lot of communes, co-operative farms…that kind of thing. Some of them were really cool,' she said quickly, 'And, you know, genuine. Others…weren't.'

Santos's fingers tightened on hers. 'Mia,' he said in a low voice, 'What are you saying?'

'Those places attract all sorts of types,' she continued, and now her voice started to sound a little wobbly, which was exactly what she didn't want.

Don't feel sorry for me.

Sometimes, growing up, it felt as though her dignity was the only thing she had. She didn't want to lose it now. 'Drug addicts, wastrels…predators.'

Santos tightened his hand on hers, so she winced as he squeezed her fingers, and he murmured an apology as he loosened his grip. '*Dios benedito*… What are you telling me?'

'There were a few dicey situations,' she admitted. 'Heaven knows, it could have been worse. I was never… Well…'

She drew in a hitched breath. 'But a couple of times it was close. Some guy would sidle up to me, or corner me somewhere alone, tell me how pretty I was, try to… Well, you can imagine.'

Santos swore under his breath, his expression turning thunderous.

'I got used to being on my guard,' Mia explained. She'd slept with a knife under her pillow sometimes. 'And used to not trusting people, I guess. Making myself invisible…

and always moving whenever I needed to, just the way my mother did.'

Santos's face was pale, his golden-brown eyes wide and dark. He looked seriously shaken. 'Mia… Dear Lord. Did you never tell your mother about any of this?'

'I tried, at first, but she wasn't really interested. She'd never actually wanted me, you see. At least, that was what she told me, but she kept dragging me around, so who knows? Maybe she did.'

She let out a sound that was meant to be a laugh, but definitely wasn't. Mia dragged in a breath, determined to recover her dignity.

'It was a long time ago, Santos, and I've moved on. I'm only telling you now because the way I grew up made a difference to who I am as a person. It made me guarded, I suppose, underneath…'

She swallowed, trying to ease the ache that had formed in her throat. She *never* talked like this.

'I ended up choosing to live like my mother—moving around a lot, keeping everything easy, but underneath I've been someone different. Someone I never show to the world. Someone I haven't always showed to you.'

'And who,' Santos asked in a low voice, his mind reeling from everything Mia had told him, 'Is that person? How is she different from the face you show to the world?'

Mia stared at him, her lovely blue-green eyes so dark and fathomless. She wore her hair back in a loose braid and a few auburn tendrils had escaped to frame a face that was far too pale. He ached to hold her, comfort her, but she was holding herself slightly apart, her hand very still in his, as if she were fragile and about to break.

Maybe she was…and he'd never realised how much.

He'd though he was able to be the light and laughing person he was in her presence because she was the same. But what if she wasn't? What if it was all an act? What did that make her, or him, or their marriage?

'Mia?' he prompted quietly.

Mia slipped her hand from his and brought her knees up to her chest, curling her arms around them and hugging them tight. A few more wisps of hair had fallen from her braid and curled about her face, making her look young and somehow vulnerable.

'I didn't mean to say all that,' she whispered.

'But you did.'

A sigh escaped her, long and lonely. 'It all sounds a bit melodramatic.'

'Your childhood was dramatic,' Santos reminded her. 'You're allowed to show some emotion.' Rather ironic advice for him to give, since he liked to keep his own emotions under such tight control, and yet Mia had changed that about him. Maybe, against all odds, he could do the same for her.

Mia gazed down at her knees, her braid falling over one shoulder. 'Like I said, I've been guarded, I suppose,' she said at last, her voice so soft Santos strained to hear it even though he was sitting right next to her. 'Careful. I've acted like I don't care about many things because then people can't hurt you.' She looked up, her eyes wide with a glassy sheen. 'But it's not the same as actually not caring. Underneath, I care. I've always cared.'

'Caring is a good thing, surely?' Santos suggested, reaching for her hand again. *'Querida?'*

She let him take her hand but kept hers limp against his palm. 'Yes, except when it hurts.'

He knew immediately what she was talking about: the

miscarriage; how he'd left her alone. Guilt swirled in his stomach like acid. 'Mia…'

'Santos, there's something else I haven't told you,' Mia said in a rush. 'About…about the baby.' She gave a little gulp. 'Part of the reason I wasn't as thrilled as you were was because I've always been scared to be a mother. To care about someone that much… And I'm afraid I'll mess it up. What on earth do I know about being a mother? I didn't exactly have the best example.' She tried to laugh, but the sound was jagged and broken.

Santos gathered her up in his arms, needing to hold her. 'Mia, I think you'll make a great mother.' He could already picture her, her face suffused with wonder and love as she gazed down at their baby in her arms. 'You have so much love to give,' he insisted. 'You just haven't been able to give it before.'

'But I mess things up,' she whispered. 'And when things get hard—when I feel like I could get hurt—I run. That's what I've always done, Santos.' She wriggled away to peer up at him, her expression turning serious, a little fearful. 'That's how I operate, how I've always operated, as a child and as an adult. Maybe I don't know any better.'

'If I can change,' Santos said after a moment, 'And become Mr Touchy Feely…' this elicited a soft laugh from her, which heartened him '…then you can learn to stop running. To stay and trust me. Because I swear, Mia, on my life, that I won't let you down. Not this time. Not ever.'

Her face softened as she gently pressed one hand to his cheek. 'It's not about you letting me down, Santos, remember? It's about the two of us together, working it out. Making it work.' Her breath hitched. 'I want to believe we can, but…'

She trailed off, shaking her head, and he frowned. 'But what, Mia?'

'I'm not exactly Aguila matriarch material,' she said after a moment. She slipped out of his arms, tucking a few tendrils of hair behind her ears as she composed herself.

'My mother will come round,' Santos insisted. He couldn't believe that was all that was bothering her. His mother was a force of nature, it was true, but she was just one person. Whatever insecurity Mia felt, it had to go deeper than that.

She let out a small sigh. 'Maybe,' she allowed. 'But what about everyone else? What about you? Once…once the novelty wears off?'

Santos frowned, struggling not to feel a sense of hurt that she thought he might be so fickle, so *shallow*. 'Do you really think that I would *tire* of you?' he asked, unable to keep from sounding insulted.

'Maybe,' Mia replied bleakly. 'I don't know. This is still new, Santos. Greece has been wonderful, incredible, but we both know it's not real life. And back in Seville my deficiencies will become all the more apparent—and I'm not just talking about not knowing what silverware to use.'

He folded his arms. 'What are you talking about, then?'

She brushed another strand of hair from her forehead as she shrugged her slender shoulders, her blue-green gaze moving around the lush garden.

'Everything. Your world isn't mine, Santos, and I'm still not sure if I truly have a place in it. And,' she continued, cutting him off before he could protest, her voice turning fierce, 'I don't want to be a problem you have to solve. I don't want to be your responsibility, another burden you have to carry that you feel the weight of, that you come here to escape.'

She turned back to gaze steadily at him, while Santos strove to keep his emotions under control. He should never have admitted how he felt, how oppressive he sometimes found his own role.

An Aguila is master of his own heart and mind.

There was a reason for that, he realised. A reason he should have acknowledged and accepted. He did not want Mia worrying about him, thinking he couldn't handle life with her.

'That's not what marriage is,' she said quietly. 'It's not what it should be.'

'We can be each other's responsibility, then,' Santos replied, although he wasn't sure he entirely meant it. He never wanted Mia to feel burdened by him.

'How will that work?'

An exasperated breath escaped him before he could stop it. 'I don't know the ins and outs of it all, Mia, and neither do you. We can't, until we try. We can hash it out, and deliberate and dither, but in the end we'll still just to have jump in and try.

'And,' he added, his tone turning implacable, although he hadn't meant it to, 'The truth is, I have to get back to Seville. To work and, yes, to real life, because you're right—this isn't it.' He knew he sounded autocratic, and he wanted to stop himself but, heaven help him, he'd bent over backwards to show Mia she could trust him. At some point, she was just going to have to do it.

Mia stared at him for a long moment, her expression pensive and a little resigned. Santos met her gaze with an obdurate one. He wasn't going to beg her to come back with him, he realised. Not this time. He'd made his assurances and his promises more than once. Mia was the one who needed to take the next step now—for both their sakes.

'All right,' she said softly and, with a flicker of hurt and treacherous annoyance, he heard how sad she sounded. 'When do we leave?'

CHAPTER FOURTEEN

THE MUSTARD-YELLOW WALLS of the Aguila estate rose up towards the achingly blue sky as the luxury SUV turned through the heavy wrought-iron gates. Santos reached over and touched her hand and Mia forced a smile. She was dreading this, and Santos probably knew it, but she would do her best to act as if she wasn't.

It had taken them three days to sail from Amorgos to Cadiz, where Santos moored his yacht. Two cars had been waiting to take them to the estate, his staff accompanying them—including Ronaldo, whose attitude towards Mia had thawed only a little.

The ninety-minute trip had been conducted mostly in silence, with Santos going into full work mode checking emails and sending messages, a furrow between his eyes as his fingers flew over his phone. He'd also reverted to Spanish when speaking to various staff, a necessity that made Mia feel more left out because, while she could get by in Spanish, she was still far from fluent. Maybe, once they were back at the hacienda, she would take lessons. It would be a way to show Santos she really was trying because, she told herself, she did want to try. Even if her stomach churned with nerves and dread as the hacienda came into view.

Not only did she have all the painful memories to deal

with but also the intense awkwardness of returning as the prodigal wife. Santos had gone to fetch her and had now brought her back. Even though their relationship was restored—mostly, anyway, although she still had her fears—Mia worried at how the optics would appear. It would be as if she was an unruly child who had been disciplined and returned with her proverbial tail between her legs. She knew she shouldn't care, because Santos didn't think that, but it still wasn't something she was looking forward to at all.

And sure enough, that was exactly how it seemed as the car pulled up in front of the magnificent mahogany front doors and Santos's mother, Evalina, came out, unsmiling and severe. She was a striking woman, slender and elegant, her dark hair, barely streaked with silver, pulled up into a chignon. She wore tailored cream trousers and a silk blouse in chartreuse, with a matching set of diamond-and-emerald earrings, bracelet and necklace. As always, she had that look of seamless elegance that Mia had noticed in so many Spanish women.

She'd taken care with her own appearance that morning, and wore a pair of wide-legged linen trousers and a bright-blue top with a scalloped edge, but she suspected compared to her mother-in-law she looked something of a mess. She suppressed a sigh as she gave Santos what she hoped was a bright smile.

'Welcome home, *querida*,' he said softly, and her smile briefly faltered. The Aguila estate did not feel like home and Mia wondered if it ever would.

Evalina now gave a fixed smile, her eyes narrowed as one of the estate staff opened the car door and Mia carefully climbed out. She forced herself to meet her mother-in-law's gaze with a smile even though inwardly she quailed at the flinty look on her face.

'Hello again,' she said, and realised belatedly how flippant she sounded by the tightening of Evalina's mouth. But that had always been one of her defences—insouciance meant she couldn't be hurt. At least, it meant she could *seem* as if she wasn't hurt.

'Welcome back,' Evalina replied in her throaty, heavily accented English. 'It has been some time.' The words were decidedly, and uncomfortably, pointed.

The staff lined up by the hacienda's door all murmured their muted greetings as Mia followed Evalina inside. Santos's hand was pressed comfortingly against her back, gently propelling her forward, which she needed. The truth was, Mia was more than half-tempted to high-tail it back down the drive. But she wasn't running any more, she reminded herself, even if she wanted to.

Inside the house, the dark wood-panelled walls seemed to close in on her, the muddy oil portraits of various illustrious ancestors blurring before her eyes. She took a deep breath and let it out slowly. She could do this. She *would* do this, for Santos's sake, for her own, for *theirs*.

'We have tapas and mint tea out in the courtyard,' Evalina said, her tone as imperious as ever. 'I thought you would be in need of some refreshment.'

'*Gracias, Madre,*' Santos said, kissing his mother's cheek. 'That sounds wonderful.'

Mia followed them out to the courtyard at the centre of the building with an ornate fountain in the middle and colonnades of Moorish arches in every direction. A table had been set up with linen and dishes, along with several chairs. Santos pulled one out for his mother and Mia before sitting down himself.

'So.' Evalina's lips stretched in a smile that most definitely did not reach her eyes. 'You have been away a long time.'

'We were in Greece for nearly two weeks,' Santo answered swiftly. 'So not as long as all that.'

Evalina eyed Mia appraisingly. 'Long enough.'

'Yes, about eight weeks, all told,' Mia agreed, striving to keep her voice pleasant. She had a feeling her mother-in-law was determined to rake her over the coals for her absence, and she couldn't entirely blame her. From Evalina's perspective, it had been a terrible thing to do, and yet even now Mia knew she couldn't have done anything else. She'd been driven to it, whether Evalina would ever understand that or not.

'Where were you, Mia, as it happens?' Evalina asked, her voice mild and yet possessing an edge.

Mia hesitated and Santos put his arm around her. 'It hardly matters, Madre,' he said with a touch of reproof. 'She's home now.'

'Yes,' Evalina agreed after a pause, her cool gaze moving from Santos to Mia. 'Home now.'

An interminable hour later, Mia practically limped upstairs, exhausted from the tension that had vibrated in the air.

'Your mother doesn't seem all that pleased to have me back,' she remarked in a low voice as they headed up the grand staircase, and Santos gave a little shrug.

'I think she was more displeased to have you gone. But don't worry, she'll come round.'

It was what he'd told her before in the same assured, dismissive way, and it made Mia feel like gritting her teeth.

But what if she doesn't? she wanted to ask, but didn't. She knew Santos would refuse to so much as entertain the notion. An hour into their return, and she was already coming up against that autocratic arrogance she remembered from before. Was he even aware of it? She doubted it.

'This isn't our bedroom,' she remarked in surprise as Santos led her to an unfamiliar room at the far end of one of the hacienda's wings. Evalina had her own private wing, while Mia and Santos had had one of the bedrooms in the main part of the house. This room was on its own separate wing, with far more privacy and space.

She glanced around the room, its shuttered windows open to the view of blue skies and vibrant orange groves, a king-sized, canopied bed with soft linen sheets the main piece of furniture.

'I thought we could do with a change of scene,' Santos replied. 'A fresh start, as well as bit more privacy.' He tugged her by the hand further into the bedroom and she went, glancing around the cool, airy space with appreciation. Their last bedroom had been dark and a bit stifling, despite its size, the walls adorned with portraits of his ancestors. They'd reminded her—and maybe Santos too—of the weight of expectation and responsibility.

'I suppose we could,' she agreed with a smile as he pulled her forward for a kiss. It was no more than a gentle brush of her lips, a tender promise, and Mia chose to believe it. It would be all right this time, she told herself. They would both make sure that it was.

Santos kissed Mia once, then twice, before settling his mouth on hers with intent and possession. He heard the soft sigh of her surrender as her body became pliant under his and he wrapped his arms around her as he deepened the kiss, sealing their vows and their future. At least, that was what it felt like. This time it was going to be different—everything was.

Admittedly, there had been tension downstairs with his mother—he'd felt it himself, although he still believed his mother would come round, as he'd told Mia. She was a reasonable woman and she'd married for love herself. Still, Santos had seen how Mia had looked at the estate with naked dread on her face as the car had come up the drive, and his heart had ached for her. He longed to reassure her... and this was the best way he knew how.

Her arms came round his neck as her body melted into his. Santos ran his hand up from her hip to her breast, cupping its fullness, enjoying the soft sigh of pleasure she gave as he brushed his thumb over her nipple.

'Santos...' she murmured against his mouth. 'They'll wonder where we are.'

'I don't care,' he replied with a growl as he pressed a kiss to her throat, and then another to the tempting vee between her breasts. 'Do you?'

'No...' The word came out in a whisper of breath as she arched back to grant him more access. 'No, I don't...'

A very pleasurable hour later, Santos was showered, dressed and heading to his estate office to check on business matters. He'd left Mia still in bed, although she'd said she thought she'd unpack. He'd offered to give her a tour of the estate, something he realised he hadn't done the first time round, and she'd said she might come and find him later.

There had been a look of wistfulness on her face that had given him a pang of uncertainty. She needed to find her place here, and he wanted to help her find ways to do it. Already his mind was casting about for ideas that would play to Mia's strengths—her friendliness, easy manner and her ability to turn her hand to just about anything. Could she be involved with the staff, or maybe the estate's social media? He didn't want to pressure her, but he wanted her to have something to do to feel involved and important. He would talk about it with her when he gave her a tour, he decided. They could plan their future here together.

In the estate office, at least, he knew what he was about. It felt good, surprisingly so, to settle back into the matters of business he knew so well—the forthcoming olive harvest, messages with suppliers and a new fertiliser to try. He spent an hour talking to his manager, Antonio, before he left him to his own devices to tackle his own overflowing inbox. Santos was steadily working through his messages when he heard a light yet authoritative tap on the door.

'Come in,' he called, his tone a bit brusque, as he was focused on his work.

'I hope I'm not disturbing you,' his mother replied tartly as came into his office.

'Madre!' Santos stood up, surprised to see his mother in the office block near the orange grove. He couldn't remember the last time she'd ventured in there; she had always left the estate work first to her husband, then to her son. 'Is everything all right?'

'You tell me, *mi hijo*,' she replied, folding her arms as she arched one eyebrow. 'I did not expect you to bring your errant wife back here.'

Santos stiffened before he forced himself to relax. When he'd brought Mia back the first time, much to his mother's shock, she'd murmured something about true love and made no objections—although admittedly he'd felt her censure, or at least her concern, in every eloquent look and taut remark. He'd weathered them because he understood why she was so worried, and he'd assumed things would settle down. Now, however, it seemed as if his mother had decided to be blunter.

Well, then, so would he. 'What did you think I would do,' he replied mildly, 'When I went to find her?'

'I thought you'd come to your senses!' his mother burst out before she pressed her lips together. Like a true Aguila, she did not like to show emotion. Sometimes Santos wondered if she even liked to feel it.

'And do what?' he asked in the same mild voice, although there was a dangerous edge to it. *Come to his senses?* He'd come to his senses when he'd found Mia, when he'd convinced her to come back with him. 'Divorce her?'

'I spoke to Rodrigo,' his mother replied, naming their family's lawyer. 'He said he thought a divorce could be dealt with quite quickly.'

Santos swore under his breath. He knew his mother was a strong-willed woman, but this was taking things too far, even for her. 'I don't want a divorce, Madre. Neither does Mia.'

'And yet she left you,' his mother pointed out ruthlessly. 'Santos, how can you hold your head up in this community with a wife like that? She has caused so much gossip—she will bring shame to this family! She already has.'

'Careful, Madre,' Santos replied with lethal softness. 'This is my wife you're talking about.'

'Very well, then, I will speak more plainly,' his mother retorted, her voice rising. '*You* bring shame to this family, Santos, by returning here with her! She is not worthy of you, of this place.' She spoke flatly now, her voice ringing out with awful certainty. 'You will never be able to hold your head up among your staff, or your peers, with this woman by your side.'

'Madre, you overstep yourself,' Santos replied. He felt his face heat and his hands balled into fists. He had had no idea that his mother felt this strongly, this *terribly*, about Mia, although he realised wretchedly that Mia had tried to tell him. 'You don't know her at all—'

'I don't *want* to know her!' his mother snapped. 'She *abandoned* you, Santos!'

He clenched his hands harder to keep himself from doing something stupid like punching a wall. His mother had never spoken so plainly, so viciously, before. He'd thought she was a reasonable woman, but now she seemed to be lashing out in emotion—emotion he resented her feeling. Her reaction left him winded, reeling and also utterly furious. 'There were reasons for that—'

'There was a reason for you to stay married before,' his mother cut across him. 'Because of the baby, as unfortunate an occurrence as that was. It was an act of God that she miscarried.'

'Don't.' Santos's voice was swift and deadly. 'Do not talk about my child like that.'

'Santos.' His mother held her arms out towards him, her expression crumpling into distress. 'I want only what is best for you, for our family, and this…this gold-digger… is not it. Of that, I am sure.'

'She's not a gold-digger,' Santos replied stonily, hating the thought that his mother could entertain such a notion, even for a second. 'She didn't even take the clothes and jewels I bought her when she left.' He thought of Mia's one battered backpack and his heart ached with love and sorrow.

'Pfft…' His mother shrugged in dismissal. 'You didn't sign a pre-nuptial agreement. She would have received a

hefty payment in the divorce settlement. She would have been counting on that.'

'And yet she came back with me,' Santos reminded her.

'Did she never suggest divorce to you?' his mother challenged. 'I'm sure she would have been canny about it, but I can guess what she wants.'

Santos was silent as he remembered how Mia had first asked for a divorce back on the yacht. She hadn't asked for money then, but would she have? He would have given it to her, he still would, but the memory of it created a splinter of doubt in his soul that he desperately did not want to feel. He loved Mia. She loved him.

And yet she's never actually said the words.

He was the only one who had, more than once. Mia had responded with kisses, with smiles, but never with those three little words. He keenly felt the lack of them now.

He wheeled round so his back was to his mother as he raked a hand through his hair. He did not want to think this way or feel this way. And yet…he did. It hadn't taken long at all for the doubts to come rushing back, and he was determined to keep them at bay. To trust his love for Mia… and her love for him, even if she hadn't said the words.

'Santos.' His mother's voice turned soft and gentle as she came to stand behind him, resting one hand on his shoulder. 'You have a reputation, a *name*, to live up to. I understand you didn't care for Isabella Ruiz, as suitable as she was, and heaven knows your father intended for you to marry her. But there will be another woman who is of our class, our station, for you to marry. Who understands what it means to bear the responsibility you do and who respects the name of Aguila.'

Santos was silent for a long moment, absorbing what his mother was saying and what it meant. Would she *ever*

accept Mia, if this was her attitude? It saddened him that
she might not, but he knew he would not be swayed. He
loved Mia and no one—not his mother, his sister, the community or anyone—could take that from him.

'It was a mistake of passion,' his mother continued, her
voice now low and persuasive. 'My God, you wouldn't
be the first man to be turned by a pretty pair of eyes!
There is less shame in that, Santos, than in staying with
a woman who can never truly understand what it means
to be an Aguila or who will never be a credit to you or to
your family.'

'Madre…' His throat was tight with anger and something like grief. He'd had no idea that his mother felt this
strongly and he hated that fact.

'Please, think about it.' She squeezed his shoulder before stepping back. 'Think about your responsibility to this
family and to your father's memory. Don't react in passion
or anger, Santos, but with the even temper and reason I
know you have. You will see sense then. I am sure of it.'

'And do what?' he asked, his voice thick with emotion
he didn't want to reveal. 'Divorce my wife?'

'Yes,' his mother replied swiftly. 'As I said. It will be
easy. Rodrigo has the papers ready.'

'Does he?' Again, Santos felt as if he were reeling. He
could not believe his mother had planned this already and
had spun a web of manipulation…

For a second Santos simply stood there, absorbing everything, letting it reverberate through him. He thought of
his place as head of the Aguila family—the expectations
not just of his mother, but of his wider family, his staff and
the Sevillian community. He thought of how Mia hadn't
felt at home here—and how could she, if this was what
she was up against?

If he divorced Mia, or if he agreed to some sort of separation, maybe, in the long run, it would be easier—not for him, but for her.

The thought of it was like a knife plunging into his heart. The sensation made him dazed with pain, but in the midst of that he felt a sudden certainty thudding through him, waking him up, clearing his mind.

'Madre…' he began, only to stop at the sound of a movement outside his office. He heard a stifled sob, light footsteps down the corridor and then a door being wrenched open.

With a sinking sensation, Santos realised Mia must have overheard the entire conversation. How much of their Spanish had she understood? Too much, he feared; far too much.

CHAPTER FIFTEEN

MIA RAN AS if the devil were on her heels, and in some ways it felt as if he were. All of Santos's mother's words, and his guarded replies, thudded through her head, an endless, mocking echo she couldn't escape from, no matter how fast or long she ran.

There is less shame in that, Santos, than in staying with a woman who can never truly understand what it means to be an Aguila or who will never be a credit to you or to your family.

A sob escaped her, raw and wild. She went back to the hacienda, thinking only to get away, to run, the way she always did, because she wasn't wanted here, and she wasn't going to stay somewhere it hurt to be. 'Always move on' had been her motto until she'd met Santos, and even then...

Mia raced up the steps of the main staircase and down the corridor to the bedroom, where just a few short hours ago she and Santos had lain in a sleepy, sated haze. Already, it felt like another lifetime. She'd only gone to find Santos because she wanted to show him she was making an effort. She had been planning to ask him to show her the olive groves. She'd wanted to hear about the estate; she'd wanted to be part of it.

No longer.

In the bedroom, Mia gazed around, feeling as if she'd

never seen it before. This house had never felt like home. She'd never been truly welcomed. Why stay and have it all play out and unravel? She and Santos only worked when they were isolated in their beautiful little bubble. That wasn't real life, just as she'd said before, and it—they— didn't work when confronted with reality. She'd been afraid of that before, and she suspected Santos was now as well.

He hadn't refuted his mother's claims, had he? He hadn't said the idea of a divorce was outrageous. No, if anything he'd sounded pensive, maybe even cautiously approving. He'd sounded as if, on some level, it made *sense*—and why wouldn't it? Santos was a sensible, rational man. Marrying Mia had been the thing that was out of character for him, not everything else. It made total sense for him to want to divorce. But she wasn't going to stick around, waiting for him to do that.

Her backpack was leaning against the suitcases Santos had bought in Barcelona for all her new clothes. It looked so small and forgotten, and yet it felt like the truest thing about herself. She grabbed it and slung it over her shoulder, and for a second she thought *this* was home—having nothing more than a single bag, running to the next new place. It was all she'd known, maybe all she'd ever know.

She turned from the room, and as she did her steps slowed. For a dizzying second, it was as if the room took on a magical sort of haze and she could see it with different eyes. On the bed, she saw Santos and her with their limbs tangled, her head resting on his chest and his arm around her. She saw herself staring out at the blue sky by the window, a beautiful new day with all its possibility. On the *chaise*, she saw herself lying with Santos next to her, their baby in her arms as they gazed down at the tiny, beloved face in wonder.

A small, stifled cry escaped her. If she ran—again—none of that would ever happen. She'd just keep running; she wouldn't have changed, learned or grown. Was that what she really wanted to do? Was that what Santos wanted her to do?

But he hadn't said otherwise to his mother. He hadn't told his mother that he loved Mia, that he wanted to stay with her. He hadn't even sounded as if he'd wanted to say those things, if he'd felt them. Santos was stubborn, Mia knew. He'd insisted he didn't have doubts, but she knew him better than that. He might not admit it but he did. He had to. And if he felt conflicted—as conflicted as she did—how could they possibly survive?

Slowly Mia looked around the room and the mirage of possibility and happiness evaporated before her eyes. She hitched her backpack further up on her shoulder and walked out of the room, down the stairs and out of the hacienda.

No one stopped her.

Santos swore under his breath as he headed for the door.

His mother reached out one hand in supplication. 'Santos…'

'That must have been Mia,' he snapped, biting off her words. 'I think she heard the entire conversation.'

His mother looked startled and perhaps a bit discomfited before she lifted her chin as she eyed him in cool challenge. 'And if she did?'

Santos shook his head slowly. 'I love her, Madre,' he said, his voice a quiet throb of feeling. 'Maybe you haven't believed that, or wanted to believe it, but Mia is my wife and I love her. I love who I am with her, who she enables me to be, and I want to spend the rest of my life with her.

There will be no divorce, not ever. And I'll thank you to speak of my wife more respectfully, because she carries the Aguila name, and *she* is a credit to *me*.'

He saw the look of blatant shock on his mother's face and found he relished it. 'And,' he finished coldly, 'If you cannot find a way to welcome her into my home, perhaps you will be more comfortable living in another one of my properties.'

'Santos…' his mother began, her face crumpling with hurt as well as shock.

'I'm serious, Madre,' Santos told her. 'Mia is and will always be my wife. *Accept it*.'

Without waiting for his mother's response, he stalked from the room.

His blood was boiling, his mind seething, as he strode towards the hacienda. He hated to think of how Mia might be feeling, but worse, what she might be doing. Her words from just a few days ago came back to haunt him:

And when things get hard—when I feel like I could get hurt—I run. That's what I've always done, Santos.

But not this time, he told himself. She wouldn't this time because they were both different now. They'd promised each other that they *would* be different, that they would try to be.

But what if trying simply wasn't enough? With his brows pulled together in a scowl to hide his fear, Santos stormed into the hacienda.

Just as before, the moment he stepped into the bedroom he knew she was gone. He'd felt it even before that, although he'd tried to pretend that he didn't. It was an emptiness in the house, inside *him*, like a cold wind whistling through it. She'd left. She must have. *And so quickly!* Once again, she hadn't had the courtesy, the *care*, to tell him or

even to leave so much as a note. To leave like that *again*…
He could hardly believe it. It made him wonder, had she
loved him at all?

How could she, to have left as she so obviously had? he
thought in misery. And this time, he acknowledged starkly,
he didn't know if he had the emotional strength to find her
and bring her back again.

As he paced the empty bedroom, Santos swore aloud.
All her suitcases were still there, the clothes she'd changed
out of when they'd first arrived discarded on the rumpled
bed. But one thing was gone, he realised: her old, battered
backpack.

Just as before.

Tears stung his eyes and he blinked them back angrily.
Once more, fury warred with hurt—and fury won. He'd
spent the last three weeks wooing and winning her, proving to her in every way possible that he could be trusted.
Why hadn't she trusted him with this? Why hadn't she
waited, at least talked to him and let him explain?

And yet, he acknowledged, what would he have said?
He'd been blindsided by the depth of his mother's determination and, he was ashamed to admit, it had caused him
to doubt, if only briefly…

But maybe those doubts weren't as traitorous as he'd
thought, because Mia had *gone*. She hadn't trusted him.
She hadn't believed they could make it work, that *he* could.
No matter what she'd said about it taking both of them to
make a marriage work, he'd made a promise—to her, as
well as to himself—and she'd been the one to break it,
right here and now.

A shuddery breath escaped him and he raked a hand
through his hair. If he called Rodrigo, he could at least get
the legal process set in motion this afternoon. He didn't

want to do that, but damn it, *where was she*? Why had she proved all the things he'd feared were true? He'd wanted them to be wrong. He'd convinced himself they were.

And yet she'd left. There was no escaping that grim reality...*again*.

Having no idea what to do now, Santos walked slowly from their bedroom. The house felt so empty without her; and, he realised, it was an emptiness in himself. How could she be gone already? Had she meant anything she'd said?

And yet she'd warned him...

'Santos.' His mother stood at the bottom of the stairs, her hand fluttering by her throat. 'Is she gone?'

His chest felt tight, his throat too, so he had to squeeze the words out. 'Yes.'

To his surprise, his mother did not look gratified or vindicated by the news; rather, she slumped, seeming disappointed and even regretful.

'I'm so sorry,' she said, shocking him all the more. 'I didn't... I didn't mean this to happen.'

Santos let out a hollow laugh. 'I think you meant *exactly* this to happen, Madre.'

'No, Santos!' Her hand fluttered again as she took a step towards him. 'I didn't...' She swallowed. 'I didn't realise you truly loved her.' Santos stared at her dumbly, having no idea what to say. 'I thought it was infatuation,' she continued. 'Beguilement. Not...not love.'

For a moment, Santos didn't reply. He was honest enough to acknowledge that his mother had had a good reason for thinking the way she had—after all, he'd only known Mia for two weeks when he'd brought her back the first time. Had it been love, even then, or mere infatuation that his mother—and Mia herself—had claimed it was? Did it even matter? He loved her now.

But did she love him?

'I love her,' he told his mother steadily. 'And I'm going to get her back.' The doubts he'd felt before, that maybe he should let Mia go, faded away into nothing. He loved her. And he thought she loved him. She might not have said the words, but she'd showed him in a thousand different ways, hadn't she? They both had—and he would fight for their marriage and their love.

But would she?

'Where do you think she went?' his mother asked and a long, low sigh escaped him.

'I have no idea,' Santos admitted heavily. And he had no idea even where to begin to look for her. Once again, a sense of hopelessness swamped him. Was love even enough? he wondered. He really didn't know if he could do it on his own if Mia wasn't going to fight for their marriage… It took two, as she'd said herself, and there was only one of them here.

So, Santos wondered as he gazed around the empty house, where did that leave them?

CHAPTER SIXTEEN

IT WAS TWILIGHT when Mia slipped back into the hacienda, her body aching, her eyes gritty, and yet her heart surprisingly at peace. She'd made her decision.

The house was dark and quiet, almost eerily so, and she felt a stirring of unease and guilt. She'd been gone a long time, she realised, at least four or five hours. She'd missed dinner, with its five interminable courses and his mother's cool-eyed gaze watching her every move. To be fair, she wasn't sorry she'd missed that, especially in light of what Santos's mother had proposed this afternoon—*a divorce*. But Santos must have wondered where she'd gone. Would he be angry?

The floor creaked as she headed towards the stairs, feeling more uneasy by the second at how *empty* everything seemed. The hacienda was huge, it was true, but there was no sign of life anywhere, neither family nor staff. Then she saw a sliver of light from the door to one of the many reception rooms which had been left slightly ajar. After a few seconds' hesitation, Mia tiptoed towards the door and peeked into the room, with its leather sofas and chairs, heavy, dark furniture and big stone fireplace.

Santos was there, slumped in an arm chair by the French doors that led out to one of the many terraces, an empty tumbler dangling from his slack fingertips. His head rested on the back of the chair and his eyes were closed. He looked exhausted, but worse, he looked despairing. Mia's heart clenched with love and fear. She shouldn't have left for as long as she had. But she'd needed the time to get her own head—and heart—straight.

She stepped into the room. He didn't stir.

'Santos,' she called softly, her heart full of love for this beautiful, proud but humble man. After what felt like an age, his eyes fluttered open. He blinked several times and then his golden-brown gaze trained on her, as focused as a laser. His lips twisted in a way that made Mia catch her breath.

'You're back.' He did not sound pleased, or even relieved. The words came out flat, toneless, and inwardly she shrivelled.

'Yes.' Mia hitched her old backpack higher on her shoulder. 'I'm sorry I was gone for so long.'

Santos's gaze flicked to the mantle clock and then back again. 'Six hours.'

Longer than she'd realised, then. 'I'm sorry,' Mia said again. 'Truly, Santos.'

'Are you, though, Mia?' Santos asked. He rose from his chair in one sinuous movement, stalking to the drinks table in the corner of the room where he poured himself two fingers' worth of whisky and tossed it down in one gulp. 'Are you really?'

'Santos…' Mia had no idea what to say. 'Yes, I am. I… I needed some space to think. After…' She paused and swallowed. 'Are you angry?'

'No.' He put down the glass and then turned to face her, his arms folded, his expression foreboding. 'I was angry at the start, I admit. I realised you'd overheard my conversation with my mother and predictably drawn all the wrong conclusions.'

'Had I, though?' Mia challenged quietly, parroting a semblance of his earlier words back to him. 'She asked you to end our marriage, Santos. You…you paused, like you were thinking about it. You didn't say no, at any rate.' She hadn't meant to lead with that, but those seconds of silence had *hurt*. They still did.

'I was shocked by what she was suggesting, Mia,' Santos replied evenly. 'It took me a moment to absorb. And yes, I admit, I thought about it for a second—but not *then*.' His gaze blazed at her, a furnace of pain. 'I thought about it a few minutes later when you left—*again*.'

Mia's mouth opened and closed and she took a step towards him. 'Santos, I wasn't—'

'*Don't* lie to me,' he cut her off, and now he sounded lethal and coldly furious. Mia didn't think, through all their difficulties, that she'd ever heard him sound like that before, and it scared her. She'd expected him to be worried, yes, annoyed as well, but *this*?

'After all we've gone through,' he continued in that same cold voice, 'All we've tried to overcome… Don't lie to me, Mia.' His voice caught and then broke, the fury gone, revealing the pain pulsing underneath, making Mia's heart ache and her throat tighten with unshed tears. 'You took your backpack,' he explained as he closed his eyes briefly, his voice a jagged splinter of sound. He opened his eyes to stare at her bleakly. 'That's how I knew.'

'Santos, I'm sorry.' She could barely get the words out. Tears crowded her eyes, and she blinked them back.

'Were you going to leave?'

Mia knew she needed to be completely honest with him, as he'd been with her. 'I… I thought about it,' she admitted in a low voice. 'Like you, for a *second*. I was—I was scared, Santos, as well as hurt, by what I'd overheard. And, like I told you, running is my gut instinct, my kneejerk response. But I didn't get very far, not even to the front door, before I realised that wasn't what I wanted.'

'What did you want, then?' Santos asked, his voice still toneless, as if he didn't really care very much about the answer. 'And why did you still go, then?'

Mia decided to answer the second question first. 'I went because I needed to clear my head.'

'For six hours?'

'Santos, please, listen,' she begged. 'I know I shouldn't have gone for so long, and I am truly sorry. But it really threw me, what your mother said, and also how *I* had responded. Not you, but me—how quickly I felt that I needed to run. I scared *myself*, Santos; that's what I'm trying to say.'

For the first time since she'd come into the room, she saw a flicker of interest in his eyes, a spark of understanding and maybe even compassion. 'And?' he asked quietly.

'And I needed to think through things,' she told him. 'I didn't want to just react when I saw you next—lashing out in hurt or choosing to stay silent, like we both did before, even though we were hurting. I wanted to be different. I still do, but I needed time.'

'All right.' He folded his arms and met her pleading gaze with a level one of his own. 'So, you couldn't have sent me a text to let me know that's what you were doing?'

Mia closed her eyes as guilt rushed through her like acid. 'I'm sorry,' she whispered. 'I should have. I suppose old habits die hard. I wanted to be completely off-grid, to be able to think without any interruption, but that wasn't fair to you. I should have let you know where I was.' She opened her eyes. 'Please believe me, Santos. I am sorry.'

'So am I,' he said heavily. He walked back to the arm chair he'd been in before and dropped into it, his head resting in his hands. 'But where does this leave us, Mia? We both struggle to break these old patterns of ours. Are we ever going to succeed?'

'I don't know,' Mia admitted quietly. 'But I want to try. That was the conclusion I came to when I was wandering around your orange groves, Santos. I looked at this land and I felt how it's as much a part of you as your heartbeat. And I realised how much I loved that and love that part of you. And I want to be part of it, of this place. I want to be part of it with you.'

Santos lifted his head from his hands, a strange look coming over his face. 'You've never said that before.'

'Said what?' Mia asked uncertainly.

'That you loved me. Or even part of me. You've never said those words to me.'

'I… I know.' Again, the guilt. She knew she hadn't said them because she'd found them so hard to say. 'I do love you, Santos. I'm not sure when I started—if I fell in love with you back on the beach in Portugal, or if it happened over time—but I do love you. And I want to spend the rest of my life with you.'

He smiled faintly, heartening her. 'I was thinking the same thing earlier. I don't know when I fell in love with you, but then I realised it doesn't really matter. The point is, I love you now.'

'And I love you now.' With each time, it became easier to say. She *wanted* to say it. She wanted him to know—and be sure.

'And do you think,' he asked after a moment, 'That love is enough?'

'Not by itself,' Mia replied. 'But with effort and hard work and hope—yes. It is more than enough.'

For a second Santos stared at her and then, to her shock, his face crumpled. 'I thought you'd gone,' he whispered, and his shoulders shook.

'Oh, Santos.' Mia flew to him, dropping to her knees in front of him as she put her arms around him and drew his head towards her breast. He came willingly, wrapping his arms tightly around her as they clung together. 'Santos, I didn't. I didn't leave you. I love you. I love you. I love you.' She would keep saying it until he believed it. Until he knew it as surely as she did.

He held her tightly, his lips against her throat. 'And I love you so much, Mia. I want to fight for this, for us. But... I don't want to go through what I did today ever again. I don't want to live in fear that you might leave me.'

She could tell it cost him something to admit this, and it made her ache all over again. 'Santos, you won't. I won't leave. I promise,' she told him, her voice throbbing with emotion. 'That was what I realised today—that I don't want to leave, *ever*. And even if I did I wouldn't because, like you said, I made a commitment. We both did. And we have to trust each other, Santos...trust that we'll honour it.' She tightened her arms around him. 'Do you trust me?'

He lifted his head to gaze at her with damp eyes. 'I thought you didn't trust me.'

'I do,' she said softly. 'I know it will be hard, especially with how set your mother is against me.'

'She isn't,' he told her, and when Mia started to protest he shook his head. 'Please, believe me. She was, it's true; I didn't realise quite how much, and I'm sorry about that. But she told me today—after you'd gone—that she hadn't understood how much we loved each other. She will come round, Mia, I promise. She already is and, even if she doesn't, we'll still be together. Nothing can change that. If my mother can't accept it, I've told her she can live elsewhere.'

'Santos, you didn't…'

'I did,' he assured her. 'And I meant it. I want you to be happy here, and I also want you to feel safe and accepted by everyone. That's non-negotiable.'

'Thank you,' Mia whispered, moved by his sensitivity and kindness. 'That means a lot to me.'

'I love you,' he told her again, and she smiled.

'I love you too. So much.'

She leaned forward to kiss him gently on the lips. The future shimmered in front of them, unknown yet not uncertain. They would find a way forward…together. 'Nothing can change that,' she echoed, and then Santos deepened the kiss.

EPILOGUE

Two years later

THE HACIENDA SPARKLED under the summer sunshine as Mia glanced around the courtyard in approval. The pillars were festooned with balloons and a drinks table with lemonade and sangria had been set up one end. In the fountain, several-dozen yellow plastic ducks bobbed for a game of Hook the Duck, and outside on the terrace there were lawn games set up for the children who were coming to the garden party, a new yearly tradition for the estate's staff and employees.

In the two years since they'd returned to Seville, Mia had worked hard to find her place there, and Santos had supported and encouraged her every step of the way. At first, she'd been cautious, not wanting to step on anyone's toes, especially her mother-in-law's. But Evalina had decided to take an extended holiday through Europe, mainly to give Mia and Santos their own space.

When Mia had discovered that the Aguila brand had little social media presence, she'd realised there *was* a need she could fill. When Santos's sister, Marina, flew in for a visit she was wildly approving, as well as fun to be with— Mia had been grateful to make a new friend. And when Evalina had returned after several months, they'd both agreed to put the past behind them, and they now respected

and liked each other. It was, Mia had decided, a relationship that would continue to grow.

Once the socials had taken off, Mia had turned to other
ideas, including events to support the Aguila staff and make
them feel more like the extended family Santos had said they
were. She'd invited every member of staff over for a social
occasion at some point during the year to get to know them,
as well as to practise her now nearly fluent Spanish, and
she'd also run some extended learning and cultural days.

Today's garden party was the latest initiative, a way to
include the many children on the estate. It was set to start
in twenty minutes.

'Does everything look all right in here?' Santos asked
as he strolled into the courtyard. He looked devastatingly
handsome as always in an open-necked blue shirt and linen
trousers. Mia smiled to see him, her heart giving that familiar little leap of love and excitement.

'Yes, I think so.'

He came to stand behind her, sliding his hands around
her waist. 'You've worked hard on this,' he murmured
against her hair.

Mia leaned back against him, savouring the moment.
'It's been fun. I've enjoyed it.' As his hands rested on her
hips, she thought with a little thrill of joy that now was as
good a time as ever to share the news she'd learned that
morning but had suspected for a few days.

'And it's good practice, you know, to spend time with
all these children,' she told him. 'Rosaria in accounts had
a baby just six weeks ago—I might need to practise my
cuddles.' And, just in case he didn't get it, she put her
hands over his and guided them to her still-flat stomach.

For a second, Santos tensed in surprise and then he
slowly turned her round to face him. He looked dazed,

which made Mia smile. 'Do you mean…?' he asked, and she nodded.

'I'm pregnant, Santos.' And this time she felt ready— more than ready. She'd gone off birth control three months ago, after they'd both decided it was time to try again.

'Mi querida…' He kissed her gently. 'How are you feeling? Are you all right?'

She laughed as she kissed him back. 'I feel fine. It's early days, though, and you know nothing is certain.' For a second, they were both sombre, remembering the baby they'd lost. 'But I feel good,' she assured him, twining her fingers through his. 'I feel happy and hopeful. This is exactly where I want to be.'

'And it's exactly where I want to be,' he murmured against her lips before he pulled her close for another kiss.

The last two years had held their challenges as they'd both learned not just to break old patterns but to create new ones. To trust each other with the little things as well as the big ones. To grow in love, and what that meant, living it out day by day. But Mia knew they were getting there, and in the meantime they were both enjoying the journey, savouring absolutely every moment.

As Santos deepened the kiss, Mia gave herself up to it—and to him, so thankful for how he'd come to find her and had fought for her in a way she'd never been fought for before. And had won her, she thought with a smile, as reluctantly she broke the kiss.

'I think,' she told him as she heard the delighted squeal of a child, 'Our guests are about to arrive.'

Santos smiled back and, hand in hand, they went to greet their guests—and their future—together.

* * * * *

MILLS & BOON®

Coming next month

GREEK'S ENEMY BRIDE
Caitlin Crews

The priest cleared his throat.

Jolie took one last look at Apostolis, soaking in this last moment of blessed widowhood before he became her husband.

He looked back, that gleaming gold thing in his gaze, but his expression unusually serious.

For a moment, it was as if she could read his mind.

For a long, electric moment, it was almost as if they were united in this bizarre enterprise after all, and her heart leaped inside her chest—

'Stepmother?' he said, with a soft ferocity. 'If you would be so kind?'

No, she told herself harshly. *There is no unity here. There is only and ever war. You will do well to remember that.*

And then, with remarkable swiftness and no interruption, Jolie relinquished her role as Apostolis's hated stepmother, and became his much-loathed wife instead.

Continue reading

GREEK'S ENEMY BRIDE
Caitlin Crews

Available next month
millsandboon.co.uk

COMING SOON!

We really hope you enjoyed reading this book.
If you're looking for more romance
be sure to head to the shops when
new books are available on

Thursday 19th December

MILLS & BOON

LET'S TALK
Romance

For exclusive extracts, competitions
and special offers, find us online:

 MillsandBoon

 @MillsandBoon

 @MillsandBoonUK

 @MillsandBoonUK

Get in touch on 01413 063 232

Afterglow Books is a trend-led, trope-filled list of books with diverse, authentic and relatable characters, a wide array of voices and representations, plus real world trials and tribulations. Featuring all the tropes you could possibly want (think small-town settings, fake relationships, grumpy vs sunshine, enemies to lovers) and all with a generous dose of spice in every story.

♪ @millsandboonuk
📷 @millsandboonuk
afterglowbooks.co.uk
#AfterglowBooks

For all the latest book news, exclusive content and giveaways scan the QR code below to sign up to the Afterglow newsletter:

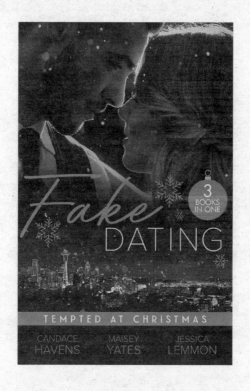